# Ryan's Return

She closed her eyes to resist the temptation, but Ryan completely filled her senses. He took over her thoughts. He became her fantasy.

She was in deep trouble. She had known the man for barely a day, yet had already been thrust into an emotional whirlpool of feeling.

"We're good together," Ryan said. His lips touched the top of her forehead, warm and promising.

"I can't do this," she whispered. She slipped out of his arms before second thoughts took her closer into his embrace.

He held on to her arm. "What happens if I kiss you anyway?"

Kara's lips parted. But she couldn't say anything, because he was lowering his head, because his mouth was hot and warm and welcoming, and she suddenly needed this kiss as much as she needed air.

*Other Avon Contemporary Romances by*
**Barbara Freethy**

DANIEL'S GIFT

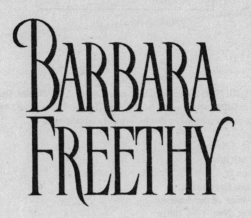

# BARBARA FREETHY

# RYAN'S RETURN

AVON BOOKS NEW YORK

RYAN'S RETURN is an original publication of Avon Books. This work
has never before appeared in book form. This work is a novel. Any similarity to actual persons or events is purely coincidental.

AVON BOOKS
A division of
The Hearst Corporation
1350 Avenue of the Americas
New York, New York 10019

Copyright © 1996 by Barbara Freethy
Inside cover author photo by Dave Dornlas
Published by arrangement with the author
Library of Congress Catalog Card Number: 96-96177
ISBN: 0-380-78531-5

First Avon Books Printing: October 1996

AVON TRADEMARK REG. U.S. PAT. OFF. AND IN OTHER COUNTRIES, MARCA
REGISTRADA, HECHO EN U.S.A.

Printed in the U.S.A.

RA  10  9  8  7  6  5  4  3  2  1

To Dorothy and Pat, two very special women
who inspire me with their patience,
strength of character, and generosity

# 1

His bed was on the sidewalk!

Ryan Hunter slammed the door of the cab, tossed a twenty-dollar bill at the driver, and ran across the busy Los Angeles intersection, dodging cars and honking horns. As he reached the sidewalk, two men emerged from his three-story apartment building with a bookcase.

"What the hell is going on here?" Ryan dropped his overnight bag on the ground, taking more care with his saxophone case and camera bag.

The moving men set the bookcase down on the sidewalk. The younger man, who wore white coveralls with the name Craig embroidered on the pocket, grinned. "Oh, hi, Mr. Hunter. Your lady's moving out. Third one in a row, isn't that right?"

"Yeah? Who's counting?" Ryan grumbled.

The older man, Walt, reached into his pocket and pulled out a bill. "I do believe you're our best account, Mr. Hunter. Shall we put this on your tab?"

Walt and Craig laughed in unison as they picked up the bookcase and set it in the truck.

Ryan surveyed the furniture strewn around the sidewalk and the steps leading up to his apartment building with a weary sigh. He had spent the past thirty-six hours on three different planes, traveling through three different time zones. All he wanted to do was sleep— in his own bed. Only his own bed was now in a moving van.

The men loaded the easy chair next, the one perfect for stretching out with a beer. Behind the chair was the big-screen television.

"Not the TV." Ryan groaned. He gave it a loving pat as the men walked by him.

Craig laughed. "You don't have much left up there, Mr. Hunter, just that old sofa with the springs sticking out, a couple of crates, and a fan. Maybe instead of getting a new woman, you should buy yourself some furniture."

"Thanks for the tip, Mack."

"The name is Craig, and you're welcome."

Ryan stalked up the steps. He met Melanie on the landing just inside the front door. She wore her usual aerobics gear, a pair of hot pink Lycra shorts, a midriff tank top, and tennis shoes. Her blond hair bounced around her head in a ponytail. She was the perfect southern California woman, tan and fit—great body, great in bed, and great furniture. Sometimes life sucked.

Melanie stopped abruptly, her bright pink lips curving downward in dismay.

"Oh, dear," she said. "I thought I'd be gone before you got home."

"Where are you going?" he demanded.

"I'm moving out, Ryan."

"That's obvious. Without saying good-bye, without offering a word of explanation?"

"Ryan, honey, you've been gone seven weeks."

"I was working."

"You're always working."

"Did you see my photographs from Israel?"

"Yes, they were on the cover of *Time*. Very impressive. Excuse me, but I have to go."

"Melanie, wait."

She shook her head. "Ryan, we've been living together for three months, and you've only spent ten nights in that apartment with me."

"It has to be more than that," Ryan said, truly surprised by the number.

"It's not. I should know. I had plenty of time to count." Melanie sighed wistfully. "You're a great guy when you're around, but you don't love me."

"I don't?"

"Seven weeks, Ryan." She poked her fingertip into his chest. "No phone calls, no letter, not even a postcard."

Melanie was right. She was a nice woman and fun to be with, but he didn't love her. He didn't love anyone. It was not an emotion that he wanted in his life. Love was too complicated, too messy.

Ryan touched Melanie's cheek, feeling genuinely sad at her departure. "I'm sorry. I hope I didn't hurt you."

"I'll live," she said with a regretful smile. "I just wish I knew what you were running from or running toward." She stood on tiptoe and kissed him on the lips. "Whatever it is, I hope someday you find it."

Ryan watched her walk down the steps. The movers closed up the van, and within minutes a big part of his life disappeared—again.

He retrieved his bags and saxophone case from the sidewalk and walked slowly up the stairs to his apartment.

The door stood halfway open. He walked inside and stared at the emptiness. His old sofa bed stood against one wall next to the lamp with the tilted, yellowed shade. The wooden crate with his antiquated record collection featuring jazz musicians Duke Ellington and Louis Armstrong, as well as an eclectic mix of rock and roll artists like Bruce Springsteen, Mick Jagger, and the Grateful Dead, spilled out onto the beige carpet.

A card table had been opened up in one corner of the living room. On top of the table lay his mail, piles and piles of it. Ryan walked over to the table and spread the envelopes out so he could see what he had—electric bills, telephone bills, sales letters, and a couple of checks from his latest photo assignments.

Dismissing most of the mail as junk, Ryan's gaze came to rest on an ivory-colored oversize envelope with his name engraved on the top. The return address caught his attention. For twelve years he had hoped for a letter with that postmark. To get one now was unsettling.

His hand shook as he reached for the card. He told himself not to be a fool, to throw it away. But he couldn't. Sliding open the seal with his finger, he pulled out the card.

*Serenity Springs invites you to attend its Centennial Celebration, February 20–23, a three-day festival of parties, games, and arts and crafts to celebrate 100 years of history. In tune with this theme, a special dinner will be held Thursday evening in honor of Serenity Springs' own Ryan Hunter, award-winning photojournalist.*

What the hell!

Ryan picked up the accompanying letter. Ms. Kara Delaney, president of the Serenity Springs Chamber of Commerce, wanted him to be the guest of honor at their kickoff dinner. Because of his world-renowned photographs and reputation as a photojournalist, Serenity Springs considered him their hometown hero and hoped he would be able to participate in the festivities.

Jesus! His father must be pissed. Either that or dead.

Ryan couldn't imagine Jonas Hunter allowing the town, *Jonas's town*, to honor his youngest son. And his brother, Andrew, was probably beside himself with jealous rage.

Ryan shook his head as he read the letter again. There was no way he would go back to Serenity Springs, a small river town a hundred miles north of San Francisco. As a successful freelance photographer, he could choose his assignments. He didn't have to go anywhere he didn't want to go.

Ryan tossed the invitation in the trash basket and pushed the button on the answering machine. Message after message came across. Two magazines wanted to send him on assignment, one to New York, the other to Hong Kong. His dry cleaning had been ready for three weeks. MCI wanted him to switch from AT&T, and he had just been named a finalist in the Holiday Travel Sweepstakes. Yeah, right.

The last message was from Camilla Harper, a woman he had met on the plane from New York to L.A. She wanted to see him while she was in town.

Ryan rewound the tape. He didn't feel like calling her back. He was tired of the dating game, tired of women moving in and out of his life. Tired of long airplane flights, no furniture, and fast food. Most of all Ryan was tired of feeling so damned tired.

He had a good life. He was thirty-three years old and had plenty of money, plenty of jobs, and plenty of hair. He smiled to himself as he ran a hand through his thick, dark brown hair. A few strands of gray maybe, but at least he wouldn't be going back to Serenity Springs as a balding, paunchy, overweight nothing. Not that he was going back.

Ryan walked into the kitchen and opened the refrigerator. Melanie had cleaned him out there, too. The only things left were a jar of pickle relish, a carton of milk, and a bottle of Gatorade.

Ryan closed the refrigerator door and returned to the living room. He sat down on the couch, wincing as one of the springs pinched his leg. He wanted to relax, soak up the silence. Only there wasn't silence. The couple next door had "Wheel of Fortune" blaring on the television set. The tenant upstairs was doing step aerobics, pounding the ceiling over his head with a relentless rhythm that matched the pounding in his head. And somewhere in the City of Angels a siren blared through the night.

He had been an ambulance chaser all his adult life, fleeing to every newsworthy event with his trusty Nikon, ready to record someone's bleakest or happiest moment. He had seen the bulls run through the streets of Pamplona, caught the last lap of the Indy 500, and watched the winning horse cross the finish line at the Kentucky Derby. But he had always been a spectator rather than a participant, traveling the world, trying to find his place in it.

In fact, he had no place, just an apartment that was little more than a stopover, sometimes furnished by the woman in his life—sometimes not. Melanie thought he was running away. Maybe she was right. He had always felt the need to keep moving—just like his mother.

Ryan's gaze returned to the garbage can. How could he go home? His father had told him to leave and never return. The last words Ryan had heard from his brother were "Good riddance."

So many angry words. So many bad memories. Yet the only family he had was in Serenity Springs. Ryan rolled his head around on his neck, feeling tense.

He was no longer a small-town guy. He liked the city with its traffic, malls, and twelve-theater cineplexes. He liked walking down a street full of strangers.

So what if he was a little lonely now and then? It was by choice, his choice.

With a sigh he reached over and took his saxophone out of the case. He blew into the instrument with passion, frustration, and restlessness. He didn't need written music or even a song, because he played by ear, by touch, by emotion, knowing instinctively the right notes to play. The music filled the empty spots in his soul, giving him an outlet for emotions that could not be expressed with words.

When he left Serenity Springs twelve years ago, he had taken nothing more than a couple of pairs of jeans, his camera, and the saxophone handed down from his grandfather, to his mother, to him. At the time, he hadn't needed anything more. Now—now he wasn't so sure.

Ryan set the instrument down on the floor and looked around the empty apartment. Maybe it was time to go back if only to reassure himself that he had made the right decision to leave. Just a couple of days, he thought. In and out like the breeze. No big deal.

Ryan got up and took the invitation out of the trash. His gaze dropped to the signature line, Kara Delaney. He wondered who she was and how she had the guts to call him back to a place where so many people hated him.

Ryan reached for the phone, suddenly curious to know the answer.

Kara Delaney struggled to hit the right keys on the piano, stretching her fingers as she had been taught, searching desperately for the rhythm that escaped her. The last two keys went down together, a screeching sound that echoed through her living room, finally ending in total silence. Kara stared down at the keys, afraid to turn her head, certain she did not want to see the face of her instructor, Hans Grubner.

Hans was in his early seventies, retired from a celebrated career as a concert pianist. Originally hailing from Germany, he had married a beautiful young American and spent forty years traveling through Europe. When a car accident crushed the fingers of his left hand, Hans and his wife, Gillian, retired to Serenity Springs, the town where Gillian had been born and raised. For the past ten years Hans had taught piano to almost every child in town, still hoping to one day find a protégée who could play the music that he longed to hear.

Unfortunately that protégée did not appear to be her. Slowly Kara turned to face her instructor.

Hans looked grim, his small black eyes haunting his

long, pale face. He opened his mouth to speak, then closed it. He waved his arms. Finally the words came out.

"You are killing me, Mrs. Delaney. You are torturing the piano. Your fingers are like clumsy elephants. The birds in the forest cover their ears when you play."

"I thought I was a little better," Kara said with a hopeful smile.

Hans threw up his hands in frustration. "Three-year-old children play better than you. Please, you must give this up. You are simply—how do you say it—no good."

Kara's shoulders stiffened at his turn of phrase. It was too familiar. "I'll practice more."

"All the practice in the world will not help. You can't do it."

"I can do it. I will do it. I want to play the piano for my guests in the evenings. My aunt Josephine always played the piano here. The Gatehouse is known for its nightly entertainment."

"Perhaps your aunt could play for you."

"The arthritis in her hands is too painful now."

"Then I suggest you buy a CD player."

Kara frowned as she looked down at her hands. Her fingers were long and slender. She should be able to master a simple instrument like a piano. "I'm not giving up," she said. "I've given up too many times in my life. No more."

Hans sighed as he reached for his hat. "I can no longer teach you. It pains me to hear you play."

"I'll pay you double."

"It is not the money."

"Please," Kara said. She looked into his eyes, willing him to understand. "I want to do this. I need to do this."

"Why? There are other instruments besides the piano. Perhaps the flute would sing for you."

"No. I want to play the piano." Kara ran her fingers lightly along the keys. "My fondest memories are of my aunt playing this piano every night before bedtime. My mother and father cuddled in the love seat. I sat on the floor at their feet. Everything good in my life happened right here, with this piano. I want to feel that joy again. I want to bring it back for my daughter, for my guests."

Hans's face tightened with his own remembered pain. "Some things cannot be recaptured, not for any amount of wishing."

"I can't give up now. I'm so close."

Hans gave her a pitiful look. "It is difficult to say no to someone with so much passion, misplaced though it may be. I will give you another month. Now I must go."

Kara walked Hans to the front door. "Say hello to Mrs. Grubner for me," Kara said. "I can't wait to hear her sing at the centennial. You two must have been really something. Your music, her voice."

"A perfect duet for forty-eight years now."

"Forty-eight years? What's your secret?"

"Apple strudel," he said.

"Excuse me?"

"Gillian hates to cook, but I love apple strudel."

"I don't understand."

"Some day you will." He tipped his hat. "Good afternoon, Mrs. Delaney."

"Good afternoon." Kara leaned against the door as Hans walked down the front steps of the old Victorian, along the cobblestone path that bordered the green lawn and the carefully tended vegetable and herb garden. She had spent the past six months refurbishing the Gatehouse and revitalizing the gardens, investing every cent of the small inheritance she had received from her mother. She was now ready to turn the Gatehouse into a profitable inn that combined the warmth of home and the seclusion of a romantic getaway along with the amenities of a five-star hotel.

She just hoped she could pull it off. As Kara closed the front door, she admitted to herself that romance and realism rarely went together, except perhaps in the

Grubners' case. Forty-eight years of marriage. She couldn't even imagine such a thing.

Her own marriage had lasted ten years, a lifetime by some standards, but not by her own. She had wanted to live the happily-ever-after life. Unfortunately her husband, Michael, had not cooperated. They had separated a year ago, and six months after that separation Kara had returned to the place of her birth, determined to make a home for herself and her daughter, Angel, in the small town, away from the pressures of the city, away from the lying smiles of her ex-husband.

Kara walked down the hall, taking pride in the shine of the hardwood floors, the scent of freshly picked flowers, the proud gleam of the grandfather clock that chimed out the hours with relentless predictability. Looking around, she knew she could count on this house, on the things she had surrounded herself with. She could be happy here.

Kara passed by the living room, the formal dining room where she served breakfast in the morning and dinner in the evening, the alcove where she set up cocktails at dusk, and the carefully carved staircase that wound up to the second and third floors, a pattern of diamonds and hearts decorating the railing.

At the back of the house was a large country kitchen with an adjoining breakfast room on one side and a sun porch on the other. The kitchen, with its oak cabinets, large center island, and decorative brass pots, was where she spent most of her time, filling the house with the scents of ginger and cinnamon.

Kara had just entered the kitchen when she heard the front door open then slam shut, characteristic of her eleven-year-old daughter. But it wasn't Angel who called out to her.

"Kara?" A man's voice rang through the house.

"I'm in the kitch—"

Andrew Hunter threw open the kitchen door before she finished speaking. A tall man in his mid-thirties,

Andrew was attractive in a clean-cut way with short brown hair, matching brown eyes, a smoothly shaved face, and neatly pressed clothes.

Andrew was a nine-to-five kind of man, one who would never take an extra minute for lunch, never call long distance on a company phone, and never kiss a woman unless he asked first. Kara found that trait comforting, as safe and warm as the house and the town she had come to cherish.

But Andrew also seemed to be a man who thought too much and said too little. Kara suspected that one day the words would burst out of him and his emotions would spill forth like the river after a nasty rain. She just hadn't anticipated being the target.

"I can't believe it," Andrew said. "I can't believe you asked my brother to come to the centennial. Are you out of your mind?"

Andrew ran a hand through his hair in frustration. His eyes reflected anger and uncertainty. He looked like a man who had just found out a murderer was being released in his hometown.

Kara took a step back from him and placed her hands on the cool brown-and-white tiles of her kitchen counter. She had expected Andrew to be upset, but she hadn't expected to see such a look of betrayal in his eyes.

"Andrew, calm down," she said. "This isn't personal. It's business. I think Ryan can help us."

Andrew looked at her in amazement. "My God, Kara, you don't know what you've done." Andrew sat down at the oak table in the breakfast room. He rested his head on his hands, no longer angry but defeated.

The other members of the centennial committee had warned Kara that Ryan Hunter could be a problem, but the advantages of inviting him to participate had seemed to outweigh the disadvantages. At least until now.

She knew Andrew and Ryan had been mixed up with

some woman years ago. Rumors of the old love triangle still made their way around town in between the daily gossip about Loretta and her fatherless baby, Aunt Josephine's true hair color, and who had spiked the punch at the high school dance.

But Ryan had left town twelve years ago. There had been a lot of water under Tucker's Bridge since then.

After a moment Kara joined Andrew at the table. "Think about it," she said, putting a hand over his. "Ryan is a celebrity. He's just the draw we need to sell tickets for the centennial dinner."

Andrew lifted his head and looked her straight in the eye. "Ryan is a troublemaker. You should have told me, Kara. I thought we were friends. I thought we were more than friends."

Andrew's gaze challenged her to reply, to admit the feelings they had yet to discuss. But that was the problem. They didn't talk about their feelings, about what mattered to them. Maybe that's why she was holding back on an intimate relationship. She wanted to be with a man who would tell her everything.

Kara reminded herself that Andrew was a good man. As a single father he knew the challenges she faced in raising a daughter on her own. Plus, Andrew was content to live in a small town, to work on the newspaper with his father. He might not be the most passionate man, but she knew she could count on him.

"We are more than friends," Kara said slowly. "I didn't tell you about Ryan, because I knew what you would say."

"If you knew what I'd say, why did you do it?"

Because her desire to restore Serenity Springs to its former glory had superseded Andrew's feelings. Saving Serenity Springs had become synonymous with saving herself. If she could make the centennial a success, if she could revive the town, then she'd be that much closer to having the home she had always wanted.

Kara lifted her chin, knowing that even though she

disliked confrontation, she could no longer avoid this particular showdown. "I'm president of the chamber of commerce, Andrew. It's my job to create interest in Serenity Springs. Harrison Winslow, the developer I told you about, is interested in building an expensive resort in the north woods. If we can show him a nearby town with the charm of the old country and the sophistication of a big city, he'll be completely won over. Think about what that would mean for all of us—our town featured in premier travel magazines, touted as a popular destination for world-weary travelers."

"I'm sure it would mean business for the Gatehouse."

"That's right, it would. And if I don't get more business, I can't stay here, Andrew. Don't you see what's at stake? It's not just me and my home that's in jeopardy. Your newspaper needs *news* to stay afloat."

"What does any of this have to do with Ryan?"

"Ryan is news, Andrew. Some of the people in town have been threatening to boycott the centennial, afraid that we're trying to turn Serenity Springs into New York City. But I think if Ryan comes to the party, they'll be more interested in seeing him than in causing trouble."

"They won't have to cause trouble; Ryan will."

"There's another reason, too." Kara paused, hating to rub Ryan's success in Andrew's face, but she didn't seem to have any other choice. "Ryan is a terrific photographer. His work is seen all over the world. If he takes photos of the centennial and sends them off to a national magazine, everyone will see how special this part of the country is. The bottom line is that this celebration, and hopefully Ryan's attendance, will mean more business for everyone, for Aunt Josephine's antiques shop, for Ike's barbershop, for Loretta's bar."

"Progress could ruin this town."

"It could also help it. I don't want our kids to grow up and leave. I want them to grow up here and stay, because there are opportunities."

"Opportunities to destroy what makes this town special—its smallness."

Sometimes Andrew could be so damned stubborn. "I don't think this is about progress; it's about your brother. I know there are bad feelings between you and Ryan, but surely after all this time . . ."

"You don't know anything about me and my brother."

"Then tell me."

"No."

Kara sat back in her seat, taken aback by his blunt answer. "How can you expect me to understand if you won't talk to me?"

"I guess I can't. It's not just me though. A lot of people in this town don't like Ryan. He was always breaking things, always screwing up, always causing trouble."

"Maybe Ryan has changed."

"I doubt it. Who else knew about this?"

"The centennial committee, Loretta, Aunt Josephine, Hannah Davies, Mayor Hewitt, Will Hodgkins, and myself."

"Loretta's probably still pining after him. Your aunt Josephine would do anything you say, and Mayor Hewitt's new in town." Andrew shook his head. "Old Hannah loves Ryan's photos, practically has a shrine set up at the library, so she wouldn't say no. But I don't understand why Will didn't put a stop to this. He's my friend."

"Will only had one vote."

Silence fell between them. "Ryan won't come," Andrew said finally. "He didn't come back when my son was born. Not even when my wife sent him a note. I told Becky Lee not to bother. But she just—just couldn't forget him."

"You can't forget him either, can you?"

"I was doing just fine until you sent that invitation. Some things are better left dead and buried."

"But Ryan isn't dead."

"He is to me."

The phone rang. Kara stood up, suddenly tense. "That's probably Angel." Andrew didn't move. The phone rang again. She picked up the receiver. "The Gatehouse. May I help you?"

"Is Kara Delaney there?"

The man asking the question had a deep, melodious voice that went down as smoothly as a cup of French roast coffee. Kara swallowed hard. She knew who it was. Deep down in her gut, she knew. "This is Kara Delaney."

"Ryan Hunter."

"Mr. Hunter. Hello." Kara turned away from Andrew.

"I just got your letter. I accept your invitation."

"You do? I mean, that's great." Kara twisted the phone cord between her fingers. Never had she imagined that he would actually attend. Now she didn't know if she should be relieved or worried.

The kitchen door slammed so hard a picture fell off the wall. She turned her head. Andrew had left. Problem number one. They were off and running. She turned her attention back to the phone.

"So you'll come?" she repeated.

"Don't make me say it twice. When do you want me?"

Kara cleared her throat. "The banquet is Thursday night, February twentieth. If you can get here the day before, we can go over the schedule."

"Fine."

"Do you need accommodations? Or will you be staying with—friends?" Silence greeted her question. "Mr. Hunter?"

"I'll need a room."

"You can stay here. At the Gatehouse."

"Crazy Josephine's place?"

"Mrs. Parker—actually it's Mrs. Kelly now—is my aunt."

"Your aunt? Kara Cox?" Ryan let out a long, curious whistle. "I haven't thought of you in years."

Kara stiffened. "Why should you? You couldn't possibly remember me. I was only seven years old when I last lived here. And you were at least . . ."

"Nine. But I do remember you. We have something in common, don't we, Kara?"

"What are you talking about?"

"Are you telling me you don't know?"

"Know what, Mr. Hunter?"

Ryan didn't answer for a long moment. "It's not important. Mrs. Delaney—is my father still alive?"

"What a strange question. Of course he's alive."

"Then hell must have frozen over."

## 2

Hell? Kara thought about Ryan's parting words as she hung up the phone. Her mother had used that phrase every time Kara had asked about her father. "He'll be back when hell freezes over," Jane Ann Cox would say. Her mother would put her hands on her hips when she said those words and glare at Kara as if it were her fault that the man they both loved had up and gone.

For a long time Kara believed it was her fault. A part of her still did, because she didn't know why her parents had split up. One day they were living happily at the Gatehouse in Serenity Springs. The next day the river flooded its banks, and a week later her mother filed for divorce. She hadn't seen her father again for fifteen years.

Kara stared at the phone. What had Ryan Hunter meant—*we have something in common?* They had nothing in common, except that they had both been born in Serenity Springs.

The grandfather clock in the hall began to ring six long, melodious, penetrating bells that counted off the hours, reminding Kara that Angel was late—again.

A gust of air blew the wind chimes on the back deck into a sudden frenzy. Kara walked over to the back door

and stepped outside, drawing her arms around her
body to ward off the chill of winter.

Normally she loved the view from the back deck, enjoying the impressive redwood trees that led down to
the Snake River a few hundred yards from the house.
Like the serpent it was named after, the Snake River
wound its way through several small towns in Sonoma
County, moving relentlessly in its downward trek toward the Pacific Ocean some sixty miles away.

The river had played a major role in the birth of Serenity Springs, giving the early loggers an opportunity
to move the massive logs downstream, and creating a
beautiful setting where loggers and their families could
make a home for themselves. The river had also drawn
tourists and vacationers from San Francisco, thus giving
the town a chance to survive once the forest had been
stripped bare.

The trees had finally grown back, some protected in
a redwood grove ten miles south, the others protected
by the people who had come to respect and cherish the
land, not profit from it.

Although, Kara guiltily admitted, she did want to
profit from the river. She wanted to share some of the
beauty of this town so that she could make enough
money to stay here, to live here.

Kara shivered again as a brisk breeze blew through
her thick red hair, drawing goose bumps down her
arms. Tonight the early-evening atmosphere was almost
spooky. Dark clouds gathered to the west, promising
more rain in the not-too-distant future.

Maybe it was the phone call from Ryan or the confrontation with Andrew, or maybe it was just nerves
over the upcoming centennial, but Kara felt uneasy, as
if something bad was about to happen.

She glanced down at her watch, her worry increasing
as she wondered about Angel.

Not that Angel wasn't often late—she was. Her
daughter had a tendency to get caught up in imaginary

games. Since her parents' divorce, those imaginary games had turned into long, involved flights of fancy.

Kara told herself there was nothing to worry about. At eleven, Angel was vulnerable, and she was probably just acting out her fears about the divorce, about their future. At least Kara hoped that's all it was. Sometimes Angel looked at her in the strangest way, as if she knew something that Kara didn't.

But that was impossible. Kara had protected Angel from most of her marital fights, always putting on a happy face, pretending that they were a normal family. And when they'd finally split up, she had simply told Angel that she and Michael would always be friends, but they couldn't live together anymore. It was only a half-truth, but the full truth was too ugly for a child to hear about her father.

A sudden crack of distant thunder rattled the house, bringing another shiver to her chilled body. Kara hated storms, the feeling of being out of control, at the mercy of something so much bigger than herself.

Kara hugged her body tightly as the wind whistled through the trees. There were shadows everywhere, in front of her, behind her, next to her. Andrew had told her that by bringing Ryan home she was raising the dead. Tonight she could almost agree.

"At night the lady rises out of the river like a ghost. She wears a long, white lace dress, and a veil covers her eyes. Her hair is black as night and floats down to her waist, with streaks of gray that shine like silver in the moonlight." Angel Delaney dropped her voice to a whisper as her fellow sixth graders looked nervously at the brown, muddy river. She had them going now. She dropped her voice another notch.

"If you listen very, very carefully you can hear her voice in the wind. It starts out soft like a whisper, then gets louder until it pierces the night like a scream. *Ah-oooh*," Angel wailed. "*Ah-ooh*."

"Stop it, Angel. You're scaring me." Melissa Johnson slid closer to Billy Hunter.

"Listen." Angel turned her attention to the river. The current moved fast with the breeze. Storm clouds blew in from the coast. "I think I can hear her."

"You can't hear anything," Billy said. "You're making it up. I've lived here my whole life, and I've never heard that story."

"It's true. And the best time to see her is when the river is rising, like today."

"My mother doesn't think I should play with you anymore," Melissa said. "She says you tell lies."

Angel ignored Melissa, concentrating instead on Billy's rapt expression. "The lady is very sad about something. When she cries, her tears fill the river."

A shrill cry pierced the night, and Melissa buried her head in her arms.

"How did you do that?" Billy demanded.

Angel shook her head. "I didn't do anything."

The sound came again, a long, lonely wail. All three children jumped to their feet. Thunder rocked the sky.

Melissa clutched Angel's sleeve. Billy had a hand on the belt loop of her jeans. Angel wasn't afraid of the storm. She liked it when the wind blew hard and the trees rattled the windowpanes on her house. It felt like God was sweeping the world clean, blowing out the cobwebs and all the other nasty stuff.

"It's okay, it's just the wind," Angel said calmly.

"Right," Billy said.

"Maybe we'll see the lady." Angel pointed to a faraway spot on the river where the clouds were so low they almost touched the water. "There she is. I see her. Look. Look," she cried. Actually she did see a shape, and it looked like a woman, but Angel told herself it was just her imagination making her own story even better.

"I don't want to look," Melissa yelled as she scrambled up the riverbank. Billy ran after her.

Angel smiled to herself. Scaredy-cats, she thought. Then a heavy hand came down on her shoulder and it was her turn to scream.

"What are you doing out here?" The man's voice sounded rough. His hand slid from her shoulder to the back of her neck. She could feel the calluses on his fingers as he spun her around to face him.

Angel swallowed hard. As tall as a redwood tree and thick around the middle, the man wore an old fishing hat on his head that barely covered his straggly black and gray hair. He had a thick beard, and his dark eyes blasted right through her.

Jonas Hunter, Billy's grandfather, and the meanest man in town. Aunt Josephine said Jonas Hunter was a lonely, bitter man. Billy said his grandfather was a grumpy bear. Angel thought he looked like Bigfoot, at least the monster she imagined in her mind.

Still, her mother had always told her to be nice to old people, so she supposed she should give him a chance. Maybe she would be grumpy, too, if she looked as ugly as he did.

"I said, what are you doing here?" His voice shook her more than the thunder.

"I, uh. I . . ." Angel looked around. Billy and Melissa were long gone. "I got lost."

"Lost? You're that kid, aren't you? That Delaney woman's kid, the one who tells all the stories."

"Angel. My name is Angel." Angel offered him her brightest, most winning smile and stuck out her hand. When he didn't respond, she stuffed her hands into the pockets of her jeans. "I came down to the river to write an essay for school on the sound the water makes when it rushes downstream. Does it sound like a roller coaster or a jet plane? What do you think?" It wasn't much of a tale, not up to her usual standards, but it was all she could think of at the moment.

"Why are you out here all alone?"

"She's not alone. I'm here, too." Billy walked slowly

out of the trees. He was shaking so bad Angel thought he might fall over.

"Billy? Is that you, boy?" Jonas roared. "Why, I should tan your hide for coming down to the river on a night like this. You got sawdust in your brains, or what?"

"Well, sir." Billy's voice shook and he started to stutter.

"Speak up now. I can't hear you." Jonas put his hands on his waist when Billy tried to get out a word, but it was completely unintelligible. "What the hell's the matter with you, boy?"

"You're scaring him," Angel said, running over to Billy's side. "How come you're so mean?"

Jonas stared at her through slitted eyes. "What did you say?"

"We're just kids, you know," Angel said defiantly, hating to see her best friend so upset. "We can come to the river if we want to. It's a free country."

"You got a tongue on you, just like your mother," Jonas said. "She ought to wash your mouth out with soap."

"And you ought to be nicer to Billy. He's your grandson," Angel replied.

"Angel, stop," Billy muttered. "You're making him mad."

"I used to wish I had grandparents. But mine are all dead," Angel said. "Maybe that's good if all grandparents are as mean as you. No wonder your own son left town and never came back." Angel stopped abruptly at the look of rage that crossed Jonas Hunter's face.

"You fixin' to see your next birthday, kid?"

"She didn't mean it," Billy said, finally getting some words through his stiff lips.

"Oh, I think she did."

Angel nervously licked her lips. So much for being nice to old people. "I'm sorry."

"Get out of here, both of you, before I tan your hides myself."

Billy grabbed Angel's hand and dragged her away from the river. "You shouldn't have mentioned Uncle Ryan," Billy said as they made their way back to town. "Nobody is supposed to talk about him, not ever."

"How come?"

"Because he's a liar and a thief."

"What did he lie about?"

Billy shrugged. "Don't know."

"Well, what did he steal then?"

"My dad wouldn't say."

"Then maybe none of it's true," Angel said.

Billy looked shocked that she would even question him. But then Billy believed most of what she told him, too.

"Of course it's true," Billy said. "My dad wouldn't lie to me."

Angel looked away, feeling terribly sad. "Sometimes dads are the worst liars of all," she whispered, but Billy didn't hear her. Maybe it was better that way.

Andrew Hunter set his beer glass down on the bar and sighed. Three beers and he didn't feel drunk, just nauseated. He never could hold his liquor. Just another thing his little brother did better than him.

"Refill, hon?"

His brain said no. His mouth said yes.

Loretta Swanson took his empty glass and filled it from the tap behind the bar. Her movements were graceful and efficient for a woman nine months pregnant. He couldn't help admiring the slender curve of her neck where her blond hair was swept up into a ponytail, or the long thin legs that came out from under her oversize sweater.

Loretta Swanson had always been the prettiest girl in town as well as the fastest. She was the Serenity Springs bad girl. She had been in Ryan's class, and for a while she and Ryan had been a pair.

Rumor had it that Loretta had laid every man in town. And even if that was an exaggeration, judging by the current state of affairs she'd slept with at least one. According to the town grapevine, she wasn't saying who the father was. People speculated that she didn't even know who the father was, and since she'd turned up knocked up most of the men took care to avoid her.

Of course, Andrew had never been with her. His father would have kicked his butt out of the house if he had ever messed with a girl like Loretta. It was bad enough when he got involved with Becky Lee. . . .

"Must be woman problems," Loretta said, offering him a warm, commiserating smile.

"Not this time." Andrew drained his glass of beer in one long draft. His stomach turned over, and his vision blurred slightly. "Hit me again," he said.

Loretta shook her head. "You're not a drinker, Andrew Joseph. So what are you doing here in my bar, shoving down beers like a thirsty man in the desert?"

It was her warm brown eyes that did it. No wonder so many men wanted her. She had a way of talking and looking that made everything seem personal. Course, he didn't approve of her life-style. He wanted a woman with morals, someone like Kara.

He tried to smile at the thought of Kara. She was just as pretty as Loretta in a different sort of way. Kara had beautiful red hair and big blue eyes, the kind of skin that burned under a winter sun, and a womanly figure that was pleasing to a man. Unfortunately she also had a stubborn streak, a tendency to laugh at the worst jokes, and a bit of a temper. Not to mention her ideas for Serenity Springs, which was why he was here in the first place.

"Cat caught your tongue, Andrew Joseph?"

"Don't call me that," he growled. "Makes me feel like

I'm in the third grade again. If you really want to know the problem, it's Ryan. He's coming home."

Loretta stared at him in shock. "I knew Kara invited him, but I never thought he'd come." She put a hand to her mouth in amazement, then self-consciously began to tuck her loose hair into her ponytail, as if Ryan might walk in any minute and catch her not looking her best.

"I don't think your hair will be the first thing Ryan notices," Andrew said, tipping his head toward her stomach.

Loretta blushed. He couldn't believe it. Her cheeks actually turned red.

"That was a mean thing to say," she said.

"You are pregnant."

"Believe me, if anyone knows that, I do. I'm the one with the backaches and this whale of a body that barely lets me get through the door. You don't have to remind me." Her eyes blurred with tears.

Andrew stared at her in amazement. "I'm sorry. But if things are so tough, maybe you should get the father of that kid of yours to help you out."

"Aw, shove off, Andrew Joseph. Go drown your sorrows somewhere else. I'm closing up."

Andrew glanced around the empty bar. Aside from old Hank Marley and Lou Osborne playing checkers in the corner, the place was dead. Still, there were glasses to wash and tables to scrub down, and Loretta already looked ready to drop. "You need any help?"

"No. I can do it alone. I can do everything alone."

"Fine." Andrew stood up abruptly, then wished he hadn't when his head began to spin.

"You got yourself a buzz, don't you?" Loretta said knowingly. "You want a cup of coffee before you go home?"

"I thought you were closing."

Loretta shrugged her shoulders. "I guess I have time. It's not like I got anywhere to go. What about Billy? He expecting you?"

"Mrs. Murray will stay till I get back," Andrew said, referring to his longtime neighbor and baby-sitter. She had been taking care of him and Billy for more than ten years now.

Loretta set a cup of black coffee in front of him. A bit of it sloshed over the rim of the cup, and they both reached for a napkin. His hand came down on top of hers, and the touch set off a charge down his spine.

When he lifted his head, he was staring straight into her eyes. Goddammit. He didn't need this, not now. He got to his feet. "I gotta go," he mumbled.

Loretta didn't smile, just nodded her head. "Running away again. You been making a habit of that, haven't you?"

"I am not running away. I have never run away. I stayed here in Serenity Springs to help my father run the newspaper, to raise my child. Ryan's the one who left."

"Sometimes running away just means turning your back, Andrew Joseph, and I've seen a lot of your back."

Andrew walked out of the bar and slammed the door behind him. The last thing he needed was pop psychology from Loretta Swanson. As he ran to his car, the rain came down on his head, sobering him up, reminding him that even after a night of drowning his sorrows, he could still remember that Ryan was coming home.

## 3

A week later, Ryan turned off the main highway and headed toward Serenity Springs. The winding two-lane road took him farther away from what he considered civilization—fast-food restaurants, video stores, and ATM machines.

Now, instead of traffic lights and billboards, he saw redwood and pine trees; thick grassy meadows and rain-filled ponds; apple orchards and Christmas tree farms; small-time restaurants with names like Joe's or Mary's; fresh-fruit stands that were nothing more than a truck, a dilapidated shack, and crates of apples, oranges, and grapes.

Ryan could feel the pace of life getting slower with each mile. Even the cars moved at a more leisurely pace. When the truck in front of him stopped to let a trio of horseback riders cross, Ryan knew there was no point in honking his horn. They would move when they moved.

Eventually the traffic thinned out until there was nothing to see in either direction but a long ribbon of asphalt leading to his final destination, Serenity Springs.

Ryan turned on the radio, hoping for a snappy tune to take his mind off his doubts. The first station had Bruce Springsteen singing "Born to Run."

Jesus! How appropriate. He had been born to run, and he was still running. Only now he was going backward instead of forward. Ryan changed the station, hoping to find some jazz or maybe some blues. That would certainly fit his mood.

As he drove over a narrow bridge, his attention turned toward the river. His first sight of the water brought back memories. He remembered the big flood twenty-five years earlier and the damage left in its wake. He had been nine years old when the river broke over its banks. The rush of water had been tremendous. The friendly creek had become a monster that could not be defeated. He had been afraid of it ever since.

His father never understood his aversion to the water, his fear of getting too far from shore or caught up in a sudden torrent. But then Jonas had no time for weakness in any form. Just another one of his father's wonderful traits.

Today, with the clouds and scattered sunshine, the river did not look threatening, although it did appear higher than Ryan remembered. Of course, it had rained last week, and according to the weather service, there was more rain on the way. He just hoped it would hold off till Sunday.

Ryan's breathing relaxed as he drove off the bridge and the road moved away from the river. It was easier to look at the far-off mountains and the empty road than the powerful and swift Snake River.

His father loved the river, respected it, feared it, and wanted to live by it all the days of his life. Ryan wondered if Andrew felt the same as Jonas. Andrew must, or he would have left Serenity Springs years ago.

Ryan smiled to himself as a freshly painted billboard greeted his eyes.

TWO MILES TO SERENITY SPRINGS, HOME OF THE WORLD'S OLDEST TEACUP COLLECTION. VISIT NEARBY SNAKE RIVER FOR THE BEST FISHING, CANOEING, AND

CAMPING MOTHER NATURE CAN PROVIDE. EXIT AT
MAIN STREET.

So old Josephine had finally found a place to boast
about her teacups. Ryan couldn't help but be amused.
He had to admit he was feeling curious about his hometown.

He pushed his foot down on the gas pedal of the red
Ferrari. The car wasn't his. He had rented it for the trip.
After all, Serenity Springs had invited the celebrity
home, not the man. They wanted him for flash and excitement. He might as well live up to his reputation.

The car burst forward under his hands, and the sense
of speed was exhilarating. Then a flash of light in the
rearview mirror caught his eye. He looked up and
swore. Damn. A cop car was chasing his dust.

Ryan slowed down and pulled over to the edge of the
highway, tapping his fingers restlessly on the steering
wheel as he waited for the policeman to approach.

The officer moved with the speed of a lumbering cow.
He opened his door, put one foot out, looked at something on the seat next to him, put the other foot out,
and finally stood up. There was something familiar
about him, but he wore a hat and dark glasses, making
it impossible for Ryan to see his face.

When the officer got to his car, Ryan rolled down the
window and took off his sunglasses. The cop put his
hand on the roof of the car and looked at him. "Okay,
city boy, let's see your—God almighty. Ryan Hunter, is
that you?"

Ryan nodded his head, squinting to get a better look
at the man. "That's me. And you are . . ."

"Will. Will Hodgkins." The man removed his sunglasses. "Don't you remember me?"

"Sure, of course." Ryan nodded his head. Will had
been in Andrew's class, one of his better friends, in fact.
Ryan wondered if Will and his brother were still close.

If so, he had a feeling this ticket was getting more expensive by the minute.

"I can't believe it's you." Will shook his head. "I never thought you'd come back."

"Yeah, well, someone sent me an invitation."

"Kara Delaney. She's stirring up all kinds of trouble."

"Sounds like my kind of woman."

"Right." Will frowned. "I wasn't in favor of the town inviting you, just so you know up front. I thought it was a slap in Andrew's face. But I was outvoted."

"I see."

Will straightened up. "But that was that, and this is this. You were speeding, Ryan, and I'm a sheriff now, so I have to give you a ticket. Can't do otherwise. Wouldn't be right."

"I understand. What happened to Dirk Anders? Did he retire?"

"Not yet. He's still my boss. But he's getting on in years, same as Jonas." Will paused. "Quite a car you got here. Those pictures you take must be worth a lot of money."

"They are to some people."

"Hannah Davies has a whole shelf of your work at the library. She's going to be happier than a flea on a dog when she sees you. Where are you staying?"

"Not with Andrew. I'm sure my brother wouldn't have me in his house, and I doubt Becky Lee would either."

Will stared at him for a long moment. "Becky Lee's dead, Ryan. Gone eleven years now."

The words took Ryan by complete surprise. Dead? Becky Lee was dead? A sudden burst of pain ripped through him as he remembered his high school sweetheart.

"No. No." He shook his head in bewilderment. "That's not possible. She's our age."

"I'm sorry. I thought you knew."

"How? She was so young. My God, it must have happened . . ."

"Before their first anniversary," Will finished. He scratched his head, clearly puzzled. "I can't believe you don't know."

"Know what?"

"She was leaving Andrew. Packed up the car and the baby and left town with a note saying she was going to find you, Ryan. Got hit by a drunk driver ten miles out of town. The baby made it. She didn't."

"Goddammit." Ryan looked into Will's face. "I didn't ask her to come."

Will stared back at him without saying a word.

"Does Andrew know that?" Ryan asked. "Does he blame me for her death?"

"What do you think?"

Ryan thought his brother had one more reason to hate his guts. "The only thing I got from Becky Lee was a baby announcement. I figured she and Andrew must be happy together if they were having kids so soon. Guess they just couldn't wait to start a family."

Will sent him another curious look, then shook his head and began to write out a ticket. "How long will you be staying?"

"A few days. I'm not sure." Ryan slid his sunglasses over his eyes, still reeling from the news of Becky Lee's death. He couldn't imagine her body still and lifeless. In his mind he could see her on the sidelines at the high school football game, cheering him on in her short red skirt with her colorful pom-poms. He could still remember her wicked smile, her teasing manner, her love of adventure.

They had necked under the grandstands, smoked cigarettes in the supply closet at the high school, and sneaked sloe gin into their 7-Up cans at the school dance. A woman more full of life he could not imagine.

Becky Lee. Goddammit.

Ryan hit his fist against the steering wheel.

Will handed him the ticket. Ryan tossed it onto the passenger seat.

"I really thought you knew," Will said.

Ryan shook his head, his mouth and jaw so tight with emotion he couldn't get a word out.

"I guess you would have found out sooner or later. Take it a little slower into town. Okay?"

Ryan nodded.

Will patted the hood of the car. "Nice wheels. They suit you."

Ryan let out a breath as Will walked away. Through his rearview mirror, he watched him get into the patrol car. Will Hodgkins, once voted class clown, was now a sheriff, and Becky Lee, the most vibrant girl in school, was dead. He couldn't believe it. And she had died on her way out of town. She had never had a chance to see the big city, never danced in a smoky nightclub the way she had dreamed about, never seen London or Paris or any of the places he had come to take for granted.

What a waste. What an incredible waste.

Will drove away long before Ryan had enough courage to turn the key in the ignition. Finally he started the car, feeling a mix of emotions. He wanted to go forward. At the same time he wanted to go back to where he had been before the damned invitation arrived, before he had learned about Becky Lee, before he had had to think about his father and brother again.

But he couldn't walk away now. He only had part of the picture, a glimpse of the past. He needed to know the rest.

Ryan pulled the car onto the highway. A half mile outside of town, he saw the graveyard behind the church. He didn't intend to stop, but at the last moment he turned the wheel and pulled into the parking lot, bringing the Ferrari to a stop in front of the sign announcing the time of the next mass.

Without allowing himself to think too long about his actions, he got out of the car and walked down the path next to the church, the one that led to the cemetery in back.

His grandparents were buried in the cemetery along with his great-grandparents, an aunt, and a cousin. He had been to the cemetery many times with his mother, who always felt it important to place fresh flowers on the graves. In fact, he could remember many a time when they had come to this place and talked about God and heaven and angels.

Isabelle had believed in all those things. She had told him once that she was afraid to go to bed angry, because she always worried her harsh words might be the last she had a chance to utter.

Ryan had thought about that more than a few times over the years, especially after she had left him without a word of explanation. How could she make sure she didn't go to bed angry, yet leave her two boys without saying good-bye?

As he walked into the yard, Ryan slowed his pace, reading the headstones with nostalgia. He remembered Mrs. McIntyre, his first-grade teacher, the one who gave out red jawbreakers on Valentine's Day. He remembered Mr. Woolsley, the janitor at the high school, who helped him clean up the glass from a science experiment gone awry.

For the first time in a long time, it occurred to Ryan that he had left some friends behind in this town. Only he had been too full of himself and his problems to see that.

He leaned down and brushed a cigarette butt off Mr. Woolsley's grave. The man had hated cigarettes with a passion, probably because he had to clean up smoke-filled rest rooms at the high school.

As Ryan straightened, he realized that the rest of the yard was in good condition with neatly trimmed grass and flowers on some of the graves. The birds sang in harmony with the nearby river, bringing a sense of peace to this spot. But it didn't suit Becky Lee at all.

Ryan searched the headstones until he found her. Then he dropped down on one knee and looked at her grave.

"I'm sorry," he whispered. He traced the name on the headstone with his finger. Becky Lee Woodrich Hunter.

She had married his brother.

Ryan squeezed his eyes shut. He didn't want to remember, didn't want to care again. All these years he had thought Becky Lee and Andrew were married and happy, raising their son. And all these years she was gone. Andrew must have been devastated. And the boy, Billy, growing up without a mother. Ryan knew firsthand how hard that could be.

"Damn you, Becky Lee. Your timing never was right," he muttered as he opened his eyes.

Ryan thought back to those last few weeks before he had left town. He had graduated from the nearby college with a bachelor's degree in journalism and an intense desire to get on with his life someplace far away from Serenity Springs. Becky Lee had wanted to go with him. She had wanted to get married. He had put her off, needing to be on his own for a while. She had paid him back by marrying Andrew. Ryan had left before the wedding.

Damn. Ryan got to his feet and took several deep breaths, forcing the emotion out of his body. Becky Lee had died a long time ago. And he hadn't really thought of her in years. It was this town, this damned town. He hadn't even driven down Main Street, and he already felt bad. What the hell was he doing here?

It was too late to turn back. Will knew he was here, and by now probably everyone else did, too.

Ryan left the graveyard and walked to the front of the church. His parents had married in the small chapel. And marriages in Serenity Springs were supposed to last forever. But not his parents' marriage. And not Andrew's marriage.

"God," he said aloud in frustration, anger, and sadness.

"He's right inside if you want to speak to him," a voice said from behind him.

Ryan turned around and stared into the face of a short gray-haired man wearing the traditional black collar of a Catholic priest. The man smiled at him, his blue eyes filled with a wiseness that came either from his faith or his age. Ryan wasn't sure which.

"Excuse me?" Ryan asked.

"God. I heard you call his name."

"Oh." Ryan tipped his head apologetically. "I—uh, I just, well, you know."

"It's nice to see you again, Ryan."

Ryan's eyes widened. "You know me?"

"I'm Father Miles. Jonathan Miles."

Ryan gave him a closer look, the familiarity of his name ringing a distant bell. "Father Miles, of course. I remember. You heard my first confession."

"That's when I got my first gray hair."

Ryan reluctantly smiled. "It got worse after that."

"Maybe you should have come back." He waved his hand toward the front door. "Would you like to come inside?"

Ryan immediately shook his head. He never went into a church unless there was a purpose, like a wedding he had to photograph or a funeral or a coronation. He never went in to pray. He didn't have a clue how to do that. Besides, he didn't hold much faith in prayers. A long, long time ago he had prayed every night before bed, squeezed his eyes shut, clasped his hands together, and tried so hard to make God hear him. But there had never been an answer, not even a whisper of one, just silence, just the sound of the river mocking him.

"Ryan?"

"What?" He turned his attention to the priest.

"I'm glad you've come home."

"Not home—just back." Ryan shoved his hands into

his pockets. "Maybe it's not a good idea after all."

"Second thoughts?"

"Oh, yeah."

"Afraid of what you will find, or what you won't find?"

"Both."

"I always liked you, Ryan."

Ryan sent him a skeptical look. "I distinctly remember having to say something like one hundred and fifty Hail Marys after my first confession, and I was only nine at the time."

"You had some catching up to do. And penance is good for the soul. I always wondered what made you so angry. Is the anger finally gone? Is that why you've come home?"

Ryan thought about his question for a long time. He didn't think of himself as angry, but something certainly drove him to the farthest corners of the world. "I came back to say good-bye."

"But you just got here."

"I never looked back when I left before. I guess there's a part of me that wants to take one last look."

"That's a start." Father Miles patted Ryan's shoulder and walked into the church.

"A start to what?" Ryan muttered. He wasn't starting anything. Not here. Not now. Not in this town.

The church door opened again, and Father Miles hurried out with a large wicker basket in his hand. "I'm glad I caught you. Could you give this to Kara Delaney for me? She'll know what to do."

"What is it? Food or something?"

Father Miles pulled back the blanket, revealing three puppies waking up from a nap. They were starting to stretch and blink their eyes open.

Ryan took a step backward in dismay. "Uh, Father, I'm not very good with animals."

"They're not for you. They're for Kara. She told me

she wanted a big family. You're staying at the Gate-house, aren't you?"

"Yes."

"Then you can save me a trip. They're orphans, poor things. Their mama died, and their owner—well, she's an older woman and she just can't handle them. They're small now, but they're golden retrievers."

"Oh, my."

"Yes, indeed." Father Miles smiled as he handed the basket to Ryan. "Go on, take them."

Ryan reluctantly took the basket. One of the puppies tried to scramble over the side, and he pushed it down with his other hand. Almost immediately the other two puppies tumbled into one another.

"Better get them in the car fast," Father Miles advised.

"Oh, Jes—I mean, gee whiz," Ryan corrected himself as he tried to maintain control of the basket and the puppies. "I don't know how to take care of puppies or anything for that matter. Just myself, you know. I just take care of myself."

Father Miles nodded as he opened the door to Ryan's car. "They can't take care of themselves, Ryan. They need you. And Kara, of course."

Kara. Right. Ryan was beginning to dislike her already. Not only had she sent him the damn invitation, but now he had to take care of her puppies. He set the basket down on the floor in front of the passenger seat. It was a tight fit, but he managed to close the door.

"God be with you," Father Miles called.

Ryan looked out at the sky. He had the distinct feeling that God had a sense of humor.

4

Ryan glanced at the wicker basket. The puppies stared back at him, big brown eyes filled with the wonder of life. He now knew where the expression "puppy dog eyes" came from. It would be difficult to deny these little doggies anything.

"Just stay right there," he warned, "or you'll be in big trouble." One of the puppies barked in obvious delight. Maybe talking to them wasn't a good idea. He didn't want them to think he actually liked them, although they were kind of cute. Nothing like Max, the German shepherd his father had raised from a pup. That dog had scared him to death. Max had not been the kind of dog you could pull on your lap or snuggle up to on a cold winter night. He had been an outdoor dog, a hunting companion for his father.

Ryan turned the key in the ignition and backed out of the parking lot. Fifty yards down the highway, one of the puppies crawled out of the basket and onto the passenger seat. Ryan tried to push the dog back into the basket, but the puppy playfully licked his hand. Ryan winced at the moisture. "Come on, little doggy. There you go."

One dog in, another dog out. Then the third. Suddenly all three puppies were crawling on the front seat, over the console, onto his lap.

"Oh, shit." Ryan tried to drive with one hand as he grabbed for the puppies. As if in reply, one of the dogs peed on his pant leg. Ryan groaned. "I'm going to kill you," he said to the puppy. "Right after I kill Kara Delaney."

The puppy put his head down on Ryan's leg with a woebegone expression. "All right, maybe I won't kill you."

Ryan took the turnoff onto Main Street. There was a new stop sign at the corner; still not much traffic, but it looked as if someone was hoping. He drove farther down the street, under the faded white arches that read Serenity Springs, past Ike's Barber Shop, Miller's Grocery, Nellie's Diner, and Swanson's Bar.

The buildings on Main Street were rundown, some in desperate need of a paint job. A few of the storefronts were boarded up. The five-and-dime was gone. The bicycle shop was gone. But there was a new yogurt shop, and some construction was going on at the corner of Main Street and Jordan Road.

Down one of the side streets he could see the banner for his father's newspaper, *The Sentinel*. Down another street he saw the post office and the bank, a movie theater still showing one of the Rocky movies, and the recreation center.

He got mixed feelings from the town. Some streets seemed deserted. Others looked on their way to restoration, as if the town was divided into two factions, people who wanted to move on and people who didn't.

At the end of Main Street, Ryan turned left. He drove down familiar residential streets. He remembered playing kick ball, trick-or-treating on Halloween, playing hide-and-seek on late summer evenings, and catching butterflies in the springtime.

The carefree days of his childhood had become less enchanted after his mother left. By the time he reached his teens, the small town had become too small for him, like a prison, barring him from his dreams.

Thank God he had gotten out.

While Ryan was reminiscing, one of the puppies started to bark, then uttered a coughing, choking sound, and finally threw up on the passenger seat.

"Great, just great." Ryan rolled down a window. This trip was already a disaster. Why on earth had he agreed to come?

He took the last couple of blocks at a faster speed, relieved to finally turn toward the river onto Laurel Lane. There were only a few big houses on this road, two- and three-story monuments to a river town gone downhill. One of them looked empty; another struggled to stay upright. At the end of the road was the Gate-house, a proud old Victorian home with fanciful turrets and gables.

As he came to a stop in the parking lot, he noticed that the house had been repainted a light beige. The garden was bursting with color even in the middle of winter, and the old white gazebo in the side yard sported patches of new wood that still needed paint.

On the large porch that wound around the house were white wicker chairs, hanging plants, and a love-seat swing. Next to the house, an old tire still hung from the oak tree. It blew slightly in the wind, reminding him of long-ago summer days when he had sat in that very swing and wanted nothing more than a hot, lazy day. Things had been so easy then.

Ryan shut off the engine. He opened the car door and the three puppies jumped onto the ground, each going in a different direction. "Hey, wait. Come back here."

He grabbed one puppy and pulled its squirming body into his arms. The second one escaped him. He saw the third playing with the end of a garden hose on the lawn.

As Ryan jogged up the grass to get the third puppy, the first puppy tumbled out of his arms. The garden hose snapped up and a small stream of water caught him in the face. He pulled back abruptly. The puppy stopped and looked at him in surprise.

"Okay, that's it. Now I'm angry," he declared. "You are puppy chow."

"What's going on?" a voice demanded.

Ryan looked up as a woman stepped out onto the porch. Her hair was a glorious shade of red, drifting down past her shoulders in thick waves that glistened in the late-afternoon sunshine. Her body was slender and supple in a pair of navy blue leggings and a soft, clingy white sweater.

For a brief moment he felt as if he were looking at her through the hazy glass of an old mirror or the fuzzy lens of a camera. She fit the setting perfectly, the old house, the big porch, the sense of past and present connected. A modern woman in an old-fashioned setting. Instinctively he reached for the camera that usually hung around his neck. Today it was missing, and he felt almost naked without it.

Ryan scrambled to his feet, suddenly realizing he was kneeling in the middle of this woman's lawn with his face dripping from a garden hose and his pants smelling to high heaven. This was not how he had pictured his arrival home.

Kara jogged down the steps of her porch as one of the puppies dug furiously in the dirt near her rosebushes.

"Excuse me, but your dog is digging up my garden," she said.

Ryan stared at her in astonishment. "That is not my dog."

"Oh yeah? Well, he's not *my* dog." Kara picked the puppy up. As she did so, the other two puppies came charging around the corner. "What on earth? How many are there?" she demanded.

Ryan managed to grab one of the puppies as it scooted by. The third remained free, barking in delight. "Three," he ground out. "And they're all yours."

"I'm sorry, but I don't allow dogs in the Gatehouse. I just redid the rugs. You know how puppies are."

Ryan sent her a wry smile and pointed to the wet spot on his slacks. "Oh, yeah, I know how puppies are."

Kara took a step closer, really looking at him for the first time. "Oh, my. You're—you're Ryan Hunter."

He nodded, taking his own time looking at her. She wasn't as pretty as the models he worked with, but he found her looks more appealing. Her clear blue eyes conveyed a sense of tranquillity. The laugh lines around her eyes indicated a sense of humor, and her wide, generous mouth was just perfect for . . . Ryan cleared his throat. If there was ever a time not to think about kissing someone, this was it. Besides, she was probably married.

"You're early," she said. "I—I wasn't expecting you until tonight. And I thought you'd be alone."

"That was my intention. The dogs aren't mine. I'm just delivering them to you from Father Miles. He said you'd know what to do."

Kara gave him a blank stare. "Know what to do? With puppies? I've never had a dog in my life."

"You've got three now."

"You must have misunderstood Father Miles."

"You are Kara Delaney?"

"Yes, but—"

"Father Miles said you wanted a big family."

"I wasn't talking about puppies. I was talking about—well, it doesn't matter what I was talking about. You'll have to take them back."

"I'm not taking them anywhere. They're all yours."

"Then I'll take them back."

"You do that." Ryan handed her another puppy. "By the way, one of them gets carsick. I can't remember which one."

"Carsick," Kara said faintly, trying to hold the two puppies in her arms. Oh, Lord, she didn't know what to do with animals. Most dogs didn't even like her. And she never heard cats meow. They usually gave her some sort of a hissing sound and a swipe of their paw. She just wasn't an animal person. There was no way she could keep three puppies. What on earth had Father Miles been thinking?

Ryan captured the last puppy and walked down to his car. He retrieved the wicker basket and set it on the porch steps. "Here you go," he said.

Kara looked at him in dismay. Before she could say a word, Angel came running around the side of the house, her long brown hair blowing in the wind, her feet bare, jeans dirty. She stopped abruptly at the sight of her mother holding two puppies.

"Mom. You got me a dog?" Angel asked in wonder. Her big brown eyes got even bigger. The look on her face turned into pure joy.

Kara groaned. Now she was in trouble.

"You said we couldn't have a dog. But you got me one anyway." Angel threw her arms around her mother and the puppies. "I love you. I love you. I love you. You're the best mother in the whole wide world." The puppies started to bark, and Angel laughed with delight as she pulled one into her arms. "They are so adorable. And you got me two, I can't believe it."

"Actually she got you three," Ryan said, holding up the third puppy.

"Wow."

Kara shot Ryan a dirty look. "They are not staying."

Angel's face fell. "They're not?"

"No."

"Oh."

Kara weakened at the sight of her daughter's face. For a moment Angel's face had filled with light, the way it used to. Now her expression was dull, pained. Kara hated that look, and she had seen it a lot lately.

Silently Angel held out the puppy to her mother.

Kara glanced over at Ryan. He was studying her thoughtfully, and she didn't care for the look of judgment in his eyes. "I'm busy," she said. "I don't have time for puppies."

Ryan shrugged. "Hey, it's no skin off my back what you do with them."

Kara sighed, feeling like the wicked stepmother. "All right. We'll keep one, just one."

"I think they're a package deal," Ryan interjected.

"Would you be quiet?"

"Just trying to help."

Kara shook her head. "Everyone said you'd bring trouble with you. I should have listened to them."

"You probably should have," Ryan agreed, his tone and expression carefully neutral.

"Well, right now we need to find a place for the puppies. Maybe the sun porch. We can close it off and cover it with newspapers for the time being."

Kara put the puppies in the basket, and with Ryan's help they got them into the sun porch without any further mishaps. Leaving Angel to play with the dogs, Kara led Ryan into the kitchen. She handed him a dry towel and watched as he wet it down with water and tried to wipe off his tan-colored slacks.

His casual clothes were wrinkled from the trip, the sleeves on his navy blue shirt pushed up above his elbows. But despite his somewhat tired look, he was a handsome man. He didn't have the chiseled look of a movie star, but rather the square, rugged face of a man who liked to get dirty, the kind you'd see on a rugby or a soccer field, the kind who wouldn't walk away from a fight.

His dark brown hair and olive skin were set off by a pair of light green eyes. His well-defined jawline implied stubbornness, his windblown hair suggested a spirit of adventure, and his confident movements made it clear that this man was used to being in charge, which was probably why he was frowning at the stain on his pants.

Kara smiled in spite of herself. He'd looked ridiculous

chasing after those puppies, not like the wild, angry young man she had heard so much about, or the jet-setting playboy photographer for that matter. He had just looked like a man—human, vulnerable, strong, sexy . . .

Kara shook her head, dismayed at the direction her thoughts were taking.

Ryan looked up and smiled. His crooked grin put her on edge. He didn't look vulnerable anymore. He looked dangerous, mischievous, and far too knowing. This was a man who knew his power over women, and that was the last thing Kara wanted in a man. Never again would she be the one to love the most. Never again would she put herself in the position of waiting for a man to come home, and wondering if he ever would.

"Why don't you sit down? Would you like some iced tea?" she asked pleasantly, deliberately putting on her innkeeper hat, at least figuratively speaking.

"Sure." Ryan slid into a chair at the breakfast room table and cast a curious glance around the kitchen. "You've done wonders with this place. Last time I saw it, the house was falling apart."

"My aunt went through some hard times with the death of her third husband," Kara said as she took a pitcher of iced tea out of the refrigerator. "She remarried last year—Ike Kelly, you might remember him."

Ryan's jaw dropped open. "Ike Kelly, ex–marine barber who talks like a sailor and drinks whiskey for breakfast—that Ike Kelly?"

Kara smiled. "Opposites attract, I guess."

"I guess."

Ryan's gaze drifted down her body, and Kara instinctively moved the pitcher in front of her breasts. This man could flirt without saying a word.

Moving over to the counter, she took two glasses out of the cabinet and filled them both with tea. "Do you take lemon or sugar?"

"Plain is fine."

Kara took the glasses over to the table and sat down across from him, reminded that only a week earlier she had sat here with Andrew and argued about Ryan. The two brothers certainly were different, one quiet and somewhat plain, the other outgoing and attractive.

"Does your aunt still live here?" Ryan asked.

"No. When she remarried she considered selling the Gatehouse, but I decided to come back and take it over."

"What did your husband say?"

By force of habit, Kara looked down at her now-empty ring finger. The tan line stood out in stark evidence.

Ryan followed her gaze. "No husband?"

"Not anymore."

"He didn't want to leave the big city?"

"You could say that."

"What on earth do you see in this godforsaken town?" Ryan leaned forward. His voice took on a harsh tone. His eyes darkened, and his face tightened with tension.

"I like it here," she said quietly.

"But there's nothing here."

"Maybe that's why I like it. Not all of us need to spend every second of our lives trying to get somewhere other than where we are. Not all of us have to grab the brass ring on the carousel. Some of us just like to go around and enjoy the ride."

"Meaning me?"

"Actually I was talking about my ex-husband, but if the shoe fits . . ."

"It doesn't. And I hate being compared to other people."

Kara realized that her innocent statement had touched a nerve, obviously a painful one. "I'm sorry."

"Forget it." He sat back in his chair. "So, how's business?"

Kara relaxed, relieved by the change in subject. "Pretty good in the spring and summer, nonexistent in the fall and winter, but we're hoping to change that with the Centennial Celebration."

"I have to say I'm surprised at the timing. February usually means rain, hardly the best time to use the river."

"But that's the point. There are still wonderful recreational opportunities here in the winter. In fact, upriver the rafting is spectacular right now. The fishing is good, too. We can't afford to have tourists just in the summer. We need them all year round if we want to grow."

"I'm surprised the town is interested in growing. When I lived here, there was a single-minded approach to keeping things exactly the way they'd always been."

Kara sighed. "There are still a few of those people left. I'm hoping to win them over."

"One of them being Jonas Hunter, I presume, and number two being my brother, Andrew."

"Andrew is being open-minded."

"Now, that surprises me. Andrew never picked a side until he knew where the apples would fall."

Kara rested her arms on the table. She liked having something solid under her hands. It made her feel secure, not that Ryan was threatening her. He wasn't even flirting with her anymore, although she had a feeling his charm could be overwhelming when put to use. He was just sitting there staring at her, and it was the intensity of his regard that unnerved her, as if he knew something about her, something about them all.

"Why did you invite me?" Ryan asked abruptly.

"I want you to photograph the centennial activities and send the photos out to be published in one of the magazines that features your work." She looked straight into his eyes when she answered his question, having learned after a lifetime of mistakes that the only way to get what she wanted was to ask for it.

Ryan started to laugh. "Good God. You have a lot of nerve. And honest as hell, aren't you?"

"You asked me why. I told you."

"Do you realize there are people living in this town who hate my guts?"

"Yes."

"How did you get them to agree?"

"I didn't tell them until after I sent the invitation. Frankly most of them didn't believe you'd come."

"I'll bet they didn't. I hope you know what you're doing."

"What I'm doing is trying to revitalize this town."

"You're fighting a losing battle."

"I'll be the judge of that."

Ryan looked down at his glass, seemingly absorbed in the color of the liquid. "How's my father?"

"Jonas? He's . . ." Kara searched for the right words. "He's older."

Ryan raised his head. "We all are. Is that the best you can do?"

She tipped her head. "Why don't you go see him?"

"I will eventually. Do you know Andrew?"

"Yes. Andrew and I are very good friends, as are our children." Kara stood up, walked over to the counter, and rinsed her glass in the sink.

Ryan didn't say anything for a moment. "You're involved with my brother?" He sounded disappointed.

"Yes."

"And Andrew let you invite me to the party?"

Kara turned to face him. "I make my own decisions."

"I hope you can live with them." Ryan stood up. "I'll get my bag out of the car."

"Do you need help?"

"No, I like to travel light—a couple pairs of pants, a few shirts, my cameras, and my saxophone."

She raised one eyebrow. "You brought a saxophone with you?"

"It goes everywhere with me."

"Why?"

"Because it's more reliable than a woman."

"But not as warm, I'll bet. Or do you use it as a tool for seduction? The every-woman-wants-a-musician fantasy?"

He grinned back at her. "You mean that would work?"

"On some women, maybe."

"On you?"

"Definitely not."

"Too bad. Actually I don't play for anyone, especially not women."

"I see. Just you and your horn."

Ryan laughed out loud, and Kara couldn't help but blush. "I didn't mean that the way it sounded."

"You don't have red hair for nothing, do you?" He paused. "See, I'd rather have a saxophone than a woman, because my horn doesn't ask questions. It doesn't want to talk at three in the morning. It doesn't want to discuss my hopes and dreams and plans for the future, and most of all it doesn't ask for commitment."

"No wonder you're not married."

"No wonder," he agreed.

"You're in room three, up the stairs to the right," she said briskly, deciding it was past time to change the subject. "The room is all ready for you."

"I'll get my stuff."

Kara let out a breath of relief when Ryan left. The room was ready for Ryan, but she obviously wasn't. What a piece of work he was—he had probably broken more than a few hearts with his love 'em and leave 'em philosophy.

Thank goodness he was leaving on Sunday. Andrew was right. Ryan Hunter was nothing but trouble.

5

Andrew Hunter took the paper out of his printer, scanned the article, and abruptly crumpled it in one hand, then tossed it in the trash basket. He couldn't concentrate on work knowing that Ryan had arrived in town, that his younger brother was probably sitting at Kara's kitchen table feeding her lies about the past.

He hated the thought of Ryan getting anywhere near Kara. But there wasn't a damn thing he could do about it.

Andrew leaned back in his chair and glanced around the newsroom. He usually took comfort in his surroundings, the furniture that hadn't changed in twelve years, the water cooler that was always empty, the telephones that rarely rang, and the photos on the wall of his father and grandfather and great-grandfather, each with his own special edition of *The Sentinel*, headlining the biggest story of his generation.

There had always been a Hunter at the helm of *The Sentinel*. Jonas's grandfather had started the paper at the turn of the century, and the tradition had been passed on through the generations down to Andrew. Only he didn't have his photo on the wall. He didn't have his story, not yet. Sometimes he wondered if it would ever happen.

He was thirty-six years old and still playing Jimmy

Olsen to his father's Perry White. They didn't have a dashing Clark Kent or a wily Lois Lane, just sixty-year-old Louise Johnson, who wrote the society page; fifteen-year-old Howard Philips, who got school credit for covering sports at the high school; and a college kid who was building his portfolio by taking photos for the paper. Andrew wrote most of the other articles and sold advertising, but his father kept the editorial page for himself and refused to discuss their financial status, thereby effectively keeping Andrew in the number two position.

Their news came off the AP wire and from the gossip counter at Nellie's Diner. There was never much local news—at least not until now. The Centennial Celebration was creating a big problem for his father. It was the biggest thing to happen to Serenity Springs in the last hundred years, but his father refused to publicize it. Jonas thought Kara was trying to ruin the town, change it into a suburb instead of the wild and rural river town it was meant to be.

Now that Jonas knew Ryan was coming back, he was fit to be tied.

There had been a time in Andrew's life, many times actually, when he had desperately wanted his father's attention on him and him only, times when Andrew had wanted Ryan to screw up in his father's eyes. He had dreamed of those moments, never expecting that one day he would get exactly what he wished for.

But now his brother was back.

Jonas walked into the office. He tossed the paper down on Andrew's desk. "What the hell is that?" he demanded.

Andrew glanced down at the article on Thursday night's banquet. "It's an article on the centennial kick-off."

"*His name* wasn't in the version I approved."

"I rewrote it." Andrew looked up at his father, seeing anger and tension written in every line of his body.

Jonas was a big, strong man. He had intimidated Andrew every day of his life. The years had not been good to Jonas, drawing more lines in his craggy face, adding more gray to his hair and beard. But he had never lost his ability to make grown men cower.

"Damn you."

Andrew stiffened under the attack. "You can't pretend he's not coming back. In fact, he's back. Will gave him a speeding ticket right outside of town about two hours ago."

Jonas allowed himself a small smile at that piece of news. "Already in trouble. Doesn't surprise me."

"Or me."

Jonas sat down at his desk. He focused his attention on a stack of papers, but Andrew didn't think his father's mind was on circulation figures or advertising. It was on his youngest son. Always had been. Always would be. It didn't seem fair that Ryan could disappear for twelve years, come back, and once again be the center of attention.

Suddenly fed up, Andrew shoved back his chair. "I'm going home."

"It's not five yet." Jonas tipped his head toward the clock on the wall.

"So dock me for twenty minutes."

"What's your problem?"

"Nothing. I'm fine. I'm great. I'm on top of the world," Andrew said.

"He always could get to you."

"Not this time." Andrew shook his head. "I don't care that Ryan's home. I don't care that he wants to play the hometown hero when we both know he's a little shit. I just don't care. That's why I put his name in the story. It doesn't make any difference to me. And it shouldn't make any difference to you either." He grabbed his coat off the rack and shrugged it over his shoulders. "By the way, the National Weather Service is predicting three to four inches of rain by Saturday night. You might want to make sure your boat is securely tied down. The river is already high."

"She can handle it," Jonas replied, always referring to the boat as a woman.

"I hope so. I'd hate to see her flood in the middle of the Centennial Celebration."

"Might be a good thing. We don't need all those outsiders in our town. We don't need their slick money or their city ways, corrupting our young folk. Which reminds me, I saw Billy with that Delaney girl down by the river. I don't know what they were doing, but they were up to no good, I'm sure of it. If I were you, I'd put a stop to that friendship right here and now. And while you're at it, you should break things off with her mother. I don't know what you're thinking—getting involved with Kara Delaney. She's against everything we stand for."

"Angel is a good kid, and Kara is a very nice woman. She loves this town as much as you do."

"That will be the day. You mark my words. Those two females are trouble. And Billy is—well, you know."

"Know what?"

"He's a little slow sometimes."

"He is not," Andrew said angrily.

"Well, he doesn't need anyone putting ideas in his head. It's history repeating itself. Becky Lee taking you down to the river, now Angel taking Billy."

"It's not the same thing. Angel and Billy are eleven years old. Becky Lee and I were grown up."

"But she got you into a hell of a lot of trouble. Just like Eve teasing Adam with the apple. Sometimes a man has gotta say no. Now, are you going to tell Billy to stop seeing her?"

Andrew smiled bitterly. "No, Father. I'm not. See, I can say no." With that he walked out the door, letting it slam behind him just so he could hear his father swear. Billy and Angel were nothing like him and Becky Lee. It was a completely different situation. Billy was a good kid. He wouldn't do anything stupid. At least Andrew hoped he wouldn't. But half of Billy's genes were Becky Lee's—the other half he wasn't so sure about.

Not that it mattered. He was Billy's father. Nothing would ever change that.

"My father has a watch like that," Angel announced from the doorway to Ryan's room. She pointed to the gold Rolex he had just placed on the dresser.

"Don't you knock?" Ryan asked, buttoning up his denim shirt.

"The door was halfway open." Angel pushed it the rest of the way open and walked inside. "My dad's rich." She scooted onto the end of his bed and sat cross-legged, resting her elbows on her knees and her chin in her hands. "Are you rich, too?"

"Yeah, I'm loaded," Ryan said. "Got more money than the queen of England." He ran a comb through his hair as he looked in the mirror.

Angel regarded him thoughtfully. Ryan stared back at her. She had the most expressive face of anyone he had ever met. He could photograph her from three different angles and never come up with the same shot. Her eyes were a deep, dark brown, her skin as clear as an airbrushed photo. Her nose was straight and pert, her lips full, her teeth still finding their way in her mouth. She had a look of Kara, something in the tilt of her chin, the direct, unflinching gaze. But the rest of her belonged to someone else. He wondered who.

Angel answered his unspoken question.

"My dad's in the CIA," she said.

Ryan raised an eyebrow as he met her glance in the mirror. "Excuse me?"

"He works undercover, foreign countries, mercenaries, wars, you know the routine. He has to travel a lot. But he always sends me these incredible postcards from exotic places like Hong Kong and Barbados."

Ryan walked over to the bed and began to unpack

his overnight bag. He didn't believe a word she was saying, but he had to give her credit for having a vivid imagination.

"My dad wears these great hats," Angel added. "He has one that makes him look like Sherlock Holmes and another one that makes him look like a fisherman. It even has hooks on the side. They're disguises so no one will recognize him."

"I guess that's important if you're a spy," Ryan said, pulling a Los Angeles Dodgers baseball cap out of his bag and putting it on his head. "Think anyone will recognize me with this on?"

Angel smiled. "Not if you grow a beard to go with it."

Ryan rubbed his clean-shaved chin. "Mm-mm, that's an idea. Not." He tossed her the cap, and she put it on her head backward. "Tell me more about your dad."

"He's really brave," she said. "Once he saved this old lady. It was in one of those bazaars—in Cairo, I think. These two bad guys tried to steal the old lady's bag of fruit. My dad ran after them and grabbed one by the neck." Angel's eyes grew wide as she told her tale. "But the man struggled free, and when he turned around, he pulled out a long silver blade with a jeweled handle. My dad said it glistened in the sunlight, so bright it almost blinded him."

Ryan sent her a long look. "What happened next?"

"My dad put up his hands, and they started to dance around each other." Angel got off the bed and began to demonstrate the moves. "Everyone came into a circle around them. All the chattering stopped. My dad said the place was as silent as a tomb. Then the man raised his arm. He rushed forward. My dad grabbed his arm and pulled it behind his back. The knife clattered against the cobblestones."

Ryan sat down on the bed. "What happened to the other guy? I thought there were two."

"There were. He had run on ahead, but when he saw

his partner was in trouble, he came back. He grabbed my dad around the neck and started to strangle him. My dad said his hands were so big and so strong that he couldn't get in even a whisper of air. Then the other man came at him. He picked up his knife off the ground and started walking toward my dad, really slow, one step at a time. Like this."

Angel took slow, lingering steps toward Ryan, her hand held up as if she had a knife in it. "My dad said he saw his life flash before his eyes. He knew he was going to die. But he wouldn't give up without a fight. When the man got this close . . ." Angel looked into Ryan's eyes from six inches away. "My dad kicked him in the nuts with his foot."

Ryan winced. "Ouch."

"The man screamed like a girl and fell to the ground. Then my dad sent his elbow into the gut of the other man. He doubled over in pain. My dad whirled around and knocked the man out with one quick blow to the head. The crowd went wild, cheering him on. My dad picked up the old lady's bag of fruit and handed it to her. She started to cry. Then she got down on her knees and kissed his feet. She was so grateful to have her bag of fruit. Otherwise she and her children would have gone to bed hungry that night." Angel sighed as she sat down on the bed next to Ryan. "I wish I could have seen it."

"So do I," Ryan murmured.

"Angel?" Kara's voice came up the stairs. "Where are you?"

Angel flung a guilty look at the open door. "I better go. The puppies are giving Mom a hard time." Angel ran to the door, then paused. "Oh, you might not want to tell Mom that story. She gets a little upset when she hears it."

"I'll bet."

Kara appeared in the doorway, looking flustered and harried. "The puppies are chewing the rug," she announced. "I still can't believe you dumped those dogs on me," she said to Ryan.

He held up his hands. "Wasn't me. Blame Father Miles."

"I'll get the puppies," Angel replied. "Don't worry, Mom. It will be okay."

Kara watched her daughter skip out of the room. "Oh, to be eleven again and believe that everything will be okay." She paused. "Do you need anything?"

"No. This room is nice. It smells like a garden. How did you manage that in the middle of winter?"

"Potpourri." She smiled somewhat self-consciously. "Sometimes I have a heavy hand."

"I like it. Everything fits together perfectly." Ryan waved his hand around, acknowledging the matching wallpaper, bedspread, and carpet. "You're quite the homemaker, aren't you?"

Kara sighed. Even though he hadn't said the word with a sneer like her ex-husband, it still rankled. So she liked to clean and cook and hang curtains. So what?

"What did I say?" Ryan asked, a perceptive gleam in his eye.

"Nothing. I'm proud of the way the Gatehouse has turned out. I want it to feel like a home, warm and welcoming, a safe haven. A place where people can find peace."

"Including you?"

"Maybe." He saw too much. She should have expected that. As a photographer he was used to studying people.

Kara walked past his prying eyes and pulled the curtains back. "Did you notice the lovely view of the river?"

"That I could live without." Ryan picked up his empty overnight bag off the bed and stashed it in the closet.

"You don't like the river?" she asked with surprise.

"I hate it."

'Why?"

"I don't know. Maybe because Andrew loves it so much."

"And you both can't love the same thing?"

"No, we definitely can't love the same thing—or the same person." Ryan's gaze traveled down her body, then back up again. "What are you all dressed up for?"

Kara self-consciously smoothed down the sides of her winter-white woolen skirt. "We're having one last committee meeting tonight before the centennial officially kicks off. Will you think about taking photos, please? It would mean a lot."

Ryan walked over to her. He stopped too close, his hard, athletic body just inches away. Kara could see a shadow of a beard along his jawline, the tiny laugh lines that creased the skin around his eyes. She could smell his after-shave, and the heavenly scent of musk made her sway slightly, as if her body knew where home was, even if her mind didn't.

But thankfully her mind took over. Kara backed up, but there was nowhere to go; she was already against the wall.

"Kara?"

When Ryan looked into her eyes, she couldn't look away. Damn. She didn't need physical attraction, not now, not with this man.

"What? What did you say?" she asked again, trying desperately to remember what they were talking about.

"I said, I'll consider it." Ryan lifted his hand to her face. Kara thought he was going to touch her. She tensed, not sure what to do if he did. But Ryan's hand barely grazed her hair, and when he pulled it away, she saw a white thread caught between his fingers.

"Thanks," she said somewhat breathlessly.

"My pleasure. I couldn't let it spoil the picture."

"You weren't taking my picture."

"I'd like to. You have great—bones."

For some reason she didn't think bones was his first

choice. Kara cleared her throat. "You can photograph me at the centennial if you like."

He grinned. "I walked right into that one, didn't I?"

"Yes, you did. So, are you going to see Andrew or Jonas tonight?"

The connection between them broke with her words. Ryan took a step backward. Kara breathed easier.

"No." He walked over to the dresser and shut a drawer that was halfway open.

"You'll have to see them sometime. It's a small town."

"They'll be at the dinner tomorrow."

"But it's such a public place. It might be awkward for you."

He turned to face her. "At least my father can't kill me in front of witnesses."

"What did you do that was so terrible, Ryan?"

His eyes narrowed. "Hasn't Andrew told you?"

"No."

Ryan tilted his head. "I thought you two were close."

"We are."

"But he doesn't confide in you?"

"Not many men do." Kara regretted that statement the moment it left her mouth, but it was too late to retract it.

"Why not?"

"Forget it." Kara headed toward the door. "There's chicken pot pie for dinner. Fifteen minutes, all right?"

"Andrew isn't coming, is he?"

"I did invite him."

"What was his answer?"

"He'd starve before he broke bread with a bastard like you."

Ryan smiled, but it didn't quite reach his eyes. "So my brother thinks I'm a bastard. What do you think?"

"I don't know. Are you?"

"Maybe you should spend time with me, find out for yourself."

Kara looked at him for a long moment. His challenging smile almost made her say yes. But she reminded herself that Ryan was a troublemaker, and she was not about to help him stir up trouble.

"You're nothing like your brother," she said thoughtfully. "Maybe a little like Jonas, though."

"God forbid."

"Of course, I don't remember your mother. What was she like?"

Ryan's face paled. Kara didn't think he'd answer her question. Andrew refused to even talk about his mother, but Ryan surprised her once again.

"She was pretty," Ryan said slowly. "She had dark brown hair, so long it almost touched her waist, and a smile so bright you couldn't help but smile back. She couldn't stand next to me without touching my hair or giving me a kiss on the cheek. She used to drive my father crazy. He wasn't a toucher." Ryan's voice hardened.

"She sounds nice."

"She was better than nice. I used to think she was magic. I remember one day I went out in the garden and I saw a butterfly land on her outstretched fingers. It was as if she were a part of nature or something."

"That's beautiful."

"But she flew away just like that butterfly." Ryan's voice held regret.

"Where did she go?"

"No one knows. Maybe back to New Orleans where she grew up. I haven't been able to find her."

"And you've looked, haven't you?"

"In just about every corner of the world."

"You're a dreamer. I didn't expect that."

Ryan shook his head as his defenses kicked in. "No. I'm a realist. I gave up on dreams a long time ago."

Kara saw vulnerability in his eyes and a deep-rooted sadness that touched her in a way that was familiar, as if he shared her feelings of abandonment and loss. She had been a little girl when her parents divorced. Ryan had been a young boy when his mother left.

She told herself that she had the same connection with Andrew, that he, too, had lost his mother. But she and Andrew had never discussed their childhoods, never shared that part of themselves.

"Aunt Josephine told me your mother had a beautiful voice," Kara said. "That she used to sing in the choir, and her solos would bring the church to absolute and utter silence. Far more effective than any sermon."

"She could sing, all right. Her whole family was musical. In fact, my saxophone originally belonged to my maternal grandfather. My mother never learned to play; she preferred to sing." Ryan paused. "I may not know where my mother went, but I do know why. Maybe someday I'll tell you."

Kara stiffened, once again struck by the belief that Ryan knew something that no one else knew. Something she might not want to hear. And it would be disloyal of her to even consider listening to Ryan. If she needed answers about anything, Andrew should be the one to provide them. He was the man in her life, the one who would still be here next week when Ryan left, when the centennial was over, when life returned to normal.

"You know, Ryan, I didn't realize when I invited you here that there were so many bad feelings. I knew you were a rebel, but I honestly thought the stories were exaggerated. I didn't know the resentment went so deep."

"Surely Andrew told you how much he hates me?"

"No, he didn't tell me. Because frankly, Ryan, Andrew doesn't talk about you at all, and neither does your father. I read about you at the library. That's where I got the idea to invite you. When I tentatively mentioned your name to Andrew one day, he just said the two of you didn't get along. But you're brothers, and I guess I thought that deep down, no matter what had come between you, you could resolve your differences and be a family again."

He looked at her in astonishment. "Now who's the dreamer?"

"Okay, so I have a tendency to believe the best about people. It's a bad habit, and I'm trying to break it." She tilted her head to one side. "You'd think I would have learned by now. I've certainly had a lot of people disappoint me."

"So have I." He sent her a pointed look. "It's not too late for me to go, Kara. I can leave tonight."

"No." The answer burst out of her before she could even consider the consequences.

"Are you sure?"

Their eyes met. Her heart quickened.

"The people in this town need you, Ryan."

"They don't need me."

"They do. They just don't know it yet."

He shook his head. "No matter what the press release says, I'm a photographer, Kara, not a hero. Don't try to make me into one."

## 6

"Ryan Hunter is not a hero. He's a murderer," Margaret Woodrich declared, her statement bringing utter silence to the centennial committee meeting. There were more than thirty people present in the high school auditorium, with the committee members seated at the head table and the rest of the townsfolk in folding chairs.

The meeting had barely begun. In fact, Kara had had difficulty bringing the group to order. Even with repeated strokes of her gavel, Kara had only gotten the attention of a couple of people.

But this woman, this plain, sharp, homely woman, had done what Kara could not: She had silenced the crowd. Because Margaret Woodrich was Becky Lee Woodrich's mother, and it was doubtful that anyone in town disliked Ryan Hunter more than she did.

Now that the group was silent, Margaret looked nervous. She held her black leather purse against her waist like a shield and rocked back and forth. She didn't seem to know what to say next, glancing down at her companions for help.

Beverly Appleborne sat on one side of her. As the wife of the town's only doctor, Beverly was the closest thing Serenity Springs had to a queen. Jeremy Woodrich, Margaret's husband, sat on the other side, a brood-

ing man who ran the local bookstore, a man who hadn't
spoken much since his one and only daughter had died.

Kara cleared her throat. She couldn't allow Margaret
to take over the meeting. She couldn't let these people,
no matter how deep their pain, destroy the centennial.
She had already sent out press releases announcing
Ryan's involvement. Reservations and bookings for the
dinner had increased by fifty percent since Ryan had
accepted her invitation to come home.

Because he had been interviewed several times on
talk shows across the country, and because his last collection of photos had made the best-seller list, Ryan was
even better known than Kara had realized.

She'd been expecting flak from Margaret Woodrich
and some of the others in town ever since she'd told the
committee Ryan had accepted her invitation. But apparently neither Mrs. Woodrich nor Mrs. Appleborne
had really thought he'd come, because they hadn't said
anything until now. Now that it was too late.

"The centennial committee has already approved the
plans for tomorrow night's dinner," Kara declared, re-
fusing to look at the other committee members, who
also seemed to be avoiding her eyes. She sought out
Andrew in the audience, but he was picking lint off the
sleeve of his shirt. No support there.

"You had no right," Beverly Appleborne declared,
rising to her feet. "This issue should have been discussed publicly before an invitation was offered. I realize you're an outsider, so perhaps you don't
understand the ramifications."

Kara inwardly cringed at the word "outsider." She
had been fighting that tag for six months. Her only saving grace was that she'd been born in Serenity Springs,
thereby giving her an edge on those who had moved to
the town when they were grown. But not everyone had
accepted her, and certainly not everyone agreed with
her progressive ideas.

In the face of such animosity, a part of her wanted to

back down, the way she had done so many times with her husband and her parents and anyone else who had intimidated her.

Who did she think she was kidding, pretending to be a civic leader when she was trembling with nerves and feeling as if she was about to throw up?

"Ryan Hunter killed Becky Lee Woodrich," Beverly added, seizing the moment. "The man should be hanged, not celebrated."

The accusation was so stark, so horrifying, and so blatantly untrue that Kara forgot her nerves. She had no idea of all the things Ryan Hunter had done in the past, but she did know that he was not the man driving the car that took Becky Lee's life.

"You're wrong," Kara said, cutting off Beverly as she attempted to elaborate. "Ryan Hunter was not anywhere near the scene of the accident."

"But he called her," Margaret Woodrich said. "He told her to come. Tell them, Andrew. Tell them."

Andrew sat up in his chair. He looked flustered and embarrassed. Kara felt sorry for him, but also a bit angry. Why the hell didn't he get up and tell them all the truth?

Loretta stood up. "Tell them, Andrew. Tell them what you think."

Kara watched Andrew's gaze shift to Loretta. She could see the battle raging within him. Finally he took a deep breath and stood up. "Ryan had nothing to do with Becky Lee's death. She was hit by a drunk driver. That driver was not my brother."

"Well, hallelujah," Loretta muttered as she sat down in her seat, approval in her eyes.

"I didn't want Ryan to come," Andrew continued. "Like most of you, I have reasons to dislike my brother. But I can't deny his success or the fact that he's here. Maybe Kara's right. Maybe the centennial is more important than one man."

Kara smiled her thanks as he sat down. "Andrew is

right. Mr. Hunter is here. The banquet is sold out. And every available room in town has been booked for this weekend. We're predicting an increase in sales receipts at our shops and restaurants of over two hundred and fifty percent during the next three days. We have already had requests for books and other literature on the town and the river," she added pointedly, looking directly at Mr. Woodrich as she did so. No one said a word.

"There are some people in this room who are upset. I apologize. But I hope we can pull together as a town, a community. I've spoken to several developers over the past few days. Their presence at the centennial has nothing to do with Ryan Hunter, but has everything to do with our town, with the land that we have to offer. I don't think I need to remind you that we all have a lot at stake this weekend. Please, give us your . . ." Her voice faded away as she saw Jonas Hunter standing at the back of the room. She stumbled on. "As I said, the committee would very much appreciate your support. Please remember that Ryan Hunter's participation is only one small part of our celebration."

The crowd looked toward Jonas, eager to see his reaction. He didn't move a muscle. But the stony expression on his face told her she would not have his support.

"Never," Beverly Appleborne declared, taking the moment of quiet for her own. "If you want the centennial to be a success, you will ban Ryan Hunter from the dinner tomorrow night and all other events. As for the developers, that is another issue that we will continue to discuss. But on the Ryan Hunter issue, we will not compromise. We know the truth, no matter what Andrew says. Obviously his interest in you has clouded his judgment. Don't you agree, Jonas?"

Kara felt her stomach twist into a knot. She could fight Beverly and even Margaret, but Jonas was a cornerstone of the town. To some, he *was* the town.

"If you want to save the town, pick up the trash, don't bring more in. Cherish the land, don't tear it up for concrete." Jonas spoke in a loud, booming voice, like a Sunday preacher calling to the sinners to repent. "We cannot trade the river for dollars. We cannot ignore the cost of progress. We cannot allow outsiders to take what is not theirs. We cannot let them turn the river into a whore, using her and abusing her, then walking away. This is our town. We must fight for it. We must protect it at all costs. Stand with me, not against me."

"I am standing with you," Kara replied, somewhat shaken by his impassioned speech, his loyalty to the town, his love for the river. "I want to celebrate our history. That's what the centennial is about."

"The centennial is about money. Money in your pocket," Jonas declared. "You're willing to sell out this town if it means booking rooms in your inn."

"He's right," someone shouted in the back. "We shouldn't sell our souls for a few extra bucks."

"And we should not honor a man without honor," Beverly Appleborne said as she walked to the back of the room and stood next to Jonas. Margaret and Jeremy followed. A few other people joined them.

Kara held her breath as the town divided into factions, those who hated Ryan and those who didn't, those who wanted progress and those who wanted things to stay the same.

When the musical chairs stopped, Andrew sat alone in the middle of the room, torn between her and his father. Kara knew how much Andrew valued Jonas's opinion. She also knew how much she wanted Andrew's support.

"Kara, perhaps we should reconsider," the mayor said quietly, apparently seeing his chances of reelection fading fast.

"Reconsider what?" she asked. "Ryan? The whole Centennial Celebration? Because of Jonas? The man is stuck in the dark ages. He has run the same damn editorial in his paper every Sunday for the past six months and probably longer than that." Suddenly furious, Kara turned back to the crowd, deliberately forcing her voice to ring through the room.

"We can have progress without chaos," she said. "We can make money without prostituting ourselves. And we can honor a man for his photographic accomplishments without dissecting his personal life, without treating gossip like the gospel truth."

"Here, here," Loretta said quietly. "Go get 'em, Kara."

Kara rapped her gavel on the table as chatter once again broke out. "Jonas is right about one thing. By standing together, we all stand taller, but we must respect one another's beliefs. We must honor our differences, and we must give this town a chance to grow, to survive, so that we can all survive. Now, let's have no more dissension. We have work to do."

She offered Jonas a challenging look. He returned it, then walked out of the room. Beverly Appleborne, Margaret, and Jeremy Woodrich went with him. The rest stayed with her, including Andrew. Kara let out a breath. It was a partial victory, but she would take it.

"You won," Andrew said to Kara as they walked up the steps to the Gatehouse later that night.

"I'm not so sure about that. Your father is a formidable man."

"And he doesn't like to lose," Andrew added. "Especially not when it concerns this town."

"How can I make him see we're on the same side?"

"I'm not sure you are."

"Oh, Andrew, if I can't convince you, how can I convince him?" Kara sighed. "I just want to make things right for everyone."

"Some things can't be fixed."

"I know, and I wouldn't put it past Mrs. Appleborne or Mrs. Woodrich to make a scene tomorrow night."

Andrew turned toward the river, his profile grim and forbidding. Kara knew that Andrew took Billy over to the Woodrichs' house every Sunday afternoon for dinner, but she had no idea of Andrew's own relationship with his former in-laws—another thing they never spoke about. She sighed, wondering why she suddenly felt she knew nothing about the man standing next to her.

"Margaret and Jeremy spoiled Becky Lee rotten," Andrew said after a moment. "They've never been able to accept her death. You can't expect them to welcome Ryan with open arms when Becky Lee made it clear that she was running off to be with him."

"And it's so much easier to blame Ryan than it is to blame Becky Lee," Kara said sharply. "For goodness' sake, Andrew, the woman had a mind of her own. She knew what she was doing when she left."

"She didn't know. She was hung up on him, so crazy about him she couldn't think straight. And he led her on, Kara. He promised to show her a big, exciting world. I couldn't compete with that." He paused. "I don't want to talk about it. Why *are* we talking about it?" His voice filled with pain. It was the most he'd ever told her about his marriage.

"Because I need to understand."

Andrew walked over to the porch railing and gripped it tightly.

"Why, Andrew? Why did she marry you? Did she love you? Did you love her?"

He swung around to face her. "She married me because she was pregnant, dammit. Because she was scared. And because Ryan didn't want to marry her. Are you satisfied?"

"She was pregnant with your child?"

Andrew didn't answer her. There was something in the way he avoided her eyes, the way he hung his head, the way he turned his body away from her penetrating question.

"Oh, my God." Kara clapped a hand to her mouth.

"No." Andrew immediately shook his head. "It's not what you're thinking."

"It's not?"

"I'm Billy's father. Leave it alone, Kara. Leave the goddamned past alone."

Andrew knew he should walk straight home, but anger at Kara and Ryan took him away from his own house. He never should have told Kara that Becky Lee was pregnant when they'd gotten married. He hadn't meant to tell her that, hadn't meant to tell anyone.

He was Billy's father. End of story.

Silently he counted to ten. Then he turned down another block and tried to walk off his frustration. He realized his mistake as soon as he saw the woman standing on the front porch of the last house on the left—Loretta's house.

He didn't want to see her now. Didn't want to deal with her and feelings that he shouldn't be feeling. Instinctively he turned away, but Loretta called his name, and he was too polite to ignore her.

"Andrew. Is that you?" Loretta called again, waving at him from her porch. She looked distressed and kept pointing to the big oak tree in her front yard.

He had no choice but to see what she wanted.

Loretta wore next to nothing, a silk robe over a T-shirt. Her legs were bare and her hair flowed loosely around her shoulders. She looked soft, feminine, sexy, as if she had just gotten out of bed, which was not something he wanted to think about. She was pregnant, for God's sake. Her stomach was as big as a basketball. What was he thinking?

"You are a lifesaver," Loretta declared as he joined her on the lawn. "Trillion is stuck in the tree."

"Trillion?" he asked in confusion.

"My cat." She pointed to one of the higher branches

where there was indeed a cat clinging to a branch. "I need you to get her down."

"Excuse me?"

"She doesn't like the wind. She senses another storm coming," Loretta explained.

Andrew glanced up at the sky. There were no stars, just thick clouds that would surely bring rain sometime in the next twenty-four hours.

"So—"

"I need your help."

Loretta looked at him in a way that made him want to help, only he wasn't sure he could. He could barely solve his own problems, much less anyone else's. "I don't know," he said. "Won't she just get tired and come down the same way she went up?"

"She's scared, Andrew. She's just a kitty."

"Why did you name her Trillion?"

"I figured it was as close as I'd get to a trillion dollars." She smiled at him again, warmly, pleadingly.

He looked at the tree. The bottom branch was a good five feet off the ground. Even if he could hoist himself up that high, he'd still have to climb halfway up the old oak. With his luck he'd fall straight into the trash cans on the sidewalk. "Why don't you call 911?"

"You think Will Hodgkins is going to rescue my cat?" she asked in disbelief. "He hasn't spoken a word to me since I started to show. Afraid he'll get named as the father, I guess, and that wife of his will toss him out on his ear."

"Is he the father?"

Loretta gave him a steady look. "Does it matter? If I say yes, you won't believe me, and if I say no, you'll still wonder if I'm telling the truth." Her voice turned hard, filled with disillusion and bitterness. "Most of the women in this town treat me like the scarlet woman. Like none of them are having sex in their cozy little houses with the shades drawn. God, sometimes I hate this place. Now, are you going to get my cat down, or do I have to climb up that tree myself?"

"You can't climb a tree in your condition. I'm just not sure I can do it either."

Loretta's expression changed from bitter and defiant to soft and caring. It almost took his breath away.

"You can do it, Andrew," she encouraged. "I have confidence in you."

God, no one in his life had confidence in him. How could he say no?

"Do you have a ladder?" he asked.

"No. When Pop died, I got rid of his tools and stuff. His ladder was falling apart, so I used it for firewood."

Great, she had just reminded him that she was all alone in the world, and he would be a complete jerk if he walked away and left her little kitten stuck in the tree.

Hands on his hips, he surveyed the tree from various angles. The cat started to meow pitifully. Andrew sighed. He grasped the branch with his hands and tried to hoist himself up. It took three tries, and he felt as if he needed an oxygen tank when he finally got up.

Loretta beamed at him. "You're almost there."

He looked over his head. The cat was a good four feet higher. Tentatively he put his foot on the next branch. It held his weight, and he breathed a sigh of relief. Another step up took him even closer. He maneuvered his way onto the next branch and finally got close enough to stretch out his hand and call to the cat.

"Here, kitty, kitty. Come on down, now."

The cat stared at him without blinking an eye or moving a muscle. She was not making this easy on him. Andrew stretched flat out on the branch, sliding his stomach along the rough-hewn oak until he could grab the cat.

"I've got you," he said. As he grabbed for the cat, she swiped at him with her paw, drawing blood from the back of his hand.

"Ouch! Dammit."

"Are you okay, Andrew?" Loretta called.

"Your cat clawed me."

"She doesn't like strangers."

"Now you tell me."

"Just sweet-talk her, like a man trying to get a woman into bed."

As if he had had much luck in that area, Andrew thought cynically.

"Okay, baby," he said softly. "Don't embarrass me. Just come along now. I'm going to take you down, then I'll go home and we'll never have to see each other again. I promise."

The cat hissed at him.

"Now, don't be doing that." He tried to hang on to his temper. "You gotta come with me."

Andrew grabbed the cat. She clawed his face. He jumped backward, completely unbalancing himself, and made a desperate grab for the branch. His hands grabbed nothing but air, and Andrew toppled from the tree.

The spiked leaves of the hedge made his landing feel like a bed of nails. The force of his fall took his breath away, and for a moment all Andrew could feel was a hundred sharp pins sticking into his body, sending pain down his back and along his legs, reminding him that he was not a kid and he should not be climbing trees.

Just as his breath began to fill his chest, the cat landed on his stomach, her sharp claws sinking through his shirt to burn a line of fire down his abdomen. He swallowed back a curse as Loretta grabbed the cat and knelt down next to him, her face a picture of apologetic thanks.

"You got her down. Thank you, Andrew."

"You're welcome." He groaned.

"Are you okay?"

He watched her squeeze the cat in a loving embrace

and wished she'd squeeze a little bit tighter, preferably around the cat's neck.

"Fine. Just great." He tried to sit up.

Loretta put the cat down and helped Andrew into a sitting position. She wrapped her arms around him as he tried to catch his breath. He rested there for a moment, enjoying the soft fullness of her body, the scent of her shampoo. Her face was just inches away. If she turned a tiny bit, his mouth would touch hers. Good God, what was he thinking?

Just then the front door of the house next door opened and shut. Ralph Kramer, one of Andrew's former classmates, came out on the porch.

"Hey, what's going on over there?" he yelled as he came down off the porch and walked over to the fence.

Andrew and Loretta broke apart.

Ralph's jaw dropped in disbelief. "Andrew Hunter. Good God. You? You're the one?"

Andrew scrambled to his feet. "Now, don't get the wrong idea, Ralph."

"I didn't think you had it in you," Ralph said with a leer in Loretta's direction.

Andrew couldn't help but move in front of Loretta, protecting her from the look of pure lust in Ralph's eyes. How could she stand living next to this creep?

"Now, hold on," Andrew said. "I was just getting the cat out of the tree."

"Yeah, right." Ralph hitched up his jeans over his beer-belly gut.

"You don't understand," Andrew said.

"Hey, I not only understand, I say go for it. From what I hear, she might teach you a thing or two."

"Now, look here, Ralph—"

"Forget it, Andrew," Loretta said. "Ralph is going to think what he wants no matter what you say."

Before Ralph could reply, his wife, Arlene, opened the front door. "Ralph? Who are you talking to? If you're making time with Loretta again—"

"I'm not. I'm talking to Andrew."

Ralph grinned at Andrew. Andrew sighed as he heard the surprise in Arlene's voice.

"Andrew Hunter? Is that you?"

"Yeah, it's me."

"Does Kara know where you are?" Arlene demanded. She didn't wait for him to answer. "I didn't think so. Well, I bet she'd like to know about this. Ralph, if you want dessert, you better get your butt back in here and take out this trash for me," Arlene added.

"I'm coming, honey," Ralph said, hurrying back to the house.

"Guess you'd better go to Kara's and explain before Arlene cuts your reputation into little pieces and feeds it to the dogs," Loretta said.

"Kara will understand."

"She probably will." Loretta paused. "I like Kara. And she's the right kind of woman for you—upright, honest, decent. It's no wonder you want her. She wears a white hat, just like you. Me and Ryan—we always wore black." Loretta walked back to her house with the kitty ensconced in her arms.

Andrew watched her go in silence. Loretta was right. He and Kara were a perfect match. Kara was the kind of woman he'd dreamed about—a woman content to live in a small town. They could have more children. They could build a life together. It would be comfortable and peaceful, not unpredictable and scary, the way it had been with Becky Lee. Becky Lee had turned his world upside down. Kara would keep it right side up.

Maybe Loretta and Ryan would hit it off again. They both had shady pasts, bad reputations, and too much to say. They didn't know when to stop talking, when to stop trying to change the rules of the game and just play them the way they were written. Yes, Loretta and Ryan were a good match. As he and Kara were.

It still bothered him to think of his little brother staying in Kara's house, eating her food, and making her laugh, no doubt. Ryan had a way with women that Andrew could only dream about. He knew he should confront Ryan, tell him to stay away from Kara. In fact, he should have seen him earlier, set things straight between them.

Andrew glanced down at his watch. It was almost eleven. He wondered if it was too late to go back to the Gatehouse.

## 7

It was almost eleven that night when Angel raised her hand to knock on the door to Ryan's room. She hesitated, taking a quick look down the hall at the door leading into her mother's bedroom. It remained closed.

Visiting Ryan probably wasn't a good idea, but she needed to talk to a man, and there wasn't anyone else around to help. Besides, she liked Ryan Hunter. He had listened to her story and not laughed or anything. That made him okay in her book. She felt as if she could trust him, and she hadn't felt like that about anybody in a long time.

Angel knocked on the door.

After a moment the door opened. Ryan looked at her in surprise. He was still dressed, thank goodness. She didn't think her mom would approve of her talking to a man wearing only pajamas.

"What's up, Angel-face?" he asked.

"I have a problem."

"Maybe you should talk to your mother."

"This is a boy problem."

"Then I think you should definitely talk to your mother."

Angel ducked under his arm and walked into his room.

77

Ryan sighed. Angel wore a long-sleeved flannel robe with big, pink, fuzzy slippers. She sat down on his bed and looked ready to settle in. Ryan deliberately left the door wide open. "Okay, what's the problem?"

"I don't know how to dance with a boy, and tomorrow night's the dinner, and I think Billy is going to ask me to dance, and I don't want to look stupid."

Ryan looked at her in confusion. "What do you want me to do about it?"

"Show me how a guy dances with a girl." She stood up and walked over to him. "Where do I put my hands?" She held them up for his inspection.

Ryan hesitated. "Look, Angel, I think you should ask your mom."

"She hasn't danced in years. And I can't ask my dad, because he's away, you know, saving our world from being swallowed up by evil dictators. Otherwise I'm sure he'd teach me how to dance."

Ryan sighed, knowing he was beaten. "All right. One quick lesson, then you're out of here."

"Deal."

Ryan took one of her hands and placed it on his shoulder. The other he took in his hand. He deliberately held her about a foot away. "This is the way you do it. Okay?"

"We're awfully far away," Angel complained, her arms straight out.

"Believe me, that's close enough at your age."

She frowned. "I'm almost twelve."

"And going on forty, I'd say."

"Huh?"

"Never mind."

"Okay, now show me a few steps."

"If I do, will you promise to leave?"

She nodded.

"All right." He showed her what he remembered of the box step.

"This is awfully hard without music." Angel stepped

away from him, walked over to the clock radio by his bed, and flipped it on. She punched the channels until she hit on a big-band station. "I think this is the kind of music the old people will dance to," she said, returning to his arms. "Okay, lead away."

Ryan tried to waltz her around the room, but they stumbled over the carpet, tripped over their own feet, and burst into a fit of laughter when the beat got so fast that Ryan ended up spinning Angel around in circles.

"What is going on here?" Kara demanded.

Ryan and Angel stopped abruptly. After a moment Kara walked over to the radio and turned it off. Silence filled the room.

"Would you like to tell me what you're doing?" she asked.

"I wouldn't." Ryan looked at Angel. "How about you?"

Angel shook her head.

"I'm waiting." Kara folded her arms across her chest.

"I think your daughter should explain," Ryan said, nudging Angel on the shoulder. "Go on, tell her."

Angel offered her mom a bright, winning smile. "It's like this, Mom. Did you know that Mr. Hunter was named the best dancer at Serenity Springs High School? He once set a record for . . ."

Ryan listened in amazement as Angel's tale took life. By the time she finished, he almost believed he had won the state dancing championship with Conchita Gonzalez.

Silence once again filled the room.

Kara shook her head once, twice, three times. Ryan felt sorry for her.

"So that's it. Good night, Mom." Angel fled from the room before Kara could catch her breath.

"What am I going to do with her?" Kara threw up her hands in bewilderment.

"Give her an A for effort?"

"She's telling lies."

He smiled mischievously. "How do you know I didn't win the dancing title with Conchita?"

"Oh, please."

"I am a pretty good dancer." He switched the radio back on, this time finding a station playing love songs. "Why don't you find out for yourself?"

"No thanks."

"Scared?" he asked softly.

"Not on your life."

"Prove it."

"I don't have to."

Ryan took her hand in his and pulled her up against his body. Kara held herself stiff, every muscle tight with tension. Her gaze fixated on his chest, and he could see the pulse beating in the base of her neck.

Ryan held his breath as Kara slowly raised her head, as a strand of her red hair brushed across his chin, as the scent of her perfume filled his senses, as her breasts brushed against his chest.

Suddenly he didn't want to dance at all. He wanted to kiss her. He wanted to make love to her.

Andrew looked up at the Gatehouse at the second-story window. There was a light on in one of the guest rooms. He could see two shadows in silhouette, standing apart, then stepping close together. His mouth turned dry. It looked like a man and woman about to embrace, about to kiss, about to make love. His heart began to race and he turned away, unable to bear the sight, to contemplate the notion of Ryan and Kara together. He walked down the street, away from her house, away from Loretta's house, away from his own house.

Suddenly he was twenty-five again and spying on Ryan and Becky Lee. He couldn't do it. He couldn't make the same mistakes.

His speed picked up. The river called to him as it always did when he was upset or worried or scared.

There he could banish his thoughts with the roaring sound of the water. There he could shout out and no one would hear, because the river kept all his secrets.

"That's enough," Kara said breathlessly as she pulled herself out of Ryan's arms. Her hand shook as she tucked her hair behind her ear and tried to look as if nothing had happened between them. But they both knew it was pretense. Something had happened. She just wasn't ready to admit it. Neither was he.

"I'm going to bed," Kara added.

"If that's what you want."

"Alone."

He tipped his head. "Of course."

Kara took a step back. "I'd appreciate it if you wouldn't encourage Angel. She misses her father, and I'm afraid she's eager for male attention."

"Is her father still in Cairo?"

"What?" Kara looked confused. "I don't think Michael has ever been to Cairo."

"I didn't think so. Where is he, then?"

"It's a long story, and it's late, and . . ."

"And I think the puppies are barking," Ryan said, putting a hand to his ear.

Kara rolled her eyes. "Oh, dear. I have guests arriving tomorrow for the centennial and a sun porch full of barking dogs who are definitely not house-trained. What else could go wrong?"

Ryan offered her a wicked grin. "Andrew could find you here in my bedroom in a very sexy robe."

Kara pulled her silk robe around her body. "Andrew trusts me."

"But does he trust me?"

"You're only here for the weekend."

"A lot can happen in three days."

A lot could happen in a few hours, Kara decided as she tossed and turned in bed that night. She felt too keyed up to sleep, too excited about the upcoming centennial, and much too attracted to Ryan Hunter.

With a groan she pulled the pillow over her head, but even that couldn't keep his image from floating in front of her closed eyes or drown out the increasingly loud beating of her heart or the sudden piercing sound of music. Music?

Kara sat upright in bed, wondering if the wind roaming through the trees was mimicking the sound of a saxophone. Then she remembered Ryan.

She swung her legs over the side of her bed, wincing at the cold floor beneath her warm feet. She grabbed the afghan off the bottom of her bed and wrapped it around her T-shirt as she walked over to the window.

She knelt on the window seat and peered out at the garden and the lawn leading down to the river. It was a night cursed with more clouds than stars, but in the pale moonlight she could make out a shadowy figure under one of the trees, and the shining gold spark of a saxophone.

After a moment she raised the window a few inches so she could hear him better.

Ryan played with power and purpose, the same things Hans Grubner had told her were essential to playing the piano. *There can be no doubt in your movements, no hesitation,* he had said. *You do not play with your fingers, you play with your heart.*

Listening to Ryan now, Kara knew that he didn't play with his mouth, he played with his soul. The music was beautiful but somewhat sad. He didn't play like a cocky, arrogant SOB. He played like a man who was lonely, who was calling out to someone with his music.

His mother? Another woman perhaps? A lover? He must have had many in his lifetime. He didn't look like a man who spent many nights alone. Then again, one didn't get that good on a saxophone without having lonely nights in which to practice.

Kara knew a lot about loneliness, about pretending to

be happy when the middle of night brought such intense feelings of aloneness that she couldn't sleep. She had thought getting married would end those feelings, but even with a man sleeping next to her, she had still felt alone and, in the end, abandoned again.

Kara leaned her head against the wall and wrapped the blanket more tightly around her as she listened to Ryan play the lilting sounds of love and loneliness, joy and anger, passion and despair. She heard them all, and she understood. She wondered if he knew how much he had just confided in her.

When she opened her eyes again, it was morning.

Jonas Hunter got up early that morning and set up his fishing pole on the old dock just below his house. The river was higher today, moving faster by the minute, but he enjoyed the rush. After baiting his hook, he cast into the water and sat back on a deck chair that creaked with his weight and protested every time he moved. It was an old chair and, just like him, showed distinct signs of wear and tear. Maybe he should get rid of it instead of trying to fix it. What was the point of fixing something that probably wouldn't last much longer anyway?

With a shake of his head, Jonas sat back in the chair, deliberately testing it with his weight. It held, at least for the moment.

For a long time he sat there, watching his line drift in the water, listening to the sounds of the birds as they woke up the other animals in the forest, as the squirrels ran up and down the tree branches, searching for food. The familiar sounds comforted him like an old song.

He heard Andrew's car pull into the driveway, but he didn't look up until his oldest son had reached the dock. Without a word Andrew took out his pole and cast it into the water. They sat without speaking as they had done almost every morning of their lives.

Andrew was a comfort, too. He didn't ask questions. He didn't rock the boat. Not like Ryan.

By all rights Jonas should love Andrew more. And he did, he told himself. But deep down Jonas had a pang of regret for his youngest son and a strange longing to see him again. Not that he had any intention of confronting his son. He either wouldn't go to the dinner or he would ignore Ryan, make him so uncomfortable that he would have to leave.

The last thing Jonas wanted in life was a mirror to look into, and that's what he got whenever he saw Ryan—sharp, twisted reflections of the past. The past twelve years had been blessedly silent after more than a decade of Ryan's relentless questions, his insatiable need to know the truth.

Maybe that's why the boy took pictures. Ryan couldn't understand something unless he had it on paper, where he could see every detail.

When an hour had passed, Jonas stood up, laid his pole down on the dock, and picked up a large Hefty trash bag and his walking stick. "You coming?" he asked Andrew, who made no move to get up.

"Not today. I have things to do."

"Things more important than taking care of our river?"

"Yes."

Jonas felt a keen sense of disappointment, though he would never admit it. "All right then."

"Kara needs help decorating the recreation center. Are you coming to the dinner tonight?"

"Maybe. Maybe not."

Andrew sighed. "If you do—just lay off the whiskey beforehand, okay?"

"Who the hell are you to tell me how much to drink?" Jonas demanded, angry and offended by Andrew's comment. He knew he had been drinking a bit much lately, but that was his business. He had things on his mind, problems made lighter by a nightcap.

"For what it's worth, I'm your son. And Dr. Apple-borne has called three times to schedule your annual physical, and three times you've canceled. The last time he called, he told me he wants you to see a cardiologist in Sonoma, a Dr. Steiner. He's worried about your heart, and so am I. You're not a kid anymore; you have to take care of yourself."

"You're my son, not my mother. Lay off."

Andrew's face shut down. "Fine, do what you want. You will anyway." Andrew gathered his things and walked up the steps that led to the house and his car. After a moment Jonas heard him leave.

God, what was he doing—driving away the only person he had left? But he couldn't seem to stop himself.

Squaring his shoulders, Jonas picked up his walking stick and headed downstream. He stopped now and then to catch a candy bar wrapper or an empty milk carton on the sharp edge of his stick and put it into the garbage bag that he carried over his shoulder.

After awhile he began to feel winded, so he sat down on a boulder and waited for the sudden tightness in his chest to go away. He didn't like the sensation of getting old, feeling weak, but the last thing he needed was some damn doctor telling him his ticker was slowing down. As if he didn't know that.

Thankfully the river wasn't slowing down. It sailed by his feet, fast and swift. Jonas loved the rush of the water. It soaked right through to his soul, giving him a thrill of excitement every time he heard it.

All of his memories were of the river. His parents had married on the grassy bank. He had been born in a log cabin where each fall the river rose high enough to wash the summer dust off the front steps. He had spent his summers learning fly-fishing from his father and testing his courage on the white-water rapids upstream. The river had been his playground. While other kids had jungle gyms and toy cars, he had had a big, glorious river to play in, and he had loved the water since his first breath.

When the sky was blue and the sunlight sparkled through the trees to dance on the water, he felt God close to his soul. This morning there were clouds, but as Jonas looked up toward the sky, they broke apart and the sun beamed down a welcoming ray of light.

The light beckoned to him like a playmate's mischievous smile. Oh, to be as free as the birds that flew overhead, that sang their songs to the melody of the river. How he would love to be flung from this mother earth and tossed up high to the treetops, to feel as light and as joyous as a new bird, feeling its wings for the first time.

But his feet still touched the ground. His heart still felt heavy, so he turned his face away from the sun and the joy and looked down at the ground, at the empty granola bar wrapper. This was reality, ugliness in his special place.

He hated the intrusion of such ugliness. He hated when things didn't work out the way they were supposed to.

Thirty-seven years ago he had married Isabelle, a beautiful young girl from New Orleans who had come to live on the river with her aunt Claire. Isabelle's parents had died in an automobile accident, and aside from her maiden aunt, she had been all alone in the world.

He had fallen in love with her on sight. She had seemed so much like the river to him—long, flowing summer dresses, a smile that warmed his heart, and a passion as exciting as a canoe trip on a wild, unpredictable river.

Isabelle had promised to love him, to stand by his side for all time. He had believed her.

She had given him two sons, and they were happy. At least he was happy. Isabelle had never quite settled into the town. There had always been a part of her that yearned for the magic of New Orleans—the French

Quarter; the jazz clubs; the stories of voodoo magic; the hot, spicy Cajun food; the whole mystical, magical life she had left behind.

Jonas got up and walked on, trying to escape his thoughts, the way he always did. But he knew it was futile. His thoughts would be there when he returned home. Even now, after twenty-five years, his house still carried her scent. The furniture he had built for her still stood solid in the house, the oak chest at the foot of his bed where she had kept her lace shawl and the boys' first shoes and all the other silly feminine things he had had no use for but couldn't seem to throw away.

The house reminded him of Andrew and Ryan, of the two sons he had watched grow into men, one so desperate to please him, the other so uncaring of his thoughts. After his last fight with Ryan, he had said good-bye to the angry young man and watched him leave. But he had never quite said good-bye to the Ryan in his heart.

"Jonas."

He looked up in surprise. A man in uniform stood in front of him, the county sheriff, Dirk Anders, a man he had grown up with, a man who loved the river almost as much as he did.

"Dirk," he acknowledged reluctantly. Although they had been friends since childhood, Jonas had kept his distance in years past. He didn't care to be reminded of happier times when he and Isabelle had double-dated with Dirk and his wife, Susan. Susan had stood by her man as promised. Isabelle had not.

"I'm worried about the river," Dirk said. "She's high from last week's storms. And there's more rain on the way."

Jonas looked at the water. "She'll hold."

"They had heavy rainfall last night in Sonoma County. The National Weather Service is predicting three to four inches by tomorrow night. We've got folks coming in from San Francisco for the celebration tonight." Dirk shook his head in dismay. "I don't know what to do."

"Cancel the damn thing," Jonas said. He didn't like the Centennial Celebration, and now it was turning into a sideshow, bringing in developers and all kinds of people who had no business in his town.

Just like that woman, Kara Delaney, had no business in his town. It was her fault things were changing. But then, she had bad blood. How could he expect more from a Cox? Just their name on his tongue turned his whole mouth sour.

"I can't cancel the centennial," Dirk said.

"Why not? You're the sheriff."

"Everything's set. Folks are counting on a good time. And the shopkeepers are hoping for lots of business." Dirk paused. "I wish you'd stop this war you've got going with Mrs. Delaney."

"I will not let her turn my town into a freak show."

"She's not doing that."

"Oh, no? She's the one who brought that Harrison Winslow to town. Did you know he's planning to put a Taco Tommy's on Main Street? We've never had fast food here." Jonas shook his head in disgust. "Next thing you know there will be a video arcade next to the church."

Dirk sighed. "Change is coming, Jonas. It's not our turn anymore. Young Will is itching for my job. And I bet Andrew would like to take a crack at running the paper."

"He's not ready yet."

"Sometimes you gotta let go." Dirk picked up a pebble and tossed it into the river. They watched it skip its way downstream. "You seen Ryan yet?" Dirk asked.

Jonas shook his head. "Nope."

"He'll be at the dinner tonight."

"So I hear."

"Look, Jonas, I don't want any trouble with you. I

already have my hands full with Beverly Appleborne and Margaret Woodrich."

Jonas stared out at the water. He didn't want any trouble either, but it was hard to change the patterns of a lifetime. No doubt Ryan was itching for a fight. What was he supposed to do? Turn the other cheek?

"I remember a time when you couldn't say enough good things about that boy," Dirk added.

Jonas felt the anger rise in his soul. He didn't want to remember when Ryan was a little boy, when he had loved him more than he had loved anything or anyone. Ryan had turned on him with a vengeance. He couldn't forget that.

"It's time to move on," Dirk said. "Let the past go."

"When I want your advice, I'll ask for it." Jonas flung his trash bag over his shoulder.

"I guess I'll be getting back to town." Dirk tipped his head at Jonas. "Watch yourself. The current is pretty swift in parts."

"I know this river better than I know myself," Jonas said. "She won't hurt me." He wished he could say the same about his son.

## 8

"Billy," Andrew called as he entered the house. A quick glance at the clock told him he'd have to hurry if he was going to get to the rec center by eleven as he had promised Kara. "Billy?"

"In here, Dad," Billy replied.

Andrew jogged up the stairs and pushed open the bathroom door. Billy stood in front of the mirror, a gangly, awkward boy of eleven who was trying desperately to slick his hair down. He had a head full of brown curls that he absolutely couldn't stand, and no matter how many times he tried to wet down his hair, the curls bounced back up. Billy had Becky Lee's hair. Andrew could still remember running his fingers through her hair. He blinked the disturbing image from his mind.

"Oh, man," Billy complained.

"Can I help?" Andrew asked.

"No." Billy stared at him in the mirror.

As usual Andrew didn't know what to say to the boy. Like his father before him, Andrew wasn't good with kids, didn't know how to show affection without looking silly. When Billy was a toddler, Andrew had left the hugs to Mrs. Murray, and as Billy grew up he seemed to expect less and less from his father. They were almost strangers now, sharing the same house, eating their meals in silence, occasionally watching a television show together, but that was it.

Maybe Kara and Angel could bring them back together. Two halves into a whole. Mother and daughter on one side, father and son on the other. They could forge a family together. He wanted a family, sometimes more than anything on this earth. He just didn't know how to make it happen.

His own family had fallen apart with Isabelle's desertion. His whole body tightened at the thought of his mother. She had ripped them apart. It was her fault. Everything was her fault.

"Did I—did I do something wrong?" Billy stammered, suddenly looking nervous.

Andrew realized he was staring at his son with a ferocious, glaring expression. "No, of course not. I was thinking about something else."

"About Mom?" Billy asked.

Andrew started in surprise. "Becky Lee? No. Why would you ask me that?"

"Because sometimes you look like that when you stare at her picture, the one on the mantel in the living room."

"Do I? I didn't realize."

"I miss her, too," Billy said. "Even though I don't remember her."

Andrew stared at his son, realizing this was the first time Billy had ever said anything quite so personal. Andrew didn't know how to respond. He was inadequate when it came to words. He was a newspaperman; words were supposed to be his business. But it was far easier to write about city council meetings than to talk to his son about the mother he had never known.

Andrew wanted to tell Billy that he understood, because he knew what it was like to lose a mother. Only, his mother hadn't died. She had left him. At least Becky Lee had taken Billy with her. She had deserted her husband but not her child. He could give her credit for that.

"Do you want to use the bathroom?" Billy asked.

"No." And the moment passed before Andrew could say anything more personal than that. "I'm going into town to help Kara decorate the rec center. Do you want to come with me?" he asked, almost as an afterthought.

Billy shook his head.

"It might be fun," Andrew added. If he couldn't talk to his son, at least he could do something with him once in awhile.

"Is Uncle Ryan going to be there?"

Andrew tried to stay calm. "I don't know. Does it matter?" Of course it mattered. Andrew and Billy had never spoken about Ryan, but Andrew was sure Billy had heard tales about Ryan all over town. That was the problem with small towns. Everybody knew your business, sometimes before you did. But despite the speculation, nobody knew the real story, and as far as Andrew was concerned, nobody ever would.

"It doesn't really matter, but . . ." Billy stumbled over his words. "I just, sort of, thought that well, you know, maybe . . ."

Andrew waited patiently for the sentence to come out.

"Maybe he'd want to meet me or something, or maybe not." Billy looked down at his hands, obviously worried about his father's reaction.

"I'm sure you'll see him before he goes," Andrew replied, not sure at all, but he didn't know what else to say.

"Grandmother Margaret hates him, doesn't she?" Billy asked with surprising clarity.

"I guess she does."

"And you hate him, and Grandfather Jonas does, too. I don't think I'll like him either. He's probably a jerk."

Andrew didn't know what to say. As much as he wanted to agree with Billy, he couldn't find the words.

It suddenly seemed wrong to talk about Ryan to a boy who . . . Well, it just seemed wrong.

"I don't think I'll go with you," Billy decided, not waiting for Andrew to reply. "Angel wants to check out the river. It's really high, almost to the bottom of Tucker's Bridge."

"Stay away from the fast parts," Andrew said, relieved at the change in subject.

"I will."

Andrew turned to leave.

"Uh, Dad?" Billy said, looking suddenly uncertain.

"Yeah?"

"Do you think I'm getting some hair above my lip?"

Andrew walked over to Billy and looked into the mirror with him. He had a feeling this was the most important question Billy had asked him in a long time.

"Yeah, I think so."

Billy ran his finger along his upper lip. "It feels kind of rough. Maybe I should shave tonight, before the party."

Andrew nodded his head solemnly. "Good idea."

"Dad—uh, do you think—uh, you could show me how—I mean, if you have time?"

"Yeah, I could do that."

Billy met his eyes in the mirror, his expression full of adolescent pride. For the first time in a long time, Andrew felt confident in his role of father.

If Andrew hadn't stopped at the pharmacy to pick up some shaving cream for himself and Billy, he would have missed Ryan. Or at least he wouldn't have had to see him for a few more hours.

But no, he had to stop. He had to go in, even after he saw the red Ferrari in the parking lot.

Ryan was talking to Harry Bender, the pharmacist, and Leslie Bender, the pharmacist's daughter. Leslie had a hand on Ryan's arm. She smiled up at him like he was a goddamned hero. And Ryan soaked it up, the way he always had.

Andrew felt his body tense. Ryan looked just the same, just as attractive, just as arrogant. It wasn't supposed to be this way, Andrew thought desperately. If Ryan was going to come back at all, it should have been as a failure, not as a rich celebrity.

The door closed behind Andrew, jangling the bell overhead. Ryan, Leslie, and Harry looked up. Their laughter stopped. Their smiles faded, as if he were the intruder. Dammit, this was *his* town, not Ryan's, not anymore.

Andrew picked up a can of shaving cream and walked over to the counter. He handed Harry a five-dollar bill. "Keep the change," he said. Then he walked out—without saying a word, without acknowledging his brother.

Andrew was still shaking when he got into his truck. He sat there for a moment, watching Ryan through the glass door of the pharmacy. Andrew should have said something to him, should have confronted him, told him to get the hell out of town or at least stay away from Kara, but he'd been a coward, the way he'd always been.

He hit the steering wheel with his hand, angry at himself, angry at Ryan for making him feel like a stupid kid again. As Ryan came out of the pharmacy, Andrew turned the key in the ignition and pulled out of the lot.

Ryan caught up to him a block away, at the corner of Highland Avenue and River Road. Andrew's ten-year-old Toyota pickup truck felt like a clunker next to Ryan's sleek red sports car, and Andrew prayed the light would change. But instead of a green light, the railroad crossing gate came down, signaling the arrival of the morning train. Dammit all! And this was the only way to the recreation center. He wondered if that's where Ryan was going.

Seeing Ryan with Leslie Bender had only reminded

him of the night before when he'd seen Kara in Ryan's bedroom, when he'd been reminded of all the old feelings of inadequacy. He had never measured up to Ryan before. How could it be different now?

Andrew took a quick glance at his brother. Ryan stared straight ahead, his profile etched in stone. Then he turned and met Andrew's gaze.

Andrew looked away, watching as the train halted in front of the station.

Ryan pushed down on the gas pedal. The Ferrari whirred a challenge.

Andrew pushed his own gas pedal before he could think of the consequences. Then he felt foolish. He was not going to race Ryan down River Road. It didn't matter that once past the train crossing and the turn that led into town, the road was long, straight, and fast. Ryan had been the king of River Road. Andrew had never done anything so reckless.

The engine on the Ferrari came to life once again.

Andrew's foot hovered above the gas pedal. In his mind he could see himself and Ryan lining up on the riverbank when they were not more than eleven and eight.

*"Race you to the house," Ryan said.*

*Andrew dug his shoe in the dirt and played with a stick. "Nah."*

*"Come on, don't be such a wuss."*

*"I don't feel like racing."*

*"I'll give you a head start."*

*Andrew took off running. "Okay," he yelled over his shoulder, hoping without hope that he would make it to the house before Ryan. He was almost there when a tree branch snapped up in his face. He lost his balance and fell down. Ryan breezed past him the last twenty yards. Andrew felt like crying. Then he saw his dad on the porch and knew he couldn't cry. Slowly he got to his feet and walked up to the house.*

*"Beat you again, did he?"* Jonas asked, slapping Ryan on the back in congratulations. *"Don't know why you keep racing him, you'll never win."*

Andrew shrugged his shoulders. He walked up the steps to the porch. Jonas grabbed his shoulder with his hard hand.

*"You ripped your jeans, goddammit,"* Jonas said. *"If I have to buy you new jeans, you'll be doing more chores next week. You can start by moving that pile of firewood back behind the house."*

Andrew looked at the firewood in disbelief. It was four feet high. It would take him hours. But he couldn't argue with his dad. He would only find himself moving it twice just for the heck of it.

*"Yes, sir,"* he mumbled as he walked into the house.

An hour later Ryan came up to Andrew as he was moving the wood. *"Want some help?"* he offered.

*"This is your fault,"* Andrew said.

*"It's not my fault you fell down. You want some help or not?"*

*"I don't need your help."*

*"Fine."*

*"Fine."*

Ryan had stormed away, and Andrew had stacked wood till his back hurt and his hands blistered. He could almost feel the pain now as he gripped the steering wheel and watched the train pull out of the station.

The Ferrari's engine stopped whirring. When Andrew looked over at Ryan, he saw his brother fiddling with the radio. Maybe, just maybe . . . It was stupid, foolish. But damn, he wanted to win, just once in his life.

The gate went up on the railroad crossing. The light turned green.

Andrew pushed the gas pedal to the floor. His truck skidded down the first part of the road. In the rearview mirror he saw the Ferrari respond, but he had a head start. The roads into town flashed by on the left-hand side. He pushed the truck to the limit, faster and faster until he left the city boundaries. The road curved.

Andrew sped into the turn. He had barely straightened when a trio of ducks ran across the road. Instinctively he turned the wheel.

Ryan's car was right there, and the truck bounced off the front fender of the Ferrari. Suddenly they were both off the road. Andrew hit the wooden fence head-on, breaking it in two as he headed across the meadow toward Miller's duck pond.

Ryan's car seemed to be clinging to the back of the truck. Andrew braked just in time, two feet short of the pond. As the truck came to an abrupt stop, Ryan crashed into the back.

Ryan jumped out of his car.

Andrew did the same.

They met face-to-face next to their locked bumpers.

"You hit my car," Ryan said in disbelief.

"What do you mean? You hit me."

"You stopped too fast."

"It was your fault. You were trying to pass me."

"You're the one who swerved."

"I didn't want to hit the ducks."

"What ducks? I didn't see any ducks," Ryan declared.

"Oh, yeah? Then you must need glasses."

"Oh, yeah? Well, I think you're lying. I think you lost control of the car." Ryan stuck his face right in front of Andrew's, like an angry baseball coach arguing with the umpire.

"Well, I won," Andrew declared.

"Don't be such a jerk."

Andrew pushed Ryan on the shoulder to get him out of his face. Ryan pushed back. And suddenly they were kids again, wrangling in the living room over control of the television set.

They pushed and shoved and landed on the ground, rolling around like a pair of school kids. The ducks flew off the pond, upset by the chaos. They landed in the

meadow, squawking around Ryan and Andrew like a
bunch of teenagers rallying around a lunchroom fight.

Ryan was oblivious to the sound of the ducks, to the
sound of a car approaching. He just wanted to get Andrew off him. He wanted to shake some sense into his
big brother, make him admit for once that he could be
wrong, that he could be the one at fault.

That's when Andrew socked him in the eye. Ryan
howled in pain. For a moment he couldn't see a thing.
Instinctively he hit back.

But Andrew was gone. There was another man in
Ryan's face. A man wearing a hat and a badge and some
kind of uniform. Ryan tried to pull his hand back, but
it was too late. His fist connected with the jaw of Dirk
Anders, county sheriff.

The ducks scattered, and silence overwhelmed the
three men.

Dirk rubbed his hand along his jaw as he straightened
up. His pulse beat frantically in his neck as he wrestled
with his temper. Andrew stood behind Dirk, as stunned
as Ryan.

"Uh, sorry," Ryan said, getting slowly to his feet. "I
thought you were Andrew."

"Did you now? Well, you just assaulted a police officer."

Ryan swallowed hard. Dirk had tossed him in jail
once before for fighting in back of Loretta's bar. He had
been seventeen then, and he had spent the night in a
cell, waiting for his father to pick him up. Jonas had
made him wait twenty-four long hours.

"Can't stay out of trouble, can you?" Dirk asked. He
glanced over at Andrew, who looked pale and stricken
with guilt. "And you, Andrew. I didn't expect this from
you."

No, Dirk only expected it from him, Ryan thought
cynically. Once a sinner, always a sinner.

Dirk tipped his head toward the broken fence. "Anyone want to tell me what happened there?"

"He did it," Andrew grumbled.

"You started it. You took off first."

"You gave me the signal."

"I was warming up the car."

"You were not."

"I was, too," Ryan shouted back.

Dirk grabbed their arms as their fight escalated.

"Get in the car," he ordered. "We're going downtown."

"Jail?" Andrew's mouth dropped open. "I can't go to jail. I'm supposed to be decorating the rec center."

"Me, too," Ryan said. "I'm helping Kara."

"She doesn't need your help," Andrew said.

"Then why did she ask me?"

Dirk sighed. "Get in the car, boys." He pushed them over to the patrol car. "Mr. Miller wants to press charges. Said he's tired of all the drag racing down this road. Afraid one of his ducks is going to get hit."

"It's his ducks that caused the problem," Ryan said.

"Nevertheless, we have paperwork to fill out and a fence to pay for before anyone goes anywhere. Not to mention assaulting a police officer."

"Look, I'll pay for the fence," Ryan said. "It was my fault. I take responsibility. And I'm sorry I hit you."

"No, I'll pay for the fence," Andrew declared. "This is my town."

"Fine, you pay."

"Not that it was my fault," Andrew reminded him.

"Then I'll pay."

"Holy Mary . . ." Dirk shook his head. "If you two don't quit arguing, I'm going to handcuff you together and throw the key in that pond over there. Now get in the car."

"You can't lock me up, I'm the guest of honor," Ryan said as Dirk started the car.

"And I'm the press," Andrew declared.

Dirk smiled as he started the motor. "I can do anything I want, boys. I'm the sheriff, and I've got the keys to the jail."

Kara checked the clock on the wall at the recreation center for the sixth time in an hour.

"A watched pot never boils," Josephine Parker Willis Caldecott Kelly stated as she placed the last floral centerpiece on the table.

Kara sighed, watching her aunt fiddle with the flowers so that each blossom could be seen from every angle of the table. In less than an hour the multipurpose auditorium had been turned into a glowing bower of flowers, candles, and polished silver. The tables were set. The crepe paper was hung. The balloons were gathered in nets along the ceiling. The room was ready. Everything was going according to plan, so why did she feel so worried?

"You've been a lifesaver, Aunt Josephine," Kara said. "I couldn't have done this without you."

"Sure you could. You can do whatever you set your mind to. Why, just look what you've done to the Gatehouse."

"It looks good, doesn't it?" Kara asked, unable to resist boasting a little. "My homemaking talents are paying off after all. Michael always said I wouldn't be able to support Angel, that I didn't have any skills. Not that he cares enough to send his child support on time."

"Michael Delaney is a loser," Josephine said flatly. "He's not worth as much as his Italian suits."

"I know. But he is Angel's father. She wrote to him again yesterday." Kara met her aunt's perceptive gaze. "He never answers her letters or returns her calls. He's breaking her heart, and there's not a damn thing I can do about it."

"The man should be shot. Maybe you ought to invite him up here for hunting season." Josephine's eyes lit up with mischief. "I've been known to miss once in awhile."

Kara couldn't resist a laugh. "You're terrible. I'm surprised Ike lets you out of the house."

"As long as I leave my shotgun at home, he's happy."

"And your crystal ball, your tarot cards, and your extra-strength vitamin syrup, which we both know is really whiskey from Bud Brodie's still. You know, Prohibition is over. You can actually buy liquor at the store now."

"Don't be smart with me," Josephine chided.

"I'm sorry." Kara checked the clock again. "I can't imagine where Andrew is. It's almost noon."

"I don't think Andrew is the one you should be worrying about."

Kara sighed. "I'm worrying about *him*, too."

Josephine positioned the last carnation within the centerpiece. "There, what do you think?"

"It's perfect, thank you."

Josephine's smile lit up her pale, thinly lined face. She was a small woman, barely five feet, but her heart was as big as the whole town. She loved most people, some better than others, which was probably why she was on her fourth marriage. Not that the others had ended in divorce. No, all three men had died, the first in the Korean War, the second of a heart attack, and the third in an automobile accident.

Although Josephine had mourned each loss, her innate sense of survival had always brought her chin back up. She was a survivor, and six months ago she had married Ike Kelly, a man of her own age, a man of strong opinions.

Personally Kara thought them a perfect match. Ike's common sense kept Josephine out of trouble. Which was a relief to Kara, who always had a feeling that her aunt was just seconds away from blowing a hole through the roof, whether she was mixing her magic love potions or practicing her shooting.

Josephine sat down and pulled out a chair for Kara. "Now. Sit down and tell me about Ryan Hunter."

"I have too much to do, Aunt Josephine. I have to finish tying the ribbons on the favors, and I should check the wine. Loretta said sometimes her supplier cheats."

"Sit down," Josephine ordered.

Kara sat down, knowing it was futile to argue with Josephine. "What do you want to know?"

"Do you like Ryan?"

"He's okay." She turned away from her aunt's sharp eyes. Josephine had a way of reading Kara's mind that gave her goose bumps.

"Okay? Goodness, girl. Most people in this town have a hundred words to describe that boy, but okay has never been one of them."

"What do you want me to say—that he's tall and strong and built like an athlete, that he has a sexy smile and incredible green eyes and a way of looking at a woman that makes her feel like she's the only one in the room? Is that what you want me to say?"

Josephine sat back in her chair and nodded approvingly. "Just as I thought. You like him."

"He's good-looking, but he's not my type."

"And Andrew is."

"Definitely. Andrew is solid. Dependable."

"Boring."

"Aunt Josephine."

"I always tell the truth, Kara, and I'm telling you now that Andrew is not right for you or for Angel."

"Don't bring Angel into this."

"She's your daughter, and her spirit would be broken in a second living with a man like Andrew."

"Her spirit?" Kara asked with irritation. "Angel is fast becoming a pathological liar. Andrew is exactly what she needs, not someone like—like Ryan, who thinks it's fun to encourage her tales." Kara got up from her chair and paced around the table. "Angel is driving me crazy, Aunt Josephine. Every time I try to talk to her, she makes up a story. She's living in a dream world, and I don't know how to pull her out of it. She has to face reality."

"Why? She's only eleven. Let her dream."

"So she can be disappointed over and over again?"

"It doesn't have to be that way."

"Show me where it says that."

Aunt Josephine shook her head. "Kara, how can you say that? You had a dream of restoring the Gatehouse, and you've done it."

"I've restored the Gatehouse, but I haven't made it a success. If business doesn't pick up, I'll lose it to the bank. I'm mortgaged up to my neck, and I'm sinking fast."

"You'll make it. The centennial will put us all in the black. You're booked for tonight, aren't you?"

"Yes, and for the entire weekend. I wish it could be like this every weekend."

"Keep the faith, Kara. That's all any of us can do."

Kara squeezed Josephine's hand, reminded of how much grief her aunt had suffered and how she had always come out fighting. "I wish I had your courage."

Josephine laughed and stood up. "Personally I'd rather have Barbra Streisand's voice, but we've got what we've got. Now I'll see to the wine."

As Josephine disappeared into the kitchen, the front door to the rec center flew open. Beverly Appleborne stormed in with Margaret Woodrich following just behind her.

More trouble. Kara's gut instinct had been right.

"Ladies," Kara said. "Can I help you?"

"We're giving you one last warning, Mrs. Delaney," Beverly Appleborne said. "If you dare to honor that scoundrel, we will walk out of this dinner with our friends, and we do have a lot of friends."

"I'm sorry you feel that way, Mrs. Appleborne, but as I said before, Mr. Hunter's part in the dinner is very small, just a five-minute speech, a few photos, and then the mayor will give him the keys to the city."

"The keys to the city, are you out of your mind?" Beverly asked.

Kara sighed. "It's just a token gift. It doesn't mean anything."

"It means we've forgotten Becky Lee. It means we've forgiven Ryan," Margaret said with a shaky voice.

"The centennial is not about Ryan; it's about this town, about moving forward," Kara replied, trying to distract them from the issue of Ryan. "Surely we can all work together—for the good of the town."

"Unlike you, we're very happy with this town exactly the way it is," Beverly said. "My husband has practiced medicine here for thirty-five years. Our children grew up in the beauty and tranquillity that is Serenity Springs. We don't want video arcades and drive-through restaurants."

"With all due respect, Mrs. Appleborne, three of our merchants went out of business last year because they could no longer make a living," Kara replied. "There are people in this town who are struggling."

"Then they should go elsewhere," Beverly declared.

"Can't we compromise, ladies? Can't we have some progress, carefully watched over so we don't disturb the uniqueness of our town, but at the same time give everyone here a chance to earn a living?"

"Humph." Beverly tilted her nose in the air.

Margaret clutched her black patent leather purse to her bosom. She looked as if she wanted to say something but wasn't sure where to begin. Finally her mouth opened, her lips trembling.

"You have a daughter. You should understand," Margaret said. "That man is responsible for Becky Lee's death. I can't stand to look at his face. It hurts me here— in my heart." She put a hand to her chest.

The simple gesture moved Kara more than words. She did understand a mother's sorrow. She knew that if anything happened to Angel, she would never be the same.

"I'm sorry," Kara said. "Truly. I had no idea when I invited Ryan here that you thought there was some connection between him and your daughter's death. Andrew never said anything. No one ever said anything."

"It's not something we like to talk about."

"Your ignorance is not an excuse," Beverly said. "You should have consulted with us before you made such a radical decision. I still can't believe Andrew let you do this."

Kara bristled at that implied insult. "I didn't ask Andrew for permission. I'm a grown woman. I'm also the president of the chamber of commerce. I make my own decisions."

"Bad ones, apparently."

"That's enough," Josephine said, interrupting their conversation. She walked toward them, her mouth set in a grim line, her eyes promising retribution. If anyone could intimidate Beverly Appleborne, it was Josephine.

"I didn't see you there," Beverly said.

"Obviously not. You can take your insults and go. Kara doesn't need grief from you. And Margaret, I can't believe you're blaming Ryan for everything. Becky Lee had a mind of her own, and you knew that better than anyone. If she left Andrew, it was her decision and no one else's. That girl never did anything she didn't want to do."

Margaret shook her head. "It was him, Josephine. She loved him so much, she couldn't think straight."

"Then she shouldn't have married his brother."

"Becky Lee was hurt. She was upset. She was just a baby herself." Margaret's shoulders began to shake.

Josephine softened. "Now, don't be doing that," she said. "This town can't take any more tears. The river's already high."

Kara smiled at the analogy. In Serenity Springs everything came down to the river.

"It's time for healing," Josephine continued. "Long past time. I, for one, am glad Ryan has come home. We could all use some excitement around here."

"You want excitement, you've got it," Beverly said. She spun on her heel and stalked out of the room, Margaret following quietly behind her.

Kara shot her aunt a worried look. "What do you think she's planning?"

Josephine's eyes glittered with anticipation. "I haven't a clue, but I hope it's good."

"Aunt Josephine, I have two hundred people coming for dinner."

"That's good. Every show needs an audience."

"I don't want a show."

"Then you shouldn't have invited the devil to your party."

"Do you think Ryan is as bad as they say?"

Before her aunt could answer, the phone rang, surprising both of them. Kara ran over to answer it. "Rec center," she said.

"Kara, it's Andrew."

"Andrew, where are you?"

"I'm—I'm in jail."

"You're *where*?" she asked in astonishment.

"In jail. It's a long story, but I need one hundred dollars to get out, and I don't have my checkbook. Could you go to my house and get it?"

"Sure, of course. I'll be right there." Kara hung up the phone. "Andrew is in jail."

"No." Josephine actually looked shocked. "I don't believe it. That boy never broke a rule in his life."

"Why do I have a feeling this has something to do with Ryan?" Kara groaned as the phone rang again. "I don't have a good feeling about this."

"Answer it," Josephine commanded.

Kara reluctantly picked up the receiver. "Recreation center."

"Kara? Hi, it's Ryan. I have a small problem."

"Don't tell me—you're in jail, too."

"It wasn't my fault."

"Oh, God, what did you do to Andrew?"

"Hey, I'm the one with a black eye."

"I'll be right there."

"Could you bring my wallet with you? I left it at the Gatehouse."

Kara hung up the phone without replying, anger and frustration stirring her blood. "Ryan's in jail, too."

"At least no one's dead."

"It's still early," Kara said darkly as she grabbed her purse and headed home.

# 9

"Kara will be here in a few minutes," Ryan announced as he set the phone down on Dirk Anders's desk. "She said she would be happy to help me."

"Only because you're a paying guest at the Gatehouse. Otherwise she would have let you sit here for the rest of forever," Andrew replied, sitting in the straight-back chair next to Ryan's.

"That's it. I've heard enough." Dirk stood up.

"You're letting us go?" Ryan asked hopefully.

"No, I'm locking you up. You two want to have at it, fine, but I don't have to listen to it." He led them down a hallway and opened the door to a cell. "Go on, get in there."

"Look, Dirk, can't we talk about this?" Andrew asked.

"No."

Ryan smiled as Andrew walked into the cell.

"You, too," Dirk said, pushing Ryan through the doorway.

"Hey, I want my own cell," Ryan said.

"This isn't the Hilton, boys."

"There's only one cot. Where is he supposed to sit?" Andrew asked, pointing at Ryan.

"That's not my problem. Maybe it's about time the two of you learned how to share."

"I'd rather sit on the floor," Andrew said.

"Then do it." Ryan walked over to the cot and sprawled across it.

Dirk slammed the door shut, and they were alone.

Neither one spoke for ten long minutes. Ryan lay on the cot and stared at the ceiling for most of that time, counting the square tiles, wondering if the sprinklers would really go off in case of a fire. His gaze moved over to the brick walls, to the dirt and grime that clung to the floor that Andrew was sitting on. He had been in this cell before, years earlier. He had been scared out of his mind then, afraid of his anger, his lack of control, and most of all afraid of Jonas's reaction.

Now Ryan felt resigned, more frustrated than angry. He shouldn't have raced Andrew, and he shouldn't have tried to fight him. Hadn't he learned anything in twelve years?

"I want you to stay away from Kara," Andrew said, interrupting his thoughts.

It was the worst thing Andrew could have said. Ryan hated it when people told him he couldn't do something or have something. "Why should I?"

"Because she's mine."

"Does she know that?"

"She knows."

But Andrew didn't sound all that certain. Not surprising, really. Ryan had a feeling Kara would never be anyone's possession. She had too much fire, too much passion, too much heart, too much stubbornness. Otherwise she wouldn't have invited him to the centennial.

He couldn't see Andrew with Kara at all. But then he hadn't believed Andrew and Becky Lee would get together either. Obviously his older brother had something that appealed to women.

The silence ate away the years between them. As the long minutes passed, the petty bickering of the past hour faded into the quiet, and Ryan's thoughts turned to Becky Lee.

"Why didn't you tell me Becky Lee died?" Ryan asked, voicing the question that had been constantly on his mind since the day before.

Andrew met Ryan's gaze head-on for the first time that day. "I figured when she didn't show up at your place, you would probably come looking for her."

He said the words as if he didn't care, but Ryan didn't believe for an instant that Andrew had taken her departure so easily.

"I didn't know she was coming," Ryan said. "I didn't ask her to come."

"That's not what she said."

"She lied." Ryan sat up and swung his legs down on the ground. "The last note I got from Becky Lee was a birth announcement. I never called her. I never wrote to her. I never said one damn word to make her leave you."

Andrew's face drew into a taut line. Ryan suddenly realized how old they both were now, how many years had passed between them. His older brother had gray hair in his sideburns and wrinkles under his eyes. There was a weariness in his expression that spoke of pain and anger, most of it directed at him.

"I never would have asked Becky Lee to leave you, not with her having a kid and all," Ryan added. "Besides, she chose you. She wanted you. That was the end for me."

He couldn't help the bitterness that crept into his voice. Becky Lee had hurt him when she married Andrew, more than he would have thought possible. Over the years he had told himself it was for the best. He wasn't the marrying kind then, and he wasn't the marrying kind now. And more than anything Becky Lee had wanted to be married. That's what he couldn't figure. Why had she left Andrew when she finally had everything she ever wanted—a husband, a home, and a baby?

"It wasn't the end for her," Andrew said so softly that Ryan had to strain to hear him.

"Why? What happened between you two to make her leave?"

"Nothing."

A man of few words, that was his brother.

"There had to be something."

"If there was, she didn't say."

Ryan wondered if Andrew really believed that. Or if his brother just couldn't stand telling him the truth. Andrew always had to have someone to blame. And it looked as if Ryan was it—as usual. Andrew had blamed Ryan for everything bad in his life—when he wasn't blaming his mother, that is.

"So, did you find her?" Andrew asked abruptly.

Ryan started at the change in topic, wondering how Andrew had followed the line of his thoughts so clearly. "Mom?"

Andrew nodded, his expression carefully guarded.

Ryan was suddenly reminded that they had another woman in common besides Becky Lee, and that woman was their mother. Isabelle's desertion had built the first wall between them. Becky Lee had built the second. For a moment he saw Kara in his mind and wondered if they were heading down the same road—if they were bound by some force, some destiny, to keep repeating the mistakes of their past.

"You looked for her, didn't you?" Andrew asked again, his voice gruff as if he didn't really care about the answer.

Ryan took in a deep breath, not sure he could talk to Andrew about his mother. They had never agreed on why Isabelle had left. Andrew had blamed his mother for walking out. Ryan had blamed his father for forcing her to choose between Serenity Springs and her dreams.

They had both been too stubborn to ever see the other side.

"I never found her," Ryan said. "I hired a private detective a few years back. He couldn't pick up a trail. Said it was too cold. It had been almost twenty years by then."

"I guess she didn't want to be found."

"It's strange, though. The detective said he never saw anyone disappear quite so thoroughly before. No trace of her anywhere. No bank stubs, no phone bills, no credit cards, nothing."

"She always was pretty good at playing hide-and-seek," Andrew said, a genius at understatement.

Ryan grinned. "Remember that time she hid in the old oak chest at the foot of her bed? We couldn't find her for the longest time. We looked everywhere. And then we heard Dad go into the kitchen—"

"And he said he was going to start dinner," Andrew continued.

"Which meant he was turning on the stove, and we suddenly—"

"Thought Mom was hiding in the oven and—"

"You went screaming into the kitchen that Dad was going to turn Mom into the Gingerbread Girl."

Andrew bit back a smile. "He got mad."

"At Mom," Ryan said, his grin fading. "Yelled at her for playing stupid games with us. Remember?"

Andrew's smile faded, too. He didn't say anything for a long moment. "I forgot about that part. But he was right. I mean . . ." Andrew stopped himself. "Actually he wasn't right. He was wrong."

"Well, that's a first for you, big brother, admitting that Jonas actually made a mistake."

"I know he made mistakes, but he didn't leave us, and she did. I can't forgive her for that."

Ryan wondered if it was time to tell Andrew the truth. But was he ready to hear it?

"Andrew? There's something—"

"Shut up, Ryan. Just shut the hell up. You always did talk too much."

"And you never did want to listen." Ryan lay back on the cot and closed his eyes. Only his mother had listened to him. Never Jonas. Never Andrew. Not even Becky Lee had really listened to him. A wave of loneliness swept through him as he and Andrew sat silently, ten feet away from each other physically but miles away emotionally.

Why the hell had he come back?

"Why are we coming back here?" Melissa demanded as Angel led them down the riverbank.

"Because this is where I saw the ghost last night," Angel replied as Billy and Melissa kept up with her. "The lady was in the trees over there." She pointed to a large oak tree with branches that swept along the surface of the rising river.

"I don't believe you saw a ghost. You're making it up," Melissa said.

Angel shook her head. "I'm not. She was sitting on the lowest branch, and she was wearing a bright yellow and red scarf with big flowers all over it. I almost thought she was part of the sun for a minute. But then she turned her head and told me to come closer."

"Did you?" Billy asked.

Angel sat down on a log. "Yes. She had the prettiest voice. It sounded like a song you would hear in church."

"What did she say?" Melissa asked.

"She said she was looking for a friend, that she was lonely. I told her that sometimes I get lonely, too, because I miss my friends back home and my dad. She told me I could come and talk to her any time."

"How come you're the only one who sees her?" Melissa asked skeptically, planting her hands on her hips.

"Maybe because I'm the only one who believes in her. Maybe if you tried believing, you would see her, too."

Melissa rolled her eyes. "I'm hungry. Let's go to my house and get some lunch."

"I thought we were going to Tucker's Bridge," Billy said. "I want to see how high the water is."

"I'm tired of looking at this stupid river," Melissa said. "I'm going home. Are you coming, Angel?"

Angel shook her head. "I'll go with Billy. But I'll see you at dinner tonight. Okay?"

"Okay," Melissa grumbled as she ran up the bank and disappeared from sight.

"Oh, shoot," Billy said suddenly. "Melissa borrowed my watch and didn't give it back."

"You can probably catch her. I'll wait here."

Angel sat down on a fallen log. She put her hands over her eyes as the sun broke through a cloud, suddenly blinding her. It disappeared almost as fast. Angel blinked at the changing light, suddenly seeing a shadow by the very tree she had used in her story.

A shadow made up of yellow and red colors. The form slowly took shape, the shape of a woman.

Angel blinked her eyes again.

"Hello, Angel."

She turned her head, but there was no one behind her, only this very odd shadow in front of her.

"You're right. I am lonely," the lady said.

Angel's mouth dropped open. "What? Who are you?"

"The lady you spoke about."

"But I—I was just making that up."

"I am sad," the lady continued. "I miss my family."

"You do?"

"Just like you miss your father and your friends. It's difficult to say good-bye to those we love, isn't it?"

Angel suddenly felt like crying. The lady's voice was so soothing. "I didn't want to say good-bye to my dad, but I had to, because my parents got a divorce. They don't love each other anymore. I—I don't think my dad loves me anymore either."

"How could he not love you?" the lady asked. "You're such a beautiful girl, so full of spirit and imagination."

"I caused trouble, you know, with him and my mom. It's my fault they split up."

"That's not possible. If they loved each other enough, there is nothing you could have done to break them up."

"Really?" Angel asked hopefully. She wanted to believe that was true.

"I need your help, Angel," the lady continued.

"You do?" Angel asked, her eyes widening.

"Yes. I lost my locket somewhere along the bank. It's gold, and it has pictures of my children inside it. Will you help me find it?"

"Uh, sure. I guess."

"It's very important," the lady said urgently, sounding desperate. "I can't leave here until I find it."

"Why not?"

"Because I can't leave them. This might be my last chance, Angel. When the river rises, everything comes up with it, everything that's been buried. . . ." Her voice faded away, and the colors of her scarf turned pale, then white, then gray, until there didn't appear to be anything left.

"Who are you talking to?" Billy asked, coming up behind Angel.

She started with surprise. "Why—I was talking to the ghost."

Billy grinned. "Right."

"No, I mean it."

"Come on, Angel. I want to take a look at the bridge."

"But she was right there, Billy. Just like I said." Angel pointed to the tree. But no one was there. Had she imagined it? Had she fallen asleep for a minute? There were a lot of shadows, and she didn't really believe in ghosts.

"Are you coming or not?"

"Coming."

But Angel couldn't help taking one last look as she followed Billy down the riverbank. The lady's voice still rang through her head. She had said something about a locket. Instinctively Angel looked down at the ground, then felt foolish. The river went on for miles, finally dumping into the ocean.

If anyone had lost a locket along this river, it was long gone by now.

"How long are you planning to keep them locked up?" Kara asked Dirk when she arrived at the jail.

He smiled at her. "What's your pleasure?"

"How about forever? I cannot believe this. I am putting on the biggest dinner this town has seen in a hundred years, and not only is the guest of honor in jail but so is the town's only reporter."

"Damned inconsiderate of them, I'd say," Dirk agreed. "Sit down, Kara."

"I'm too angry to sit down." But she did anyway, because Dirk had a way of getting people to do what he wanted without raising his voice. He was the perfect sheriff—smart, calm, and patient.

In some ways he reminded her of her father. Dirk had the same broad girth as Harry Cox, the same twinkling blue eyes. But Dirk had stood by his wife and his children for a lifetime. Harry had left a long time ago.

More water under the bridge, she thought with a sigh, wondering if it was the centennial that was bringing all the old stuff back to the surface, when it would probably be better off staying buried.

"I'm worried about the dinner tonight," Dirk said.

"So am I."

"Maybe Ryan shouldn't go."

"Oh, Dirk, it's too late to change things now."

"I could make it easy for you. I could say you couldn't find his wallet, couldn't bail him out."

"There are so many people coming to see him."

"Then maybe we should keep Andrew locked up."

"Maybe you should put me in there so Mrs. Apple-borne and her cronies can't tar and feather me and send me out of town."

"You sure did open up a can of worms."

"I sure did. But it's done now."

"I suppose you're right." Dirk stood up and jangled the keys. "Guess we better let 'em out, then."

Kara followed him down the hallway. "You didn't put them together, did you?" she asked in amazement.

"I sure did. Figured they'd either start talking or kill each other. Either way works for me."

He opened the door. "The cavalry has arrived, boys."

Kara looked first at Andrew. He gave her a pleading, apologetic smile. "I'm sorry, Kara."

She turned to Ryan. He simply shrugged and put a hand to his blackened eye. For a moment she felt sorry for him, then her pity turned to annoyance. Ryan was in jail. He had a black eye. That was going to look great on the front page of tomorrow's paper.

"You hit him?" she asked Andrew, still not sure how it could have happened. Andrew was the least violent man she knew. When he got angry he got silent, not physical.

"He sure did," Ryan declared.

Andrew shot him an angry look. "You deserved it."

"I didn't do anything."

"You two sound like a pair of five-year-olds," Kara declared.

"Sometimes families bring out the worst in one another," Dirk said. "Don't know why that is, but it is."

"It should be just the opposite," Kara said.

Ryan simply smiled. It was the last straw.

"You think this is funny?" she demanded.

"You have to admit—"

"You think I don't have better things to do than come running down here to bail you out of jail? Stop laughing," she said in complete frustration as Ryan's grin grew.

He pointed to her shoe. There was a red streamer stuck to the heel. Good Lord, she had walked down Main Street and driven across town trailing a stupid piece of red crepe paper.

In anger and embarrassment, Kara threw Ryan's wallet at his face. He tried to grab it but missed. A pile of credit cards flew onto the floor. Ryan knelt down, but instead of picking up the cards, he reached for Kara's foot. "Here, let me help you."

"I'll help her," Andrew said immediately.

Andrew tried to push Ryan away, but in his haste he missed Ryan and knocked Kara in the face with his elbow. The force sent her backward, and she landed hard on her buttocks.

The three men turned to stone.

Kara grabbed her stinging right eye and bit back a cry of pain. Her bottom hurt. Her eye hurt. And her pride hurt most of all.

Dirk held out a hand, and with as much dignity as she could muster, she got to her feet.

"I'm sorry," Andrew said, looking suitably horrified.

"Me, too," Ryan added. "How can I make this up to you?"

"You can both go to hell. That's what you can do."

Ryan looked at Andrew as Kara stormed out of the jail. "I think we're already there," he muttered, and for once Andrew appeared to agree with him.

# 10

"Lighten up, this is a party," Loretta said to Andrew as they stood against one wall of the recreation center, watching Kara greet the arriving guests.

Andrew stared down at his beer. "More like a wake," he replied gloomily.

"Who died?"

"Me."

Loretta punched him in the arm. "Oh, come on, it can't be that bad. At least you don't have to pee every thirty seconds like I do."

"Loretta!"

She smiled unrepentantly. "Well, it's true. Things could be worse, you know."

"I don't think so. I spent most of the day in jail."

"I heard. And now you're in the doghouse, huh?"

"Kara has a right to be angry. I let her down. Not only that, I gave her a black eye."

"You hit her?"

"Accidentally. I was aiming for Ryan."

Loretta tried not to laugh, but she couldn't hold back a big grin.

"It's not funny. Why do I act like a fool every time I see Ryan? In one second I go from being a responsible adult to a stupid kid."

Her smile turned to one of understanding. "He just gets to you, that's all."

Andrew took a sip of his beer. "It was like I'd seen him yesterday, instead of twelve years ago. Like we were still fighting over comic books, still swiping each other's clothes."

"He's your brother, Andrew. Disliking him doesn't make all that go away. You shared a lot of years together. You have a past, a history."

"But that's the point. It is the past. And I don't want him in my present or my future."

"Why? What are you so scared of?"

"I'm scared of being found out," Andrew said. He bit down on his lip, holding back any further confession. Why did the words flow so easily with Loretta?

"Found out that you're human and you made a mistake, and that you loved someone who didn't love you back?" Loretta asked.

"I don't know what I'm saying. Forget I said anything."

"Just because Becky Lee didn't love you doesn't mean you aren't worth loving."

Her words brought his eyes up to meet hers. The warmth of her gaze crept under his skin. The glow of her smile made him stand a little straighter.

"Loretta," he said impulsively, then stopped, not sure what he wanted to say next.

"What, Andrew?" she asked softly.

Jesus, was that desire in her eyes—for him? A rash of goose bumps raised the hair on his arms. He suddenly wanted to bury himself in her warmth, in her honesty, in her generosity. But she was pregnant. God, what was he thinking?

Loretta wasn't the right woman for him. In some ways she was another Becky Lee, passionate and single-minded, somewhat selfish. Maybe Loretta had slowed down a bit because of the baby, but once she had the kid, who knew what she would do?

He stiffened when she laid a hand on his arm. "Is that how you did it?" he asked.

"Did what?" Her voice grew tense.

"Got all those men to want you? By telling them they were worth loving? By making them believe in things that weren't true? Is that how you seduced them all?"

Loretta stepped back as if he had physically hit her. He realized belatedly that the strength of his question had silenced the crowd around them, making them the center of attention.

"You want to know how I did it, Andrew? I stripped for them, talked dirty, and did anything they wanted, and I do mean anything."

"Loretta, hush," Andrew implored.

"Why should I hush? I'm the town whore, isn't that right? And a good man would never be caught dead with me, at least not in the light with his pants down. After dark you'd be surprised how few really good men there are in this town." She rubbed her stomach defiantly. "Isn't that right, Mrs. Appleborne?" Loretta threw Beverly a wicked smile as she walked defiantly to the bar and ordered a drink.

Andrew met Kara's shocked eyes across the crowd. Damn, he had done it again. Caused another scene. This was not his day. This was definitely not his day. And he felt guilty as hell for what he'd done to Loretta. She hadn't deserved his words. She'd only tried to help him. But he didn't want her help. He didn't want anything from her.

With Loretta gone, the crowd dispersed. Music suddenly filled the room as Hans Grubner sat down at the piano to accompany his wife, Gillian. Although he couldn't play the way he used to, Hans still commanded the piano like no one else. And Gillian's sixty-eight-year-old voice rang through the room—clear, strong, and passionate.

She sang an old tune and a new one, "Unforgettable,"

first made famous by Nat King Cole, then by his daughter Natalie.

Andrew sat down in one of the chairs along the wall and leaned his head back. Unforgettable. So many people in his life were unforgettable—Ryan, Becky Lee, Loretta. Andrew wished he could leave, escape the memories, the madness. But there was no more running away. The monster was now within him, and somehow he would have to find a way to vanquish it.

Their music spoke of love. As Hans's fingers ran across his beloved keys, Gillian smiled at him with her heart in her eyes. Kara caught her breath at the sight of their love, still so strong after forty-eight years of marriage.

Kara's tension eased as the music inspired the crowd to relax, to sip their wine, to share the moment together, to forget that Andrew and Loretta had just engaged in nasty comments, and that Mrs. Appleborne and her crowd of followers were wearing black dresses as if mourning the death of Serenity Springs, rather than celebrating its birth.

While the music played, while the two people who knew each other so well filled the room with their love and passion, everything else was forgotten.

This was what Kara had wanted most from the dinner—a coming together, the community celebrating its history and its future. Of course, she wanted the developers, like Harrison Winslow, to throw money their way, and of course she wanted the tourists to be inspired by the town, but what she most longed for was the feeling of family that had been missing in her life.

She turned her head and saw Angel and Billy huddled together with several other children, their foreheads almost touching as they whispered to one another. Kara smiled to herself, thankful that Angel had made friends, that their move to this small town had been the right one.

At least for Angel.

As Kara's gaze moved on to Andrew, her own feelings became less clear. For a moment she thought of joining him. But tonight he seemed isolated, distant from her, a stranger almost. She supposed that was partly her fault after leaving the jail so abruptly. But he had deserved her anger. Imagine racing his brother, running his truck off the road, and landing in jail on one of the most important days of the year. Not to mention giving her a black eye.

With a tentative hand Kara touched the slightly puffy swelling around her right eye. Two layers of makeup had hidden the bruise, but it still felt tender.

Andrew's reaction at the jail had surprised her as much as it had angered her. Ever since she had told him Ryan was coming to town, Andrew had changed. Even tonight the passion he had displayed in his argument with Loretta had made her realize that she and Andrew rarely fought over anything, and certainly not with that kind of enthusiasm.

Maybe it was Ryan's fault. His presence had thrown Andrew completely off balance, as it had Jonas. Kara's gaze drifted over to the bar, where Jonas was drinking shots of whiskey. He seemed intent on getting drunk, and a drunk Jonas would be even more dangerous than a sober one.

Kara looked down at her watch. Ryan was late, and the catering manager had already begun to set out the salads. She didn't want to start the dinner with one conspicuously empty seat at the head table, but in a few minutes she would not have a choice. Maybe it would be better for everyone if Ryan didn't show up.

But even as the thought crossed her mind, she knew it was untrue. No matter what happened, she wanted Ryan to come. She wanted him to see the results of her efforts. She wanted him to feel a bit of the magic that was Serenity Springs.

The music ended on a high note. Gillian leaned over and kissed Hans on the lips. The crowd broke into ap-

plause. When the clapping ended, a man stood alone at
the back of the room. Heads turned. Hearts quickened.
Voices hushed.

No one seemed to know what to do now that the
moment had come. Kara least of all.

Ryan looked straight at her, and despite his confident
stance, the quiet sophistication of his sleek black suit,
she could tell he was nervous. She didn't know how she
knew, but she did. There seemed to be a connection
between them that went deeper than words.

It was up to her. She had invited him here. And he
had come.

With deliberate, purposeful steps Kara walked up to
him and extended her hand. "Thanks for coming," she
said with a smile.

Ryan took her hand and squeezed it. "You look terrific."

Kara couldn't help feeling pleased. It was a throw-
away comment, the kind any man would make at a
function like this. Nothing to get worked up about. But
when his gaze traveled down her midnight blue cocktail
dress with glowing approval, she felt every nerve in her
body tingle as if he had stroked her with his fingers
instead of his gaze. "You look good, too," she whispered. "Come on in. Stay a while."

He smiled, but it didn't erase the tension in his eyes
as he looked around the room.

Most people were hanging back, not sure what to do.
Finally Josephine stepped forward. "Ryan, it's nice to
see you again. You remember Ike Kelly, don't you?"

Ryan nodded as Ike shook his hand. "Congratulations. I heard you two are newlyweds."

Ike muttered something about being newly hog-tied,
but a sharp look from Josephine made him simply raise
his glass to his lips.

As Josephine stepped aside, Kara took Ryan over to
meet the press people and the developers. The crowd
came to life again as people began to chatter among

themselves. She didn't consciously avoid Andrew or Jonas, but it seemed easier to move away from them than toward them. Eventually they ended up at the bar, face-to-face with Jonas.

He was drunk, Kara realized with dismay. Jonas's eyes glittered with anger, despair, and a myriad of other emotions. His face seemed to get redder with each breath that he took, each loud, angry, frustrated breath. Jonas was itching for a fight. She could see it in his hands clenched at his sides, in the upward thrust of his chin, in the beads of sweat clinging to his brow.

Ryan squeezed her hand so tightly it hurt. She squeezed back, trying to lend him whatever support she could. Whatever was between these two men, this father and son, it was obviously strong enough to scare both of them.

Neither man spoke for long, tense minutes. There seemed to be a silent battle going on as to who would say the first word. The rest of the room disappeared into shadowy silence, the crowd hushed as if the curtain had opened on the first act of a play.

Finally Jonas opened his mouth. "Get out," he said. "Get out of my town."

Kara caught her breath, casting a quick glance into Ryan's stony face. The challenging words had made his hand flinch within hers, but otherwise he gave no visible reaction. In a way it was the worst thing he could have done, because it made Jonas even angrier.

"I said, get out," Jonas repeated.

Kara silently prayed that Ryan would respond, that he would somehow smooth things over so the entire party would not be ruined.

Finally Ryan spoke. "No."

Simple, direct, completely unacceptable.

"How dare you? How dare you come back here? This is my town. My town." Jonas pointed to his chest. "I will not honor you, not tonight, not ever."

"And I won't honor you," Ryan said. "Because you have no honor."

"You son of a bitch!"

Kara gasped as Jonas threw his whiskey in Ryan's face.

Ryan didn't move a muscle. He didn't wipe the liquid off his cheeks or his mouth. He just stared at his father, his fingers still tightly entwined with Kara's. She wondered how he could stay so calm, how he could act so indifferent in the face of such bitter rage.

Kara would have thrown her own drink back at Jonas. Unfortunately she didn't happen to be holding one. Fortunately Josephine did, and before Kara could think of stopping her, Josephine tossed the contents of her wineglass into Jonas's face.

"You need to cool off," Josephine said.

Jonas sputtered with indignation. "Good Lord, woman," he roared.

"Oh, stop your barking," Josephine snapped back. "I've known you since we shared a playpen together, and I've had it up to here with your ranting and raving. If you can't be nice, then go home."

Jonas looked as if he was about to have a heart attack, Kara thought worriedly. He was flushed and jittery, nervous. Maybe even more nervous than Ryan.

Andrew suddenly appeared at her side, a little late but she was still glad to see him. "I'll drive you home, Dad," he said quietly.

"Get the hell out of my way. I'll drive myself home. I don't need you. I don't need any of you," Jonas shouted. "This is my town. My town."

Andrew tried to take his arm. Jonas shook him off, but he did walk out of the rec center. For that Kara was grateful. She thought the fireworks were over until Beverly Appleborne stood up and made a sweeping motion with her hand. "We want everyone here to know that along with Jonas, we will not honor this man. Serenity Springs will never welcome Ryan Hunter into its midst, or accept what he represents—big-city ways, lying, and cheating." She walked over to Kara. "And we will not let you change this town. You will fail. Just as this dinner has failed."

With that she left. Kara held her breath as one person after another stood up to leave. When the door finally closed on the last individual, the room was half full.

"I'm sorry," Ryan said.

"It's not your fault. It's mine." Kara handed Ryan a napkin from the bar so he could dry off his face. "Believe it or not, I didn't invite you here for public humiliation. I owe you a big apology."

"Actually Kara, you're one of the few people here who doesn't owe me an apology," Ryan said as he glanced over at Andrew.

Andrew stiffened, but instead of acknowledging Ryan's comment, he turned to Kara. "Do you want me to take you home, Kara?"

Take her home? Run away from this disaster of a dinner? No way. She hadn't done anything wrong, and if she had learned one thing from her failed marriage, it was to stop taking the blame for things that were not her fault.

"Are you kidding? This is my party. Let's eat," she said defiantly. "Aunt Josephine, please tell the caterers to serve."

"Atta girl," Josephine said.

"Now, are you and Ryan capable of sitting at the same table without insulting each other or dishing out miscellaneous black eyes to anyone who happens to come between you?" Kara asked bluntly, looking from one to the other.

Ryan smiled at her candor. Andrew scowled. Neither one said a word, but she took that for agreement and led the way to the head table. She put Ryan on one side of her, Andrew on the other.

After a moment Hannah Davies, the librarian, came over to sit next to Ryan, then the mayor and his wife,

then Loretta, and Will and his wife, until the head table
was full and dinner was served.

When the band began playing just after nine, Kara let
go of the last bit of her tension. The people who had
stayed at the dinner seemed to be having a great time.
Harrison Winslow had pulled her aside to tell her that
his plan for building a resort in the north woods was
moving along nicely, and he would have a proposal on
the table by the following week.

In addition to Harrison's support, some of the other
developers Kara had invited to the party had also
stopped by to let her know that they were interested in
the future of Serenity Springs and would be in touch.
Of course, it helped that most of the town's progressive
supporters had stayed at the dinner while the detractors
had left. Little did Beverly Appleborne realize that by
leaving she had actually made the centennial dinner an
even bigger success.

The developers didn't care about Ryan's infamous
past, so his presence at the dinner made no difference
to them. The local reporters did care, but the father-son
scene had only added more color to their stories. In fact,
they had all taken photos of Ryan and interviewed him
about everything from his recent trip to Bosnia to his
love life and his relationship with his father.

Ryan parried their questions with ease and confidence, telling them just enough to satisfy without giving
away anything deeply personal.

Kara would have felt ecstatically happy if Andrew
hadn't spent most of the evening by her side, stoically
silent. When anyone made an attempt to engage him in
conversation, he simply refused to say anything more
than "no comment."

In fact Andrew's response had become so rote that
when Kara asked him what he thought of the music, he
said, "No comment," not realizing his mistake until he
caught her staring at him in amazement. Then he stam-

mered out an inconsequential answer that left Kara wondering what he was thinking about. It certainly wasn't her.

Men. She wondered if she would ever figure them out. "I need some air," Andrew said as her gaze drifted over to him. "I'll catch up with you later."

"All right."

"I don't get it," Angel said with a sigh, slumping down into the chair next to Kara's as Andrew excused himself.

"What's wrong, honey?" Kara asked as she smoothed an errant strand of hair behind Angel's ear.

"Billy hasn't asked me to dance. And I even practiced." Her sigh spoke a volume of disappointment.

Kara rubbed her shoulder. "Maybe he hasn't had a chance yet."

"He has already danced with Melissa twice and Paula once. He must think I'm stupid or ugly or . . ."

"Now, stop that, you're beautiful."

"You have to say that because you're my mother."

"I'm saying it because it's true."

But Angel didn't believe her. Her face was as long as the day. Kara wanted to say the right thing, but it was obvious that Angel needed a boost from someone besides herself.

As Kara looked around the room, she noticed Ryan dancing with Loretta. His arms were around Loretta's waist. Loretta's arms were around his neck. They were smiling at each other. It wasn't the first time they had danced that evening either. Of course, Ryan had barely stopped dancing.

He had some nice moves, Kara grudgingly admitted. And he had a way of looking at people as if they were special. Like now, like the way he was looking at Loretta.

Kara felt a sharp stab of anger. It wasn't right, Ryan flirting with Loretta. Although why it wasn't right she couldn't quite define.

Angel sighed again, and this time Kara sighed right along with her. Then she caught her daughter's eye and smiled. Angel grinned back.

"We're quite a pair, aren't we?" Kara asked.

Angel nodded.

"We could dance with each other," Kara suggested.

"I'd rather die."

"Don't die yet," Kara said as Billy walked up to them.

"Hey, Angel."

"Hey."

"Do you—uh—I mean—do you—want to dance?"

Angel beamed. "Sure, I guess."

Kara smiled as her daughter made her way to the dance floor. At least one of them was happy.

The music went on for another minute, then ended to a round of applause. Angel and Billy ran over to get a Coke as the band began to play a love song. Kara was relieved to see them choosing soda over slow dancing. Time enough for that later.

Kara felt lonely sitting by herself at the head table. She wondered where Andrew had gone and why she suddenly seemed to be the only single woman in a roomful of couples.

Her success as hostess of the dinner felt rather hollow. No matter how hard she worked, how busy she kept herself, there was always a moment when she realized she was truly alone. Sometimes it caught her off guard.

It was the music, she told herself, and the candles, and the late hour, and the dwindling crowd. A perfect setting for romance. For lovers. Her gaze drifted to the dance floor. No Andrew. No Ryan.

Then a hand came down on her shoulder, and a voice whispered in her ear, soft and sexy, "Dance with me."

She turned her head, and his lips grazed her cheek. Ryan. She swallowed hard. "I—I'm waiting for Andrew."

"He's out front talking to Loretta."

"Oh."

His eyes searched hers. "Jealous?"

"Of Loretta? No."

"Dance with me, Kara."

"I'm not sure that's a good idea."

"Why not? We did it last night—in my bedroom."

"Ryan!" Kara looked around to make sure no one had heard him. "Someone will hear you and get the wrong idea."

"Come on, dance with me."

Kara wanted to resist him, but the music was too sultry, the night too long. When Ryan took her hand and led her to the dance floor, she went with him. He held her too close, pressing her breasts against his chest, caressing the small of her back with his hand. Kara tried to pull away, to put some space between them, but Ryan would have none of it. Unwilling to cause yet another scene, she stayed in his arms.

Ryan rested his chin against her hair, and Kara realized how well they fit together, how every long, lean muscle of his body seemed to welcome her every curve. Ryan danced like a lover. Kara swallowed hard at that thought, reminding herself that it was just a dance. That they were surrounded by other people. That nothing was going to happen.

She tried to focus on something else, on someone else—on Andrew. Andrew had lots of good qualities. He was kind to animals. He was never late. Andrew was . . .

Kara couldn't remember anything else, not with Ryan's cheek brushing against hers, with the tantalizing scent of champagne clinging to his breath making her want to taste his lips. She closed her eyes to resist the temptation, but without the other dancers to distract her, Ryan completely filled her senses. He took over her thoughts. He became her fantasy. Maybe that was the problem. He so closely resembled the man of her dreams—strong and sure, ruggedly handsome, confident, caring, loving, tender.

Oh, God, she was in deep trouble. She had known the man for barely a day, yet she had been thrust into an emotional whirlpool of feelings, caught between Ryan and Andrew, between Ryan and Jonas.

"We're good together," Ryan said. His lips touched the top of her forehead, warm and promising.

They were good together. Too good. So good she was suddenly terrified. "I can't do this," she whispered. "I can't." She slipped out of his arms before second thoughts took her closer into his embrace.

"Kara, wait!" Ryan caught up with her at the back door of the rec center. "Don't go."

"I have to. This is wrong."

He held on to her arm. "It feels right."

"Leave me alone, Ryan. I don't play with matches anymore." She shrugged her arm free.

"Then how are you going to start a fire?"

"I'm not." She walked out onto the patio. He followed her, and the quiet intimacy of the dark night was worse than the dance floor.

"What happens when you get cold?" Ryan asked with a seductive smile.

"I'll buy a blanket."

"What happens when you get lonely?"

"I'll wrap my arms around my pillow."

"What happens if I kiss you anyway?"

Kara's lips parted. But she couldn't say anything, because he was lowering his head, because his mouth was warm and welcoming, and she suddenly needed this kiss as much as she needed air.

It was the thunder that broke them apart, the sudden flash of lightning that illuminated their mistake. He was the wrong man. She was the wrong woman. And when the heavens opened up in a torrential downpour, the fire was finally doused.

## 11

It was still raining at 2 A.M. when Kara finished cleaning up the recreation center and returned home. It was still raining when she put a sleepy Angel to bed and went down to the kitchen to make sure she had breakfast fixings ready to go in the morning for her guests. It was still raining at 3 A.M. when she finally got to bed, and it was still raining at 4 A.M. when the puppies began to howl.

Another thunderstorm had hit Serenity Springs, and the puppies did not like the noise. After assuring each one of her annoyed guests that she would do something about the howling, Kara took up residence in the sun porch.

"Come on, guys, give me a break, huh? It's just noise—like when you bark."

As if in reply, the puppy called Rex began to bark.

"That was not a command," Kara said in a stern voice.

Rex looked hurt at her sharp tone and crawled under the chair. She felt guilty, but at least he was quiet.

She pulled Rosie into her arms as the female puppy began to whimper. "You're okay." The dog whimpered louder. "Stop acting like such a wimp," she said tiredly.

133

"She's a female, what do you expect?" Ryan asked from the doorway.

He wore faded blue jeans, the top button still undone, drawing her gaze to a place she did not want to think about. She raised her head, unable to resist noting the tight fit of his T-shirt, the broad chest, the well-defined biceps in his arms. His hair was tousled, his green eyes still sleepy. He looked sexier now than he had in his suit. Was God trying to torture her?

"That's a sexist comment if I ever heard one," Kara said, stroking Rosie's head with the palm of her hand. The puppy continued to howl.

"I tend to get very sexist at four in the morning. Isn't there anything you can do to shut them up?"

"I could shoot them," she suggested.

"Where's the gun?"

"Ah, I didn't mean it. I didn't mean it," Kara said as the third puppy, Oscar, whimpered in fear. "I know you can't help it. You're just little and scared, and it's so loud." Her arms tightened around Rosie as lightning lit up the sun porch, followed by a loud crack of thunder.

Ryan sat down on the floor across from her and ran his hand down Oscar's back. The puppy immediately responded by burrowing his head into Ryan's side.

"I think he likes you," she said.

"Nah. They probably just bond with the first person who puts them in a car. Any taxi driver would have their love."

"I hardly think so." Kara gripped the puppy in her arms as another clap of thunder rocked the house.

Ryan sent her a shrewd look. "You don't like storms either, do you?"

"Okay, so I'm a wimp, too. It just reminds me of . . . never mind."

"What? You might as well talk to me. It doesn't look like we're going to get any sleep," he added as Rex began to howl again.

Kara pulled Rex out from under the chair and into

her lap next to Rosie, hoping the warm bodies would make them all feel better. "Do you remember that big storm we had twenty-five years ago when the river flooded?"

Ryan nodded, his expression more somber than before. "Yes, I remember."

"The rain went on for days. I didn't think it would ever stop. Everyone was tense. My father and mother were constantly arguing. I felt as if my whole world was falling apart. Then the sheriff came and told us to move to higher ground. My mother started to cry. My father told us to go ahead, that he would finish moving the furniture to the upper floors. So my mom and I went to the rec center. I can still remember how narrow the cot was, how the edges felt, clutched between my fingers. I wanted my father to come and tell me things would be all right. But he never did. My mom disappeared for hours, too. I have no idea where she went. I just know it was the longest night of my life." She took a deep breath, trying to shake off the bad memories.

"The next day Mom and I went to San Francisco to stay with one of her girlfriends. She told me my father would join us once he made sure the theater was all right. Do you remember the Galaxy Theater down on River Road?"

"The first movie house in town. Your father owned it, right?"

"Yes. It was a grand old place. He used to play old movies, and the popcorn had real butter on it."

"But the Galaxy was damaged in the flood," Ryan said. "A few months later it was torn down."

"He couldn't save it. And he couldn't save his marriage either. My dad finally came to see us in San Francisco a few days after we had left. He and my mother stayed up all night arguing. I couldn't hear what they said. I just knew something was terribly wrong. In the morning my dad was gone, and my mother said they were getting a divorce."

"Did you see your father again?" Ryan asked.

She was so intent on her story that his question took her by surprise. "I did see him again, but not for years, not till I was grown."

"When did you see him? Where?" Ryan asked.

"Why are you so interested?"

He shrugged. "Just curious."

Somehow she sensed there was more to his interest than curiosity, but she didn't see any point in evading his question. "I saw him again right after Angel was born. He came to the hospital. He cried when he saw her. I cried when I saw him. He looked so old, so used up. I found out then that he had been a drunk for years. He said something about chasing a dream that couldn't be caught. I don't know what he was talking about, and frankly I didn't care about his dreams, not after spending my life without a father."

"Was he alone? Was he alone all those years?"

She looked at Ryan searchingly. "What are you asking me?"

Ryan uttered a nervous laugh. "If you don't want to say . . ."

"I don't know if he was always alone. But he was when I saw him. And it sounded like he had been that way for a while. I don't know what happened between him and my mother. She never said. I learned pretty quickly not to ask too many questions."

"Did you ever ask him where he had spent his life?"

Kara thought about his question. When her father had first come back, she had still felt such a sense of betrayal that she hadn't wanted to show him any interest. She had let him hold her baby, but that was all. After a few weeks, when she had begun to realize that this old, failing man was not the heroic father she had held in her heart, some of her anger had faded away, but not all of it.

"I put it off too long," she said. "My father died three months later from cirrhosis of the liver."

"I'm sorry."

"Why? Because it was all so pointless?"

"No, because you lost your father, not once but twice."

Kara's eyes clouded over with unexpected tears. "It was so unfair. And the worst part is that I never really said good-bye."

"I know." He looked into her eyes with complete understanding.

"You do know, don't you? Because of your mother."

"Yes."

"I've done the same thing to Angel. I took her father away from her."

"Did you take him, or did he leave?"

"Does it matter? He's still gone."

"I think it does matter."

Kara shook her head, not wanting to get into a discussion about Michael. "No. What matters is making things right from now on. Giving Angel the family she deserves, the security and the home she was meant to have."

"With Andrew."

"Maybe. He's a good man. I know he won't leave me."

"That's probably a safe bet."

"What about you? Do you want to get married?"

"Me? Hell, no. I don't think I could eat the same breakfast every day for forty years, much less kiss the same woman." Ryan's grin lightened his words.

"You'd be lucky to find someone who'd want to kiss you for forty years."

"Was my kiss so bad?"

He looked at her mouth in such a way that she felt as if he were kissing her again.

"Yeah, it was pretty terrible," she said huskily. She looked down at the puppy in her lap, suddenly realizing she had petted the puppies into falling asleep. The other one had conked out in Ryan's lap. "We must be fascinating conversationalists."

"At least they're quiet."

"Only problem is, we can't move."

"Trapped in the sun porch by a trio of puppies. News at eleven," Ryan said with a laugh. He leaned his head back against the couch.

"Tell me about you, Ryan. Is it exciting to travel all over the world, to tell stories with your camera?"

"It's the best," he said simply. "I've been everywhere. I've seen everything. But . . ."

"But," she encouraged.

"But sometimes I don't feel as if I've really experienced what I've seen. It's like reading a good book, wanting to know the characters, wanting to touch them and hold them, but no matter how hard you try, you just can't get in the pages. It's someone else's story, not yours."

"I know what you mean. Sometimes I feel that way here, trying to live in this town, where I belong and yet I don't. I think if I push hard enough, I'll begin to fit in."

"And if you don't, will you leave?"

"No. Because this is what I want. And I believe this is my story."

Ryan grinned. "I have the sudden urge to turn to the end of your book and see what happens."

"That would be cheating," she said, shaking a finger at him. "Besides, as Aunt Josephine says, it's the getting there that's the fun. The destination is the last bite of pie, not the first."

"Who else is in this story with you?"

"Angel, of course. These wonderful, mischievous puppies who have already eaten through two of my shoes. Andrew, Billy. The whole town."

"Even me?"

"You—you are an unexpected plot development."

He raised an eyebrow. "Major or minor?"

"Minor."

"Why minor?"

"Because this is my story, not yours."

"Somehow I have a feeling it might be ours."

Ryan stared at her so long, she felt her body begin to tremble. The desire was back in his eyes, the connection between them stronger than ever.

Kara drew in a breath, then slowly let it out. She didn't want to talk about their story, didn't want to admit to him or to herself that they could share anything together. She tipped her head toward the clearing sky outside. "Looks like the storm is over," she said.

"For a while anyway."

"What does that mean?"

"I don't know." Ryan grinned. "I guess you'll have to turn to the next page and find out."

Ryan was right. The storm returned with a vengeance at noon on Friday, one hour before the arts and crafts fair was due to open. When Kara arrived at the high school, the vendors stood huddled under an overhang, their station wagons and vans still loaded. Puddles large enough to wade through covered the front lawn and the parking lot.

So far the Centennial Celebration was turning into a survival test.

"Hi, honey," Josephine said as she waited patiently near the front door of the school with Ike. Josephine was scheduled to have her teacups on display as well as other knickknacks and antiques that she wanted to sell. "Did you sleep well?"

"No."

"The storm kept you awake?" Josephine asked perceptively.

"Among other things," Kara replied.

"Ah, that sounds interesting."

"You best save it," Ike interrupted as a group of vendors walked over to them.

Cole Jackson, one of the painters, spoke for the group. "Looks like a bust, Mrs. Delaney. We'll need refunds if you're going to cancel."

"I'm not going to cancel," she said. "We'll move it inside."

"Where? We won't all fit in the cafeteria. And the principal won't let us use the gym floor. We spoke to him a few minutes ago. He said they just redid the floor for basketball."

Kara knew that was true, because she had already had more than one conversation with the principal about that very matter.

"We'll start in the cafeteria and overflow into the classrooms," she said, trying to sound decisive.

The vendors eyed her doubtfully. Even Josephine looked skeptical.

"The classrooms?" Cole stroked his bearded chin. "I don't think that will work. There are desks and books, and the lighting certainly won't do anything for my paintings."

"There's nothing I can do about the lighting, but at least your paintings will be dry," Kara said with stubborn determination. Why did she seem to be climbing mountains alone? You'd think she was the only one in town with a vested interest. "We don't have any other choice. We can't disappoint our visitors. Let's make the best of things. Need I remind you that there is money to be made?"

The mention of money eased the grumbling. No one had anything better to do. They were ready for action. They might as well set up shop as best they could.

At one o'clock the fair officially opened. Kara had found more streamers to decorate the front hall, and she hoped the trophy case would add a touch of glamour to the setting. After all, she wanted the developers to know that they had an excellent school system, small though it might be. It was quality all the way.

The first few visitors were mostly relatives of the vendors. Ticket sales were slow, and nobody seemed to be buying. Either the town was still waking up from the previous evening or the arts and crafts fair was a bust.

Kara hoped it was the former.

Unfortunately the slow ticket sales and lack of people gave her too much time to think. There was only so much wandering she could do from vendor to vendor before she caught up with her thoughts.

And that meant thinking about Ryan. She shouldn't have kissed him, and she shouldn't have sat up half the night talking to him. Now she knew that not only was he sexy and a great kisser, but he could also listen, and it was that quality that most appealed to her.

Actually it wasn't just that he listened, it was that he talked. Give and take, the way two people were supposed to communicate. With Andrew she felt as if she did all the talking. Getting him to say anything remotely intimate was harder than playing the piano.

Setting her elbows on the table, Kara rested her chin in her hands, suddenly feeling weary. Every second of her day seemed to be a test. What the hell was she trying to prove? Deep down, she knew she wasn't a superwoman. She couldn't save the town single-handedly, raise her daughter, run the Gatehouse, learn to play the piano, reunite the Hunter family, and still retain her sanity. She was trying to do too much, but now that she had started, she didn't know how to stop.

The last thing she wanted to do was fail. Stopping anything she had undertaken would mean failure. She had no choice but to go on.

The flash of light startled her. For a moment she thought the lightning had returned; then she realized it was the flashbulb on Ryan's camera.

"You didn't take a picture of me, did you?" she asked in alarm. "I'm a mess." She pushed her hair behind her ears.

"I like messy. It's more interesting than clean."

She made a face at him.

Ryan snapped another shot.

"Stop that."

"Hey, you're the one who insisted I take photos."

"But not of me. Of the fair, of the vendors, of the townspeople."

"You are one of the townspeople. One of the prettier ones, I might add."

"You're a charmer, I'll give you that."

He walked over to the table. "How's it going?"

She held up the large circle of unsold tickets. "Slow. Very slow."

"The weather, no doubt."

"No doubt."

"Guess I'll wander around," Ryan said. "Unless you'd like some company?"

She wanted to say yes. He looked good in his forest-green twill slacks and tan shirt, and his eyes had their usual sparkle. She realized then that he was always lit up, a man who lived life to the fullest, who loved adventure, who always played offense.

She felt pale next to his tan, listless next to his energy, insecure next to his confidence. She wondered if Andrew felt the same way, if that's why he had such a difficult time dealing with his brother.

"If you don't need me, I guess I'll go," Ryan said when she didn't answer.

"Sure, walk around. Take some shots." She glanced through the front door, where she could see all the way out to the sidewalk. "Why don't you go now?"

Ryan stepped behind her so he could look out the door. Andrew and Billy were walking up the steps. They stopped to wave to someone else. Then they smiled at each other as they waited for that someone to join them. Seeing them together, side by side, touched Ryan in a way he couldn't fathom.

Father and son. His eyes blurred with emotion, and for a moment Andrew looked like Jonas and Billy looked like Andrew or himself as a young boy.

Ryan had never felt the need to re-create himself until this very second, until it finally occurred to him that the only way he would ever have a family was to build his own. There was no room for him now with Andrew or Billy or Jonas. They didn't want him and they didn't need him.

As he looked away from Andrew, he glanced over at Kara's face. She was watching them, too, but her expression looked troubled instead of joyful. He wondered what she was thinking. He wondered if he was partly the cause of the frown that creased her forehead.

He shouldn't have kissed her last night. He should have stayed the hell away from that sun porch. Because getting to know her had only made him want to know more of her. He couldn't see her with Andrew at all. She was a redhead, for God's sake. She had a temper and passion and an unbelievable amount of stubbornness. She would drive Andrew crazy in a second.

Andrew was too methodical for Kara, too organized, too predictable, too stuck in his own ways, in the old ways. Why couldn't they see that they were wrong for each other?

Just like Becky Lee and Andrew.

God, it was happening again.

And if push came to shove, Kara would pick Andrew, because Andrew knew one very important thing: He knew how to give a woman what she wanted, and Ryan didn't. He couldn't figure out what he wanted, much less what a woman wanted.

Ryan backed away from Kara, away from Andrew and Billy and the past that was creeping up on him. When Andrew reached the front door, Ryan turned and jogged down the hall. He didn't stop until he got to his old locker, until he saw the scratching in the corner and the initials BLW and RH wrapped around a heart.

He couldn't escape. Everywhere he looked there were memories. He couldn't hold them back any longer. They were everywhere. He saw the janitor's closet and remembered when he had smoked his first cigarette. He walked down the hall and saw the fire extinguisher that the principal had used to put out his first cigarette. A smile curved his lips at the thought.

At the end of the hall, he jogged up the stairs past Mr. Conrad's classroom, where he had taken ninth grade algebra and fallen in love with Kristie, or was it Donna Jean?

The next classroom had belonged to Hannah Davies. She had taught English then, and she had forced him to read by offering him a deal he couldn't refuse. For every chapter he read in *War and Peace*, she would let him publish a photograph in the school newspaper. He had jumped at the chance, because Jonas refused to publish any of his photos in *The Sentinel*. And Ryan had wanted to prove that he was a good photographer, so he had finished that damn book, every last page.

The experience had changed his life, not the reading really, but the photography. That's when he had first thought of making a career for himself away from the town, away from his father's newspaper.

Ryan lifted his camera and took a shot of the hallway, of the artwork, of the drinking fountain, of the desks and the books and the lockers, of everything that was high school, everything that was youth. He could almost see a pictorial in his mind, the rites of passage at a small-town American high school.

Damn. He caught himself just in time. He was starting to think like Kara, to believe that the outside world would have an interest in a town like Serenity Springs.

But the shots were taken, and he couldn't help loading another round of film. It was easier to look at the school through the lens of his camera. He could divorce himself from his surroundings. He could keep the memories on the other side of the lens. He could remind himself that he was only a spectator, not a participant. Only the players could feel pain and joy, not the people watching.

He tried to hang on to that thought as he prowled the hallways of his past, trying desperately to focus on the people who were there now, and not on the people he remembered.

# 12

"This place brings back a lot of memories," Andrew said as he sat down next to Kara at the front table.

"Good ones?" she asked, pleased that Andrew had initiated some personal conversation.

"Mostly." He looked down the hall to where Ryan had vanished. "I wonder what he thinks."

Kara barely caught the softly spoken words and doubted that Andrew intended to say them aloud. "Ryan probably thinks the school is smaller than he remembers. When I first came back, everything seemed smaller. Of course, I left as a child, and Ryan left as an adult, so maybe it's different."

Andrew shrugged. Sharing time was apparently over. He handed her a white paper bag.

"What's this?" she asked.

"A turkey and cranberry sandwich from the diner."

She smiled at him with pure delight. "My favorite."

He nodded, looking extremely pleased with himself. "I thought you might be hungry."

"I'm starving."

"Why don't you take a break? I'll sell tickets for a while."

"That's sweet of you." Impulsively she kissed him on the cheek. His skin felt smooth beneath her lips and somewhat cool, chilled from the storm, she supposed.

Andrew touched her cheek with his hand. It was the most intimate gesture she had had from him in several days.

"I want to make you happy," Andrew said, his tone somber. He had none of Ryan's humor. No sparks of light firing from his eyes. No hint of mischief just beneath the surface.

"You do—make me happy," she said, realizing he was waiting for an answer. She just wished she sounded more definite, less wishy-washy.

"I'm sorry about yesterday, about the jail, your eye, everything."

He sounded sorry, and Kara couldn't help responding to his tone. He was a good man, she told herself fiercely. He was trying hard to please her even in the midst of the impossible situation she had thrown him into. How could she have doubts?

She touched her eye. It was still tender but no longer swollen, and the bruise had faded. "I'm okay. Just remind me not to get between you and your brother again."

Andrew stiffened, and she realized her mistake.

"I don't want you between us," Andrew said. "I don't want you anywhere near him."

"Ryan can't get between us if we don't let him." *And if I don't kiss him again.*

"Ryan has a way with women," Andrew said. "I can't explain it. They just fall at his feet."

"Well, I'm still standing. Actually I'm sitting, but you know what I mean." She tried to smile, but Andrew didn't respond. "I think I will take a break." She stretched her arms over her head. "I'll be in the teacher's lounge if you need me."

"Okay. Oh, I almost forgot." He handed her a copy of *The Sentinel.*

A montage of photos from the banquet covered the front page. The newspaper photographer had caught·

the excitement of the moment and none of the tension.
There was no sign of Ryan, however.

"It's nice," she said. And it was nice. It was just a
little bland, a little too safe. Not that she wanted con-
troversy, but she also didn't want boring.

"The other papers will use Ryan's picture. This is the
best I could do."

Kara tried to shake off the feeling of disappointment.
"I understand."

"My father. He could barely do this. It goes against
the grain."

"I thought he was a professional. I thought you
were—" She stopped herself just in time. "I'm sorry.
I'm tired, and I didn't mean that. I better take that break
before you're sorry you came down here."

He was already sorry, Andrew thought as he watched
Kara walk away. She looked beautiful in her floral skirt
and teal blue sweater, as gorgeous as any woman in any
city. And not just good-looking but smart, too. He was
proud of what she had accomplished, proud that he was
with her. Proud. But even reinforcing the word in his
mind didn't make it ring true.

In fact, he was more worried than proud, afraid that
Kara's determination to bring progress to the town
would ultimately destroy what they both loved. He also
worried about their future as a couple. With Jonas angry
at Kara, and Ryan itching to cause trouble between
them, Andrew knew anything could happen.

He wanted the centennial to be over. He wanted the
outsiders to go home so his father could relax and Ryan
could disappear. He wanted back the Kara that he
loved, the woman who cooked and baked and moth-
ered the kids and still had time for him. It was okay
that she had the Gatehouse. He understood she needed
independence and a source of income, but he didn't like
her work for the chamber of commerce. He didn't appreciate it when she put the interests of the developers
before his own. He wanted her to think the way he

thought, to believe in the things he believed in. Was that too much to ask?

Andrew shifted his position, feeling restless and disturbed by his rampaging thoughts. He wanted this relationship to work. He wanted Kara to be the right woman, yet he had doubts, not just about her but about himself. His mother had left him. Becky Lee had left him. What if he wasn't man enough for Kara? What if she left him, too?

But Andrew couldn't tell Kara how he felt. He couldn't let her see how insecure he was deep down inside. He had to keep his distance emotionally until she was committed to him, until he felt safe enough to open up to her. Only then could he tell her the truth.

"I'm telling you the truth," the lady said as she hovered above Angel, her long black hair blowing in the wind.

Angel stared at the ghost through wide, disbelieving eyes. "You're not real," she said. "I'm just imagining you, like I imagine everything." She shook her head as she looked at the river and the trees and the threatening black clouds on the horizon.

She had come down to the river to see if the water had reached the bottom of Tucker's Bridge, the lowest bridge over the river, and it had. The sight scared and excited her. All that power rushing by. It made her feel as if she could change the world by herself. It made her want to believe in anything.

"I need your help, Angel. You're the only one I can trust."

"Why?" Angel looked up at the ghost.

"Because you're willing to believe in me."

"I want to," Angel said carefully. "But my mom doesn't believe in ghosts."

"She used to believe in love. So did Ryan and Andrew—even Jonas. But nobody believes anymore. No one but you. We have to change that. Please help me,

Angel." She pointed to a fleck of gold in the dirt by the corner of the bridge. "In another hour the water will cover it up again. You must get it now."

Angel hesitated. This was getting weird. Was she imagining the whole thing? Was this just the best story she had ever told, so good that she felt as if she was living it?

"Angel, please don't be afraid."

"I'm not afraid—not exactly. Okay, I'll get it. Is it your locket?" Angel asked as she walked over to the bridge.

"No, but it's very important."

Angel brushed through the dirt with her hands. Excitement swept through her as she saw a sparkle of light. She dug her fingers into the dirt and pulled out— a kid's watch with Mickey Mouse hands. "It's a watch," she said, somewhat disappointed.

"Yes, it is."The lady started to cry, and her tears fell like raindrops on the river. "Give it to Ryan," she said, and her words carried on the wind like a song as she faded away.

"Wait, don't go!" Angel cried. But the lady was gone.

Angel turned the watch over in her hand. There was something written on the back. She caught her breath at the words. *To Ryan. Love, Mom.*

Ryan stared at the sprawling house he had called home for the first twenty-one years of his life. A large deck on the first floor wound around the front of the house, overlooking the river. There was a smaller deck on the second floor, two actually, one outside his father's room and one outside his old room. Andrew's room, on the back of the house, didn't have a deck. Ryan would have felt claustrophobic without an escape route, but Andrew apparently had never felt the need to escape.

Ryan sighed as he wondered again why he had come.

Of course he knew why. Because he couldn't leave without seeing his father again.

He didn't need Jonas's approval, but he did need to say "I told you so." It wasn't honorable. It wasn't pretty. In fact, it was damn stupid, but Ryan still had a burning desire to say those words to Jonas's face, to make his old man realize that he had made it without him, without the town, without the goddamned river.

His adrenaline pumping, Ryan stalked up the steps to the house. He knocked on the front door, his heart pounding against his chest. No one answered. He knocked again, then pushed the doorbell. Nothing happened.

Jonas wasn't home.

What a letdown.

Ryan instinctively tried the door. The knob turned. Of course Jonas hadn't locked the door. He lived in a town where crime was nonexistent. He lived in a state of mind that allowed no room for fear or caution. But that world was slowly disappearing. Ryan wondered if Jonas would ever catch on.

After a momentary hesitation, Ryan walked inside. The house was neat as a pin. No dust. No clutter. Just stark furniture and stark white walls. The only paintings were of the river. The only rugs were handcrafted by local artisans. The only photos on the mantel were of Andrew and Jonas and Billy.

It was a masculine house, yet there were still a few surprising traces of his mother—the bud vase Jonas had given Isabelle on their wedding day; the needlepoint pillow his mother had struggled to make all those years ago, now worn and somewhat yellow, but still there.

Ryan walked upstairs and saw his mother's oak chest at the end of his father's bed. He wondered for the first time why Jonas had kept so many of her things. For a man supposedly filled with bitterness, he had lovingly cleaned and dusted the furniture he had built for Isabelle.

Why?

Ryan realized he had never noticed these things before. Maybe because they had always been there. Maybe because he had never stopped to consider there was another side. Now, without his father's domineering presence in the house, things seemed much clearer.

Ryan moved down the hall to the next room, inexplicably drawn to his old bedroom. He slowly turned the knob, trying to prepare himself for whatever he would see.

The room was dark, the storm clouds and heavy foliage blocking most of the daylight. Ryan switched on the light and caught his breath as his past hit him hard in the face.

It was the same. Everything was the same. His posters—an eclectic mix of baseball players and jazz musicians—his collection of mysteries and school yearbooks, his baseball signed by Willie Mays, and his photograph of his mother.

Ryan grabbed the edge of the desk and steadied himself as he looked at Isabelle. He had meant to take the picture with him years ago, but in the haste of leaving he had left it behind; he'd been too proud to go back for it. He thought Jonas would have burned it by now. It had been a source of contention between them for years. But here it was, and not a speck of dust on it. Which meant Jonas had come in here. He had cleaned the room. He had touched Ryan's things over and over again.

Suddenly it was too much. Ryan walked out of the room and pulled the door shut. He ran down the stairs. He had to get away—to think. But when his foot hit the last stair, Jonas walked in.

Ryan stopped abruptly.

Jonas did the same.

The ticking clock echoed through the room, counting off the seconds, the minutes, and the years since they had last seen each other.

"I see you let yourself in." Jonas tossed his car keys on the table.

"I see you still don't lock the door."

His father's gaze burned a hole right through him. Ryan wanted to look away. He wanted to hide. But he forced himself to stand tall and straight and proud. He didn't have anything to apologize for. His father was the one who had broken up the family. His father was the one who had driven him from Serenity Springs. If anyone should apologize, it had to be Jonas.

"Why the hell did you come back?" Jonas asked.

"I was invited."

"That isn't the reason."

Ryan shrugged. "I wanted to see the old homestead."

"More like you wanted to show us what a big man you are now. Too bad nobody cares."

Big man? Talking to his father, Ryan felt nine all over again. But he'd be damned if he'd let it show. "Enough people cared to give me the keys to the city. I don't think they've ever given you the keys, have they?"

His father headed toward the kitchen.

"Don't walk away from me," Ryan shouted. He would not be dismissed that easily. He followed his father. "You can't admit you were wrong about me, can you?"

Jonas washed his hands in the sink. "Wrong about what? As far as I'm concerned, you ran away, deserted a pregnant girl, and left your brother to pick up the pieces. You're selfish through and through."

"Becky Lee was pregnant?" It was the only part of his father's statement that stuck with Ryan, maybe because it was so shocking. He had thought he knew everything back then. But he hadn't known that.

"As if you didn't know," Jonas said scornfully.

"I—I didn't."

Jonas opened the refrigerator and pulled out a beer.

"Did she tell you she was pregnant?" Ryan asked.

"Yes."

"Did Andrew know?"

"Yes."

"I wonder why she didn't tell me," Ryan said, speaking more to himself than to his father.

But Jonas heard him, and he couldn't resist offering his own explanation. "Knew she couldn't count on you, that's why. Just like I couldn't count on your mother."

"My mother? She wasn't the problem. You were."

"She left you. I didn't."

"You sent her away." It was the same argument that had driven him away twelve years ago. Ryan hadn't meant to bring it up, hadn't wanted to get into a fight. He had meant to stay detached, in control. But suddenly that seemed impossible. "You may have fooled everyone else into believing you had nothing to do with her leaving, but you and I both know differently."

"I didn't take away your mother, boy. She left you same as she left me. She didn't love any of us."

"That's not true. It was your fault. You wouldn't let her sing. You knew what a great voice she had, the opportunities she gave up to stay here with you."

"She could sing right here."

"But she wanted more. She wanted to go home."

"This was her home."

"She wanted to go back to New Orleans. But you wouldn't even take her back there to visit her friends. Too expensive, you said. But we both know the real reason. You were afraid to let her go, afraid she'd never come back. And your worst fear came true."

"I gave your mother food and clothing and a home. I tried to make her happy, but it wasn't enough. It was never enough. She was spoiled and selfish, just like you. And she left with that man. She chose him over all of us."

"She didn't. I don't know where she went, but she didn't leave with him. I hired a private investigator to find both of them. He couldn't pick up a trail on Isabelle, but he followed the man all the way back to the day he left this town, through his divorce to the day he died, but they were never together. Never."

"That's not true."

"It is true. She left because of you, because you told her to get out, just like you told me to get out. You're the one who broke up this family, not her."

"Get out of my house."

"No."

"I said, get out," Jonas screamed. He threw his beer bottle against the wall in rage.

Ryan jumped back as the remaining beer splashed across the room. Then his father's face turned pale. He clutched his chest and sank to the floor.

"What's wrong?" Ryan asked.

Jonas struggled for breath. His eyes began to flutter.

Ryan rushed to his side. "Dad? Dad?" he cried out, suddenly terrified. "What's happening?"

"Heart," Jonas gasped. "Pills. Counter."

Ryan frantically searched the kitchen counter for pills, knocking over a stack of mail and a bowl of oranges before he found the small bottle next to the phone. His hand was shaking as he tried to open it, and he swore as the childproof lid balked at his efforts. Finally he got it open. He handed Jonas a pill and ran for a glass of water. By the time he got back to his father, Jonas had swallowed the pill.

Ryan felt helpless watching his father struggle to breathe. "What should I do?"

"Appleborne. Find Appleborne," Jonas moaned.

Ryan reached for the phone. Dr. Appleborne was unavailable. So he called 911 and prayed that they would arrive in time.

When he hung up the phone, Jonas tried to say something to him, but he couldn't catch his breath.

"It's okay. Just rest," Ryan said, kneeling beside his father.

Jonas closed his eyes. His head fell to one side, and his hand reached out to Ryan in a silent plea for help.

The front door slammed behind them. Ryan looked up, praying it was the ambulance. It was his brother.

Andrew stopped in the kitchen doorway. His face turned white at the sight. He had to swallow three times before he could speak. "My God! You killed him."

# 13

There was no hospital in Serenity Springs. The ambulance took Jonas to Sonoma, a twenty-minute ride. Ryan and Andrew followed in the Ferrari. They didn't speak one word the entire time, both caught up in their own thoughts.

Ryan had been in emergency rooms before, usually to photograph victims of some horrendous accident, some nightmarish act of God. But he hadn't known those people. He had seen their blood, but he had never felt their pain.

He didn't want to feel pain now. He didn't want to feel anything for the man they had wheeled behind the double doors a few minutes earlier. He hadn't wanted his father's ashen face to mean anything to him, or to have his stomach turn over at the sight of his father's limp body.

This was not the man who had raised him. This was not the Jonas who had towered over him like a tree, who had roared at him like the river, who had never weakened in the face of any storm, any danger, any heartache.

This Jonas had trembled, had been forced to his knees with pain, had needed him to help. Seeing his father like that had scared the hell out of Ryan.

He still felt shaky inside, almost nauseated. He was afraid that his father was going to die. It was ridiculous to have such feelings of desolation for a man he hadn't seen in years, but the feelings were there. He couldn't stop the memories, and each one eroded the wall he had built to protect himself.

His father had taught him to play basketball, given him his first camera, watched him score the winning run at the high school baseball game.

Jonas hadn't talked much, hadn't showed affection, but he had been there. He had fed them and clothed them and put a roof over their heads. Ryan didn't want to feel thankful for any of that, but at the moment that's just what he felt, along with a sense of regret that this might be all there was, that Jonas might truly die and their relationship would be over.

Father and son.

He had once wanted the relationship with desperation. He had once walked away from it with determination.

Father and son. The words rang through his head until he put his hands over his ears.

Andrew and Jonas were the true father and son, two men so alike they were almost mirror images of each another. Ryan didn't belong. He had never belonged.

Why had he come home? Why the hell had he come home?

Andrew sat down in the chair across from him. Ryan didn't know what to say. Why was it so hard to talk to his brother, to talk to his father? Why was it so hard for him to have a family?

"He's going to be okay," Andrew said, repeating the one and only phrase he had uttered in the past half hour.

"I hope so," Ryan replied.

Another long silence. More people entered the waiting room—a little girl crying over her swollen wrist, a man coughing and sneezing, a pregnant woman and her devoted husband. One by one they went through the double doors, leaving their loved ones to wait and wonder.

"This is your fault," Andrew said. "Why did you go there? Why didn't you just leave it alone?"

"I wanted to see the house. I wanted to see my father."

"After all these years—why?"

"I was curious."

"About what?"

"Everything." Ryan tilted his head to one side, studying Andrew with an intensity that made his older brother flinch. "I thought I took all the secrets with me, but they were here all along."

"What are you talking about?"

"Why didn't you tell me Becky Lee was pregnant?"

Andrew looked down at the ground. "It wasn't any of your business."

"Wasn't it?"

"No. It was my baby. My responsibility. It had nothing to do with you. Nothing." Andrew got to his feet. "I'm going to see what's taking them so long."

Ryan thought about calling him back, about forcing the issue, but a doctor came through the doors and beckoned them over.

Dr. Robert Steiner, a cardiologist, had been called in to consult. After introducing himself to both Ryan and Andrew, he spoke briefly and bluntly.

"Your father suffered a heart attack," Dr. Steiner said.

"How bad?" Ryan asked.

"Bad enough to scare the hell out of him. But not bad enough to do him in. He said he was arguing with his son. That would be . . ."

"That would be me," Ryan finished bitterly. "So he blames me for this, too."

"Blame is not important. What is important is getting your father to realize that he needs to take care of his heart. He was supposed to see me weeks ago. Dr. Appleborne went over his case with me at Christmas. Why didn't he come in?"

Ryan looked over at Andrew. His brother shrugged helplessly.

"He doesn't like doctors," Andrew said. "He thinks he can take care of himself."

"I see. Well, since he's here now, I'd like to keep him here for a few more days. Run some tests and give him a thorough workup. Then we can talk about proper diet, exercise, and rest."

"That sounds good," Andrew said. "Can I see him?"

"You can, but he's sleeping at the moment. Come back in a couple of hours. Let things cool down a bit. And try not to upset him."

"All right." Andrew turned to Ryan when they were alone. "Dad is not going to want to stay here. He hasn't missed a day at work in thirty years."

"Looks like you'll have to put out tomorrow's edition of the paper," Ryan said.

Andrew looked taken aback, then nodded. "Yeah, looks like I'll have to do that."

"Want any help?"

"From you? I don't think so."

"Why not? I worked on the paper as much as you did when we were growing up."

"But you don't work there anymore, I do. Why don't you leave? Go home. You've done enough damage for one weekend, don't you think?"

"I'll go when I want to go. And since you're going to be busy with the paper, I'll keep Kara company." Ryan couldn't resist that last shot. He didn't like being told he should stay away from his father and the newspaper and the town he had grown up in.

"You stay away from Kara."

"I don't have anything else to do. You don't need me. Jonas doesn't need me."

"Kara doesn't need you either."

"Maybe I need her."

"What do you want?" Andrew asked again. "To come back and ruin my life for a second time?"

"I didn't marry your girlfriend, Andrew. I didn't steal the woman you loved right out from under you. So where do you get off acting like the injured party?" Ryan nodded slowly, as if he had suddenly seen the light. "You're just like Jonas, blaming me for what you did."

Andrew flushed at the charge. "I didn't steal Becky Lee. She made her choice."

"And why did she make that choice?" Ryan asked again. "Because she was having your child? Or because—" he lowered his voice—"because she was having mine?"

The blood drained out of Andrew's face. "Billy is my son," he said haltingly.

"He better be, Andrew. He better be."

Billy hung up the phone in Kara's kitchen and looked over at Angel and Kara. "My dad says Grandpa had a heart attack, but he'll be okay. He has to stay in the hospital for a couple of days, though."

"Oh, dear." Kara looked at Billy's troubled face and her heart went out to him. He had to be confused by all the animosity flowing through the Hunter household. Poor kid, probably didn't know what to make of his family.

"I think Uncle Ryan made him sick," Billy said. "Dad told me not to talk to him if he calls me or anything. I guess he's afraid he'll make me sick, too."

"Why would he do that?" Angel asked with her own sense of unerring logic. "Ryan is a nice guy."

"You don't know him," Billy replied.

"I know him better than you."

"Do not."

"Do too."

"Time out," Kara said. "Let's leave the fighting to Andrew and Ryan. It's their business, not ours."

"I bet they're fighting because they found out that Ryan is not really a Hunter," Angel said, using her best story-telling voice. "That his father is an Italian count who came to America to find his lost love, only to discover that she was already married. They knew they couldn't be together, but before they left, they had one incredible night of passion, and . . ." Angel's voice faded away as she looked at her mother in alarm.

Kara realized she was staring at her daughter with her mouth hanging open. "Incredible night of passion? What have you been reading?"

"Nothing," Angel said quickly.

Even Billy was staring at Angel as if she had suddenly grown two heads.

"That is enough," Kara said. "More than enough. Go to your room."

"Can Billy come with me?"

"Absolutely not," Kara replied, her mind still focused on that last line, one incredible night of passion. What did her eleven-year-old daughter know of such things, and just how close were these two kids? "You better go home, Billy. You and Angel can see each other later."

"Mom," Angel protested.

Kara shook her head, opening the back door for Billy. "Good-bye, Billy."

"Good-bye," he mumbled.

Kara turned to her daughter. "Are you still here?"

Angel's eyes grew teary. "How could you do that? How could you make my one friend in this stupid town go away?"

"He just went home for dinner. He'll be back."

"No, he won't. You make everyone go away," Angel declared.

"I do not."

"You made Dad go away. You wouldn't cook him dinner, and you wouldn't take his clothes to the cleaners. And he had to ask that other lady to do it for him. And now he won't even write me, and when I call him he won't talk to me. You made him hate me."

Kara's mouth fell open for the second time in less than five minutes. "I didn't—your father doesn't hate you."

But Angel wasn't listening. She was running up the stairs to her room. Kara started to go after her.

"Let her go," Ryan advised, closing the back door behind him.

"When—when did you come in?"

"Right before Angel said you made her father go away."

Kara flushed. "That's not true. I have to make her listen."

"I don't think she'll hear you right now, no matter what you say."

"But she has it all wrong."

"Don't we all."

"What does that mean?"

Ryan sat down at the table. He looked exhausted.

Kara thought about Angel and decided Ryan was probably right. It would be easier to talk to her once she calmed down.

"How's your father?" she asked.

"Still breathing."

"That's good."

"Yeah." He rubbed the muscles along the back of his neck.

"How did it happen?" Kara asked.

"I went to the house. Jonas wasn't home when I got there, so I went inside." Ryan looked at her through pain-filled eyes. "He kept my things, Kara. My room was exactly the same as I'd left it. And it was clean, not a speck of dust anywhere. Tell me Jonas has a cleaning lady. Tell me Mrs. Murray goes over there once a week and cleans his house."

"I can't tell you that, because I don't think it's true. As far as I know, Jonas cleans his own house. In fact, Andrew once mentioned that Jonas is a nut for neatness.

That you two used to have endless chores every Saturday, and that you couldn't play until Jonas could bounce a quarter off your bedspread."

"That's true. But I don't understand, Kara. Why didn't he throw my things away? Why did he keep them? Why did he dust them?"

"Maybe he was hoping you'd come back one day."

Ryan laughed bitterly. "And that's why he threw a drink in my face last night? To welcome me home?"

Kara sighed. "I don't understand Jonas any better than you do. The one thing I do know is that the Hunter men are filled with pride, way too much of it as far as I'm concerned." Kara paused. "You still haven't told me how Jonas came to have a heart attack."

"We started fighting. I guess this time he got the last word."

"What were you fighting about?"

"The old stuff." He looked at her with a bewildered expression in his eyes. "All this time I thought I knew the secrets, but I didn't." His expression turned thoughtful. "Maybe Angel knows, too."

"Knows what? Your secrets?" Kara asked in confusion.

"Not mine, yours."

"I don't have any." But they both knew she was lying. Kara picked up the knife on the kitchen counter and began to slice carrots, her motions getting faster and faster until her knife hit the cutting board so hard the carrots scattered across the counter.

Suddenly Ryan's hands were on her shoulders. She turned into his embrace, and they held each other for a long moment. A port in a storm, his arms felt strong and safe. She wanted to linger in his embrace, in a place where the past couldn't touch her and the future was out of reach.

But Ryan moved away. He didn't protect her. He forced her to open her eyes, to lift her head.

"What did he do?" Ryan asked.

"I don't want to talk about it."

"Fine, don't tell me. Tell Angel. Don't make the same mistake my father did. Angel is a smart kid. She probably knows more than you think."

"The truth is so—dirty," Kara whispered. "I don't want it to touch her."

"I think it already has. That's why she makes up stories about her father and everyone else. She doesn't like your world, so she's inventing her own."

Kara wondered if he was right. Angel had always had imagination, but she had never told lies, not until the divorce. She wanted Angel to stop, and yet in some ways she didn't. It was easier to hear Angel boast about her father the CIA agent than wonder what Angel would be saying about her father if she knew the truth.

"I can't," Kara said. "It's too hard."

"You don't run from challenges. You face them head-on. I saw you do it last night at the dinner. I saw you stand up to those people."

"But I didn't stand up to my husband, not until it was too late. I was a coward. Maybe I'll tell Angel the truth when she's older."

"How old? Is there a magic age when we don't feel pain anymore, when we don't feel connected to our parents?"

"Yes. I think so."

"How old are you, Kara?"

"I'm thirty-one, why?"

The look came back into Ryan's eyes, the one that made her think he knew something about her. "Do you think you could handle anything I told you about your own father?"

Her entire body tightened. She didn't like the expression on his face. She didn't like the tone of his voice. She didn't like the question. "What could you tell me? You don't know anything about him."

"But I do. The question is, do you want to hear it?"

Before Kara could answer, the back door opened again. An overwhelming scent of lilac perfume was followed by her aunt's entrance. Josephine dumped two large suitcases on the floor with a decisive thump. Then she carefully removed her broad-rimmed floral hat and placed it on the kitchen counter.

"Aunt Josephine, what are you doing here?" Kara asked in alarm. "And why do you have your suitcases?"

"It's over," Josephine said dramatically. "Mr. Kelly and I are finished."

"What are you talking about? You're not finished. You and Ike are still newlyweds."

"I don't feel like a newlywed. I feel like I'm nearly dead." She wagged a finger at Ryan. "I don't need you laughing at me."

Ryan erased the smile on his face, but Kara could see the twinkle in his eyes. He might think this was funny, but she didn't. The last thing she needed was for her aunt Josephine to run away from home. She had enough to handle with the centennial, the feuding Hunters, and her rebellious daughter.

"Now, Aunt Josephine—"

"Don't you 'Aunt Josephine' me. I know what I'm doing. I'm getting a divorce."

Kara put a hand to her heart. "You can't do that."

"Why can't I?"

"You never have. Ike Kelly is your fourth husband."

"I should have stopped with three. Three's the charm, they say. Four is just one more." She walked across the kitchen and proceeded to fill the empty teapot with water. "Do you still have some of that herbal tea I gave you for Christmas?"

"Second shelf," Kara said.

Josephine helped herself while Kara exchanged a pleading look with Ryan.

"What exactly did Ike do?" Ryan asked, responding to Kara's silent query.

Josephine's mouth turned down into a frown. "He said my tea tasted like castor oil. And when I read his tea leaves, he refused to listen to me. I told him there was danger on the horizon, that someone we both love was heading straight into danger. But what did he do? He turned on the television set to that show he always watches with the women. 'Baywatch,' I think they call it. As if an old goat like him could get some sexy thing in a bikini. Who does he think he is?"

"A man," Kara said darkly.

Ryan cleared his throat. "Uh, do you think you're jumping the gun here? Maybe you should talk to Ike."

"As if I didn't try. I packed my suitcases right in front of him. You know what he said? 'If you want to be an old fool, go right ahead.' Now, I may be a fool, but I am not old." Josephine turned on the gas under the teapot and tapped her long, pale-pink fingernails against the kitchen tiles.

"Aunt Josephine, you can't get a divorce," Kara said, trying desperately to come up with the right words.

"Why not? You did. Your mother did. Ryan's father did." Josephine tilted her head to one side. "Why, come to think of it, I may be the only woman in this town who hasn't gotten a divorce."

"That's not true. Think about the Grubners. Hans and Gillian have been happily married for forty-eight years."

"Only because she makes him that damn apple strudel."

"What does apple strudel have to do with it?" Ryan asked.

"I have no idea," Kara said as her aunt took a cup and saucer out of the cabinet.

"Do you want some tea, dear?" Josephine asked. "What about you, Ryan?"

Kara ignored her. "Dirk and Susan," she said, snapping her fingers. "They're going on thirty-nine years, I

think. And the Applebornes have been together a long
time and the Woodriches, too."

"Only because no one would else would have Beverly
and Margaret," Josephine said.

"She might be right about that," Ryan added.

Kara shot him an irritated look. "You're not helping."

He grinned at her without any sign of being sorry.
"You said you came here to create more of a sense of
family. Looks like your family is moving right in."

"That's right," Josephine said, sending Ryan a look
of approval. "I'm moving in with you, Kara. I'm going
to help you run this place, and I can watch Angel for
you, too. It will be perfect."

"Aunt Josephine, I have a full house tonight. I don't
have any empty rooms." Kara could not even contemplate having Josephine under the same roof. Not that
she didn't love her aunt, but Josephine was forever
causing problems with her tea leaves and crystal ball
readings and occasional séances. The Gatehouse had
once been the favorite haunt of many a supernaturalist.
It was not the image nor the clientele Kara wanted.

"I'll sleep with Angel," Josephine said. "She has a
trundle bed. We'll be cozy as two peas in a pod. Unless—you don't want me here?" Josephine gave Kara a
sharp look.

"Of course I want you. I just hate to see you make a
mistake. Ike loves you. And I think you love him."

"Love! Piffle! Who needs it anyway? Now, where is
my great-niece?"

"I sent her to her room."

"What did she do now? Tell more stories?"

"Yes."

Josephine shook her head. "Sending her to her room
won't solve anything."

"It will give her time to think about what she's doing," Kara replied.

Ryan leaned against the counter, resting his chin on
his hand. "More likely give her time to come up with

some better stories. Why, she's probably in there telling her dolls that her evil mother has locked her in the tower without bread or water.''

Kara put her hands on her hips and glared at him. ''You're as bad as she is, encouraging her all the time.''

''Me?''

''Yes, you. I heard you telling her about China and Africa and all the places she's not likely to see.''

''And why shouldn't she see them?'' Ryan challenged.

''Because those places are a long way from Serenity Springs. Angel is going to stay right here and help me run the Gatehouse. One day she'll get married and have a family and live down the road or right here if she wants.''

''That's exactly the kind of thinking that will drive her away,'' Ryan said, straightening up. ''God, you sound just like Jonas.''

''I do not.''

''You do, too.''

Kara turned to her aunt. ''I don't sound like Jonas, do I?''

''A bit, dear,'' Josephine said.

''I just want her to have a good life,'' Kara protested.

''Then let her live it her way,'' Ryan said.

''She's eleven years old. She doesn't know what her way is.''

''She needs space to grow, Kara. Don't lock her into your dreams. Let her have her own. Trust me, I know what I'm talking about.''

Ryan looked too earnest to argue with. Kara sighed. ''I can't think about this right now. I have a million things to do. I have to make dinner and get it on the table before six so I can get down to the rec center for the show tonight. I don't have time to talk about anything else right now. And I mean anything,'' she said to Ryan, remembering his earlier comment about her father.

Ryan threw out his hands. ''Fine, bury your head in

the sand. Be like everyone else in this town."

"I'm not doing that. I'm just busy."

"Fine, I'll talk to Josephine then."

Josephine beamed. "Good idea. We have lots to catch up on." She led Ryan toward the door, then glanced back at Kara. "Can you bring us a cup of tea when it's ready?"

Kara threw her dish towel at the door as it closed behind Ryan and Josephine. Bring them a cup of tea. Jeez. As if she didn't have enough to do.

And she was not going to think about what Ryan had said. He didn't know anything about her father. He was just trying to startle her, to make her uncomfortable so she would tell Angel the truth about Michael.

There was no deep, dark secret about her father. At least—she hoped there wasn't.

# 14

Angel opened her window and leaned her head out. The branches from the oak tree brushed against the side of the house. They were big, thick, sturdy branches, strong enough for climbing on. If she climbed out on the ledge and scooted over to the side, she could do it. She could use the branch to escape.

Pulling her head back inside her window, she picked up her backpack and checked the contents. She had her wallet, an extra shirt, another pair of jeans, her Raggedy Ann doll, her diary, and a slip of paper with her father's address. Taking a deep breath, she tried not to think about her mother downstairs.

Angel could smell the beef stew that had been simmering on the stove since morning. She could almost taste the tender chunks of beef, the soft carrots, the potatoes. Her stomach rumbled at the thought. She was a little hungry. But she had her stash of candy, she told herself, digging into her bottom drawer for a bag of Skittles and a box of Junior Mints. They would have to do.

She couldn't risk a trip to the kitchen. Her mother would be setting the table and welcoming the guests downstairs. She could already hear the shower going in the next room. Someone down the hall laughed. And in the distance the puppies barked at something or someone.

Angel looked toward the door, torn by the sound of the puppies, the welcoming smells of home, and the desire to run away to find her dad. He hadn't answered any of her letters, and he never returned her phone calls. It was driving her absolutely crazy. She felt so frustrated she wanted to scream. She wanted another chance with him to tell him she was sorry and that she loved him.

Angel pulled her sweatshirt over her T-shirt. Then she scribbled a note for her mom.

*I'm not hungry. I'm taking a nap. I'll come down later and get something to eat.*

She stuck it on her door with a piece of tape, then locked her door.

Next, she threw her backpack out the window, watching it land on the long, soft grass below. At least it wasn't raining. But the window ledge was wet, and when she crawled out onto the branch, drops of water sprayed in her face. She blinked back the moisture and clung to the tree. Carefully she descended, not really afraid, not even when the wind blew the branch she was on back against the house.

When Angel reached the ground, she turned on her flashlight. It was almost six. With any luck, her mom would go ahead with dinner and not notice she was gone till the morning. She would follow the river south, and sooner or later she would find a bus to take her the rest of the way to San Francisco.

Angel took off running. She wanted to get away from the Gatehouse before anyone caught up with her—before she had second thoughts.

Kara looked over at Angel's empty seat and lost track of the conversation around the dinner table. She was tempted to go upstairs and drag Angel out of her room, but what purpose would that serve? Maybe it was better to let her sulk for a while. Angel had to realize that she couldn't live her life by telling lies all the time.

As the grandfather clock in the hall struck six, Kara drummed her fingers restlessly against the tabletop. Her stew sat uneaten before her. The conversation became a gentle hum of background noise. Her thoughts were with Angel and—Michael.

She thought about the dinners they had shared together as a family. She thought about the times she and Angel had eaten alone. Now she didn't have her husband or her daughter. Just a bunch of strangers.

Not that Aunt Josephine was a stranger. She was family, and it was nice to have her at the other end of the table entertaining the guests.

Ryan was talking to Aunt Josephine. His green eyes sparkled in the candlelight. He was so vibrant, so passionate. She saw it in the way he threw his hands out when he spoke and heard it in the laughter that edged his voice.

Earlier that day she had watched him working the crafts fair and had been captivated by the way he chose small, seemingly insignificant things to catch on film: a child holding an ice cream that tilted dangerously off the cone, a painter washing his brushes rather than putting paint on canvas, a vendor packing his crafts into big brown boxes to move on to the next fair.

Real people. Real life. Ryan had a knack for seeing beyond the obvious. At least he had the knack with his camera. Without it he sometimes seemed blind to what was right in front of his face.

Not that she wanted him to look at her, she thought worriedly as his gaze came to rest on her face. She didn't want his attention, didn't want his careful scrutiny, didn't want to hear his secrets or to tell him hers. He was getting under her skin, sneaking past her defenses when she least expected it. She had to put a stop to it.

"Would anyone like more stew?" Kara asked, forcing herself to concentrate on the mundane details of her life. The guests shook their heads as Josephine stood up to clear the table.

"I'll get this, Kara. Why don't you relax for a few minutes?" Josephine said.

"What about coffee or dessert?" Kara asked.

"There will be dessert after the show," Josephine said.

"That's true." Kara set her napkin down on the table. "If nobody needs me, I think I will take a break." She walked out of the dining room and into the living room. It was quiet here, and quiet was exactly what she wanted—a few minutes of peace before she had to change her clothes and deal with Angel.

One of the photos on top of the piano had fallen on its side. Kara straightened it, then impulsively sat down at the piano. She hadn't practiced in a few days. Maybe she could do it now. Maybe the music would suddenly flow from her fingers.

She placed her hands above the keys and began to play. The first two notes weren't bad, but the third and the fourth collided. The fifth shrieked like a banshee and the sixth sounded like a cow in labor. Kara sighed as a hand came down on her shoulder. She couldn't have failed in private? She had to do it in front of *him*?

"Did you say you took piano lessons?" Ryan asked.

Kara nodded. "Yep. For the past three months."

"You're terrible."

Kara tilted her head to look at him. "You're supposed to say it wasn't that bad."

"It was worse. Speaking strictly from one musician to another."

"Gee, thanks."

"Frankly I'm relieved there is at least one thing you're not good at. I was beginning to wonder." Ryan sat down on the bench next to her.

"One thing? Stick around a while. I fall on my face about three times a day." Her casual comment caused the light in his eyes to fade.

"I can't," he said. "Stick around, I mean."

She tossed off his comment with a shrug of her shoulders. "Why not? You work for yourself, don't you?"

"It's not that. I can't stay in one place for very long. I get itchy feet."

"One place or this place?"

"I don't really have a home anywhere. My apartment in L.A. is pretty much empty these days. I don't even own any furniture."

"What do you sleep on?"

He sent her a wry smile. "It's a long story."

"Oh." She looked away, focusing on the vase of dried silk flowers on top of the piano. "You probably have someone waiting for you back in L.A."

"No. She got tired of waiting." Ryan played a couple of notes on the piano, his long, thin fingers making a mockery of Kara's clumsy efforts. "They all get tired of waiting," he added. "You would, too."

She met his gaze, knowing that he was only reinforcing what she had told herself. Conversely she hated someone else making decisions for her. If she wanted to wait for a man, any man, it would be her choice, not his.

"Maybe you just never had a good enough reason to come home," she said.

"Maybe." He paused, giving her a long, intense look. "I'd like to photograph you."

"Oh, please." Kara tried to turn her head, but he caught her chin with his hand, holding her in profile.

"You have great bone structure."

She uttered a somewhat nervous laugh. "I've never heard that compliment before."

"Your skin is so clear, I can almost see through it. But it's your eyes that would take over the whole shot. Even if I photographed you from twenty yards away without zooming in on your face, your eyes would still be the central point. Big, beautiful blue eyes that show every emotion, every desire."

"Don't," she whispered.

His fingers traced the line of her lips. "Soft," he muttered. "I can't resist."

"Don't," she said again, but this time she meant something entirely different. She wanted him to kiss her, wanted to feel his mouth on hers, to get lost in his light and his fire and his passion.

Ryan lowered his head and kissed her, tentatively at first, so gentle, so light, she felt herself moving forward, wanting to get closer, wanting more than he was giving her. She slid down the piano bench until their thighs touched, until his arms locked around her waist, until her breasts pressed against his chest, until she could feel the line of his muscles, taste the wine on his lips, rub her cheek against the shadowy stubble of beard that haunted his jawbone. She opened her mouth and invited him inside. He came willingly.

One kiss turned into two, then three, until there was no stopping, no ending of one or beginning of another, just a long, endless, breathless tasting.

Kara forgot about everything but him. There was just one man, one need.

"Let's go upstairs," Ryan muttered, his tongue sliding along the curve of her ear.

She wanted to say yes. She wanted to race him up the stairs. She wanted to pull his shirt apart with her fingers and watch the light in his eyes fill with desire for her.

"Kara?"

His voice broke the spell. Closing her eyes, she leaned her head against his chest. "I have responsibilities," she said. "My daughter, my aunt, my guests, the town." She lifted her head to look at him.

"What about the responsibility to yourself?"

"I'm thinking about myself, too." Kara paused for a

long moment. "I loved my ex-husband a lot in the beginning. I couldn't see his faults. I was blind to everything but passion. And I loved him so much more than he loved me. I can't do that again. I can't open myself up to rejection."

"So you're rejecting me instead." Ryan shook his head. "You know, Andrew always thought I could get any girl I wanted. But I didn't get Becky Lee, and I guess I can't get you."

"You didn't want Becky Lee," Kara said. "You wanted adventure. You wanted to see the world. Isn't that right?"

"Maybe," he conceded.

"And you don't really want me either, because it's the same choice. Just a different woman and a different time."

"With the same result. You end up with Andrew."

"And that's what bothers you the most."

"I didn't kiss you because of Andrew."

"I'd like to believe that."

He met her eyes with pure honesty. "Believe it."

"Everything changes, but in a lot of ways it stays the same—that's what Aunt Josephine always says."

"She's a smart lady. And so are you."

"If I were smart, I'd ask you to leave tonight."

"Yeah, and if I were smart, I'd go."

"Angel." Kara knocked on the door to her daughter's bedroom several minutes later and waited for a reply. "Come on, honey. We'll be late for the show. Billy's going to be there," she added. No answer. She looked over at Josephine. "I don't suppose you know how to pick locks?"

Josephine smiled. "Why don't you go on ahead, Kara? Angel doesn't need to see the show, and neither do I. When the house is quiet, she'll come out and have dinner."

"I'm sure you're right." Kara hesitated. "But I don't

have a good feeling about this." She glanced down at her watch. Although the local talent show wasn't due to start for almost an hour, she needed to set up the chairs and take tickets. Even if she could drag Angel out of her room, she would have a sulky daughter by her side, which wouldn't make anyone feel good. She knocked one last time. "I'm leaving, Angel. If you want to go with me, you have to come now."

"Looks like she made her choice," Josephine said.

"Why is everything so difficult?"

"Because life is more interesting that way."

"Speaking of life and interesting, Ike has called three times already."

Josephine frowned. "Probably just wants his dinner and noticed I wasn't there cooking it."

"The man is crazy about you. I don't know why you can't see that."

"He loves his truck more than he loves me. He's always working on it, every Saturday and every Sunday. He cleans it, waxes it, pats it down with his hand almost like he's caressing some woman's body. It's downright disgusting."

Kara smiled. "You can't be jealous of a truck, Aunt Josephine."

"I'm not. I'm tired of being taken for granted, Kara."

"Well, I know how that feels."

"Where is Andrew anyway? Why isn't he picking you up?" Josephine demanded. "And why didn't he come for dinner?"

Kara heard the criticism in her aunt's voice and couldn't help defending the absent Andrew. "His father is in the hospital, and he has to get the paper ready for the morning."

"So he puts you aside."

"I don't need him, Aunt Josephine. It's okay."

"That's right, you don't need him." Josephine nodded as if she had just made Kara confess to murder.

"I don't need him tonight," Kara corrected as she walked down the hall toward her room.

"You don't need him at all. He doesn't make your eyes light up. He doesn't make you shiver."

"Oh, please," Kara said. "I'm a grown woman, a mother. I'm done with shivering. I'll settle for dependable and reliable."

"Why should you have to? When the real thing is staring you in the face."

Kara stiffened at the knowing look in Josephine's eyes. "If you're talking about Ryan . . ."

"Of course I'm talking about Ryan. I read your tea leaves, Kara. You're about to fall head over heels in love."

"With Andrew," Kara maintained.

"Goodness, no. You're more likely to fall head over heels in the river than fall for Andrew. Wake up and smell the tea, Kara."

"That's coffee, Aunt Josephine, and maybe if you stuck to coffee, you'd stop all this nonsense."

Josephine tossed her head in the air, obviously deeply offended by Kara's comment. "You can call it what you want. The leaves don't lie. Only people do."

Kara fumed as Josephine left. Sometimes her aunt drove her crazy. You couldn't tell if someone was about to fall in love from the leaves in a teacup or from the number of goose bumps on her arms. Shivers, indeed, but she couldn't help casting one last look at Ryan's closed bedroom door as she walked toward the staircase.

Ryan checked his camera bag one last time as a knock came at his door. His heart quickened for a moment. He wondered if Kara had changed her mind. That fantasy faded at the sound of Josephine's voice.

"Come in," he said. One look at her agitated face told him something was up. "What's wrong?"

"Angel. She wouldn't open the door to her bedroom."

"She'll come out when she gets hungry enough."

Josephine held out a bobby pin in the palm of her hand. "I picked the lock. Angel is not in her room. She's gone."

Ryan looked at Josephine in confusion. "Gone where?"

"Apparently out the window and down the branches of that tree next to her room."

Ryan rushed over to his window and looked out. Angel's room was on the same side of the house, just farther back. Sure enough, the tree branches did reach right out to her window. But it was a sheer drop to the ground. The kid would have been crazy to try a stunt like that.

Crazy or mad or frustrated—as he had been when his mother didn't come back, when Jonas sent him to his room, and he could smell the air of freedom just outside the window, too tantalizing to resist.

Angel was gone all right. Damn. The least she could have done was wait until morning.

"I want you to look for her," Josephine said.

"Me? I don't know where she went."

Josephine held up a child's address book. "The page with her father's address is torn out."

"Her father? That's it. Forget it. Count me out. I can't help you. Call Kara. I'm not getting in the middle of this family problem."

"Why not? Kara is in the middle of yours."

"She chose to be. It was her idea to invite me here."

"But you're the one who can't leave her alone."

Ryan saw the perception in Josephine's eyes. He didn't know if she had read it in his tea leaves earlier that afternoon or just knew it in her heart, but somehow she sensed the growing attraction between Kara and himself.

"I'm trying," he said finally.

"Try harder. It's dark and it's going to rain again."

"Where does this guy live anyway?" Ryan asked.

"San Francisco."

"You want me to go to San Francisco?"

"No, I want you to go to Tucker's Bridge and bring Angel home."

"I don't understand."

Josephine put her hands on his arms. "She wants to see her father, but she's afraid that she won't be welcome. She'll stop to think, and the longer she thinks, the more uncertain she'll become."

Ryan nodded. Yes, that's exactly what Angel would do, just what he had always done. He wanted to find his mother, yet he didn't. Because there was always a question in the back of his mind that maybe his father was right, maybe she really didn't want him.

He shook his head. These were two different situations, two different kids, but he grabbed his raincoat on the way out the door.

## 15

The Serenity Springs talent show went off without a hitch, and long after the final note had been played, the final song sung, people lingered in the aisles, chatting about the town, beaming their pride in wide, open smiles.

The only person missing from the event was Ryan. His absence disturbed Kara. She had hoped he would photograph some of the performers, but apparently he had chosen not to come. She wondered if it had anything to do with her—anything to do with her saying no. Maybe he had left, packed his bags and headed south to L.A. to his empty apartment and no-commitment life-style.

Her depressing thoughts carried into her actions as she folded each chair with a decisive thump, irritated with herself as well as Ryan. It shouldn't matter to her what he did. The man would be gone in two days. So what if he left early? He had done what she asked, maybe not all of it, but enough to make a difference. A small one anyway.

"Kara." Dirk Anders called her name.

She waved him across the room, taking careful note of his wet slicker.

"You missed the show," she said.

"Mother Nature is putting on one of her own."

"Is it raining again?"

"A bit. The wind has kicked up. We've had gusts up to fifty miles an hour."

"I guess that means no river events tomorrow."

"The river may be the main event. It's washing over Tucker's Bridge."

"But that bridge is low."

"We checked the high points, too. She's riding high, a couple more inches every hour."

"What are you trying to say?"

"I think she's going to flood."

"That hasn't happened in twenty-five years."

"Doesn't mean it can't happen now."

"Just the lower roads, right?" She desperately wanted reassurance, but he couldn't give her any.

"I hope so. I cleared out the folks along River Road. We'll start sandbagging tomorrow, see if we can't protect the downtown area."

"And the Gatehouse."

"You could be in trouble, Kara. I won't lie to you. The Gatehouse is at the end of the lane."

"And for me it's the end of the line. I can't lose the Gatehouse."

"Then you better start praying for sunshine."

Dirk stepped to one side as Andrew joined them.

"Hi," Kara said, taking Andrew's hand. "You okay?" He looked tired and worried.

"I've had better days."

"Dirk was just telling me about the river."

Andrew nodded, exchanging a long look with Dirk. "I haven't seen her this fast in years. She's roaring with passion."

Kara was beginning to get irked by the pronoun "she." "The river is not a person."

Dirk and Andrew looked at her blankly.

"You keep saying *she*."

"She's just like a woman," Dirk explained. "She gives

life, brings peace, nurtures the land. And when she's angry, all hell breaks loose."

Kara sighed as Dirk and Andrew nodded in complete accord. There was no point in trying to change their minds. The Snake River was as much a passionate woman to them as it was a dangerous serpent to Kara. She didn't love the river. Oh, she enjoyed the water. But deep down she was scared of all that uncontrollable power.

"This could be a disaster," Kara said. "I wanted the media to cover the centennial, not get front-row seats for a natural disaster."

"Well, at least we have more folks in town to fill sandbags," Dirk said, looking at the bright side. He turned to Andrew. "How's Jonas?"

"He's holding his own, demanding to go home, threatening to kill someone if they don't give him back his pants."

"That's good. He's on the mend." Dirk tipped his hat. "You both take care now."

Andrew turned to Kara. "I finished the paper. I think it will be okay. I had to make some last-minute decisions that I'm not sure Jonas will agree with, but— Kara?"

"That's nice," Kara said, distracted by a conversation going on at the other end of the room between Harrison Winslow and Mayor Hewitt. They seemed to be arguing about something.

"It's the first edition I ever did completely on my own," Andrew continued. "I think you'll like it."

"I'm sure I will," she said, without really hearing his words. "Would you excuse me? I think I need to interrupt that conversation over there."

"But Kara, I want to tell you about . . ."

"Can you tell me tomorrow?" She offered him a pleading smile. "I want to catch Harrison before he leaves. I have my car, so I don't need a ride."

"Sure, fine." Andrew watched Kara leave with a

heavy heart. So much for rushing over here to share his news. He dug his hands into his pockets and walked outside.

When he got in his car, he hesitated before turning the key. He was still tense and excited, nervous about his father and the paper. He didn't feel like going home. He needed to unwind, to talk to someone. Down the street, he saw the sign for Swanson's Bar. Maybe just a quick drink.

"Harrison," Kara said with a smile. "I'm glad you didn't rush out. I wanted to get your impressions of the centennial."

"I think it's terrific," Harrison said. "Unfortunately the mayor seems to think my plans are too progressive."

"How so?" she asked, trying to sound calm.

"He wants to tear down half the woods, Kara," Mayor Hewitt said angrily.

"That's an exaggeration," Harrison proclaimed in his smooth, somewhat arrogant voice.

"I'm sure when Mr. Winslow presents his plans to the city council, they'll be well within our guidelines," Kara said, "at least for the city-owned land."

"I certainly hope so," Harrison said.

The mayor mumbled something conciliatory and went to join his wife, who waited patiently by the door.

"You're one of the few people in this town with vision," Harrison said, eyeing her with more personal appreciation than was appropriate.

"I'm not afraid of change," Kara said diplomatically. "Others don't feel the same way."

"Why don't we have a drink and discuss it?"

Kara felt certain he had more than a drink in mind. "I'm afraid I can't. I need to get home to my daughter."

Harrison's eyes lost their warmth. "I'm not about to change my plans, Kara. Frankly I don't need to. Most of the land I want is privately owned. You've convinced me that Serenity Springs can offer a touristy appeal to my guests. As far as I'm concerned, the resort is a done deal."

"I'm sure we can peacefully coexist. You want a thriving resort. I want a thriving town. We both want the same thing."

"Maybe." Harrison didn't look convinced. "Sometimes it just looks that way on the surface."

"What do you want?" Loretta asked abruptly as Andrew sat down at the bar.

There was a large group of outsiders drinking over by the pool table and a smaller, quieter group of locals sharing beers across the room, but there was no one at the bar except him and Loretta.

She looked tired. Her hair was falling out of its ponytail, and as he watched she pursed her lips together and blew a few strands off her hot face.

"Come on, Andrew. I don't have all day," she said.

"Sorry. I'll have a beer, whatever is on tap."

While Loretta got him a beer, Andrew looked around the place. It was certainly more lively than he had seen it in awhile. Business had picked up for the centennial, despite the rain.

"Still wet out there?" Loretta asked as she pushed his mug across the bar.

"Yes. The National Weather Service is predicting steady rain for the next four days."

"Oh, dear." Loretta looked at him through worried eyes. "Last time it flooded we lost everything."

Andrew nodded. Loretta's house was down toward the river by Jonas and Kara. His own house was on higher ground, so he probably wouldn't have to worry, unless the whole town went underwater.

"Maybe you should start packing just in case," Andrew suggested.

"And go where?"

"I don't know. You must have some friends or family somewhere else, don't you?"

She looked him straight in the eye. "No."

"Oh." He paused. "I'm sorry about last night," he said, referring to the scene at the dinner.

Loretta shrugged. "Doesn't matter. I know what you think of me. I know what everyone thinks of me."

"You don't." The words burst out of him before he could consider the consequences.

"What does that mean?"

"It means . . ." Instinctively he looked around to see if anyone could hear him, but no one was paying any attention to them. "It means I think you're a nice person."

Loretta laughed. "Gee, I'll have to remember that for my tombstone. There goes Loretta Swanson, a nice person."

Andrew flushed angrily. "I take it back."

"You didn't mean it anyway."

"You know, it's your own fault that people don't treat you better," Andrew said. "Here I am trying to be a friend, and you laugh at me."

Her expression turned serious. "Are you really trying to be a friend, Andrew? Honest?"

He nodded.

She stuck out her hand. "Shake on it?"

When he took her hand, he found he couldn't let go. Her skin was so soft. He wanted to pull her closer, across the bar and into his lap. He wanted to take down her ponytail and run his hands through her hair. He wanted to trace her lips with his finger. His breathing came faster with each treacherous thought.

Loretta pulled her hand away and turned her back on him. She seemed to be trembling, as if he affected her as much as she affected him. But how could that be? Someone like Loretta wouldn't get turned on by a simple touch of his hand. She had probably had sex every way known to man. He was a fool for thinking she could want him. He couldn't satisfy a woman like her; he would be afraid to try.

Picking up his glass, Andrew drank it down. Loretta suddenly got busy behind the bar, tallying up cash receipts and filling drink orders. It was a good five minutes before she spoke to him again.

"How's Jonas?" she asked. "I heard he had a heart attack."

"He's all right for now, but the doctor said he needs to get his blood pressure and his cholesterol down and start taking it easier."

"Who's going to put out the paper tomorrow?"

"I am. I mean, I did. It's done."

"You? Now there's a refreshing thought. If I have to read one more editorial on preserving this town and the river exactly the way they are, I'm going to puke. What did you write your editorial on?" she asked, eagerness lighting up her tired face.

"I wrote about preserving the river and the town exactly the way they are," Andrew said slowly.

Her face fell. "Oh, well. I'm sure it still has a fresh twist to it."

"No, it doesn't. I wrote the thing like a memory, Loretta. I've heard and read the words so many times, I just turned on the computer and my fingers knew what to do." He hit the edge of the bar with his hand. "God, I am so stupid, thinking I'm putting out my own paper now, and all I'm doing is putting out the same damn paper. No one will even notice Jonas didn't do it."

"It's okay," she said soothingly, touching his hand with hers. "You just need some warm-up time. Do something special for Sunday's paper."

"Like what?"

"I don't know. Write about something that's important to you."

What was important to him? His son? His family? Kara? The river? Loretta? His mind fixated on the last word as he watched Loretta fill another drink order.

Her hands were quick and efficient. He wondered if she had ever had a doubtful or cautious moment in her life, or if she had always known just what to do and when to do it.

"I did put Ryan's picture on the front page," Andrew said when she turned her attention back to him. "Kara wanted him to get coverage. And it's ridiculous to ignore his presence when the rest of the county is covering him in their papers."

"So you did it for Kara," Loretta said with a smile that seemed rather unwilling. "That was sweet of you. I'm sure she'll love it." She picked up the dish towel and began to wipe down the bar.

"I hope so." He ran a finger around the edge of his glass. "It felt good to be at the paper all alone, nobody looking over my shoulder, nobody telling me I'm doing it wrong. The truth is, I could put out that paper in my sleep. Why can't my father see that?"

"He doesn't want to let go. He's hanging on for dear life to that paper and the way this town used to be. But things are changing, Andrew Joseph."

"Why are you still here? I would have thought you'd have left a long time ago."

"I did leave for a while in my twenties, just after you married Becky Lee. I went to Berkeley. It was like stepping onto a movie set. Nobody cared what you wore or how you talked. It was free there."

"That actually sounds kind of nice. I've often wondered what it would feel like to live in a place where no one knew me."

"It feels good. Real good." Loretta rested her arms on the bar. "I had to come home when Pop got sick. There was no one to take care of him. I never expected he'd linger for six years. By the time he finally passed on, it seemed too late to go back. But someday I'll get out of here. I want to see Los Angeles and San Diego, maybe go somewhere exotic like Bermuda or Tahiti, or somewhere cool like Switzerland."

"I wouldn't know what to do in any of those places."

"That's the beauty of it, Andrew. Learning new things. Being someone different."

"It might be lonely, going alone."

"Maybe I won't go alone. Haven't you ever considered leaving this place?"

"No. Not really. Well, sometimes," he prevaricated as he saw the challenging glint in her eye. "Okay, I confess, I've thought about it."

"Where would you go—if you could go anywhere in the world?"

"I'd like to go to New York City."

Her eyes widened. "You, in New York City? That's a picture."

"I'd like to go somewhere fast, where everything moves at the speed of light."

"Me, too—where you can feel the blood rushing through your veins and your heart pounding against your chest," Loretta agreed.

Andrew felt drops of sweat bead along his brow. He could almost see the two of them dancing in some dark nightclub in New York City, their bodies rubbing up against each other, her bright red lips leaving marks all over his body. He took in a deep breath and tried to remember where they were—a small-time bar in a small-time town. "Yeah, well, neither one of us is going anywhere, especially you. You're having a baby."

"Tell me something I don't know," she said wearily.

"You have to be realistic, Loretta. You're going to have a child to support. It's not easy being a single parent. I know."

She tossed the dish towel at him.

"Hey, I'm just telling the truth."

"You're depressing me. I don't want to be realistic." She patted her stomach. "False labor pains every other hour is realism, along with a huge stomach, night sweats, and the complete inability to sleep. That's real life. I'd rather dream."

"You're having a rough time, aren't you?" Andrew felt a deep sympathy toward her and a longing to take away her worries. He just didn't know how.

"I'm okay."

"Are you?"

"Some days I am. I do want this baby. I love her so much, it scares me. See, this baby doesn't know anything about me. It's like starting off with a clean slate. This baby won't care that I've made mistakes in my life. She won't care that no one likes me. She won't—" Loretta's voice broke. "There I go again. Just ignore me," she said, wiping a tear from her eye. "It's these darned hormones. They make me want to cry all the time. I need a tissue." She turned and fled into the back room.

Andrew looked over at the table of old-timers sitting against the wall. "Hey, Stu. Take over the bar for a sec, would you?"

"What's up with Loretta? You say something nasty to her again?"

"No."

The old white-haired man walked up to him. "See that you don't. She's a good girl, taking the blame for a lot of bad boys."

"I think you're right." Andrew walked around the bar and down the hall toward the office. It was a combination work area and supply room. Invoices and other papers covered the desk. Stacks of booze reached from the floor to the ceiling. Loretta sat in the chair behind the desk, her head on her forearms, her shoulders shaking as sobs tore out of her throat.

Andrew didn't know what to do. He didn't understand women. He had been completely baffled by his mother, then by Becky Lee. Even Kara had him scratching his head in confusion most of the time. And Loretta was, well, she was one of a kind.

He walked over and clumsily stroked her blond hair. It felt soft and silky beneath his fingertips. The strands glistened against his somewhat dirty fingers. He thought then that he had no right to be touching her hair, to be touching her at all. But he didn't want to stop. He wanted to run his hand down to her neck, to the tight muscles in her shoulders. He wanted to ease her discomfort.

"Loretta. You okay?" he asked finally.

She shook her head, still not looking at him.

"Come on, now. Don't cry." He walked behind her and rubbed her shoulders for a long five minutes.

"You're awfully nice, Andrew Joseph," she muttered, lifting her head to look at him with tearstained cheeks.

"So are you."

She stood up. "I feel all alone sometimes. But I'll be okay."

They stood there for a long moment, close but not touching. After a long mental debate, Andrew hauled her into his arms and pressed her face against his chest. "You're not alone tonight," he muttered.

Andrew closed his eyes and rested his chin on top of her head. Loretta fit perfectly in his arms. As if she had come home. Even the large curve of her stomach felt right. He remembered trying to hold Becky Lee when she was pregnant, but she had hated him getting close. Said she already felt as if her body was invaded; she didn't need a man pawing her on the outside as well. But this felt good. This felt more than good.

Loretta lifted her head. "I'm sorry, Andrew. I shouldn't be dumping on you like this. I guess I'm more tired than I thought."

"It's all right. These shoulders don't get much use anymore."

"That's a crime. They're very nice shoulders." She ran her hands up his arms and across his chest. "And you have a very nice chest." She tilted her head so she could see him more clearly. "And nice eyes and a really, really nice mouth."

Her gaze settled on his lips.

Andrew couldn't stand it anymore. He bent his head

and kissed her hard. She tasted like the butterscotch candy she kept in an ashtray on the bar, sweet and tantalizing and definitely not good for him. But he didn't care. He couldn't resist her anymore. He couldn't resist himself.

Loretta kissed him back with the same desire, the same hunger. She moved her mouth in a way that left him breathless. And every time he tried to pull away, he came back for one last kiss.

Her body moved against his in a way that was no longer platonic but completely sexual. He wanted to have her naked beneath him. He wanted to bury himself inside her. He wanted . . . What he wanted was absolutely impossible. Impossible. He finally broke away.

"Andrew." She reached for him again, but he stepped back. The desire in her eyes was replaced by hurt. "Don't say it. Please don't say you're sorry."

"I am sorry."

"Stop. Just stop," she cried out.

"We can't do this, Loretta."

"Do what? We were kissing."

"But I wanted—"

"You did?"

"Yes."

"Until you remembered who you were kissing."

"No, until I remembered who I wasn't kissing. I'm involved with Kara."

Loretta crossed her arms in front of her well-endowed chest. "You're just like the others. You want to have sex with me, but you want to marry someone else. I don't know why I'm surprised. You did it once before. Why not now?"

"What are you talking about?"

"The Sweethearts Dance, a month before your wedding. You were hard as a rock in my arms."

"Loretta, please. I was a kid then."

"You were hot for me, but you couldn't admit it. In

fact, you only danced with me because Ryan was watching."

"That's the only reason you danced with me—to make him jealous."

"I danced with you because I wanted to."

"You did?"

"Yes. But you were afraid of me then and you're afraid of me now."

"We wouldn't be compatible."

She smiled. "I think we would be very compatible."

"In bed, maybe, but not out of it. We're not the same type. You want to travel, to see the world. I like it here. I have everything I need. There's no reason to leave. What could the world offer me that Serenity Springs couldn't?"

The words flowed out of his mouth—too easily. They were his father's words, not his. Just like the editorial. He could see in Loretta's eyes that she knew it only too well.

"When are you going to start living your own life, Andrew Joseph?"

"I am living my own life. I'm doing exactly what I want to do, and I'm going to marry Kara."

"If you're going to marry Kara, then why are you here with me?"

"Hell if I know. But I'm leaving right now. And I won't be back."

"Yes, you will," Loretta said.

He slammed the door on her words but he heard them, and he hoped to God she wasn't right.

# 16

"What are you doing here?" Angel asked the question without turning around. She sat on a large boulder a couple of feet above the river. Her backpack lay at her feet, and her gaze focused on the water washing over Tucker's Bridge.

"I'm looking for you, what do you think?" Ryan asked.

"Go away."

Ryan could barely hear her over the rush of the water. The wind had picked up, covering Angel's hair with a fine mist. In a few more minutes she'd be soaked through. Not to mention the fact that the boulder she was sitting on would soon become an island.

"I'm not leaving without you," he said. "It's dangerous out here."

"I like it."

She finally looked over her shoulder at him, her face a picture of pure youthful defiance. He instinctively reached for his camera, but it wasn't there. Damn. Over the years his camera had become more important to him than his wallet, but since arriving in Serenity Springs, he had found himself without it more often than not.

"Come on, kid, give me a break here." He stepped gingerly across a few of the rocks to get closer to her.

He didn't like the sound of the river or the wet, heavy smell of the air. It reminded him of the past, of the flood that changed his life, of the nightmares that haunted him for years. The monster was awakening, stretching and groaning, waking up from a twenty-five-year sleep to reclaim the land from those who would call it their own.

"I'm not moving," Angel declared, folding her arms across her chest as she sat cross-legged on the flat rock.

"You're moving if I have to throw you over my shoulder and carry you back to the Gatehouse."

"Yeah, right."

Ryan looked at the river, at the slippery rocks separating him from Angel and then up at the sky, hoping divine intervention would be forthcoming. It wasn't. He couldn't leave Angel out here. She was a reckless, impetuous, angry young girl who wanted to run away, but this wasn't the place to run to.

"Why couldn't you go to the bus station like a normal person?"

"Last bus left at five o'clock. Won't be another one till tomorrow."

"Okay, you want to play hardball, right?"

Angel shrugged.

Ryan stepped over the rocks, taking care not to fall. By the time he reached Angel he was breathing heavily, not so much from exertion as from anxiety. It was stupid to be afraid of the water. He could swim. He could handle himself if he had to.

Angel stared at him thoughtfully. "You're scared, aren't you?"

"Me? Nah." He held out his hand to her. "Come on, get down."

"Can't you swim?"

"Course I can swim. I'm just not a big fan of white water." He grabbed her hand. "And if you don't get off this rock, we're both going to have a chance to ride the rapids without a raft."

"All right, but only because you're scared." Angel took his hand and slid off the rock. Together they made it back to higher ground. Ryan breathed more easily, even though Angel stubbornly sat down on a log instead of continuing up the path toward the Gatehouse. Finally he sat down next to her.

"So, what are you doing out here?" he asked.

"I'm waiting to see the river lady. She comes out when it starts to storm. She's my friend. My only friend."

Ryan cleared his throat and dug his hands into his pocket, not quite sure how to deal with this latest tale. "What does she talk to you about?"

"Different things. She's lonely."

*Too.* He muttered the last word under his breath.

"You don't believe me, do you?"

"Should I?"

"I don't care."

"Look, I'm not stupid. You packed a bag, locked your bedroom door, and climbed out the window. The way I see it, you're running away from home, and I don't think it has anything to do with this ghost."

"I'm going to see my dad," Angel admitted.

"Really? Might be hard to find him if he's undercover in Cairo or India or someplace."

Angel gave him a reluctant smile, still filled with the innocence of youth. No matter what she had been through, there was still a part of her that dreamed. Thank God for that.

"He's not really in the CIA," she said.

"No?" Ryan put a hand to his chest in mock surprise. "You knew all the time."

"What does he do, then?"

"He sells computer parts. He does travel a lot." Her smile faded. "All the time, in fact." She picked up a stick and began to dig in the moist dirt by her feet.

"You miss him?"

"I'm not supposed to."

"But you do?"

"Yeah. Sometimes I wish . . ."

"What?" Ryan nudged her with his elbow when she didn't continue. "What do you wish?"

"It's silly."

"So? No one will hear but me and the river."

"I wish he was a secret agent instead of just a jerk."

"You think your dad's a jerk?"

Angel gave him a solemn look. "I saw him with another lady." She licked her lips and gazed out at the river. "I came home early from school one day. They were in Mom's bedroom. I thought it was Mom at first. They were laughing, and I liked the sound of it because my parents didn't laugh much. So I just opened the door without knocking. And . . . and it wasn't Mom in bed with Dad, it was someone else. They didn't have any clothes on. The lady screamed when she saw me." Angel paused. "She had the biggest boobs I've ever seen."

Ryan didn't smile. He could see the heartbreak just beneath the surface. "That must have been tough on you."

"My dad shoved me out the door and slammed it right in my face. He told me not to tell Mom. I ran out of the house, and I didn't come back until his car was gone from the driveway."

"You didn't tell your mom, did you?"

"No. But a week later Mom told me they were getting a divorce because they didn't love each other any more. I think they got a divorce because . . ."

Ryan put a finger over her lips. "They did not get a divorce because of you."

She looked at him with agony in her eyes. "It's because I went in the room. My dad got mad. He thinks I told Mom. He—"

"He was wrong, Angel. He made a mistake. But it had nothing to do with you. Nothing." Ryan gave her a little shake. "You have to believe me."

"Why?"

"Because I wouldn't lie to you."

Angel thought about that for a long time. "My dad lied to me all the time. He would say he was going to come home early and watch me play soccer or that he'd help me with my science project or come to an open house. But he never did any of those things."

"You're right. He was a jerk." Ryan patted her leg. "You know, Angel, sometimes people screw up all on their own without anyone's help. And some people just aren't meant to be parents. It's not because they don't love their kids, it's that they don't know how to show it. They don't know what to say."

"Did your dad ever screw up?"

Ryan caught his breath at the simple question, and this time he was the one who looked away from a pair of sharp little eyes that would see right through any phony answer. "Yeah, he screwed up. Lots of times. In fact, I always blamed my dad for making my mother go away. That is, when I wasn't blaming myself."

He ruffled her hair as she looked back at him with complete understanding.

"Why did your dad make your mother go away?"

"Because my mother wanted things that she couldn't get in this town, and he refused to leave." It was only part of the answer, but the only part he could deal with right now.

"He's pretty mad at you, too, isn't he?"

"Yeah."

"I just want a normal family," Angel said. "Why can't I have a normal family?" She rested her head on his shoulder.

"Maybe your mom will get married again," Ryan replied. *Maybe she'll marry Andrew. Then I'll be the only one without a family.*

"Maybe," Angel conceded, sending him a thoughtful glance. "If she married Andrew, then Billy and I would be brother and sister. That would be cool. And you would be my uncle." Angel smiled at him. Her even white teeth and the glow in her eyes lit up the dark sky. At that moment she reminded him of his own mother, of the light and the magic that had always been Isabelle. He could see a little of it in Angel, and in Kara, too. But Kara was different from his mother. Kara had her feet firmly on the ground. She was planting roots, not reaching for the stars. She was cultivating her dreams, not chasing after them.

He wondered why he found that so appealing. Why it felt so good to have Angel's head on his shoulder, why the last two nights at the Gatehouse had made him feel like he was sleeping in a real home when in reality it was just an inn, just a single stop in a lifetime of stops.

"I guess the lady isn't coming tonight," Angel said. "I did want to see her again. She's beautiful."

Ryan followed Angel's gaze out into the shadowy darkness of the river, but he could see no sign of a lady or anything else.

"My dad's not coming back either," Angel added in the same lonely, wistful tone. "Is he?"

"Probably not."

"Or your mom." Angel turned her head abruptly. "I can't believe I almost forgot. I have something for you." She unzipped her backpack and searched frantically through the contents. "I brought it with me, in case I saw the lady again. She's the one who showed it to me."

"What are you talking about?"

"This." Angel took out the watch and held it in the palm of her hand. "It's yours. Take it."

Ryan stared at it in shock. He had thrown that watch into the river twenty-five years earlier. He had never wanted to see it again. "No," he cried, jumping to his feet.

"It is yours." Angel turned it over and showed him the back. "It says, *To Ryan. Love, Mom.*"

Ryan started walking. He could hear Angel call his name. He paused. "Go home, Angel. Just go home."

"But where are you going?" she cried.

"Away from here. As far away as I can get."

But Ryan couldn't get away from his thoughts. After a couple of hours of walking, he was finally tired enough to think he could sleep without dreaming, without remembering.

The Gatehouse was quiet when he returned, a cozy light on in the living room and another on the upstairs landing, but everyone appeared to be asleep. Ryan instinctively looked down the hall, noting Angel's partly open door. He couldn't help checking on her one last time.

As he peeked into her room, he saw Angel lying on her stomach across the bed, dressed in her granny nightgown, her arms wrapped tightly about a Raggedy Ann doll that had definitely seen better days.

The expression on her face was peaceful, innocent, and he felt a rush of emotion just looking at her. What would it be like to have a daughter? To bring children into the world and watch them grow?

His earlier restlessness returned in a different way. The loneliness gnawed at his gut like the hunger that came from an empty stomach. He wanted to fill it; he just didn't know how. With tentative steps he walked over to Angel's bed and pulled the quilt over her body. She stirred at the motion, opening her sleepy eyes.

"Mom?"

"Sh-sh, it's me, Ryan. I just wanted to make sure you got back okay."

"I'm okay. I—I like you, Ryan."

"Yeah, I like you, too, Angel-face. Go to sleep now."

Angel smiled and fell back asleep before her eyelids had fully closed. Ryan intended to go to his room, but an open door at the end of the hall drew his attention. There were stairs leading into the attic, and a gleam of light. He wondered if someone was up there or if Kara had simply forgotten to turn off the light.

Ryan walked down the hall and up the stairs. The attic was empty, but a window at the far end was wide open. He walked over to close it, but when he reached for the handle, he saw Kara sitting on the roof, wrapped in a blanket.

After a moment's hesitation, he crawled out on the roof with her. She turned to him in surprise. "What are you doing out here?"

"I could ask you the same thing."

"Counting the stars. They're easier to see from up here."

"Well, you gotta to be able to do that," he said with a grin. "It looks like the clouds have parted long enough to give you a few stars."

"Thank goodness. Maybe the storm is over."

"Maybe, or just building up steam for the next time." He paused. "You know, I was thinking awhile back that you had your feet planted firmly on the ground. Now I find you sitting on the roof, wrapped in a blanket, counting stars."

"Sometimes I need to get away from it all," Kara said. "Up here, I feel free. I can see for miles."

"I thought you were happy just seeing down the street."

"I am. Most of the time."

He put his arm around her shoulders and pulled her close.

"Ryan, I don't think—"

"That's the problem, you do think—way too much. Hush now and let me hold you. I'm cold."

"Maybe you should go inside."

"Without counting the stars?"

Kara smiled at him. "There are too many to count."

"I know, I've tried."

"You have?"

"Lots of times. In some parts of the world, the sky is endless; in others you can barely see the stars for all the lights and skyscrapers. My mother used to play that game, 'Wish I may, wish I might—' "

" 'Have this wish I wish tonight,' " Kara finished. "Then you pick the biggest star in the universe to wish on."

"Only the star I pick to wish on usually turns out to be an airplane."

Kara laughed. "How appropriate."

They sat there for a while in companionable silence. Ryan didn't want to break the connection between them. It felt so right being with her, so absolutely and utterly right. And yet she was the wrong woman for him. They both knew that.

"Did you see your father tonight?" Kara asked after a moment. "I missed you at the show."

Ryan shook his head. There would be time to tell her later about Angel. "No, I was talking to your aunt."

"She's quite a character, isn't she?" Kara said. "I don't know what's gotten into her lately. She has never ever run out on her marriage before. I'm totally surprised."

"I'm not."

"That's because you're a cynic."

"Realist."

"Cynic. Disillusioned, bitter, maybe even a little lonely."

Her words struck right to the heart of him, and Ryan suddenly realized that he had been a cynic since he was nine years old. That's when he had stopped believing in Santa Claus and the Easter bunny, and happily ever after.

"And why aren't you a cynic?" he asked, pulling her face around so he could look into her eyes. "You come from a broken home, a bad marriage. Yet you're still up here wishing on stars."

"I said I was counting, not wishing. Okay, I was wishing. I can't seem to let go of that last little bit of idealism, Ryan. I know deep down in my heart that someday I will have the family I always wanted."

"You already have a lot—a daughter, an aunt, a bunch of dogs, who by the way are curled up in the middle of my bed."

Kara laughed with delight. "I know, I saw them. I tried to get them out, but they like you."

"Yeah, right."

"But I don't have everything. I don't have a—lover." Her voice dropped down to a husky murmur. His heart skipped a beat.

"Maybe I could solve that problem for you."

"The only problem is, I don't want just one night. I want a lifetime."

"I can't give you a lifetime. We're too different."

"We're not different at all. We both grew up lonely. We both like music. We both care about people."

"How do you know I care about people?"

"You let Aunt Josephine read your tea leaves."

"I couldn't stop her."

"You listened to Angel's wild stories and never made fun of her."

Ryan smiled. "You mean, those stories aren't true? Damn." He pulled Kara into his arms and held her tight. She was right. He did care about people. He cared about her, and it was killing him.

"Ryan." Kara lifted her head from where it rested against his chest, where her warmth had taken away the chill around his heart. "The past doesn't matter. It's the future that counts."

"I wish I could tell you what you want to hear, Kara."

"But you can't. I know. That's why I'm sitting on the roof wishing on stars." She impulsively kissed him on the cheek, then got up. "Good night, Ryan."

"Good night."

She paused at the window. "Are you coming?"

"In a minute. I think I see an airplane with my name on it."

# 17

Kara awoke Saturday morning to the sound of someone pounding on the front door with such determination that she thought the wood would splinter and crash to the floor.

She threw on her silk robe and ran down the hall. A few guests poked their heads into the hall, but she assured them she would take care of the problem, whatever it was.

As she ran past Ryan's room, she heard a brief, colorful curse as the puppies began to bark. She couldn't help but smile at the thought of Ryan sleeping with a bunch of puppies. The man was definitely a soft touch where children and animals were concerned.

When Kara finally reached the front door, she heard a man yelling. She hoped to God it wasn't Jonas. Turning the knob, she threw open the door. The man on the other side almost fell into the entryway.

It wasn't Jonas. It was Ike Kelly, and judging by the smell of his breath he had been drinking, probably all night, since it was only six o'clock in the morning.

"Ike. What on earth is going on?" she demanded.

Dark circles framed his eyes. His forehead creased with worry, anger, and despair as his eyes darted back and forth from her to the staircase. "Where is she?"

"Upstairs, asleep. At least she was asleep."

Ike moved to get past her.

"Now hold on a second. You can't just barge into my house like this."

"I came to get my wife, and that's what I'm going to do. You got a problem with that?"

Kara backed up a step. Although she had never known Ike to get violent, he was an ex-marine, and he knew how to intimidate.

"Well, I do have a problem with that. I don't think Aunt Josephine wants you to get her."

"That's right, I don't." Josephine stood regally on the first landing of the staircase. Even dressed in a white terry cloth bathrobe with a pair of fluffy pink slippers on her feet and matching curlers in her hair, she still looked like a queen addressing a lowly subject.

"Now see here—" Ike began.

Josephine interrupted him with a wave of her hand. "I'm divorcing you, Ike Kelly, and nothing you can say will change my mind."

Ike stared at her for a long, agonizing second. "I love you, Josie." His voice softened to a plea. Gone was the Rambo attitude, the arrogant swagger, the cocky talk. He was a man without his woman.

Kara saw vulnerability in his eyes, fear, regret, a million things she had felt herself over the years. "Maybe you should listen to him," she said.

Josephine's voice trembled slightly. "I want him to listen to me."

"I will," Ike promised.

"You'll let me read your tea leaves again?"

"Oh, Christ, woman."

Kara sighed.

"Is that a yes or no?" Josephine asked, no longer any sign of weakness in her voice.

"I won't discuss it here. Now get on down those stairs and come home where you belong."

"I'll come home when I'm good and ready."

"You'll come home now."

"I won't."

"What the hell is going on?" Ryan jogged down the stairs, followed by the puppies and a wide-eyed Angel.

"I'll tell you what's going on," Ike roared, striding toward the stairs. "My wife is coming home."

"No, she's not," Josephine said firmly, clutching at the railing with one hand. "You don't need a wife. You need a maid. I'm tired of picking up your clothes and making your dinner and washing your socks while you watch those half-naked women prancing around on the beach."

"What half-naked women?" Angel asked curiously.

" 'Baywatch,' " Kara replied, meeting her daughter's gaze. "Can you take the puppies outside, honey?"

"Sure, Mom." Angel whistled to the puppies, leading them out to the back porch.

"Now, Josie, come on. This has gone too far," Ike said.

"It hasn't gone far enough," Josephine declared. "I read your tea leaves, Ike Kelly. There's trouble brewing in this town, and you won't listen to me. If you don't believe in me, if you don't respect my vision, then we have nothing to talk about."

"Josie, for crying out loud, you can't tell the future in a bunch of leaves. And I don't like tea. I like coffee, strong and black."

"But I like tea, and I hate coffee."

"Looks like we've reached an impasse," Ryan stated. "One wants coffee, one wants tea. What can they do?"

"Make apple strudel?" Kara said, not really sure what it meant, but it seemed to work for the Grubners.

"I don't like apple strudel," Ike said.

"Neither do I," Josephine replied with a glare.

"Well, that's good, you have something in common," Kara said brightly.

Ryan started to laugh. "All this talk of food is making me hungry. Anyone for breakfast?"

"I'm sure Mr. Kelly would like a cup of coffee," Josephine said.

"And you probably want some of that herbal potion tea," Ike retorted.

Kara held up her hand. "We'll all drink orange juice, okay?"

"I'm not thirsty. Until Mr. Kelly believes in me, we don't have anything to say." Josephine turned and walked up the stairs.

"She's crazy," Ike declared, looking at Kara for confirmation. "What am I going to do with her?"

"Maybe you should try believing in her."

"But it's nonsense. She got all spooked looking at my tea leaves. Said she saw a boat, like my old rowboat, and terrible danger, like someone was going to die. She's driving herself crazy over nothing." Ike looked up at Ryan. "Don't you think so?"

"I think I'll stay out of this one."

"So much for our small, quiet town," Kara said as Ike stormed out of the house.

"It is more lively than I remember." Ryan paused, letting his gaze drift down her body. "Nice outfit."

Kara self-consciously tightened the belt of her short robe. "I like silk."

"I like silk, too—on you."

"Jeez, I'm barely awake, and you're already flirting."

He grinned. "I can't help it around you."

"Do you want coffee or tea?"

"I'll stick to coffee this morning."

Ryan followed her into the kitchen and leaned against the counter as she ground coffee beans and poured water into the coffee maker. Within minutes the aroma of freshly ground coffee filled the cold kitchen.

Kara handed him a mug and watched him take a sip.

"God, you're good," he said.

"And not just at making coffee."

He mockingly chalked up an imaginary point for her. "Not bad. You're learning." Ryan took a deep breath, inhaling the aroma of the coffee as he closed his eyes, an expression of sensual pleasure on his face. Kara watched him with complete fascination. She wanted to see that look on his face again. She wanted to send him to heaven with more than a cup of coffee.

She started as the door between the kitchen and the sun porch opened. Angel slipped through, shooing the puppies back inside with her foot, then closing the door behind her. "Is everything all right?" Angel asked.

"It's fine, honey."

Angel looked over at Ryan. "Did you tell her about last night?"

"What about last night?" Kara asked.

"Nothing." Ryan scowled at Angel. "Maybe you should go back to bed. I don't think you're awake yet."

Angel smiled. "You're okay."

"Yeah, I am totally cool."

"Totally." She giggled.

Kara rapped the spatula on the counter. "Excuse me, what am I missing?"

"Nothing," Angel said.

Kara gave her a suspicious look. "I think we need to talk about yesterday."

"Okay, but not right now. I'm still sleepy." Angel stretched and yawned in a very unconvincing way. "Oh, Ryan." She paused. "About the watch."

"Keep it or throw it away. I don't want it."

"What watch?" Kara asked. "Come on, you guys, this isn't fair."

Ryan sighed. "Angel found a watch along the river that my mother gave me a long time ago."

Angel pulled it out of the pocket of her robe. "This watch, Mom."

Kara took the watch and silently read the inscription. "Your mother gave this to you?" she asked Ryan.

"Actually Jonas gave it to me for my ninth birthday, which came about a week after my mother left. I guess she had hidden the watch away. She was always one to buy Christmas presents in July. Anyway, I didn't want the damn watch. I wanted her. So I went to Tucker's Bridge and threw it into the river. I thought it was gone, dead and buried."

"But everything comes up when the river rises," Kara said softly. She looked down at the watch in her hand. "How odd it should appear now. If Angel had found it a week ago, she wouldn't have even known you."

"I'm a lucky son of a gun, aren't I?"

"The lady showed it to me, Mom. She's the reason I found it," Angel said.

"What lady?" Kara asked.

"The river ghost. She comes out at night, usually before a storm, and she's looking for something. She asked me to help her find it." Angel's eyes filled with excitement. "And I did. It was right where she said."

"Oh, Angel. More tales?"

Her daughter's face fell. "I knew you wouldn't believe me."

"I don't believe in ghosts. They're not real."

"But I saw her, Mom. She found the watch. She pointed right to it. Then she started to cry. At least it looked like she was crying. It might have been the rain," Angel added, determined to get the story right.

"I'm sure it was the rain you saw and the wind you heard and the moonlight through the trees that made you think you saw something. That's the only logical explanation."

"Why does there have to be a logical explanation?" Ryan asked as he sat down at the table.

"Because there does."

Angel looked from one to the other. "I'm going to get dressed." Angel walked out of the kitchen, letting the door slam behind her.

Kara sighed. "Maybe I should go to her. I should probably speak to Aunt Josephine, too. No doubt she's upset about Ike."

"Let her be," Ryan advised. "Josephine has to know

what she's missing before she knows what she wants."

Kara raised an eyebrow. "She does?"

"We all do. That's why I came back here."

"And now you know what you want?"

Ryan didn't answer.

"Do you want this?" Kara put the watch down in front of him.

"No." He refused to touch it.

"Are you sure? Your mother gave it to you. She had it inscribed. She wanted you to know that she loved you."

"If she loved me, she wouldn't have left." Ryan shook his head. "That's the first time I've ever admitted that out loud. What is it about you, Kara? One look from you and I spill my guts."

"I don't know. I've never had that effect on anyone."

"I can't imagine why."

Kara cleared her throat. "I thought you didn't blame your mother for leaving."

"I don't. Well, I do, sort of." Ryan gave her a weary smile. "I'm not sure who I blame anymore. That's the worst of it really, the mystery surrounding her disappearance. Why did she leave? Where did she go? Why didn't she ever come back?"

Sitting down in the chair across from him, Kara picked up the watch. "I think you should keep this, Ryan."

"It's a two-bit Mickey Mouse watch. It doesn't even work anymore."

"That's what it is, but not what it stands for."

Ryan held up his hand as Kara's argument began to build. "All right. I'll take it, if only to shut you up." He picked up the watch. "Are you happy now?"

"Do whatever you want," she said, somewhat hurt by his answer. "Why should I care?"

"Now you're mad."

"Of course I'm not mad. Why would I be mad?"

"You're mad."

"It's none of my business."

"I appreciate your interest and your concern."

Her anger eased at his tender tone. "You do?"

He nodded, taking a sip of coffee.

"I'm sorry I butted in. I just can't help feeling sorry for your mother," Kara said.

"Why?"

"Because it's obvious that she wanted you to know that she loved you for all time." *

"Nice play on words."

"I didn't mean it that way." Kara thought for a moment, wanting him to understand. "Sometimes I look in on Angel when she's asleep, and I think of how sweet and innocent she is. I want to protect her from the future, and I want to assure her that she'll always be loved, and I guess deep down in my heart I want to believe that if anything happened to me, she would remember that love and it would mean something to her."

"My mother didn't die."

"Maybe she did. Maybe that's why she never contacted you. Are you sure Jonas doesn't know what happened to her?"

Ryan hesitated before answering. "No, I'm not sure. I'm not sure at all."

The phone rang. Kara instinctively looked at the clock. "Another early bird," she muttered as she reached for the phone. "The Gatehouse. Can I help you? Just a minute." She put her hand over the receiver. "It's for you. Someone named Wallace Graystone from *Time* magazine."

Ryan took the phone from her hand. "Wally. What's up?" He listened for a long time. Wally spoke in his usual rambling manner, taking a good three minutes to get to the point. While Wally talked about the key happenings in Europe, Ryan watched Kara begin breakfast.

She pulled various bowls and food items out of the cupboards with confidence. This was a woman who knew her way around a kitchen, who felt comfortable in the role of homemaker. He liked watching her move, especially in the short, silky robe that molded itself to her body. Even with no makeup and her hair tousled from sleep, she looked gorgeous, real. Not like the women he had spent most of his time with in the past ten years. Their makeup cases had taken up as much room as their furniture. And they wouldn't have been caught dead sticking their manicured fingernails into a pile of bread dough the way Kara was doing now.

She kneaded the bread with loving, determined hands. She put one hundred percent of herself into every project, no matter what the sacrifice. He couldn't imagine why any man would let her go.

Didn't Michael Delaney know that a real diamond was strong enough to cut glass, to withstand incredible pressure without breaking? Kara was a diamond. And Kara deserved a diamond in return, a long-term commitment, a man who would share her breakfast every morning. Not a man like him.

"Ryan, are you there?" Wally demanded.

"When do you want me?" Ryan asked. Kara's hands stopped moving at his question. Did she care when he was leaving? Did it matter? His pulse raced at the thought. He tried to catch her eye, but she turned her back on him.

"I'm not sure," he said to Wally. "I'll get back to you. I know. It's a once-in-a-lifetime opportunity. I'll call you later."

"A once-in-a-lifetime opportunity? That sounds too good to pass up," Kara said brightly as she put the dough into a bread pan and placed it in the oven to bake.

"It might be. The royal family of Japan has agreed to allow me an intimate look at their daily life."

"Wow. You must be thrilled."

"Who wouldn't be? Can I have more coffee?" He set his cup on the counter.

Kara wiped her hands off on a towel and poured him

another cup of coffee. "Have you been to Japan before?"

"Lots of times. Which is probably why they requested me. I made friends the last time I was there."

She shook her head, a look of complete bewilderment on her face. "What are you doing here?"

"You invited me."

"But you could be anywhere. You could be dining with kings. My country inn must seem like a slum to you. My baskets of potpourri must make you laugh."

"Kara—"

"My needlepoint pillows must make you cringe, and the gingham curtains in the bathroom must make you feel like you're in the most hokey inn in America," she added, her bottom lip trembling with sudden anger.

"Stop it, Kara."

"Stop what?" she asked. "You're just like Michael. I could never compete with his world. Whatever I had at home was never good enough." She put a hand to her mouth in sudden horror. "God, where did that come from?"

Ryan looked into her eyes and saw right through to the heart of her, to the insecurity, to the open wound of past rejection. She usually covered it so well, but for a second it was all there for him to see. But he couldn't acknowledge it. That would only make her feel worse. Instead he said lightly, "Guess I hit a button."

She took a deep breath and let it out. "I'm sorry—again. Maybe I should go back to bed and start over."

"It's okay."

"I just realized how different our worlds are, and it reminded me of Michael and how much he hated the home I made for him."

"Kara, I haven't felt more comfortable anywhere in this world than I have right here in your home. Because this is a home, not just an inn. It's filled with your warmth, your joy, your passion, everything that's you."

"But it's not exciting. It's not Japan. I'm not royalty."

"You're better."

"Oh, come on, don't patronize me. We don't live in the same world."

"The world isn't that big. I know; I've been around it a few times. Royal families are a lot like everyone else. I've done intimate portraits of world leaders dozens of times. And you know what—they all sleep at night, they all go to the bathroom, they all love, they all hate, they all fight with their families, and they all wonder why they're not happy when it seems as if they have everything."

"Really?" The anger faded in her eyes.

"Really. Just like you and me."

"You're not happy, Ryan?" She answered the question before he could. "Of course, that's why you came back—to find out what you were missing so you could decide what you want," she said, repeating his own words.

"But maybe I can't have what I want," he said, watching the emotions flow through her expressive blue eyes and across her beautiful face.

"That depends on what you want."

"What if I said I wanted you?"

"What if I asked you to stay?" she countered.

"What if I said no?"

"What if you said yes?"

God, he loved talking to her. She was so quick, so sharp. They communicated almost as if they were sharing one mind, one voice. Yet they were two very different people, and they wanted different things.

"Kara, I can't stay here." Ryan's gaze traveled to the calendar hanging on the wall. "I've already accepted assignments for March and April, even some in June and July. They're all over the world."

"Serenity Springs could be your home base. You could travel from here. And when your job is over, you would have a nice place to come back to. Your family is here, too."

"A family that doesn't want me in it."

"Maybe that would change with time."

Ryan rubbed his chin with a weary sigh. "People don't change. They are who they are."

Kara took a carton of eggs out of the refrigerator and broke them into a bowl. "I don't believe that, Ryan. I changed. I used to be a wimp. I never fought back, never demanded what was mine, never tried to make things different, never yelled at Michael like I just yelled at you," she added with a rueful grin.

"Why not? It sounds like he deserved it."

"I was afraid of rocking the boat, afraid of following in my mother's footsteps. My father left me, so I felt I had to hang on to Michael, no matter what he did."

"What did he do, Kara?" Ryan asked.

Kara took in a deep breath, then let it out. "A lot of things. He was in sales, so we moved a lot. I pretty much followed meekly behind. It took me years to realize that some of those moves were mandated by the mistakes Michael made."

"What kind of mistakes?"

"Women. Michael loved women, especially those who were taken, those who belonged to someone important, like his boss."

Ryan raised an eyebrow. "He liked to live dangerously."

"Yes. He cheated on me from the first month of our marriage. After awhile, it became a game. We'd go to a party together, and he'd disappear. One time I stood around so long, I got disgusted enough to leave. I found Michael zipping up his pants in the front seat of the car."

"Kara, you don't—"

"But what really got to me was when he brought someone home to our house, to our bed. . . ." Her voice caught as she struggled for control. "I couldn't risk Angel finding him there. I couldn't destroy her illusions about her father, so I asked for a divorce and I got out."

"Good for you."

Ryan's gaze held respect, admiration, all the qualities
Kara had longed to see in a man's eyes. Michael had
never looked at her that way, but then Michael had been
too caught up in himself to even consider her feelings.
And to be honest she hadn't done all that much to earn
his respect or his admiration.

"I made a mess of things," Kara said. "I wanted to
be married so bad that I overlooked everything—
lipstick marks, credit card receipts for flowers I had
never received, hotel stubs—you name it, it was all
there. And besides the women, we had other problems.
Michael didn't want to be married, and he didn't want
to be a father, either. He neglected Angel long before
the divorce. Now he doesn't even answer her letters."
She sighed. "I made a lot of mistakes, Ryan, and I'm
afraid Angel is still paying for some of them."

"The important thing is that in the long run you did
what was best for Angel. You took her out of a bad
situation and brought her into a good one."

"Too little, too late, maybe."

"I don't think so."

Kara smiled at him. "Thanks."

"For what?"

"For making me feel better."

"I'd like to make you feel a lot better," Ryan replied,
offering her a devilish grin.

"I'll bet." Kara turned her attention back to breakfast.
"So, when are you leaving?" she asked. "Today?"

"No, not today. I still have some photographs to take,
slices of small-town America that the world desperately
needs to see."

"You'll do it?"

"For you, yes."

"You are good at what you do, Ryan. Your talent is
amazing, the way you capture life in such a way that
all the truths are revealed. Every image is truly a moment captured for all time."

"The camera does the work."

"Hardly. I take pictures. I don't see what you see, and neither does my camera."

He smiled with genuine pleasure. "Now it's my turn to thank you."

"For what?"

"For understanding that what I do is important to me."

"Of course it's important. Why else would you do it?"

"Money."

"I don't think you're motivated by money. If you were, you'd have more to show for it than a rented Ferrari and an apartment in L.A. that apparently doesn't have any furniture."

"How did you know the car was rented?"

She grinned at him. "Lucky guess. You don't look all that comfortable getting in and out of it."

His expression turned serious. "You see too much, Kara. I'm not sure I like it."

"Why, because I see through you?"

"I haven't let anyone get close to me in a long time."

"I'm not close to you. And you're not close to me. For that we would need time, which is exactly what we don't have." She paused, making her expression cheerful and bright. "Now, would you like pancakes or eggs?"

"Pancakes, with butter and syrup. I think I'll need my strength. After breakfast I'm planning to visit Jonas."

"I'll make you a big stack." Kara paused. "You know, Ryan, you should take your father's picture."

"What on earth for?"

"So you could see him objectively. The way you would look at any other subject. Capture the man on film."

"So that all the truths are revealed," Ryan finished, repeating her earlier statement. He shook his head. "I don't think so. I used to want the truth. Now I think I'd settle for a good lie."

# 18

Jonas pulled a pair of faded blue jeans over his white cotton briefs. He cast a quick look at the hospital room door, but it remained closed. Thank God. He actually had a few minutes' peace from Helga the nurse from hell, or whatever her name was. He walked over to the closet and took out his shirt. His fingers fumbled with the buttons as he hurried to get dressed.

With any luck the cab he had called would be waiting downstairs, ready to take him home. He would worry about paying the hospital bill later.

As Jonas headed for the door, it opened in front of him. He looked up, expecting to see one of the nurses or the doctor, but it was his son, his youngest son, the one who reminded him of all the mistakes he had made in his life.

"What the hell are you doing here? I don't see you for twelve years, and now I'm tripping over you every time I turn around."

Ryan's mouth curved into a reluctant smile. "It does seem like that, doesn't it? I came to keep you company, but it looks like you're on your way out."

"Damn right. And don't try to stop me."

"As if I could."

Jonas heard the bitterness in Ryan's voice. He pretended he didn't. "Get out of my way then."

Ryan didn't move. "How are you getting home?"

"I called a taxi."

"Ah, the getaway car. I don't suppose the doctor knows you're leaving."

"I don't need his permission. I feel fine, and I'm going home. I heard on the radio that the river is rising. I'm sure as hell not going to stay here when my house may be going underwater."

"It's not in any danger at the moment, and even if it was, what could you do? Hold the river back with your bare hands?"

"If I have to. At the very least I can put some sandbags out."

"No, you can't."

Jonas tried to walk past him, but Ryan grabbed him by the arm. There was as much determination in his eyes as Jonas had ever seen.

"You can't fill sandbags. You just had a heart attack," Ryan said.

"You going to do it for me?" Jonas challenged. Ryan didn't answer. "That's what I thought. You don't care about our home. You never did."

"Yes, I did. I cared about it when Mom was there. I cared about it when I was growing up. It was never the house that made me want to leave. It wasn't the town either, for that matter."

"Then what? Are you still afraid of the river?"

Ryan flinched but didn't say anything. Jonas was almost sorry to see the self-control. He had the upper hand when Ryan lost control. When he didn't—well, he'd call it even.

"You would like it if I said yes, wouldn't you?" Ryan asked. "Because it would be easy to call me a coward. Well, I'm not a coward. I'll swim in the damn river if you want me to. If that's what it takes to get through to you."

Jonas cleared his throat, not sure where this conversation was heading, not sure he wanted to go with it. "You do what you want." He looked away from Ryan's sharp, penetrating green eyes. They reminded Jonas of Isabelle's eyes, and for a moment he thought he was looking at her. He blinked hard. "I'll be on my way then."

"Fine." Ryan opened the door. The sound of voices came clearly through to both of them.

"Goddammit," Jonas swore.

"You know you should stay and let them do their tests. Dr. Steiner said you may need surgery at some point."

"I don't need tests, and I sure as hell don't intend to let anyone cut me up. I just need to be home where I can see what's happening with the river."

"Yeah, I guess you do. The river and the house always meant more to you than anything. More than Mom. More than me. Now more than your own life."

"My life isn't worth anything without that house."

"To you, I guess not. All right. Let me see if the coast is clear." Ryan poked his head out to check the corridor. "You're in luck. Everyone is gone."

Ryan helped his father to the elevator, down to the lobby, and out the front door. They managed to avoid running into anyone they knew. However, when they reached the curb in front of the parking lot, there was no taxi waiting.

"I'll give you a ride," Ryan said.

Jonas held back, his dark eyes filled with suspicion. "Why are you helping me?"

"Because you need help."

"I don't need *your* help," Jonas said, still unable to accept the fact that Ryan was trying to be nice. He was convinced that his youngest son had an ulterior motive; he just couldn't figure out what it was.

"Actually you do need my help if you want to get back to Serenity Springs any time soon."

"Fine. I'll take a ride."

"Gee, thanks," Ryan said dryly, leading him over to the red Ferrari.

Jonas looked at it with distaste. "You always did like expensive toys."

"Would you believe me if I said it wasn't mine?"

"No."

"That's what I figured."

Once Jonas got in the car, Ryan realized his mistake. He had just agreed to drive his father home, a thirty-minute trip in the quiet intimacy of the car. He wasn't sure either one of them could stand being so close for so long. But he had no other choice.

Jonas didn't speak for a good ten minutes. Ryan didn't either. He stared straight ahead at the road, wondering what he was doing. He had gone to the hospital to visit his father, not spring him.

"Andrew won't like this," Ryan said more to himself than Jonas, but his father heard his muttered comment.

"So what?" Jonas asked.

"So maybe you should care about his feelings. He certainly seems to care a lot about you, sticking by your side all these years. Andrew would do anything for you, and I'm not sure you would give him the time of day if he asked."

Jonas drummed the fingers of his left hand against his thigh. "He's a good boy."

"Yeah, Andrew is the best. Not like me, right?"

"What do you want from me?" Jonas turned to look at him.

Ryan noticed again how his father had aged, the crow's feet around his eyes, more white whiskers than gray. Although Jonas's eyes were still sharp with intelligence, they also held weariness. The man was old and tired. He also looked confused, as if he truly didn't know what Ryan wanted from him.

Maybe that was understandable. Ryan wasn't sure what he wanted anymore either. At one time he had wanted an apology, an acknowledgement that Jonas had been wrong. But now he wondered what the hell an apology would do for any of them.

"Maybe I just want to know you again," Ryan said finally. "You're my father. I'm your son. It seems as if we should be closer than we are." God, it was so difficult to say the words. He had to force each one through tight lips, but he felt a driven need to get them out, to speak them before it was too late.

"How close?" Jonas ground out, turning his head away from Ryan. "Are you back to stay? Or just back to gloat?"

"I'm not staying. I have a career. It requires that I travel."

"Then nothing has changed."

Silence fell between them, and Ryan felt a helpless rage, an inability to get through to this man. He got along with all kinds of people the world over, but he couldn't get along with his own flesh and blood. Why? Why?

"You're impossible," Ryan said. "It has to be your way or no way. You can't compromise. You can't bend. You can't think about anybody but yourself. That's why Mom left. That's why I left."

Jonas didn't answer for a long moment. "That's not why you left."

Ryan remembered their last angry scene and knew that Jonas was partly right. But now that he had begun the conversation, he wasn't sure he wanted to finish it. Jonas's skin was pale, almost chalky, and there was a slight tremor in the hand that rested on the seat, reminding Ryan that his father was not supposed to be out of the hospital, much less in the middle of an argument. "Forget it," Ryan said. "I don't think we should be talking about this now. You should be resting."

"I'll rest when I want to."

Ryan sighed and switched on the radio. His father always had to get in the last word.

A short while later, Ryan pulled up in front of Jonas's house and shut off the engine. The big frame house stood straight and proud in the midst of tall, elegant redwood trees, years of Hunter traditions deep within its foundations. The last flood had soaked through the first floor, but Jonas had cleaned up, recarpeted, and remodeled in exactly the same style, so that no one would ever notice anything had happened.

It was part of the denial. Isabelle had left during the flood, but Jonas had put her things back on the refurbished floors as if she were coming home. Again Ryan questioned why. If his father truly wanted her to leave, why had he kept the reminders?

Jonas opened the car door and stepped out. Ryan did the same. Apparently there would be no good-byes.

"Wait," Ryan said.

Jonas reluctantly glanced back. "What?"

"Why did you keep my things? I saw my room. It's exactly the same."

"I couldn't be bothered to go through your stuff."

"But you could be bothered to keep it clean?" Ryan held out his hands. "Maybe the question is—what do you want from me?"

"What I've always wanted."

"Which is what?"

"If you don't know, I'm not going to tell you."

"Oh, Jesus, I hate when you do that."

"Some things can't be told." Jonas shuffled over to the stairs, then paused. "I'm sorry about the drink the other night. I shouldn't have done that." Shaking his head, he walked up the stairs and into the house.

Ryan leaned his arms on the hood of the car, completely taken aback by his father's unexpected apology. He couldn't remember when Jonas had last said he was sorry. Maybe there was hope after all.

Before he could get in the car, Andrew pulled up in his truck, and if the spitting gravel was any indication of his mood, he was not a happy man.

"Where is he?" Andrew asked, slamming the door shut.

"Inside."

"I can't believe you took him out of the hospital."

"Take him? I stopped him from hitchhiking. He was dressed and heading for the door when I arrived. I thought it was better to go along with him than try to fight him."

"He should be in the hospital. He's sick."

"I agree. But Jonas has a mind of his own."

Andrew ran a hand through his hair in frustration as he looked up at the house. "Dammit all. What if he has another heart attack when he's alone? What if he can't reach the phone to call for help?"

"Why are you telling me? Why don't you tell him?"

"Because he won't listen. He never listens."

"Then maybe you should just let him be."

"I can't do that. I can't turn my back on him, no matter how difficult he is. He's my father. He's family."

A sharp pain cut through Ryan's gut. "You turned your back on me. What's the difference?"

"You're the one who left," Andrew replied. "If anyone turned his back, it was you."

Ryan put his hands on his hips. "Is that it, Andrew? Whoever leaves is the one at fault? Did you ever stop to think that someone's driving that person away?"

"No one drove you away."

"Not me, Mom."

"I don't want to talk about her."

Andrew tried to move past him. Ryan grabbed his arm. "That's too bad, because for once you're going to listen."

"Let him go." The voice came from the porch, and both Ryan and Andrew turned at the same time.

Ryan's grip tightened on Andrew's arm. He didn't want to let Andrew go. He wanted to tell him the truth, to set things straight.

"Don't upset him," Andrew said quietly.

"Why the hell are we always so worried about up-setting him? Maybe he's upsetting us." Ryan let go of his brother's arm, knowing it was futile to persist.

"How are you feeling?" Andrew asked his father.

"A hell of a lot worse now that I've seen this." Jonas held up the newspaper in his hand. "What did you do to my paper, Andrew? It looks like a piece of shit." Jonas tossed the newspaper off the porch toward the trash can below and stomped into the house.

"Why, that goddamn, arrogant son of a ..." Andrew's voice broke off.

Ryan nodded. "Go on. You were saying ..."

"You wouldn't understand."

"I'm the only one who would understand." Their eyes met, and Andrew slowly nodded.

"Maybe you would."

"Jonas asked Mom to leave," Ryan said. "The day before I left town, before you married Becky Lee, I found a letter from Mom to Jonas. She begged him to change his mind. He told her to get out of the house, to never contact us again."

"You're a liar!" But Andrew's words lacked convic-tion. "Why would he do that? He loved her. He was devastated when she left. Don't you remember the nights he used to sit on the deck and stare at the river, holding that bud vase in his hands?"

Ryan didn't want to be reminded of that image of Jonas. He wanted to think only of the man who had sent his mother away, the man who had been too proud, too selfish to keep their family together.

"Jonas didn't love her, not as much as he loved the river or even the house, for that matter. Mom had a chance to sing with a blues ensemble touring through San Francisco, led by an old friend of her father's. She would have had to go to San Francisco for a week to rehearse. Don't you remember?"

"That was long before she left."

"A few months, yes, but it was the beginning of the

end. It was when she finally realized she was trapped here. That she could never sing again."

"She could sing here."

"God, you sound just like him. It wasn't enough for her to sing in the choir or to walk the streets singing Christmas carols. She had a talent that begged to be used, but she couldn't use it, because he wouldn't let her."

Andrew gazed at the river. Like Jonas, he turned to the water for comfort. But Isabelle had found no comfort along the banks of the river, only unhappiness and despair. Her home had become a prison, her husband the jailer. Even Mother Nature had taunted her with weeks of unrelenting rainstorms, fog, and clouds that made her feel as if she were lost in a place that had no contact with the outside world.

"She was desperately unhappy, Andrew," Ryan said. "She started to take long walks. And on one of those walks she met someone. A man."

"No."

"Yes. A man she could talk to, a man who understood her dreams, her desires."

Andrew said nothing, his back as straight and proud as one of the redwoods.

Ryan walked around him to face him. "Jonas saw them together one afternoon, and he became enraged. He told her to leave. She said she would go, but only if she could take us with her. That night after she went to bed, Jonas woke us in the middle of the night. He took us to that old cabin in the north woods."

"To get us away from the water," Andrew said, but his voice held doubt.

"To get us away from her. He left us alone there all night and the next day, too." Ryan's voice grew gruff. "When he finally came for us, he said Mom went to visit an uncle in New Orleans. A week later he told us Mom was gone for good, that she didn't love us anymore."

Ryan swallowed hard, fighting back years of accumulated pain and anger. Deep down inside he still felt like a little, lost, lonely boy, waiting for his mother to come back. It was pathetic.

Andrew took in a deep breath and let it out. "Why should I believe you?"

"Why would I lie?" Ryan countered.

"Why didn't you tell me before?"

"I was going to, but then I saw you with Becky Lee. She told me you were getting married, remember?" Ryan asked, bitterness still evident in his voice, but he couldn't hold it back. "I had no one left to turn to, no one to share the letter with, so I left. And all these years you and Jonas acted like I committed some crime. But all I took was the letter, Andrew. You took my girl. Jonas took my mother. So tell me, why the hell am I the bad guy?"

"It wasn't like that."

"It was exactly like that."

"I was protecting Becky Lee. I was offering her a home, a family. You were offering her nothing."

"You weren't protecting her; you were protecting yourself. You're the one who wanted the home and the family. More importantly, you wanted to beat me."

"I loved her. Don't ever say that I didn't."

"You might have come to love her, but you didn't love her then. I'll never believe you did. She was just another bone between us, another competition, egged on by Jonas, no doubt."

Andrew didn't say anything for a long moment. When his words finally came, they surprised Ryan. "Jonas thought you might stay here if you wanted Becky Lee bad enough. And of course, he knew you would want her more if I wanted her, too. He played us off against each other. Just like the other times when he wanted one of us to do something for him."

"But she was a woman, Andrew, not a toy, not some pawn in a game. How could you go along with it?"

"I didn't know it then, Ryan. Jesus, what kind of person do you think I am? Hell, I think I just figured it out this second."

Ryan looked into his brother's eyes and knew Andrew was telling the truth. His eyes always gave him away, which was why Andrew had taken the blame for most of their scrapes. He couldn't tell a lie or keep a secret. The truth always won out.

Ryan looked at Andrew with new respect. At least Andrew had the guts to admit this one thing. It was more than Ryan had gotten from Jonas.

Ryan dug into his pocket and pulled out his wallet. He took out an obviously worn, yellowed piece of paper. "I kept the letter from Mom. Read it. Everything is in there." Ryan paused. "Including the name of the man our mother was in love with."

Andrew took the letter reluctantly. "Who was it?"

"Harry Cox. Kara's father."

## 19

Kara set her picnic basket down on the blue-and-white checkered tablecloth just before noon. Three large tables had been pushed together in the center of Castaway Park to hold the box lunches for the auction. The money raised would be put toward buying new computer software for the high school.

Although they had rigged up temporary awnings over the picnic tables, Kara cast an anxious glance at the sky. So far the weather was holding. There were high clouds but no rain. With any luck they could get through lunch without moving everyone inside. The last thing she wanted to do was hold another event at the rec center.

Kara gave her picnic basket one last critical glance. Forgoing the usual sandwich fare, she had provided roasted chicken, three different kinds of cheese, her own home-baked rosemary rolls, a fruit salad, a bottle of California chardonnay, two wineglasses, and a chocolate truffle for dessert. She hoped it would bring a good price.

Loretta came up next to her. "Nice job, Kara. Only the best from you homemaker types."

Kara smiled, not taking offense. She liked Loretta's straight-talking, shoot-from-the-hip attitude. It was refreshing to be with someone who didn't always say the right thing. "Making a home is one of the few things I do well. It's not worth much in the real world though."

"I don't know about that," Loretta said. "I'm quite impressed with the way you pulled off the centennial. Folks have been talking it up at the bar all weekend."

"Really? What have they been saying?"

"That things are turning out great. Everybody's business has tripled, including mine. I just wish they weren't all leaving tomorrow."

"Hopefully they'll be back."

"Right." Loretta grimaced and put a hand to her stomach.

"Are you all right?"

"False labor. I'm not due for another three weeks." She let out a sigh. "That's better. You know, after I saw Dr. Appleborne last week, Beverly paid me a visit. After her usual self-righteous arguments, she left me some booklets on putting the baby up for adoption."

"You're thinking about giving it up?" Kara asked in surprise.

Loretta's face tightened with stubborn pride. "Not a chance."

"Good. Because I think you'll be a great mother."

"Why would you say that?"

"Because you have so much love to give. And I think up till now, you've been giving it in the wrong places."

Loretta smiled weakly. "You can say that again." She opened the large utilitarian metal lunch box she had brought with her. "Well, here it is, such as it is. We might get a buck for it."

"What did you bring?"

"Roast beef sandwiches, potato salad, pickles, and chocolate chip cookies. Oh, and a couple of beers."

"Sounds good to me."

"Of course, no man will bid on it if he knows it's mine. Maybe I should put a scarlet A on it and get it over with."

"Don't be ridiculous. There are worse things in life than being single and pregnant."

"Like what?" Loretta asked.

"Like being married to the wrong man and being pregnant. My ex-husband gave Angel a last name, but not much more."

"So who needs a man anyway?"

Kara laughed, waving her hand at the box lunches. "Today, it looks like we all do."

"Next year, the men make lunch. Got it?"

"Got it."

Loretta whistled lightly. "Look who's here. Mr. Hunk himself. Maybe Ryan will bid on my lunch. I wouldn't mind sharing a picnic with him."

Kara followed Loretta's gaze, watching as Ryan made his way through the group, shaking hands, kissing cheeks, allowing an elderly woman to tweak his cheek. He was good with people, fun, friendly, outgoing. Besides Loretta, half the women in town were hoping he would buy their lunches. In fact, Kara wouldn't put it past some of them to whisper a few choice words in his ear about which box to choose.

"Did you two ever—date?" Kara asked, trying to sound casual, when in fact she was more than a little bothered by the thought of Loretta and Ryan together. Not that it would surprise her. They had both played fast and wild through their teenage years.

Loretta smiled. "Date? That's a cute word. What does it mean?"

"You know, dinner, movie, necking on River Road."

"Does one out of three count?"

"Depends on which one."

Loretta tilted her head thoughtfully. "You're awfully interested."

"Just curious. It's no big deal." Kara fiddled with the edge of her picnic basket, looking away from Loretta's perceptive eyes.

"Ryan is an excellent kisser." Loretta paused as Kara

looked up. "But Andrew is better. You should stay with him."

"You—you've kissed Andrew?"

"Well, it wasn't like it was yesterday or anything. . . ." Loretta turned away. "I have to go."

Kara crossed her arms in front of her chest, completely irritated at the thought that Loretta had kissed both Hunter men. Okay, so she had done the same thing. But that was different. Totally different.

"Kara?"

Mayor Hewitt waved to her from his position in front of the microphone. His expression was more worried than excited. Her heart sank. Something else was wrong.

"I spoke to Dirk Anders this morning," the mayor said when she joined him. "He wants us to get folks sandbagging this afternoon along the lower spots. He was thinking maybe we could turn it into a centennial event, keep things low-key so people don't take off before the big parade tomorrow afternoon."

Sandbag? Kara's stomach turned over at the thought. "Is it that bad?"

"Not yet, but there's more rain expected tomorrow and another storm loading up out over the Pacific that should be here by midweek."

Kara looked around the park. They had set up seats auditorium style, and most of them were full. The mood was upbeat, cheerful. Folks were ready to picnic, not fill sandbags and worry about their homes.

Josephine walked up to Kara wearing one of her ridiculous hats, this one made of straw with a blue jay sitting amidst a pile of flowers.

"What's the holdup?" Josephine asked.

"Dirk wants to start sandbagging today," Kara replied.

"Oh, dear."

"Maybe we can work it into the historical tour this afternoon. We were planning on hitting the high spots, talking about how Serenity Springs developed from an early logging town to what it is today. I guess at some point we could discuss the possibility of flooding and give everyone a chance to fill sandbags." It was off the top of her head but not bad, Kara decided.

"That might work," Josephine said. "In the meantime, why don't we get the auction started? Folks are hungry."

The mayor nodded and stepped up to the microphone. Kara and Josephine retreated to the sidelines as the crowd settled down.

Angel slipped into the seat next to Ryan. "Hi," she said.

"Hi." Ryan nudged her arm. "Which one of those boxes is yours, Angel-face?"

Angel rolled her eyes in response.

"You didn't make one?" Ryan asked in mock surprise.

"No. I can't cook. In fact, I don't want to cook."

"Why not? You like to eat, don't you?"

"Cooking is not worth anything. I want to do something important, like fly to the moon."

Ryan ruffled her hair as he smiled. "Big dreams, huh?"

"Why not? My mom says girls can do anything."

"Your mom is right." Ryan glanced around at the crowd. "Looks like they're about ready to get this show on the road."

"Whatever you do, don't bid on the picnic basket with the chicken and the wine," Angel said. "I think my mom wants Andrew to buy it."

"Oh, yeah?" Ryan folded his arms in front of his chest, years of competing with his brother automatically kicking into gear. He looked up as Billy joined them. "Hello, Billy. I've been wanting to talk to you."

"Uh, well, okay," Billy said, not looking at all pleased

to see him. "But I—I have to go in a minute. I—I'm looking for my—my dad."

Angel put a hand on Billy's arm, obviously concerned about her friend. "It's okay, Billy. Why don't you sit down?" She scooted over next to Ryan, making room for Billy on the edge of her chair.

Billy sat down. He stared straight ahead, obviously uncomfortable with the situation. Ryan wondered what Andrew had told Billy about him. Probably more lies, he decided, if Billy's nervous stammering was any indication.

"Are you going to bid on any of those lunches, Billy?" Ryan asked, trying to put the boy at ease.

Billy shook his head.

"We're going to have a picnic down by the river," Angel volunteered. "I'm hoping to see the lady again. Billy doesn't really believe there is a river ghost."

"I'm sure if anyone can convince him, you can."

They sat quietly for a moment as the auction began. Once in a while Ryan would glance over at Billy, struck by the similarity of this boy to Becky Lee—the same long face, the pert nose, the freckles. There wasn't much of Andrew in this boy. Even his eyes were hazel, almost a light green. But then Becky Lee's eyes had been hazel; they could have come from her. Or—from himself.

No, Becky Lee would have told him. And Andrew couldn't have lived out a lie all these years, not without cracking. He didn't have it in him to hoard such a secret. Billy belonged to Andrew and Becky Lee. That's all there was to it.

Although—Ryan's mind drifted back to the past. He had made love to Becky Lee many times. She had been a passionate, loving girl, no inhibitions, no restraint. But she had never been particularly promiscuous, at least as far as he knew. To think that she had slept with both Andrew and himself at the same time seemed impossible to believe.

Ryan tilted his head to one side and realized Billy was

staring at him, too. They both looked away at the same time. Some things were just too damn scary to face head-on.

"Billy, I see your dad," Angel said, pointing toward the far end of the park.

Ryan turned his head, watching as Andrew got out of his truck and walked slowly over to the edge of the group. He seemed to have aged in the last hour. Which meant he had read the letter. Andrew finally knew the truth, at least what there was of it to know. The rest was locked inside his father's head, and inside his mother's heart, wherever she might be.

Ryan should have felt a sense of relief, of vindication, but in truth he just felt tired. All these years he had held on to blame like a shield protecting him from more pain. Now not even the blame could stop him from feeling again. He had grown up without a mother, and so had Andrew.

They both knew why she had left, but they still didn't know why she had never come back. Maybe they never would.

Andrew saw Kara standing with her aunt Josephine. He knew he should join her, find out which basket was hers and bid on it so they could have lunch together. But he couldn't make his feet move.

Her father's name still rang through his head.

Harry Cox.

The man his mother had fallen in love with. Kara must have known, just as Ryan had known. Andrew was the only one in the dark. They had kept it from him, forcing him outside their circle.

Andrew had never felt a part of any group at school, never been fully accepted by anyone. He was still considered Jonas's son, Billy's father, but not himself, nothing in his own right.

He felt a wave of anger at Ryan and Kara and his father. It peaked when he thought of his mother, when he thought of her betrayal. He hated her for leaving. Knowing that she had also been unfaithful didn't make it easier to bear. Excusing the fact that Jonas had probably trapped her in his life still didn't make it right for her to leave her children. He couldn't forgive her for that.

And even if Jonas had forced her to leave, why hadn't she ever come back? She couldn't have been that afraid. So many years had passed. Hadn't she ever wanted to see them? Hadn't she ever wanted to see her grandchild? The pain of rejection hit him so hard, he thought he might keel over.

The only thing holding him upright was his son. He could see Billy across the park, and he knew that at least Billy loved him. But when he looked beyond Billy, he saw Ryan. His son, his brother, both with dark hair and eyes that . . .

Andrew suddenly felt sick to his stomach. Putting a hand to his mouth, he turned to leave. Loretta stood in front of him.

"What's wrong?" she asked, concern filling her warm brown eyes.

"I have to get out of here," Andrew replied with a sense of desperation.

"You can't leave yet. Kara's basket is coming up."

"I can't talk to her right now."

"Then bid on the silver lunch box, Andrew. I promise I won't ask questions. You can sit and brood if you want."

His tension eased at the understanding in her eyes. "God, where have you been all my life, Loretta?"

She smiled somewhat wistfully. "I've been right here."

"I never thought you liked me very much."

"I didn't, because you always looked down on me, like I was something to be ashamed of. A girl to kiss in a dark closet, but not one to bring to the church social."

"That's not true." But it was true. He couldn't have

dated Loretta without getting heat from his father, so he had avoided her.

"I guess it still wouldn't be right," she continued. "After all, now I'm not just fast, I'm pregnant too, proclaiming to the world that I've had sex, as if everyone else in this town was the Virgin Mary."

"Not everyone thinks that way." But Andrew knew he couldn't bid on Loretta's lunch. In the eyes of the townfolk, he and Kara were a couple. To bid on anyone else's lunch would be unacceptable.

But the thought of eating with Kara was also unacceptable. Her father's name still echoed through his head. He didn't know if he could handle this connection between them. Her father—his mother. It made him sick just to think about it.


"There's Andrew," Josephine said to Kara, pointing to the other side of the park.

"I know, I saw him." And he had seen her, too, but he made no move to join her. Kara wondered why.

"Is he still mad at you for bringing Ryan home?"

"I have no idea. But I can't worry about it anymore. Your lunch looks lovely, by the way. I think the herbal tea might be a dead giveaway, though. Or is that the idea?"

"Humph. Absolutely not. I want nothing to do with Mr. Kelly. As soon as Monday comes, I'm calling my lawyer."

"You don't have a lawyer," Kara reminded her aunt.

"Then I'll find one."

"You are so stubborn."

"Must be where you get it from." Josephine waved at an older gentleman sitting in the first row.

Kara followed her actions with a troubled eye. "What are you up to now?"

"Stuart looks a little lonely," Josephine said. "Maybe I'll sit with him."

"Ike will punch Stuart's lights out if he buys your lunch."

"Oh, piffle. Mr. Kelly is all talk and no action. Besides, this is for charity. I'm only trying to bring in a good price for my lunch."

"And cause a little trouble at the same time. Everyone here knows that if a man doesn't bid on his wife's box, he'll spend the night on the couch."

"Stuart's a widower. He can sleep wherever he wants."

"But you can't," Kara said pointedly.

Josephine put an arm around Kara and gave her a quick hug. "Stop worrying so much. Oh, dear, my lunch is up for sale now."

Kara glanced at Ike. He was staring straight ahead, his expression grim but determined. She might not have her aunt's sixth sense, but she knew trouble was on the way.

"Let's begin the bidding at ten dollars," the mayor said.

Stuart immediately raised his hand. "Ten dollars."

Ike glared at him. Stuart slid down in his chair.

"Do I hear fifteen?" the mayor asked.

"Fifteen," Ike said.

A man at the back yelled out twenty, another man upped it to twenty-five. Ike rose to his feet. "Fifty dollars."

The crowd hushed for a moment as Ike sent a challenging look around the group.

"Do I hear fifty-five?" the mayor asked. He paused. "Going once, going twice—"

"Just a minute there, Mayor," Ike interrupted. "Before I go and buy that lunch, I want to say something."

Josephine stiffened next to her. "What is that old goat up to?" she muttered.

Ike walked up to the microphone, carrying one of Josephine's teacups. "I just want everyone here to know that Josephine Kelly is the best damn woman in this town, and she's my woman. No matter what she thinks." He cast her a stern glance. "And to prove that to her, I want her to come up here right now and read my tea leaves."

Josephine grabbed Kara's arm, suddenly needing support.

"Are you all right?" Kara asked as the crowd turned to them, shouts of encouragement ringing from every corner.

"I—I didn't expect this. I don't know what to do."

"Meet him halfway," Kara said. "Go on. He's waiting."

Josephine walked slowly up to the front of the group. Ike handed her the cup, which was empty save for the tea leaves at the bottom. "I poured the water out just like you showed me."

"Ike, don't do this,"

"I have to do it, Josie. I respect you and I love you. And I want the whole damn town to know it. Now tell me, does it say I'm going to have the woman I love by my side for the rest of my life?"

Josephine hesitated, then turned the cup upside-down, letting the leaves fall to the ground. "It doesn't have to say that, because I will." And she kissed him full on the lips.

Kara wiped a tear from her eye, touched by Ike's generosity, by his willingness to be flexible, by the depth of the love that allowed him to stand before God and his country, or at least Serenity Springs, and declare himself to the woman he loved. Maybe love wasn't really about the Grubners' apple strudel or Aunt Josephine's tea; maybe it was about compromise.

The mayor finally broke up their kiss with a jovial nudge, and Ike and Josephine walked into the park with their arms wrapped around each other.

"Now, let's move on," the mayor said. "Although I'm not sure we can top that." He picked up Kara's basket. "Look what we have here—wine, cheese, chicken, a

gourmet offering. Let's start the bidding at fifteen dollars."

Stuart tried again. "Fifteen dollars."

Kara sighed, her sense of romance deflating abruptly.
Just what she needed, lunch with an old man whose
hands roved as much as his eyes.

Will Hodgkins bid twenty from the back of the room.
Harrison Winslow upped it to thirty dollars.

Kara waited for Andrew to bid. He had to know the
lunch was hers. He had seen the picnic basket a dozen
times. Andrew finally raised his hand.

"Forty dollars," Andrew said.

Kara breathed a sigh of relief. Andrew was her an-
chor, the one predictable factor in her life. He had come
through for her again. She wanted to get things back on
an even keel with him, put the whole business of Ryan
away and go back to the way they had been.

One of the men staying at the Gatehouse bid forty-
five dollars.

Then Ryan stepped in with a bid for fifty.

Kara's heart came to a thudding stop. Ryan couldn't
buy her lunch. She looked over at him, silently telling
him to back off. He simply grinned, as did Angel, who
was sitting next to him. Good grief, her own daughter
was conspiring against her.

Why couldn't Angel have chosen Andrew to adore?
Why Ryan?

Andrew stood a little taller at the sound of Ryan's
voice. He bid sixty. Mayor Hewitt turned to Ryan.

"Seventy-five," Ryan said.

The rest of the bidders fell silent, as if sensing the
battle was only meant to be waged between these two
players.

"Eighty-five," Andrew replied.

"One hundred," Ryan challenged.

Andrew hesitated. "One hundred and ten."

Kara held her breath. *Let it go, Ryan,* she pleaded silently.

"One hundred and fifty dollars," Ryan said.

The crowd hushed. Even Mayor Hewitt stumbled over the figure.

"I have one hundred and fifty dollars," the mayor said. "Do I hear two hundred?"

Andrew didn't speak.

"Going, going, gone, to Ryan Hunter for one hundred and fifty dollars."

Kara stared at Ryan in shock. One hundred and fifty dollars for her picnic basket? She barely heard the auction move on, so fixated was she on the fact that Ryan had just bought her lunch and Andrew had let him.

In fact, Andrew was now bidding on Loretta's lunch, and he won it for sixty dollars. Kara tried to smile, knowing that Andrew and Loretta were friends, and Loretta probably needed a friend right now, but deep down she was hurt that Andrew had let her basket go to Ryan.

At the end of the auction, Ryan waited for her with a gleeful expression. Kara picked up her basket, shoved it into his outstretched arms, and walked away from him, carefully avoiding Andrew and Loretta.

Ryan followed her through the park. He knew she was angry. He could see it in the thrust of her chin, the stormy light in her blue eyes, and the way she stalked across the picnic grounds without saying a word to anyone. She was no longer the conciliatory president of the chamber of commerce or the gracious hostess from the Gatehouse. She wasn't even the conscientious mother or the bitter ex-wife. No, this time she was simply Kara, a woman, passionate, angry, glorious.

His pulse began to race. At this moment he wanted her more than he had wanted any other woman.

Unfortunately she didn't seem to want him at all. She stopped at one point, hands planted on her hips. "Where the hell do you want to eat?"

He grinned. He couldn't help it.

"Are you laughing at me?"

"No."

She stormed over to the last picnic table and sat down, tapping her foot rapidly against the ground.

Ryan set the basket down on the table. "How about some wine?"

"How about a punch in the nose?"

"I'd rather have wine."

"Why? Just tell me why."

"Because I'm thirsty."

"Why did you buy my lunch?"

"Because I wanted to eat with you." And that was the complete, unvarnished truth. He wanted to have lunch with Kara, and dinner and breakfast, too. He wanted to spend every waking second with this woman. The thought caught him off guard, and he sat down on the bench, feeling suddenly weak. Wanting to spend all of his time with a woman was not his style. Even with his long-term, live-in relationships, he had always cherished his own time, his own space.

"You didn't want to eat with me," Kara continued. "You wanted to stake a claim. You were grandstanding. Using your money to beat Andrew. I think you're disgusting."

"I think you're beautiful when you're angry."

"Hah! You think that line is going to work on me? Forget it. I can see right through you, Ryan Hunter. And I will not be pulled back and forth between you and your brother like some wishbone."

"Who are you really mad at? Me or Andrew?"

"You, him, both of you," she shouted.

"That narrows it down."

"I will not be put in the middle of your stupid feud. I will not be some prize that goes to the best, the strongest, the whatever."

"That wasn't my intention."

"Oh, to hell with you." She jumped to her feet and took off down a path leading into the forest.

"Wait up," Ryan called, running after her, but she

continued on, stumbling over rocks and brush until only the sound of rushing water brought her head up.

When Ryan reached her side, he knew why she had stopped, why the anger had suddenly fled, why she couldn't move, and why he couldn't move either. The river was more than just a few feet higher. It was half-way up the bank and churning with an anger and energy that overwhelmed them both.

"My God," he said, more to himself than her. "The monster returns."

Kara put a hand on his arm. He barely felt her touch. "Ryan? Are you all right?"

The words came from a lifetime ago. They were Andrew's words. His brother had said them over and over again as they waited in the old cabin for their father to rescue them. Ryan hadn't been able to answer his brother then, and he couldn't answer Kara now.

"Ryan." Kara touched his face. He jerked away. He had to get away. He could hear her calling after him. He could hear Andrew. The past and present became one. All he knew was that the river was after him, and if he didn't escape, he would die.

## 20

"Ryan," Kara called as she ran after him.

Ryan didn't take the path to the park, but headed deeper into the woods. She didn't know what had set him off, but the anger she had felt toward him now turned to concern and worry.

The branches tore at her arms and face as she barreled through them. She had to save Ryan from whatever or whoever was chasing him. She was the one who had brought him back to the river. That made him her responsibility.

Despite her repeated cries to stop, Ryan kept going. Finally, using her last bit of energy, she tackled him like a linebacker and sent them both flying onto the rocky, uneven ground.

Kara landed on top of Ryan. A dozen sharp pine needles stabbed her hands where they landed on either side of Ryan's body, drawing tears to her eyes at the painful stinging sensation.

A pack of birds scattered in squawking protest at their invasion, and a family of squirrels scrambled into the trees, escaping the chaos below. Then the sounds of nature disappeared, replaced only by the sound of their breathing, fast and furious.

"Ryan, are you all right?" Kara asked as she picked some of the needles from her hands.

Ryan groaned. "If you wanted to jump me, you could have just told me."

She laughed with relief. "You scared the hell out of me." She slid off his back.

"So what? I think you killed me." He rolled over onto his back. "Did we just land in a pit of knives or what?"

"Pine needles."

"Same thing." He closed his eyes.

Kara studied his face for a long moment. It was a strong face with a square jaw, well-defined bones, and thick, bushy eyebrows softened only by impossibly long black lashes. There was a fine scar under his chin and another off to the corner of his right eye.

Several pine needles clung to his chin. Carefully she pulled them away from his skin, noting several red scratches that would linger for the next day or two.

Scars and flaws, she thought. The man had too many to count. He shouldn't have been appealing to her at all. But he was. Probably because he wasn't perfect, just human, and probably because he had the greatest pair of eyes she had ever seen, the sexiest lips she had ever tasted.

"Kara?"

She started. "What?"

Ryan sat up. He brushed needles off the front of his denim shirt, carefully avoiding her questioning eyes.

Finally he spoke. "Did I just embarrass myself?"

"Completely."

"You couldn't lie?"

"No." She looked him straight in the eye. "Now, do you want to tell me what your little dash through the forest was all about?"

Ryan sat back on his heels. "The river. It—"

"It what?"

"It terrifies me."

"Why?"

Ryan pulled at the collar of his shirt, as if he were choking on his emotions. "You ask too many questions."

"That's not an answer."

"It's stupid."

"Tell me, Ryan. Tell me why you don't like the water."

Ryan got to his feet and walked over to a tree. He peeled off a piece of bark and worked at it with his fingers as he thought about what he wanted to say. Kara waited patiently, trying not to push him but desperately hoping he wouldn't brush her off, wouldn't tell her that she couldn't possibly understand.

She wanted to understand, to know him as a man, not as a celebrity or a rebel son or a black-sheep brother, for that matter. She wanted to make her own decision about him, not clouded by the judgments of others.

"The last time the river flooded, Jonas took Andrew and me to an old cabin in the north woods. He said we would be safe there." Ryan's mouth tightened at the memory. "Jonas stayed away that whole day. Andrew didn't care that we were alone. He wanted to watch the water rise; he was as fascinated by the river as Jonas was. But I didn't like it, so I stayed indoors. I wanted my mother. I even wanted Jonas at that point. But he didn't come back, not even when it got dark. The next day the river grew higher." Ryan closed his eyes as the memories washed over him.

*Andrew flung open the door to the cabin, his eyes alight with excitement. "The river is hitting the bottom step, Ryan. Come and see."*

*Ryan stood behind one of the kitchen chairs, holding on to the arm with a grip so tight his knuckles turned white. "I want to go home."*

*"We can't go anywhere. The driveway is flooded."*

*Ryan licked his lips. "Dad will be back soon, right?"*

*Andrew gave him a look that was a mixture of pity and triumph. "Are you scared?"*

*"No."*

*"You are scared."*

*"I am not."*

*"Are too."*

*Andrew grabbed Ryan's hand and pulled him toward the door. Ryan dragged his feet, but his older brother was too strong, too determined.*

*"I don't want to see it," Ryan said. "Let me go."*

*Andrew pushed him into the doorway. "Look at her, Ryan. She's roaring."*

*Like a snake, the river lifted its head and snapped its tongue at them, showering the front steps with water as if intent on devouring them. It was the monster of his nightmares. It was unstoppable. Ryan ran away from Andrew, into the back bedroom, into the bathroom. He locked the door and began to cry.*

*Andrew pounded on the door, demanding to be let in. Ryan wouldn't open it. He sat in the corner of the bathroom, counting the dirty tiles, concentrating on the spider weaving its web in the corner of the window, contemplating the yellow stain of urine around the toilet bowl. He hated this bathroom. He hated this cabin. He hated the stupid river.*

*He didn't know how long it was before Andrew knocked on the door again. This time his voice sounded panicked. "Open up, Ryan. I need your help."*

*Ryan was going to refuse until he saw the water seeping under the door frame. The river was inside the house.*

*He opened the door and looked into the face of the monster. "We're going to die," he wailed.*

*"We have to get on the roof," Andrew said. "Come on, we'll climb up the trellis out back."*

*Ryan followed his brother, wading through six inches of water on his way to the back door. The weathered rose trellis was old and splintery and looked as if it*

*could fall apart, but the water swirling around their feet
sent both their heads skyward.*

*"You go first," Andrew said.*

*"I can't do it." Actually under normal circumstances
Ryan probably could have climbed to the roof faster than
Andrew. But he couldn't think. He was mesmerized by
the river, watching it eat away everything it came in
contact with.*

*"Come on," Andrew yelled at him over the roar of
the river. "Move it, you jerk."*

*"You go," Ryan ground out between tight lips. He
couldn't move. He was paralyzed. He was going to die
in this very spot.*

*Andrew pushed him toward the trellis, forcing him
to move, calling him a chicken and a coward and a
stupid idiot and every other name he could come up
with until Ryan forgot about the river and just wanted
to get away from Andrew.*

*When Ryan finally reached the roof, he sprawled out
on the shingles, trying to catch his breath as Andrew
landed somewhat clumsily next to him. They looked out
at the river. There was no land in sight. They were all
alone in a swirling, churning sea of brown, muddy water.*

*They clung to each other on that roof through the
long, lonely hours of the day, two brothers who could
only count on each other.*

"Andrew saved your life," Kara said, startling Ryan
out of the past.

He tossed the piece of bark onto the ground. "Yeah,
I guess he did."

"So you didn't always hate each other?"

"No. That came later. We were never that bad when
it was just the two of us, but when Jonas was around,
he'd pit us against each other. I don't know, maybe
Becky Lee did the same thing."

Kara walked over to him. "I'm sorry, Ryan."

"For what?"

"For what you went through." She paused. "I remember that storm, too. I was more afraid of the thunder and the lightning than the water. I thought the end of the world was coming. I remember those nights at the shelter. The old men snored, the old ladies grumbled, and the babies cried. I just lay there, feeling alone."

He touched her hair. "How did you get through it?"

"I hid under the quilt my aunt Josephine made for me, telling myself stories, pretending the outside world didn't exist. I wanted my dad to come to the shelter and hold me in his big, strong arms and make everything bad go away. But my mother said he was trying to save the theater and he would come when he was done. He never came, and we eventually left to go to the city. I never saw the river the way you did. So all my memories of the town were good ones. The only good ones, because once we moved the rest of my life fell apart." Kara took a breath. "I guess the flood changed both our lives."

"More than you know," Ryan said, his voice suddenly husky, his body too close to hers, his fingers entwined in the strands of her hair. "I want you, Kara."

The statement was so bold, so abrupt, Kara didn't know what to say. But a reply wasn't possible, because Ryan's mouth covered hers and he kissed her as if his life depended on it, as if she could give him back what he had lost, as if he could do the same for her.

And maybe he could. Because she kissed him with the same sense of desperation. Time was running out. She could feel it in her bones, in her heart, in her soul. She couldn't hold back the river, and she couldn't hold back the desire she felt for this man. She wanted him, too.

She wanted to make love, to taste his mouth, to feel his lips against her breasts. She wanted to wrap herself around him, to take his power and strength and make them hers. To give him back the softness, the loving that she sensed he needed, even though he would never admit such vulnerability.

Ryan slid his mouth along her jawline. He nipped at the edge of her ear with his teeth and ran his tongue along the tip, bringing a shudder through her soul.

"Don't stop," she whispered.

Strangely enough, it was her words that made him stop, that made him lift his head and question her with his eyes.

"No?" he asked.

"No."

He dropped his hands from behind her neck and took a step back. "I can't believe this. You're saying yes, and I'm saying—no."

"Actually I just said no." Actually Kara was totally confused and more than a little annoyed. "What are you—some kind of a tease?" she demanded. The words came out of her past, from her ex-husband's mouth. She knew exactly how deep they could wound. Only Ryan didn't look wounded; he looked amused.

"I've never been accused of that." He paused. "Kara, you're a nice woman, and I'm leaving in the morning."

She tossed her hair back over her shoulder. "I'm tired of being a nice woman," she said, feeling as foolish as her words, but it was too late to take them back. "Maybe I just want a fling. Maybe I don't care that you're leaving. Maybe I prefer it that way. I happen to like sex."

"I'm glad to hear it."

"You're laughing at me."

"A little." Actually he wasn't laughing at her as much as he was enjoying her. She was a lovely, passionate woman, as down-to-earth as the ground they were sitting on, her eyes as blue as the sky, her hair as red as the trees. And redwood trees lasted forever. They were strong and tough and glorious. Just like Kara. They were also too beautiful to be messed with.

"Let's go back," Ryan said.

"No." When Ryan started to walk away, Kara pushed him back. He lost his footing and landed flat on his back, moaning for the second time that day. Kara took advantage of his situation, straddling him with her legs, her inner thighs caressing a very sensitive part of his body. Ryan instinctively hardened against her. "What the hell are you doing?" he muttered.

"Taking charge," she said with a pleased smile. "I'm tired of men making all the decisions. You get to kiss me when you want and stop when you want. What about what I want?"

He placed his hands on her shoulders and pulled her down on top of him. "What do you want, Kara?"

"You," she whispered. "I know it's crazy and irresponsible and the absolute wrong thing to do. But I want it anyway."

"That kind of thinking can get you into big trouble."

"I'll take that chance." She kissed him on the mouth, taking her time, taking what she wanted; and Ryan let her, even though it was painfully difficult not to strip her sweater from her body, push down her jeans and get inside her.

But as much as Ryan wanted to hurry, he also wanted the moment to last forever. And he had never wanted anything to last forever. That thought scared him to death. Suddenly he wasn't worried anymore about hurting her. He was worried about hurting himself.

Kara didn't appear to be worrying about anything as she caressed the side of his face with her hands and pressed her lips against his jawbone, his nose, his eyes, his forehead. Every time she touched him, a flashbulb went off behind his eyes, illuminating his feelings, bathing his desire in a bright light that he couldn't escape behind. He wasn't taking the photograph. He was in it.

And like a Polaroid, he was coming alive, each second bringing him heightened awareness, heightened desire.

He grabbed her shoulders and held her away from him so he could see her expression. The same emotions were written in her eyes, the same need, even the same fear of getting involved. They were both wary. They were both scared. But damn if they weren't great together.

Kara lifted her head as raindrops began to fall on her hair, clinging to the red strands like clusters of diamonds. It was a perfect opportunity for her to move, for them to laugh off the moment.

Kara did move. But instead of getting off him, she pulled her sweater over her head and tossed it on the ground, revealing a black lacy bra that barely covered her lush white breasts and a stream of freckles that absolutely fascinated him.

He cupped her breasts with his hands, watching her face, watching her come alive for him.

"Make love to me, Ryan."

"It's raining, Kara."

"I want to get wet—with you."

"Oh, God," he groaned. "I thought you would be the sensible one."

"And I thought you would be the one ripping my clothes off. Looks like I'll have to do everything," she teased, unbuttoning his denim shirt with deliberate and purposeful fingers.

He grabbed her wrist. "Are you sure?"

"No, but let's do it anyway."

She pulled his shirt apart and stroked his chest with her fingers, eyeing him like some kind of dessert. Ryan suddenly wondered if he could satisfy her. He had never doubted his ability to please a woman before now, when it had suddenly become important to please this woman.

The rain came down harder, slicking her hair against her head, running in rivulets down the side of his face and chest. Kara unfastened her bra, letting the edges dangle teasingly against the sides of her breasts. She watched Ryan's face, taking delight in the way he let her control the pace. He met each of her moves with one of his own, but he didn't toss her on her back, didn't roll on top of her and take her before she was ready. He waited and watched, moving his fingers, then his mouth against her breasts.

Ryan's hands worked at her blue jeans, unfastening her belt, the snaps, pushing them down over her hips while he tortured her breasts with his mouth.

She pressed down on him, not wanting his jeans between them either. Not wanting anything between them. But he made a liar out of that thought when his fingers came between them, and she could think of nothing but his stroking fingers, his teasing mouth, the pressure building within her. She cried out his name as her body shuddered and shook with the force of her desire until she finally came to rest on top of him.

He gave her a wicked smile. "You called?"

"That wasn't fair. I wanted to do it together." She tugged on his jeans.

"Kara." His voice turned serious.

"What?"

"I don't have anything with me. No protection," he added when she gave him a blank look.

Protection? As in condoms? As in pregnancy? As in AIDS? Kara suddenly realized what she was doing. "Oh. But—"

"It's okay." He pulled the edges of her bra back together and fastened the clasp.

"It's not okay. Unless you don't—" She couldn't finish the sentence out loud. All her doubts and insecurities came back to haunt her. Michael had never been satisfied with her. Maybe Ryan wouldn't be either.

Maybe he didn't even want her to begin with. She had practically attacked him.

Kara got up abruptly, pulling up her jeans and reaching for her waterlogged sweater, which was now covered in pine needles. Apart from Ryan she felt the cold run right through her.

"I do want you," Ryan said as he stood up. "More than you can imagine."

"Obviously not enough to throw caution to the wind."

"Is that what you want? Because we can do it right here, right now, and to hell with the consequences. That's how I've lived most of my life. But I don't think it's the way you live your life, is it?"

"No."

"We can go back to the house," Ryan said. "We can go up to my bedroom and take up exactly where we left off."

They could, but she knew they wouldn't. The moment had passed. Back at the house she would be reminded of everything she was supposed to be—mother, niece, innkeeper, girlfriend, community leader, and everything that she wasn't supposed to be—sexy, free spirited, and completely uninhibited. Maybe that's why she was attracted to Ryan. She wanted what he had. She wanted it so bad she could almost taste it. She could almost taste him.

Then the rain came down in a torrent and washed away the lingering scent of his mouth on hers.

"I remember the first time I parked at this spot with Brian Sayers," Loretta said, rubbing the steam off the front window of Andrew's truck so she could see the river again. "Just like last time, everything's all fogged up."

Andrew smiled at her. "But we're not having as much fun."

"We could be."

"I'm not seventeen anymore." Andrew finished off the last bit of beer and stashed it in the now empty lunch box. "That was good."

"You look tired," Loretta said. "Rough night?"

"Rough weekend. I had another round with Ryan this morning. He got my father out of the hospital."

"I figured Jonas wouldn't stay put for long." She paused. "Do you think Ryan could have stopped him from leaving?"

"He could have tried harder."

"You can't give him a break, can you?"

"Why should I? All these years he . . ." Andrew's voice drifted away. He tapped his fingers against the steering wheel, debating his options. He needed to talk to someone about the letter, someone who would be on his side. Finally he reached into his pocket and pulled out the folded piece of paper. He held it up in front of Loretta's curious eyes. "Ryan gave me this. It's a letter my mother wrote to my father twenty-five years ago. Take it."

"I couldn't. That's private. Between a man and a woman."

"I want you to read it. I want you to help me understand it."

Loretta took the paper out of his hand and opened it. She sat back in her seat as she read the words of passion and despair, the words his mother had penned so many years earlier. Andrew could almost see her sitting at the desk in her bedroom, the tip of her pen pressed against her lips as she looked out the window and thought about what she wanted to say.

Had she been thinking of him at all? Or had all her thoughts been of Jonas and her lover? The word tore him apart. He felt incredibly jealous of that lover, of the man she had wanted more than Jonas, more than Ryan, more than himself. Why couldn't his mother have loved him the way he loved her? What had he done wrong?

Loretta's hand shook as she lowered the letter to her

lap. Tears gathered in her eyes, and a look of pain and understanding spread across her face. "Oh, Andrew. That's so sad. To love someone and not have them."

"But she had us." Andrew couldn't believe how bitter he sounded, how hurt and disappointed. "I guess we weren't enough."

"She loved you, Andrew. Didn't you read that part?" Loretta glanced down at the letter again. "Didn't you hear her talking to you in her sweet voice as she wrote the words, 'I love my children more than life, how can I be parted from them? Please, Jonas, I beg you not to separate me from the boys.'" Loretta paused. "She didn't want to leave you, Andrew."

"But she did. You can tell me it was Jonas's fault. But dammit, Loretta, she had a choice, and she made it."

"Yes, she did."

Loretta ran her hand down the side of his face, a loving, poignant gesture that reminded him of his mother, of all the touches he had missed. He grabbed her wrist, not wanting to be reminded, not wanting to need that affection again. "Don't," he said.

"I feel so bad for you, Andrew. I remember losing my mother, but that was different. She was so sick at the end, it made it easier to let her go. Pop, too. But the way you lost your mother, so sudden, in such an unexplainable way. How you must have hurt."

He had hurt deeply, silently, unable to share his burden with anyone, not his brother, not his father, not even Becky Lee. But with Loretta he suddenly felt he could let it out. He could tell her the truth.

"She just didn't love me—enough," Andrew said, his voice catching on the last word.

Loretta threw her arms around his neck, put her head on his chest, and began to cry. Her sobs tore at his heart. And suddenly he was crying along with her, silently shaking as the tears ran down his face, releasing the pain of a lifetime. They stayed that way for a long time until they were both spent, until the rushing sounds of the river calmed them both.

"I can't be with Kara," Andrew said. "Not after this. Not knowing it was her father who . . ."

"This letter has nothing to do with Kara. She was a child at the time."

"It was her father who broke up my family."

"Maybe she's the one who can bring you back together."

Andrew thought about that for a moment. "Maybe," he said somewhat reluctantly. It was hard to think of Kara while he held Loretta in his arms.

Loretta grimaced and put a hand to her stomach. She sat back and took a deep breath.

"What's wrong?" he asked.

"Nothing. Just false labor. I'll be okay."

That's right. She was having a baby. How could he keep forgetting that?

"We better go," Andrew said.

"Wait." Loretta suddenly looked nervous. "I want to tell you something."

"Okay."

Loretta didn't speak for a long moment.

"What is it?" he encouraged.

"I want to name the baby Andrew if it's a boy."

Loretta's words shocked the hell out of him. "Why? You should name the kid after someone you love—I mean, someone in your family or something."

"I love you, Andrew."

She said the words with such stark simplicity that he couldn't believe he had heard her right.

"What?"

Loretta's eyebrows drew together in a serious frown as she stared out the window. "It's okay. You don't have to say it back. I know you want Kara. You want the kind of life that she can give you. But I won't pretend anymore."

"You can't love me. We've never even been together."

"Maybe that's why I love you." She took in a deep breath. "It's funny, really. All those years I kept looking for love in sex. I thought that was the only way to get it. But I never really felt anything. Never. Not even with this baby's father. I tried so hard to feel something, Andrew, but it never came. The other night when you kissed me, and when you held me in your arms just now, when you trusted me enough to cry, I knew that I had found what I have been missing all these years."

"Loretta, you don't know what you're saying."

"It's okay, Andrew. I'll probably regret this in the morning." She tried to laugh, but it came out as more of a sob. "Like I've regretted so many things in the morning. I know you can't love a woman like me. Anyway, that's it. I want to name the baby Andrew, but I won't," she added. "Because then everyone would think—well, you know what they would think."

That he was the father. Suddenly that didn't seem so bad.

"Anyway, end of confession," Loretta said with determined cheerfulness. "Let's go back."

Andrew started the car. He wanted to say something to fill the silence between them, but he was truly lost in his emotions, torn between the woman he wanted and the woman he knew he should want more.

"I'm afraid of making another mistake," he said as he pulled out onto the highway.

"I'm not Becky Lee."

"No, but you're like her. I was a big disappointment to Becky Lee. She couldn't wait to get away from me. I expect you would feel the same soon enough. Becky Lee probably would have left earlier if it hadn't been for the baby. Of course, she probably wouldn't have married me in the first place if it hadn't been for Billy."

"She was pregnant?"

"Yeah." The word fell out of his mouth like a lead weight. "She was pregnant and scared and madly in love with my brother."

"Then why did you marry her?"

"Because it was the right thing to do." His hands gripped the steering wheel as he turned toward Castaway Park. "I did care for her. And when Billy was born, I fell in love with both of them. I wanted to be a good husband and father, but she didn't give me a chance."

"You are a good father."

"No, I'm not. I'm turning into Jonas, a man who has no idea what to say to his son. And it's worse now with Ryan here. I wish he would leave. I want Ryan out of this town and out of my life and as far away from Billy as I can get him. I can't lose my son, too."

"Why would you?" Loretta asked. "What would Ryan want with your son?"

Andrew didn't answer her. He couldn't say it out loud, not even to Loretta.

She didn't say anything more until they reached the park, and he turned off the engine. "Billy is your son, isn't he?"

"Of course Billy is my son." Andrew threw her a quick glance and saw the doubt in her eyes. "He is. Becky Lee told me I was the father."

"But she was sleeping with both of you. How could she know for sure?" Loretta asked with piercing logic.

"She knew."

"Maybe she lied."

"Why would she do that?"

Loretta sat back in her seat. "We both know the answer to that." Subconsciously she put a hand to her belly. "Some women can't stand the thought of being pregnant and alone."

Andrew heard the fear in her voice and knew she was relating Becky Lee to her own situation. But he also knew that Loretta had more courage than Becky Lee. She would never tell someone he was the father of her child if it wasn't true.

"Ryan isn't stupid, you know," Loretta continued,

turning to face him. "The longer he's in town, the more he's going to think about things, the more he's going to question."

"All the answers died with Becky Lee."

"He could force DNA testing."

Andrew felt the sweat bead along his brow. "I won't allow it. I am Billy's father. End of story."

Loretta sighed. "Oh, Andrew, somehow I don't think this story is anywhere near the end."

## 21

Kara went to bed that night wondering where Ryan had disappeared after the picnic, wondering why he had missed dinner and still hadn't returned home when it was past eleven. There weren't many places open this late, except Loretta's bar.

Maybe he had gone to Loretta's. Maybe he had sought comfort with some other woman, someone who knew the score, who knew to carry condoms in her purse and . . .

Tears welled in her eyes. She had kept them away for so many hours; there was no stopping them now. She cried for a missed opportunity. She cried for a man she shouldn't want and for every stupid mistake she had made in her life. The list seemed to go on forever. Most of all she cried because she felt helpless.

The river was rising. Ryan was leaving. Angel was growing up. Andrew was pulling away from her. Kara couldn't stop any of it. She felt powerless. So she did the only thing she could do; she pulled the covers over her head and tried to pretend the outside world didn't exist.

By morning the outside world was back again. A call from the mayor awoke Kara at 7 A.M. By 8 A.M. she had canceled the pancake breakfast. By nine she had organized groups of volunteers to start sandbagging around the library and the civic center, and called off the Centennial Parade.

By eleven she had set up a command post in the rec center, called the Red Cross to find out their procedures should the river actually flood, and by twelve she had poured more cups of coffee than she could count. So much for a leisurely Sunday.

Ryan spent the morning taking photographs. He had already caught her on film a few times, once with a bullhorn to her mouth acting incredibly bossy, and a second shot of her pouring coffee like a happy homemaker.

For some reason that thought irritated her. She untied her apron. Ryan snapped her photo again. She glared at him. He took another shot.

"Stop it already," she said with annoyance. "Take some pictures of the real workers."

Ryan raised an eyebrow. "What happened to Miss Congeniality?"

"She's tired." Kara pulled the tie out of her hair so the waves fell loosely against her shoulders. She rolled her neck to one side, then the other.

"Why don't you take a break?"

"I'm planning to do just that."

Ryan followed her over to a bench just outside the library. She scowled at him. "I thought you were leaving."

He sat down next to her. "I've got all day. Anything I can do to help?"

"Just hold the river back, Superman."

His expression sobered. "I tried that once, remember? It didn't work."

She put her hand over his, suddenly feeling guilty. "I'm sorry. I shouldn't have said that."

"I'm sorry, too—for yesterday."

"You were right. It would have been a mistake."

They sat in quiet for a while. Ryan played with her

hand, teasingly, caressingly, like a lover. She pulled her
hand away and slid down to the end of the bench.

"Are you sure you're far enough away?"

"I need space, Ryan. I feel claustrophobic."

The edges of her life were closing in on her, not just
the water but Ryan and Andrew and Angel and the
townspeople, all with their own demands, their own
needs, their own desires. How could she hope to please
everyone when she couldn't even make herself happy?

"Why don't you come with me?" Ryan said suddenly. "We could go anywhere you want. You could be
anyone you want to be—bad girl, nice woman, whatever."

"It's tempting, but no."

"Why not?"

"Because you can't chase happiness. My mother did
that. We moved every other year. I've lived in big cities,
Ryan. Oh, I haven't been to Paris or the wilds of Africa,
but I've been to L.A."

"Which is close."

She smiled reluctantly. "Besides, I like the sense of
community and family that we have here. I don't want
to leave."

"Not even now with the river threatening to destroy
everything in its wake?"

"River people are tough. They're survivors. They
stand up and fight, and even when they lose they get
back on their feet and rebuild. They start over, no matter how many times the river comes up—"

"Because living by the river is worth the risk of losing
everything," Ryan finished bitterly. "Spare me, Kara.
I've heard it before, many times."

Kara fell silent, knowing there was nothing she could
say to change his mind. Ryan had spent more of his life
here than she had. If he didn't know what the town had
to offer by now, then he never would.

Ryan leaned forward, resting his hands on his knees.
"What if you fell in love with someone, Kara? Someone

who didn't want to live here? Would you go with him? Hypothetically speaking, of course."

Kara glanced down at her hands, at the tan line that still reminded her of her wedding ring. She had promised to love Michael through better or worse, in sickness and in health. And she had broken those vows. The good hadn't been good enough and the bad had been much worse than she could handle.

But even though her first marriage had ended in failure, she knew that someday she would try again, that being married and loving one man for the rest of her life were exactly what she wanted. Could she give up this place, this haven she had chosen for herself and Angel? Could she put it all aside for the love of one man?

"Well?" Ryan prodded.

She sighed. "Would I follow the man I loved to the ends of the earth? Is that what you're asking?"

"At least down the road and onto the highway?"

"I'm not sure. I would be afraid, Ryan, to love someone more than he loved me. I know Michael turned out to be a big loser, but I did love him once, more than I had ever loved anyone. I went wherever he wanted. I tried to make a home in every dreary little apartment he took me to. I don't want to do that again. I don't want to be dependent on a man for my happiness."

"Then you wouldn't go. Of course, you don't have to go. We both know Andrew would rather die than leave this place. And you and Andrew are a couple, right?"

"Right." Kara could not look him in the eye, not after yesterday, not after she had practically seduced him by the river.

"But you haven't slept together."

Kara cleared her throat. "I don't think that's any of your business."

"You made it my business yesterday. Has Andrew seen you naked? Does he know about that cute freckle just above your left breast?"

"Stop it, Ryan."

"How can you marry him when you want me?" Ryan shook his head in complete bewilderment. "What does the guy have that I don't?"

"Staying power."

"Sweetheart, you don't know anything about my staying power."

Kara couldn't stop the flush from spreading across her cheeks. "I'm not talking about sex. I'm talking about staying here."

"And that's enough for you?"

"Yes. Besides, what about you? Would you stay in a place you hated if the woman you loved didn't want to leave? Hypothetically speaking, of course."

His lips curved into a regretful smile. "No—for the same reason. I would be the one who loved more."

"We're both cowards."

"I guess."

Kara stood up. "We might as well say good-bye now." She stuck out her hand. Ryan reluctantly shook it. But when she opened her mouth to say the words, he shook his head, his expression suddenly pained.

"I hate good-byes," he said. "I take after my mother. She couldn't say good-bye either. You know, Kara, this town has broken up a lot of marriages. My parents', your parents'. Are you sure this is where you want to be?"

"I think so."

"This isn't a Norman Rockwell painting. The people here are real, and they can be nasty as hell. When you get past the cozy shops on Main Street and the friendly diner down the road, you'll find the same problems in this town as anywhere else. Serenity Springs is not a quilt you can pull over your head to make your problems go away."

"But that's what I want it to be," she whispered. "I can't help it."

"What are you so afraid of facing?"

"Look, this isn't getting us anywhere. Thank you for coming to the centennial. I hope you enjoyed yourself. Maybe you could send me some of the photos, if you want to, that is."

His face tightened with anger at her cool tone. "Of course. That's why you invited me, isn't it?"

Ryan dug his hands into his pockets. Kara shifted her feet.

"Well, see you later," she said.

"Later."

As Kara turned her head, she suddenly became aware of a woman staring at them from the library steps. It was Margaret Woodrich.

Ryan stiffened. Kara could feel his tension. When he moved, she impulsively put a hand on his arm. "Don't," she said.

"I have to talk to her. I have to set her straight before I go."

"She won't listen. She doesn't want to understand."

"Too bad. I've spent the last twelve years being the bad guy. I think I deserve a chance to tell the truth."

"Which is what?"

"I didn't kill Becky Lee."

"You weren't driving the car, but she was going to see you."

"I know, but that wasn't my fault. I didn't ask her to come." Ryan looked at Kara in desperation. "What do I say? How do I convince her?"

"Maybe you could start by saying that you loved Becky Lee," Kara suggested. "You did, didn't you?"

"For a few months, more than life itself."

"Then tell her that. It won't be enough, but it will be something."

Something, Ryan thought as he walked over to Margaret Woodrich. He did owe this woman something. An explanation at the very least. Margaret stiffened, but she didn't walk away. One good sign.

"Mrs. Woodrich." Ryan stopped in front of her. She was smaller than he remembered, and older. Becky Lee and her mother had always been close, like sisters, and Margaret had never been able to say no to her only child. Even when Becky Lee missed curfew or cut school, her mother always gave in.

"Go away," Margaret said. "I have nothing to say to you." Ryan put a hand on her shoulder. She jumped. "Don't touch me."

"I'm sorry." Ryan hesitated, wondering if he shouldn't just leave, but he had been running for so long. His feet were tired of moving. "I just wanted to tell you that I'm sorry Becky Lee died so young. She deserved a lot more."

Margaret's eyes came alive with anger and pain. "She deserved more than you."

He winced at the direct hit. "You're right, she did, and she got it. She got Andrew. The better brother, the better son, and the better husband. I don't know why she left him. He would have done anything for her."

Margaret's mouth dropped open, obviously surprised by his attitude. "She didn't love Andrew," Margaret said. "She loved you. God help her."

"And I loved her. But we were young. We knew nothing of life. I couldn't stay here and marry her."

"Why not?"

"Because I wanted to see the world. And I couldn't take her with me. I had no money, no job. I had nothing."

"You had my daughter. You slept with her. She told me," Margaret said bitterly. "What kind of a man are you—to sleep with a young girl, then walk away from her?"

Ryan felt as if she had kicked him in the stomach. "I was the same age as Becky Lee. I wasn't taking advantage of her. We did what we did together."

"I have her diary, you know. She raved about you, the first time you spoke to her at school, the first time you kissed her." Margaret's voice caught on the word. "I tried to tell her you were no good, but she wouldn't listen."

"Of course she wouldn't. Becky Lee listened to only one person, and that was herself."

"How dare you criticize her?"

"I dare because I loved her, too. Okay? I loved her. How do you think I felt when she chose Andrew, when she agreed to marry my brother? I couldn't stick around and watch that. It hurt too much."

"Hurt? What do you know of hurt? You didn't lose your child. You didn't bury a beautiful young girl behind the church. You didn't hold her baby in your arms and listen to the pitiful cries of a child wanting his mother."

Ryan felt as if she were ripping him apart with each word. She was right, so right. He had photographed all the events she was describing, other people's pain, other people's misery. He had hidden behind his camera, playing it safe, staying objective, but now it was hitting him in the face. Actually Margaret was poking him in the chest with the tip of her finger, emphasizing each point.

"You didn't read her letter where she told of her deep unhappiness, her longing for a man she couldn't have," Margaret continued. "You didn't watch Becky Lee's father fade into a shadow. You didn't see the empty place at our dining room table. You don't know what hurt is. You have to love someone to feel pain. But what do you know of love? What do you know of anything?"

Margaret left, but her words stayed with him for a long time.

Kara turned away as Ryan and Mrs. Woodrich finished their conversation. She had no idea what had been said, but judging by the expression on Ryan's face, it was obviously painful. She wanted to go to him but didn't. They had said good-bye. It was time to move on.

In her hurry to get away, she stumbled and ran into someone's chest. She lifted her head in surprise. "Andrew." It seemed like ages since she had spoken to him.

"Are you all right?" he asked.

"Yes, I'm fine. I'm just taking a break."

He nodded, his expression strained. He looked at her as if she were a stranger, someone he had never seen before. "Is something wrong?" she asked.

"No, of course not."

"Are you sure? I didn't get a chance to talk to you at the picnic yesterday."

"It was crowded. I couldn't get to you."

Kara nodded, knowing deep down they were both lying. What had happened? When had things changed? When had they become so distant?

Andrew shifted his gaze, focusing on the volunteers shoveling sand into burlap bags that would be used to protect their homes and their lives.

"It's going well," Kara said. "People seem to have forgotten their differences and are pulling together as one team. Of course, we're barely making a dent. I'm hoping we won't have to do more."

"So am I."

"How is Jonas? Is he back at work?"

"No, but he is home. Ryan brought him home yesterday—without the doctor's permission, of course." His tone turned bitter. "I'm sure Ryan told you."

"No, he didn't." Kara moved to the edge of the sidewalk so people could get around them.

"He didn't tell you at the picnic or last night when you were alone at the Gatehouse?"

Resentment filled his voice, but instead of making her feel bad, it just made her angry. "No, Ryan didn't tell me at the picnic, and we wouldn't have even had lunch together if you had bought my basket like you were supposed to."

"He bid one hundred and fifty dollars."

"So it was the money that stopped you?"

"What else?"

"Maybe you wanted to eat with Loretta?"

"Don't be ridiculous."

"Is that what I'm being?" She put her hands on her hips.

"Yes," he said belligerently, as if he wanted to pick a fight with her. "You've been acting stupidly ever since you invited Ryan here."

"Stupidly? Now I'm stupid, too? Gee, I didn't know you had such a high impression of me."

"I did have a high impression. Until I found out you couldn't be trusted."

Kara felt his words like a slap on the cheek. "Because I invited your brother here?"

"No, because all these months you've made a fool out of me. Pretending we could have a relationship."

"I wasn't pretending. Although at this moment I have serious doubts."

"Doubts? I could never be with you, not when your father . . ."

Kara felt a sudden heaviness sink through her body. Her father—again. Ryan said he knew something about her father. Now Andrew. "When my father what?"

Andrew took a deep breath. "When your father screwed my mother."

Kara's jaw fell open. "What?"

"Your father broke up my family. He took my mother off to the big city, filling her head with promises of excitement and adventure. He convinced her to leave her children, for God's sake. The man had no decency."

Kara didn't know what to say. She understood the words coming out of his mouth, but they didn't make sense. Her father—his mother? Lovers? She put a shaky hand to her mouth, suddenly caught off guard by a wave of nausea.

No, it was impossible. She tried to remember, but there were so many faceless years in between when she hadn't seen her father, when she hadn't known him at all. Maybe she had never known him.

"I—I didn't know," she said slowly. "Are you sure?"

"Don't pretend. You had to have known."

"I didn't. And I'm not pretending. But I don't understand. How could your mother and my father, both married, have had an affair here—in a town where gossip runs faster than the river?" She paused. "And why didn't you ever tell me before?"

His eyes narrowed into slits. "Because I didn't know. Because my brother kept it to himself. All these years I thought I was the one closest to Jonas, but he and Ryan had this big secret." Andrew pulled the letter out of his pocket. "Here, read it for yourself. It's all there."

Kara stared at the paper, not sure she wanted to read it. "I can't."

Andrew shoved it into her hand. "Take it, Kara. You started this. You invited Ryan home. Now you have to pay the consequences along with the rest of us."

"Why are you so angry with me?" she whispered, truly taken aback by the viciousness of his tone.

"Because he's your father, dammit. He's your flesh and blood. When I look at you, I think of him, of what he did. How can I be with you? How can we make love? In the back of my mind, I would be seeing them instead of us."

"So that's it? Ryan hands you a letter about a twenty-five-year-old affair, and we're through? I guess we didn't have much to start with, did we?" She uttered a bitter laugh. "I've spent this entire weekend worrying that Ryan would somehow break us up, but lo and behold my father did it instead, and he's been dead for ten years." She paused. "And where is your mother, Andrew? Where is this woman whom my father supposedly led astray? I sure as hell never saw her with him, and he never mentioned her, not once."

"They must have broken up after they left here."

"Or maybe they were never together at all. Maybe this is not the truth. Maybe it's a lie."

"I don't think I can tell the difference anymore. Maybe I never could."

## 22

"Tell us another story," Melissa said as she ran down to the river next to Billy and Angel.

"It's not a story; it's the truth," Angel declared as they stopped a good ten feet from the water's edge. They couldn't get close to Tucker's Bridge today. It was almost completely covered, and the water had risen at least six more feet up the bank. "Isn't it wild?" Angel asked. "I love it like this."

Billy hung back, not wanting to get too close. Melissa also looked concerned. "Don't go any farther," Billy said. "You might get washed away."

"I'm not scared of the water. I wish I could take a raft out on it right now."

"You're crazy," Melissa stated. "No one can boat on the river when it's like this. Maybe we better go back."

"Wait. I didn't tell you about the ghost. I saw her again."

Melissa looked at her with disappointment. "Tell us a new story, Angel. That one is boring."

"It's not a story," Angel protested again.

"What did she say this time?" Billy asked with a long-suffering sigh of loyalty.

Angel hesitated, then plunged ahead. "She said she was an Indian princess when the first white man came to the river. She fell in love with one of the loggers, but she couldn't tell her parents, because they would never let her marry a white man. So they met in secret on the bridge every night at midnight. Until one night, when he didn't come back. She cried so many tears that the river rose two feet; then she went home and waited until the following night when she could go back."

"Was he there?" Melissa asked, suddenly caught up by the new twist in the story.

Angel shook her head. "No. She waited until dawn. She cried and cried until her heart was bleeding. The river rose two more feet. The next day, the third night, she returned to the river. And the same thing happened. By the end of the week, she had given up all hope of ever seeing the man she loved. She knew her father had done something terrible to him, that he might be dead, and she couldn't bear to live without him."

"What did she do?" Melissa asked with a hushed voice.

"On the seventh night, under a full moon, she cried until the river rose so high it washed over her body. She was swept off the bridge and into the dark, swirling waters. And as she looked back at the bridge, she saw him. He had finally come for her, but it was too late. He reached out his hand for her, but she couldn't grasp his fingers. He cried out her name and jumped into the water after her. She struggled to get to him, but she couldn't do it. The water held her down until she could no longer breathe."

Angel pointed toward the bridge, where only the top railing was visible. "She's still there, and at night, every night, she comes looking for him. Because she knows that somewhere in the river he waits for her, and that one night they'll be reunited for all of eternity."

"Oh, wow," Melissa breathed. "That is so romantic."

"I thought you said she was looking for something," Billy interrupted.

"She is. A necklace, she said. I think he gave it to her

the first night they met. She has to find it. Because once she has it in her hand, he'll come back to her, and they'll be together forever and ever. We have to help her." Angel took two more steps down the bank.

"You can't go down there," Melissa said. "You'll drown just like she did."

"But we can't leave her trapped for all of eternity."

"I can," Melissa said. "I have to go home. My mom will kill me if she finds out I got this close to the water."

Angel turned to Billy as Melissa left. "Are you leaving, too?"

"It's spooky down here. Let's go."

"You don't believe me, do you?"

"No, I don't," Billy said somewhat apologetically. "Come on, Angel."

Angel crossed her arms in front of her chest. "I'll find the necklace by myself. You're just a chicken anyway."

"I am not."

"You are, too."

"Why do you make up all these stupid stories?" Billy asked with anger in his voice. "Everyone knows they're not true."

"They are true."

"My dad says your dad isn't a spy," Billy added. "He's a traveling salesman. That's all he is."

Angel sucked in a deep breath as his words hit her hard. "That's just his cover."

"And I heard your mom talking to my dad one night. Your mom said your dad had lots of other women. That he never wanted to come home."

"That's not true. She's lying," Angel cried.

Billy stared at her in shock, suddenly realizing what he had said. "Uh, An-Angel," he stuttered.

She glared at him, forcing the tears back behind her eyelids. "Go away."

"I'm—I'm sorry."

She picked up a stick and tossed it at him. "I don't want to talk to you ever again." She ran down the bank until she was at the edge of the water. She knew Billy wouldn't follow her there. And he didn't. He kept calling her name. Finally he stopped. And when it had been quiet for a long time, she turned around. He was gone.

Angel wiped the tears from her cheek with the cuff of her sweater. She couldn't believe her mother had told Andrew about her father. How could she tell all their secrets?

"Angel."

The soft voice filled her with warmth, and she lifted her head. The lady floated above the bridge, her expression loving but sad.

"Why are you crying?"

"I don't know. I think I hate my father." Her face got so tight, she felt an ache through her cheekbones. "And I hate my mother for marrying him, and most of all I hate myself for making everything bad happen."

"You? A beautiful little girl who tells stories that light up the heavens?"

Angel smiled reluctantly. "Did you like it?"

"I only wish I were an Indian princess. To think that the man I loved would have died for me rather than let me go. But I fear that kind of love is only true in stories. And I suspect that perfect families only exist in stories too. Is that why you tell so many of them?"

"I guess. They make me feel better."

"You miss your father, don't you?"

"Yes. At least I miss having a father. I just want a family again, a mom and a dad, the way it's supposed to be."

"Maybe I can help you."

"How?"

The lady moved closer to the tree, so close that she almost blended in with the branches. If she hadn't been wearing the yellow and red scarf, Angel probably wouldn't have been able to see her at all.

"Did you give the watch to Ryan?" the lady asked.

"Yes. He didn't want it though."

"I had hoped . . ."

"What? What did you hope?"

"It doesn't matter anymore. I still need the locket, Angel. Time is running out. The river will flood by Thursday."

"How do you know that?"

"I just do. You must tell everyone to move to higher ground. You must tell Jonas Hunter, especially. The river will not bend to his will, not this time."

"Mr. Hunter?" Angel asked doubtfully. "I don't think he'll listen to me."

"We must find the locket, Angel. Perhaps if you take it to him, he will understand."

"Understand what?"

"What it means to love someone. Then perhaps Ryan and Andrew will also understand, and you will have a chance at getting that family you want."

"Really?" Angel stood up and began looking among the rocks and bushes, but she saw nothing. "I don't think I can find it for you," she said, feeling hopeless at the prospect.

"You must try every day in the evening, at dusk. I will help you. Promise me you will come back, Angel."

"I promise." Angel didn't know why she said yes. She didn't even know why she was talking to what was probably a low cloud caught in the branches of a weeping willow.

"And Angel, promise me one more thing."

"What?"

"That you won't stop believing in happy endings. I wish I hadn't stopped believing. Maybe then things would have been different. But I gave up, Angel. Don't ever give up on the people you love. Go after Billy and make your peace. Kiss your mother good night. And if you can't forgive your father, then lock his bad deed away in a place where it can't touch you again."

The lady's voice rose and fell like a melody, a soothing lullaby, so soft that Angel kept blinking her eyes.

She must have fallen asleep for a second, because she suddenly opened her eyes and she was sitting on the ground, and there was no ghost. There was no one around.

A shiver ran down her spine. Billy was right. This place was spooky. And the river was getting higher. Would it really flood by Thursday? Could she really tell Jonas Hunter to leave his house? He would never believe her—not in a million years. But maybe her Aunt Josephine would.

Kara stormed into her aunt's antiques shop, knocking over a basket of papier-mâché eggs and a silver tin full of assorted buttons. Aunt Josephine sent her a mild, undisturbed smile.

"Hello, dear. I'm making some tea, would you like some?"

"No." Kara put the letter down on the counter, carefully smoothing out the edges. "What I want is an explanation—of this."

"What is it? I can't read without my glasses."

Kara reached around behind her and pulled her glasses off the shelf. "Here."

Josephine reluctantly put them on. She read silently for several minutes while Kara drummed her fingers relentlessly against the glass countertop. She still couldn't believe what she had read. Her father and Ryan's mother—how could such a thing have happened, especially in this small town?

Finally Josephine looked up. "I always wondered about Isabelle."

"Are you saying you didn't know my father was having an affair?" Kara demanded. "How can that be? You know everything. You even have a crystal ball, for God's sake. How could you have missed something as important as this?"

"I didn't miss it. I just never knew for sure."

"But he was your brother."

"I know you want an explanation, but I'm not sure I can give you one."

Kara paced restlessly around the space, wishing she had more room, wishing she could break something, wishing she wasn't continually caught off guard by the people in her life. "I thought my parents loved each other," she said finally. "I thought everything was perfect when we lived here. They were happy together. I remember them sitting on the couch, listening to you play the piano. Dad would stroke Mom's hair. She would kiss him on the cheek. They would laugh together. Was it all just an act?"

"Not all of it," Josephine said. "But your parents obviously had problems. They got a divorce."

"But not till they left, not till the Gatehouse was flooded and the theater couldn't be rebuilt. Dad couldn't start over with us in the city. He was too depressed, too restless. That's why he took off."

"I don't think that's how it happened," Josephine said gently. "I think your father and mother had problems that went much deeper than where they were to live. I can't tell you what they were. Harry didn't confide in me. Oh, I would hear them argue now and then, but I wasn't privy to their confidences."

Kara tossed her hair in an angry, frustrated gesture. "I don't understand. I came back here to find the happiness I once had, only to discover now that it was all an illusion. My father was screwing Mrs. Hunter."

"The letter doesn't say that, and you don't know that they ever acted on their emotions. Love is sometimes beyond our control."

"Not when you're married. Then you have to control it."

"Yes, but I rather doubt that Harry and Isabelle had an actual affair. When she writes of him in this letter, she speaks almost poetically. In her words he's more than a man, he's practically a god. Now, Harry was a lot of things, but he definitely wasn't a god. Which leads me to believe they didn't know each other all that well."

"I don't understand."

"I think Isabelle loved the way Harry made her feel more than she loved him. And that was probably the attraction for Harry, too. Isabelle was a beautiful, passionate woman. She was warm and affectionate, all the things that your mother wasn't. Not that I didn't care deeply for your mother. She wasn't a bad person, just difficult to get close to."

Kara didn't need to be reminded of that fact. When her father left, so had all the warmth in their family. Not that her mother was mean. She just didn't touch, and she didn't like to be lazy, and she didn't have a loud laugh that made you feel as if you had told the best joke in the world. But she had been a good mother in her own way.

"Another thing I don't understand is where Mrs. Hunter went. She supposedly left with my father, but he never showed up with her, and I distinctly remember him spending the night with us in San Francisco. Where was she?"

"Maybe they split up once they got to the city."

"No wonder Mom couldn't stand to talk about him," Kara said after a moment, retracing the past as quickly as she could. "She must have known that he had fallen in love with someone else. I wish she had told me, maybe not when I was a child; but later there were so many opportunities. Right before she died, I told her I thought Michael was cheating on me. And do you know what she said?"

"I can't imagine."

"She told me to look the other way, to accept the good with the bad, to try and hang on to him. How could she give me such advice?"

"Maybe she wished she had hung on to Harry."

Josephine walked over to the hot plate and picked up the kettle, which was beginning to steam. She poured two cups of tea and handed one to Kara.

The aroma of herbs, cinnamon, and spices soothed her jangled nerves, and Kara took a grateful sip of the tea.

"Where did you get the letter?" Josephine asked as she settled onto a stool behind the counter.

"From Andrew, who got it from Ryan, who apparently stole it from Jonas all those years ago."

"That's what Ryan stole? My goodness. All these years Jonas made it sound like Ryan had taken his life savings, when in fact all he had taken was a letter from his mother."

"Andrew broke up with me. He said he can't bear to touch me, knowing that my father was with his mother."

"He's a damn fool," Josephine said sharply. "What does that have to do with the price of tea in China?"

"Apparently it means a lot to him."

"Andrew wasn't the right man for you anyway," Josephine said. "Especially when you're in love with his brother."

Kara stiffened. "That's absurd. I barely know the man. Besides, Ryan has probably left town by now. Speaking of men, I noticed you didn't come back to the Gatehouse last night."

Josephine flushed like a teenager in love. "I couldn't leave Ike—not after what he did at the picnic."

"He was pretty magnificent," Kara agreed.

Josephine looked ashamed. "Ike was right. I was being an old fool. He doesn't have to like tea or believe in my fortune-telling. He just has to love me as much as I love him. For a while I thought that if he didn't love tea, he didn't love me."

"It's not the same thing."

"No. I got scared, Kara. My other husbands didn't talk back to me the way Ike does. They didn't challenge my ideas. They didn't question me. I called the shots. I made the decisions. With Ike it's different."

"Maybe it's different in a good way."

"I know it is. But when Ike started taking me for granted, I began to think that he'd lost interest in me. I'm not a pretty young filly anymore, you know."

"You're a beautiful mare," Kara said with a warm smile. "And Ike adores you. That's obvious to everyone."

"It is?" Aunt Josephine looked as giddy as a schoolgirl.

"Yes, it is. Especially after yesterday. I'm glad you two made up."

"So am I. I'll tell you something, Kara. Ike may not be my richest husband or the most good-looking, but he is definitely the best at making up—if you know what I mean."

This time Kara blushed. "Aunt Josephine."

"So, if you don't mind, I'll be moving my things back home later tonight."

Kara gave her a hug. "I don't mind at all. I was beginning to think that life was black-and-white, that arguments couldn't be resolved, that marriage couldn't work. But it can, can't it?"

"Yes. I'm sorry if I gave you doubts. I never had any real intention of divorcing Ike. I just wanted to get his attention. I'm madly in love with him. And if anyone believes in marriage, it's me. There are lots of happy marriages, Kara. It's just the failed ones that make the headlines. Look around this town. You'll see plenty of good examples."

"I'm trying, Aunt Josephine. But after today I'm not sure I can trust my own eyes."

"Then trust your heart."

Whatever that means, Kara thought wearily. "I better check on our sandbagging operation and find out what my daughter has been up to the last few hours."

"Wait." Josephine reached for Kara's empty teacup and swirled the leaves around in a familiar circular motion.

"Oh, Aunt Josephine, I'm not in the mood."

"Your aura is so strong today, Kara. I must see what the leaves say."

"You can tell me later."

"You can wait."

Kara sighed, deciding it was simply easier to hear the reading than be scolded about leaving. "All right. What does it say?"

Josephine lifted her head, her expression serious. "I see a snake, which indicates misfortune."

"Probably the river."

"And a bridge."

"Back to the river again."

"No, a bridge means there's a decision to be made." Josephine paused. "And a bird's claw, which means danger."

Kara cleared her throat, trying to dispel the heaviness of Josephine's words. "We're all in danger from the river flooding. Your cup probably says the same thing."

"We can read it, but the leaf patterns are created by the force of your energy, Kara. They apply only to you."

"I'll let you in on a little secret, Aunt Josephine. I don't believe in this stuff either."

"Maybe you should. Maybe it's time to believe in what you don't understand, what you can't see. Look beyond the surface, Kara. Take a chance. Open yourself up. You might be surprised at what suddenly becomes crystal clear."

The door jangled with a new arrival, and Kara looked up warily, expecting to see an evil man in a black hat and cape in keeping with her aunt's fortune-telling. But it wasn't a man. It was Angel.

"I saw her again, Mom," Angel declared with excitement. "The ghost lady. She came back, and she told me the river is going to flood by Thursday. We have to warn everyone, especially Mr. Hunter, Jonas Hunter."

Oh, great, another fortune-teller. Kara threw up her hands in disgust. "What am I going to do with you two? I can't run down to the rec center, get my bullhorn, and announce that my aunt has seen danger coming in the bottom of a teacup and my daughter is talking to a ghost about when the river is going to flood."

"She's real, Mom. She's not a story. And she's looking for something—a necklace. I think it might be a locket. Because she said something once about there being a picture inside."

Josephine's expression turned thoughtful. "What does this ghost look like?"

"She has long dark hair. She doesn't really seem to have a whole body. She sort of floats. But sometimes when she turns a certain way, I can see her eyes, and they're green. Kind of like Ryan's."

Kara straightened, a sudden shiver running down her spine. She told herself not to be silly, that Angel was just telling another story.

"Oh, dear," Josephine said.

"What?" Angel asked.

"It's just that Ryan's mother used to wear a locket."

"Aunt Josephine," Kara said imploringly. "Don't encourage her."

Josephine ignored Kara's protest. "Jonas gave it to Isabelle when Andrew was born, and on the inside she kept baby pictures of both boys. She wore it all the time. In fact, she told me once that she would never take it off. But it couldn't be the same locket. She left town years ago—unless . . ."

"Unless what?" Angel asked, her eyes round with anticipation.

"Unless she never left town."

"Of course she left. It's in the letter," Kara said.

"The letter just says she's thinking about leaving."

Angel grabbed Kara's arm. "The watch, Mom. Remember the watch? It said, *To Ryan. Love, Mom.* It was hers. She gave it to him. That's why she cried when I found it. That's why she asked me what he said when I gave it to him. It's her, Mom. The ghost is Ryan's mother."

# 23

Jonas backed a dump truck up the driveway and stopped it as close to the house as he could. Lifting the lever, he released the bed of the truck, dumping a pile of sand onto the ground. This was his third load. He just hoped he had enough sand to protect the basement and first floor of the house. The water had already risen ten feet. By tomorrow it would be up another ten. At this rate, by Tuesday or Wednesday the river would be licking at the driveway.

With a weary groan, he stumbled out of the truck, suddenly feeling light-headed. He bent over, his hands on his knees, hoping the dizziness would pass. After a moment it did. He walked around to the back of the truck and pulled on a pair of beat-up leather gloves. Then he grabbed his shovel and began to fill a burlap bag with sand.

By the time he had filled three bags, he was sweating like a pig and breathing fast. The task ahead of him seemed insurmountable. But he couldn't quit now. The house was all he had left. He had to save it.

A honking horn made him pause. Ryan turned into the driveway too fast, spitting up loose gravel and dirt. His youngest son was out of the car and up the drive before Jonas could gather the energy to move.

"What the hell are you doing?" Ryan demanded. "Trying to kill yourself?"

Jonas didn't answer him. He simply bent over and proceeded to fill the next sandbag. Ryan ripped the shovel out of his hand.

"You can't do this. You're sick," Ryan said.

Jonas stiffened with anger. "I'm not sick, and I can do whatever I want."

"You are so stubborn."

"That's right. Give me back the shovel."

"No."

Jonas stared at Ryan, saw the determination in his eyes, the stubborn set of his jaw, the cockiness of his stance. Ryan was no longer a kid, but a man, and it seemed almost impossible to intimidate him. Jonas tried his sternest glare, the one that made Andrew shake. Ryan just smiled and held on to the shovel.

"I can still kick your butt," Jonas grumbled, knowing deep down that he couldn't kick anyone's butt anymore. The years were catching up to him. He couldn't stay ahead of the pace anymore, and he wasn't sure he wanted to try.

"Sure you can," Ryan agreed. "I could never beat you. We both know that. You're the best at everything. Even at shoveling shit."

Jonas had to fight back a smile. That had always been the problem. Ryan had the ability to make Jonas laugh. He had talked himself out of many a spanking that way. "You're pretty good at shoveling shit yourself."

"I learned from the master."

"Why are you doing this?"

"Maybe this place means something to me, too."

Jonas couldn't believe what he was hearing. "And maybe the Pope is Jewish."

"He's definitely not Jewish. I took his picture last year, and he's as Catholic as they come."

Jonas couldn't stop the inexplicable sense of pride

that came with Ryan's words. "You took the Pope's picture?"

"Yeah."

"You were in the Vatican?"

"Not bad for a worthless, two-bit kid, huh?"

Jonas knew he had called Ryan that many times over the years. He also knew he had never meant it. It had been his way of keeping Ryan in check, keeping him at home where he belonged. Although that strategy had worked with Andrew, it had never worked with Ryan. Telling Ryan he couldn't do something had only made him work harder. Trying to keep Ryan at home had only made him want to leave.

When Jonas didn't reply, Ryan grabbed the next bag and began to fill it with sand. Jonas watched him for a good ten minutes, not saying a word, not moving a muscle. It wasn't until Ryan rolled up his sleeves and rubbed the back of his arm across his forehead that Jonas moved. He walked into the house and slammed the door.

For a long time Jonas stared at the living room, at the worn couch, his comfortable armchair, the bud vase he had given Isabelle on their wedding day. He remembered Ryan asking why he had kept her things. The answer was simple. Deep down he had always hoped that someday she would come back for her things—if not for him. He had kept Ryan's stuff for the same reason.

And Ryan had come back.

Jonas peeked out the curtain, wondering if Ryan was still working now that he didn't have an audience. If anything, he seemed to be working harder.

This was not the same angry boy who had left town all those years ago, trashing the house on his way out the door, stealing the letter from Isabelle, calling his father and brother names, and leaving them to clean up his mess.

No, the boy who had run away from home had returned a man. One Jonas could be proud of, if he let himself. But Jonas was afraid to show Ryan love, afraid it would be tossed back in his face. He had raised Ryan, fed him and clothed him and shoved chicken soup down his throat when he was sick. He had been there for Ryan every day of his life. But who had Ryan wanted all those years? His mother. His damned mother.

Jonas closed his eyes, feeling his blood pressure rise again. He shouldn't have sent Isabelle away. Her departure had torn a hole in his heart that could never be repaired. She had taken everything that was good in him right out the door with her. Once she left he had been unable to find simple joy in anything. Only the river had brought him moments of peace. Now even those moments were fleeting.

He was old. And as Ryan said, he was sick. The doctor had told him that unless he had surgery, he probably wouldn't last out the year. There was a tiny part of him that was almost relieved at the thought. It would be easier to die than to watch everything he loved change before his eyes. It was already happening at the paper. Andrew was doing things that he would never do. And the river was changing as well as the town. His time was passing.

With a heavy heart and heavy steps, he walked up the stairs and into his bedroom. He lay down on the bed and closed his eyes. He saw Isabelle's sweet face, her lovely smile. He heard her laugh and reached for her outstretched hand. Yes, he wanted to go with her to a place where dreams came true. Within minutes he was fast asleep.

Ryan's arms were aching when Andrew's truck pulled up next to his Ferrari. He stopped for a moment, resting one arm on top of the shovel.

Andrew didn't say anything, just shook his head and disappeared into the house.

Ryan stared after him. He had been thinking about Andrew since yesterday, remembering again how close they had once been, how Andrew had saved his life that day. Somehow he had forgotten that. After years of brotherly bickering and constant competition, Ryan had forgotten that there had been a time when his older brother was also his hero.

Ryan shook his head and went back to filling bags with sand. The sky overhead turned dark. The clouds began to toss and turn in preparation for an angry, restless night. Ryan was supposed to be on his way back to L.A. The centennial was over.

But he couldn't leave. The town and the people had gotten under his skin, welcoming him back like a long-lost family. Not his family, of course, but the rest of them. He'd missed that sense of belonging, of community.

Ryan lifted his head as Andrew came out of the house with another shovel. They worked together in silence for almost an hour, piling the bags around the garage and the foundation of the house.

It was almost five o'clock when Jonas stepped onto the porch with two beers. He tossed one can to Ryan and the other to Andrew. Then he disappeared back inside.

Ryan smiled to himself as he popped the tab and took a long drink. Even Andrew seemed somewhat amused. But the amusement faded when Andrew spoke.

"I gave Kara the letter," Andrew said. "I can't be with her, knowing that her father and our mother—" He shuddered. "I can't handle that."

"You broke up with her? Are you crazy? She's one of the finest women you'll ever meet. She's strong and independent, beautiful and passionate and—God, have you lost your brains?"

Andrew looked at him in surprise, his eyes narrowing thoughtfully. "You're in love with her."

"Don't be stupid. I've known her for four days. No

one falls in love in four days. You've known her for what, six months? How can you let her go?"

Andrew shook his head somewhat shamefully. "I know you'll laugh, but the truth is Kara makes me nervous. She has the craziest ideas, and her family—Angel and Josephine—are practically certifiable."

"Angel and Josephine are great."

"They're exhausting. I have trouble enough dealing with Billy. I can't handle Angel, too."

Ryan squeezed the empty beer can between his fingers. He didn't know why he was arguing for Kara. The last thing he wanted was for Andrew and Kara to get together. On the other hand, it would be much harder to leave knowing they weren't together, that he couldn't use their relationship as an excuse to stay away.

But there was no future for him in this town, not even with the most wonderful woman on earth. He would suffocate here. He would go back to being that two-bit worthless kid. And speaking of kids—his thoughts turned to Angel and to Billy, to a boy who looked a lot like him.

Were there still more secrets to be uncovered? He wasn't sure he could handle any more.

"Ryan." Andrew suddenly looked disturbed. His gaze went to the river, then back to Ryan again. "Forget it."

"Forget what?" Ryan asked sharply.

"When are you leaving?"

"Tonight."

"We better get finished then."

Andrew started to shovel sand, but Ryan didn't move, knowing that he couldn't leave Serenity Springs without the answer to at least one of his questions. "Andrew, is Billy my son?"

"No," Andrew said abruptly, but there was doubt in his voice, in the way he avoided Ryan's eyes.

"Are you sure?"

Andrew stopped shoveling. "All right, I'm not sure.

I might be Billy's father or you might be, or some other schmuck that neither one of us knew about."

There was a gasp from behind them. Ryan whirled around. Angel and Billy stood at the corner of Andrew's truck.

"Billy." Andrew stepped toward his son, but Billy put up his hand.

"St-stay a-away from me," Billy stuttered, looking horror-struck.

"It's not true, is it?" Angel asked.

"Let me explain," Andrew said.

"Explain what?" Billy demanded. "That you're not my father? That you don't know who my father is? I hate you. I hate both of you." Billy took off running. Angel followed on his heels.

"Go after him," Ryan said.

Andrew hesitated. "I think he's your son, Ryan. I've thought that for a long time. Maybe you should go."

"Me?" Ryan asked in shock. "But—no, he's your kid. You raised him. He doesn't want me to go after him. He wants you."

"I think that's why Becky Lee was leaving me," Andrew said, taking one last second to explain. "She wanted to tell you about Billy. She had a long talk with Jonas, and the next morning she packed up her things and left."

"Jonas? She talked to Jonas?"

"He never said what about."

"Good God. Jonas could have told her anything." Ryan looked toward the house. "That old man has a lot to answer for. Come on, we'll find Billy together, and we'll deal with this together."

"We will?" Andrew looked doubtful.

"We're brothers. Isn't it about time we remembered that?" Ryan saw the look of surprise on Andrew's face, but he didn't comment. He simply headed down the driveway, hoping they could find Billy and somehow make everything right for this innocent kid who was caught in the middle.

Angel put a hand on Billy's arm as he huddled on the ground by the river. Angel was surprised to find Billy close to the water, but he was so upset, he didn't seem to notice.

She wanted to ask him if he was okay, but she was afraid to say the words. She knew what it was like to find out your father wasn't who you thought he was.

"I can't believe he lied to me all this time, pretending to be my father," Billy said finally. He looked at Angel with a face wet from tears. "I hate him."

"I know."

"I don't have anybody now. No mother. No father."

"You can stay with us," Angel suggested. "My mom always has room for one more. And she's a pretty good mom."

"She won't want me. Nobody wants me."

"I want you." Andrew's voice rang out between them. Billy stiffened. Angel stepped aside so Andrew could talk to Billy.

Andrew sat down on the ground next to his son. He didn't say anything for a long moment; then he tipped Billy's chin up with his hand. "I loved you from the first minute you were born, with your red face and your dark hair and your long, scrawny legs." Andrew's voice caught. "I loved your mother, too. When I drove you and your mother home from the hospital, I was so proud. I didn't think I could be any happier. I had wanted a family so bad. And I finally had one. But things didn't work out between your mother and me. And when she died, I was devastated. The only thing, the only person who kept me going was you."

"But you're not my real dad. He is." Billy pointed a shaky finger at Ryan.

"No, I'm your father, now and always."

Andrew looked over at Ryan, daring him to argue.

But Ryan didn't have any intention of arguing, especially not after seeing the depth of his brother's love for this child. He stepped forward.

"Andrew is right, Billy. You didn't hear our whole conversation. If you had, you would have known that you're Andrew's son. You also would have learned that I loved your mother, too, and that I'd like to be friends with you, if you'll let me."

Billy wrestled with those words, his adolescent mind trying to grasp each and every fact. "You're not going to take me away? Make me have blood tests or something?"

The thought had occurred to him, but Ryan knew that it would serve no purpose. Being a father was about much more than biology. Besides that fact, there was a part of him that couldn't believe Becky Lee would have kept such a secret from him. She would have used it to her advantage, to go with him or make him stay.

Ryan realized Billy was waiting for an answer. "No blood tests. We don't need them. You belong with your father, with Andrew. But I would like to be your uncle. What do you think about that?"

"My dad hates you," Billy said flatly. "So does Grandfather."

Another kid torn between the people he wants to love and the people he's supposed to love, Ryan thought, knowing that it had to end. "I don't hate you, Billy. And I don't hate your father or your grandfather. Not anymore. See, we had a fight, and it's been so long we've forgotten what we were fighting about. Maybe it's a good time for the fighting to stop."

"I agree," Andrew said. "Ryan is right, Billy. We don't hate each other, not anymore. Maybe we never did."

Billy flung his arms around Andrew's neck. "I don't want to leave you, Dad."

"You don't have to leave me. And I don't intend to

ever let you go," Andrew said fiercely. "You're my son. I love you."

Ryan felt a rush of emotion at Andrew's words. How he had longed to hear his own father say those three words, but they had never come. To see Andrew and Billy together made him feel lonely. Of course, it was by his choice, but he was still alone, dammit.

Then Angel slid her arm around his waist, and his feeling of loneliness eased. He put an arm around her shoulder, and they watched Andrew and Billy walk up the bank together.

"I wouldn't mind if you were my father," Angel said after a moment.

"You wouldn't?"

"No, I like you. Mom likes you, too."

And he liked Kara, more than he should. "Yeah, well, your mom is all right. So are you." He ruffled her hair, knowing that he would miss this wild-eyed, fanciful child who almost made him believe in the impossible things she talked about.

"I wish you weren't leaving."

Ryan felt the lump in his throat grow bigger. "I have to go back to work." Why did that suddenly sound dismal, when he had found joy in his work for years, when he had once preferred his camera to everything else?

"Maybe you could just stay for a couple of days. Maybe until Thursday," Angel persisted.

"Why Thursday?"

"That's when the lady says the river is going to flood."

"Oh, right. Well, I definitely don't want to be here when the river floods. I'm not a big fan of rushing water."

"I'll protect you. I don't mind the water at all." Angel took his hand, and Ryan knew that she probably would try to protect him, because like her mother, Angel was loyal as hell and just as courageous.

Angel suddenly pointed toward the water. "Look, she's there."

Ryan squinted his eyes. "I don't see her."

Angel sighed. "She's gone again."

Ryan shrugged. "Easy come, easy go, huh?"

"You don't believe in her either."

"At this point I'm not sure what I believe."

Angel opened her mouth, then closed it. Ryan was struck by the sudden indecision in her face. She was itching to tell him something. Although he wanted nothing to do with another tall tale, he couldn't bring himself to cut her off. "Okay, tell me about her."

"She's looking for a locket, Ryan. It has a picture of her babies in it. I told Aunt Josephine about it, and she said your mother always wore a locket."

Ryan's lips tightened. He could handle any story except one about his mother. "What are you trying to say?"

"I think the ghost is your mother."

Ryan snorted in disbelief. "Come on, that's quite a whopper, even for you. Besides, my mother isn't dead." Or was she? The question had haunted him for a long time.

Was Isabelle dead? Is that why she had disappeared so completely? But there would have been a record of her death, and the private investigator he had hired had turned up nothing.

"I'm going to ask her," Angel said. "The next time I see her, I'll ask her if she's your mother."

Ryan felt a sudden urge to tell her no. Because deep down he did not want his mother to be dead. He didn't want her to be a ghost. Not that he believed in such things, he told himself. This was Angel talking—Angel with the secret agent father. Why was he even thinking about this?

"Let's go home. Kara is probably worried sick about you." Ryan urged Angel up the bank ahead of him. When he got to the top, he couldn't help looking over his shoulder, but there was no one there.

# 24

Kara paced back and forth across the porch at the Gatehouse, trying to keep her imagination under control. Angel was fine. She was too smart to get caught by the river. She was just late—again.

Ryan's car turned into the parking lot. Kara sighed with relief at the sight of her daughter with Ryan. When Angel got to the porch, Kara pulled her daughter into her arms and gave her a fierce, loving hug. "Where have you been? I was so worried about you. And Aunt Josephine is waiting to take you to dinner at the diner. You were supposed to be home an hour ago, remember?"

"I'm sorry. I was looking for Billy, Mom. He was upset. I couldn't just leave him."

"She couldn't," Ryan agreed. "Not this time."

"Why? What happened?"

Before Angel or Ryan could reply, Josephine stepped onto the porch. "There you are. Wash your hands and face, Angel; I want to get to the diner before Nellie starts telling her stories. Then we'll never get our food."

"I love Nellie's stories. They're almost as good as mine," Angel said with an impish smile as she fled into the house.

"What happened with Billy?" Kara asked again.

"Billy overheard Andrew and me talking about who his father is."

"Who his father is?" Kara echoed. "Please, I don't think I can stand another revelation today."

"Hush, Kara, I want to hear more," Josephine said.

Ryan smiled at Josephine's curiosity. "Becky Lee slept with both of us. I guess that's no surprise. Apparently there's some question as to which one of us is Billy's father."

"Becky Lee didn't say?" Kara asked.

"She told Andrew he was the father."

"Then I don't understand."

"Becky Lee didn't always tell the truth. Andrew knows that as well as I do. But . . ." Ryan took in a deep breath and let it out. "But as far as I'm concerned, Andrew is Billy's father in every way that counts. He has taken care of him and loved him for twelve years."

"But if he's your child . . ." Kara started, not really sure what she wanted to say. Was biology more important than love and caring? No. Michael had fathered Angel, but he had never been a father to her. "You're right, Ryan. Andrew is Billy's father in all the ways that matter."

"Besides, I'd probably make a lousy dad," he said.

"No, you wouldn't," Josephine said. "You would make a wonderful father. Remember when I read your leaves the other day?"

"I remember something about being at a crossroads or a railroad crossing; I'm not sure which."

Josephine rolled her eyes. "You don't know which because you're not ready to choose your path. But one day, probably sooner than you think, you will have to choose."

"I've already picked my path."

"Some roads come to an end."

"And some go on forever."

"Only in photographs."

"That's good enough for me."

"Well, I think you did the right thing with Andrew
and Billy," Kara interrupted. "How is Billy handling
it?"

"He's still a little shocked. I wish it hadn't come out
this way. For that matter, I wish it hadn't come out at
all. But it did."

"When the river rises, the secrets of years past are
washed ashore and brought to life," Josephine said quietly. "Rebirth. That's what rivers are all about. That's
what life is all about."

"Do you want children, Ryan?" Kara asked curiously.

Ryan tilted his head to one side, looking more
thoughtful than usual. "A week ago I would have said
absolutely not, but I have to admit seeing Andrew and
Billy together made me feel envious. Andrew gets another chance at having a family with his own son. I'm
still left with Jonas."

"Lucky you." Kara paused. "Speaking of our parents,
Andrew gave me the letter. Quite an eye-opener. How
could you resist telling me about our parents' mutual
lust for each other?"

Ryan cleared his throat, glancing over at Josephine for
help.

"Don't look at me," Josephine said. "I didn't know a
thing."

"I was going to tell you when I first came back, but
I never found the right time. I wasn't sure how you
would react. Actually you seem pretty calm," Ryan
said.

"I wasn't at first. I felt betrayed—again. But then the
men in my life have a habit of disappointing me. I never
really knew my father. I certainly don't know what happened between him and your mother, and I never will,
because the letter only states what they planned to do,
not what they did. Their infatuation may not have
lasted past the city limits. Who knows?"

"Not me."

"I guess passion can drive people to do strange things."

Angel opened the front door, and Kara hoped her daughter hadn't heard her last comment. Angel seemed to have an affinity for the word passion.

"I'm ready," Angel said, her hair neatly combed, her face washed. "Can we get a chocolate sundae for dessert?"

"Absolutely," Josephine said with a bright smile.

"Don't stay out too late. Tomorrow is a school day," Kara said.

"I'll have her back by nine," Josephine replied. "You two have a nice time now, and please see if you can find something to talk about besides your parents. It's not their lives you're living, it's your own."

After Josephine and Angel left, Ryan sat down on the porch railing, leaning his back against one of the pillars. "Looks like it's just you and me," he said softly. "What do you want to do?"

With that look in his eyes, with that smile on his face, Kara knew there was only one thing she wanted to do—strip every last piece of clothing off his body. Her heart pounded against her chest as she tried to think of a better answer, a safer answer.

"I have lots of things to do," she said, infusing a note of calm into her voice. "Cleaning, cooking, sewing, all those homemaker things. Besides, I thought you were leaving today."

"I can leave tomorrow—if that's okay with you."

"The other guests checked out this afternoon, so it's just family now."

Family. The word hit him hard. Ryan suddenly realized that he wanted to be a part of this family. He wanted it so bad he could almost taste it. He wanted to live in this house that smelled like fresh baked bread and cinnamon cookies. He wanted to spend his nights making love to Kara under the big down quilt on his bed. He wanted to listen to Angel's stories and drink endless cups of tea just so he could watch Josephine spin her own tales of the future.

"Except for you, of course," Kara amended, not realizing how much the exclusion hurt him. "Oh, I almost forgot—you have a message from someone at the *San Francisco Chronicle*. It's on the hall table. They said something about getting photos of the river from you."

"I'll call them tomorrow."

Ryan didn't move, and Kara didn't either. He could barely see her face in the soft, dark light. There was no moon tonight, no stars, just a spill of light coming from the house onto the porch. He held out his hands to her. He could do nothing else.

Kara hesitated. "I don't know, Ryan."

"I don't either."

After a moment Kara walked slowly into his arms, sliding her hands around his waist. He lowered his head and kissed her longingly, lovingly, making it last. She turned her body into his, her breasts pressing into his chest, her hips fitting into his, her softness, his hardness. God, had he ever wanted any woman more than this one?

He laced his fingers through the thick, silky strands of her hair, tilting her head back so he could ease his mouth along the corner of her jaw, past her earlobe, down to the sensitive area of her neck and shoulders.

Kara uttered a soft moan as she closed her eyes, a look of pure pleasure on her face. He wanted to make her happy. He wanted to hear her cry out his name again. He wanted to see her tremble and shake, and this time he wanted to be with her, on top of her, underneath her, inside her.

"One night," he muttered. "Just one night."

She opened her big, beautiful blue eyes. "Yes."

He didn't think he had heard her right. "Yes?"

She smiled in the soft, sexy, innocent way that belonged solely to her. "Angel and my aunt won't be back for a few hours. Can the night start now?"

"You bet it can," he said, swinging her up into his arms.

She laughed as she flung her arms around his neck. "What on earth are you doing?"

"I'm carrying you upstairs."

"I can walk."

"You can also run away, so I'm not taking any chances."

Ryan carried her into the house, kicking the door shut with his foot. He headed for the stairs and would have made it without any problem if Kara hadn't decided to kiss his neck with her sweet, hot mouth. He dropped her to her feet at the first landing and pressed her against the wall.

"I thought we were going upstairs."

"Too far away," he muttered, taking her mouth into his. "I want you here, now."

His words excited her more than his actions, the desperation in his voice, the longing. She had never been the kind of woman to drive a man to distraction, beyond reason, beyond caring, and she had never gotten so caught up in a kiss that she was ready to strip off her clothes without asking. But when his fingers reached for her sweater, she helped him pull it over her head.

He gazed at her breasts with extreme and utter fascination, stroking her nipples until she closed her eyes and began to sway, wanting to pour herself into his hands and into his body. His mouth followed his hands. Kissing, sucking, teasing until she was a quivering mass of emotions.

She reached for his belt buckle and pulled it apart, then the snap and the zipper to his pants. She tried to push them down over his hips, but he stopped her.

"Wait, I need something," he whispered, reaching into his pocket and pulling out a condom. "I wanted to be prepared in case you decided to seduce me again. Do you want to go upstairs?"

"No, I want you here, now." She took the package out of his hand and ripped open the corner, enjoying the look of surprise on his face, reveling in her sense of control and power and complete desirability. With this man she could be anyone she wanted, including herself. "Let me," she said. Kara reached down and brought him into her hands, running her fingers over the long, silky shaft. He was so hard, so big. He would feel perfect inside her.

"Hurry up," Ryan said, his voice shaky. Then he leaned over and kissed her as his hands raised her skirt, as his fingers peeled off her panties, as his knee nudged her legs apart, and his fingers pressed against her most intimate place.

He prepared her with his fingers until she was clinging to him, wet with desire, anxious with need. Then he came inside her, filling every empty, lonely spot of her body and her heart. And as they moved together, as they came as one, Kara knew that she had finally found the part of her that was missing.

An hour later Kara rested her head on Ryan's chest and listened to the sound of his breathing, the pounding of his heart. They had finally made it to the bedroom. She knew Ryan wasn't asleep, but she didn't want to talk. She just wanted to enjoy the moment, to savor every part of him that was pressed against every part of her.

She had lied before when she told him she liked sex. But Ryan had turned her lie into the truth. He had made her feel like a sexy, passionate woman, forcing her to give him everything, to lose herself in him, to trust him completely. And she did.

She would never regret their actions. Even if he left her with nothing but this one memory, she would hold it close to her heart and know that at least for one moment in her life she had had it all.

"When is Angel coming back?" Ryan asked lazily, running his hand through her hair.

"Another hour or so."

"Mm-mm."

Kara propped herself up on her elbow, suddenly remembering everything that had happened earlier that day. "Did Angel talk to you, Ryan?"

His eyes flickered open. "About what?"

"It's silly really, but Angel thinks your mother is a ghost. I tried to tell her there're no such things as ghosts, but I don't think I convinced her, especially since Aunt Josephine refused to lend her support."

"Yeah, Angel told me."

Kara sent him a thoughtful look. "Do you think your mother is dead, Ryan? I mean, how could she disappear so completely, without a trace?"

He shook his head. "I don't know."

"I wish there was someone I could ask about all this."

"But your parents are dead, too."

"That leaves Jonas," Kara said, trying to keep her voice even and calm.

"Don't even think about talking to Jonas."

"He has to know, Ryan. He's the only one who would."

"Even if he does, he's not going to tell you anything. You're the enemy, or at least the daughter of his enemy."

"Maybe he'll tell you."

"Whatever Jonas knows is locked inside himself. I'm not sure he even has the key anymore."

"I hate having unanswered questions."

"So do I. That's why I've spent the last twelve years looking for my mother. But maybe it doesn't matter anymore. Even if we knew, what would be different?"

Kara thought about his statement. "I've made so many decisions based on something that wasn't true. I came back here because I wanted to recapture the happiness of my youth, to go back to the place where my parents were madly in love. Only now I find out they weren't madly in love, and this calm little town is looking a lot like Peyton Place, with secrets scurrying out from every dark corner like rats in the night."

"You don't have rats, do you? I can't stand the little suckers."

Kara playfully punched him on the arm. "Be serious."

"I can't be serious. And I can't keep asking questions that won't be answered or looking for a woman I'll never find. I have learned one thing though. . . ."

"What's that?"

"That it's possible to want someone so much that nothing else and no one else matters."

He looked into her eyes when he said the words, and she swallowed hard. "I know exactly what you mean." She touched her lips to his chest.

"Kara, if you do that again, I won't be responsible for the consequences."

"Good." She ran her tongue around the circle of his nipple.

He closed his eyes. "You're killing me."

"I thought men were ready any time, any place, for any reason. Gee, I'm a little disappointed," she said, dragging the tips of her nails down his stomach toward the thick dark curls of hair between his legs.

Ryan opened his eyes at that. Taking her by surprise, he tossed her on her back like an awakening lion, pressing both of her hands back against the bed. Then he stared at her long and hard, so intently she wondered what he was seeing in her face, in her eyes.

"You're staring at me," she said.

"I'm memorizing you."

"So you won't forget." She couldn't keep a note of sadness out of her voice.

"I'll never forget you. I just want to remember every detail, every glorious inch of your face, your body, your heart." Ryan put his lips to her heart, kissing the beats as they came faster and faster.

"Oh, Ryan, love me."

"I intend to."

Then he spread her legs and buried himself inside her. "I never felt like I had a home until now. This I could call home," he whispered.

Ryan released her hands and she pulled him down to her, stroking his back with her fingers, pulling his buttocks more closely into the curve of her hips until there was nothing separating them.

Kara barely made it into her bedroom before Angel and Josephine came home. She dashed into her private bathroom and turned on the shower, hoping to avoid questions, to disguise the joy in her eyes, the pleasure in her face, and any other signs that she had spent the last two hours making love to a man who was leaving in the morning.

She sighed, letting the water pour over her head and down her face, her skin still sensitized to Ryan's touch. She could remember every moment of their lovemaking, every mutter, every cry. He had been a generous lover, a man willing to give as much as take.

The moisture welled up behind her eyes. She was not going to cry, she told herself firmly. She had gone into this with her eyes open. One night he had asked for, and one night she had given him. It would have to be enough.

When the water began to run cold, Kara stepped out of the shower and wrapped herself in a peach-colored terry cloth towel. She walked into the bedroom and began to comb her hair. She could hear Angel talking to Ryan and hoped her daughter hadn't burst in on him unawares. But they were laughing about something, and Ryan didn't sound embarrassed or annoyed. He sounded amused.

Ryan and Angel got along well, their sense of humor and adventure connecting them. And beneath it all they had an underlying respect for each other. Kara hoped his departure wouldn't hurt Angel again. The last thing Angel needed in her life was more rejection, especially from a man.

Kara slipped into her silk robe and tied the knot. She hesitated at the door, torn between wanting to be alone and her motherly duty of getting her daughter ready for bed.

"Kara? May I come in?" Josephine asked with a brief knock.

"Of course." Kara opened the door. "How was dinner?"

"It was nice. Angel told lots of stories. She should write them down. They're wonderful."

"Yes, they are."

"You didn't eat dinner," Josephine said, her sharp eyes taking in Kara's appearance. "Are you all right?"

"I'm fine. I wasn't hungry."

"I'll put Angel to bed before I go, if you like."

"Thank you." Kara felt an inordinate sense of relief. She felt so many emotions at this moment, happiness mixed with regret, desire and longing, and a terrible sense of guilt. She was supposed to be a responsible parent. She wasn't supposed to make love to a man just passing through.

Josephine smiled with the wisdom of her years. She touched Kara's cheek in a gesture of affection. "Don't be too hard on yourself, Kara. You're only human."

"I'm supposed to be sensible and logical."

"Who said that?"

"I don't know, but I'm sure someone said it."

"Probably someone sensible—"

"And logical," Kara finished as they laughed together in commiseration. "Why is the love stuff so hard?"

"It's not. That's the secret. You just have to let it happen." Josephine turned to leave. "Oh, Kara, the walls are pretty sound in this house—if you know what I mean."

"Aunt Josephine!"

Kara turned to the mirror as Josephine left, noting the flush on her cheeks, the light in her eyes. Aunt Josephine didn't need a crystal ball for this one. Love was written all over her face.

It was almost two in the morning when Ryan walked into the garden and sat down on the bench under the old oak tree. The rain had stopped, but the plants and bushes still dripped with raindrops, and the scents from the garden were accentuated by the cool night breeze.

He felt closer to Kara here. She smelled like this garden—sexy, beautiful, and lush. How could he leave her? How could he walk away from this house, from the people who lived here, from Angel and Josephine and the puppies that crawled all over him in bed every night, somehow finding their way out of the sun porch and up to his room.

But how could he stay? He was a man who prided himself on having no furniture, no ties, no commitments. A man who had sworn never to live in a town smaller than Los Angeles. A man who fell asleep to the sound of sirens, not the sound of crickets.

Then there was the river, the heart of his bad memories. But in the past four days he had made new memories. He had talked to Angel by the river and been helplessly captivated by her imagination, her innocence, her loneliness. He had made love to Kara, drowning his fears in the warmth of her skin, the sultriness of her mouth. And he had made peace with his brother by the river.

Ryan sat back on the bench and picked up his saxophone, desperately needing an outlet for the emotions ripping through him. The air filled with music as he played all the things he wanted to tell Kara and couldn't. Maybe she would hear the music. Maybe she would understand.

\* \* \*

Kara curled up on the window seat in her bedroom and looked out into the garden. The scattered clouds parted and the moonlight lit up Ryan's shadowy figure. She opened the window wider so she could hear him play. The music didn't sound as lonely tonight, not as blue. There was more melody, more harmony, more joy.

She closed her eyes and fell asleep to the sound of his saxophone, dreaming of the two of them together, making their own kind of music.

# 25

As Kara flipped pancakes the next morning, she reminded herself that she would be cool and calm when Ryan left. No tears. No regrets. Maybe a kiss on the cheek good-bye, a friendly smile, but that was it. He would never know that her stomach was churning, that the thought of not seeing him again was breaking her heart.

She looked up at the clock, wondering how much time she had left. It was past eight. Maybe it would be better to go upstairs and say good-bye in private, but the thought of seeing his bed again, remembering how much love they had made there, convinced her that the kitchen was a much better setting for good-byes.

With quick, deft hands Kara slipped the pancakes off the griddle and onto a plate. She was about to cook the next batch when the doorbell rang. Wiping her hands on a towel, she went to answer it.

A man and a woman stood on the front step, one with camera equipment, the other with an overnight bag.

"Can I help you?" Kara said.

"Madeline Mills from Channel 7 News in San Francisco," the woman said, handing Kara a card. "And that's Warren O'Brien. We've just arrived to cover the flood, and we need a place to stay the night. Do you have any openings?"

The woman spoke in crisp, no-nonsense, unemotional terms. Her expression was as cool as her frosted blond hair and ice blue eyes. Even at eight o'clock in the morning, her face had the spotless, pimple-free complexion of a television personality, and Kara instinctively reached toward her own face, wondering if she still had flour on it.

"Well?" Madeline tapped her foot impatiently.

"Of course I have rooms available, but as you can see we're not far from the river. We may have to evacuate."

"No problem. Do you have any rooms with a view of the river? Maybe Warren can take some shots from there."

"Yes, you're in luck. Most of the guests left yesterday after the Centennial Celebration."

Madeline brushed past Kara. She cast a sweeping gaze around the house. "Quaint," she said.

Kara cleared her throat and walked over to the desk. "If I could get some information from you and a credit card." She handed Madeline a form to fill out. When she was done, Kara inputted the data into her computer and rang up the credit card. As she finished the transaction and handed Madeline a key, Ryan walked into the living room.

Her heart skipped a beat. He looked impossibly gorgeous, his hair still wet from a recent shower, his face bright and shiny, his eyes so green. And he looked at her in such a way that told her he was remembering every second of their time together. Her entire body tingled as if he had touched her with his hands instead of his gaze.

"Ryan Hunter?" Madeline said, stepping between them, breaking the connection as abruptly as an unexpected downpour.

"Madeline?" Ryan's voice revealed his surprise. "What are you doing here?"

"Covering the flood. You, too?"

"No, this is my hometown."

"This little place? I can't believe it. Warren, can you believe that Ryan Hunter grew up in Serenity Springs?"

Warren shook his head. "No, but man, I love your work. Great stuff. Some of the best."

"Thanks. Since when does Channel 7 cover a small town a hundred miles north of San Francisco?"

"Since the weather service predicted another hundred-year flood sometime this week. We have people up and down the river. I think my boss got something on . . ." She turned to Kara. "What was it you said just ended?"

"The Centennial Celebration," Kara said.

"That's it. Carl thought it would be cute to use some of the stuff we got off the wire about the centennial and show how people are now suddenly fighting for their lives. What a difference a day makes, that kind of thing."

The possibility of a flood was not a "cute" story; it was a potentially life-threatening situation, Kara thought with disgust, but she tried to be pleasant. "Can I help you with your bags?"

"In a minute." Madeline took Ryan's arm. "You're staying here, too?"

"Actually I was planning on leaving today."

"Where are they sending you?" Madeline asked, her face lighting up with the kind of adoration Kara was becoming used to seeing on other women's faces.

"I don't have an immediate assignment, although I may go to Japan in a few weeks," Ryan replied.

"Japan. I'd love to travel more. I'm hoping to get in at CNN. I have an interview with them next week."

Kara's heart grew heavy as Madeline and Ryan talked about their respective careers, about a world that was so far removed from hers, Serenity Springs could have been Mars for all they had in common. She had been kidding herself to think even for a moment that Ryan could be happy here with her. He needed so much more than this small town. He needed the whole damn world. She could hear it in his voice as he told Madeline about his last trip to Greece, and the boat that sank and the train that derailed and the wedding of two ninety-year-old people.

"Kara?"

Ryan's voice brought her head up. "What?"

"I thought I might stay a little longer, maybe till tomorrow or Wednesday."

"Really?" Her heart sped up as she met his questioning eyes.

"Is that all right with you?" His question went way beyond the surface words, and Kara wasn't sure how to answer. She had prepared herself to say good-bye. She had promised herself a good cry. Now he wanted to stay.

"You do whatever you want to do," she said carefully. She would not ask him to stay. It had to be his decision.

"Then I think I'll stay."

She couldn't hold back the pleasure that his words brought forth. "Good."

"Maybe you can show me around, Ryan," Madeline said. "Introduce me to the right people."

"You've already met the most important person in this town, Kara Delaney," Ryan said, giving her a tender smile. "She's the president of the chamber of commerce and the heart of this town."

"Well, that's great," Madeline said. "When can we talk?"

"After breakfast," Kara said, touched by Ryan's respect for her, his faith in her. "You're welcome to join us."

"I'll just get my things. Warren, can you help me out?" Madeline asked.

Ryan turned to Kara as soon as they left. "I packed my bags, but I couldn't bring myself to carry them downstairs. I never thought it would be so difficult to leave."

"Because of the flood? Because of the news media arriving in town? Is that why you're staying? To capture the story on film for one of the magazines you work with? I mean, suddenly you have this great opportunity to—"

"To what?" Ryan demanded, his expression turning suddenly angry. "To further my career? I don't need Serenity Springs to do that."

"You have to admit you're in the right place at the right time."

"To get a photograph, maybe. To get you, no. If this were really the right place and the right time, I wouldn't be leaving in a few days."

"You don't have to go."

"I do." His eyes filled with pain. "It's in my blood. I have to keep moving."

"That's just an excuse. You don't have to do anything. You can make a choice. You can make a decision to stay, but you're afraid."

"You don't know what you're talking about."

"I've been where you are, Ryan. I know how easy it is to drift in life, to keep doing what you're doing because it's just too damn scary to try something else."

"That's not it," Ryan said. "I like my life the way it is. I'm doing exactly what I want to do." Ryan wished he felt as strong as his words.

"Then there's nothing more to say." Kara paused. "Except this. You can travel around the world, Ryan, but I guarantee you will never find anything that's better than this."

Kara stood on her tiptoes and kissed him on the mouth with passion and persistence and determination, all the things he had come to love in her. And when she broke the kiss, when she walked away from him, he had a feeling she was taking his heart with her.

*     *     *

By noon on Monday, Ryan was more concerned with his aching arms than his heart. For three solid hours he had shoveled sand into bags, helping a grim line of volunteers place them around the lower parts of the city.

Although he had planned to shoot some photos, Ryan quickly realized that while there were more than enough photographers recording the events, there were not nearly enough active participants, and for the first time in a long time he chose to participate instead of observe.

By one o'clock the river had risen another two feet. By three o'clock heavy winds had knocked out some of the electricity in the downtown area, sending residents to the local stores to stockpile canned goods and bottled water. With the exception of the media, most of the tourists had gone home, leaving the townspeople to battle the river. This was no longer a game or an event. They were fighting for their lives, for their homes, for their memories, for their futures.

There was no more division in the town. The raging river brought both sides together. It no longer seemed to matter who wanted a Taco Tommy's on Main Street. There wouldn't be a Main Street if the river flooded. So they worked together, the men and the women, the old and the young, the Applebornes and the Woodriches and the Hunters. And Ryan stayed right in the middle of it, sweating, straining, living each moment.

At five o'clock Kara stopped by. Her face was as dirty as his, her eyes filled with worry and exhaustion. "Angel and I are going home for a while," she said. "Are you coming?"

"Later. I want to check on Jonas."

"Okay."

Ryan caught her hand and squeezed it, wanting to kiss her, to hold her tight, to erase the lines of worry that creased her face. But Angel was watching them as well as the rest of the town, so he let her go.

"I thought you'd be taking pictures, not shoveling sand," Kara said.

"I think I can do more good filling these bags."

"You do care about this town, don't you?"

"Maybe a little."

"I'm glad." Taking Angel's hand, Kara led her daughter away. Ryan watched them go, wishing he could go with them. But he needed to see Jonas. He needed to make sure his father was all right.

When Ryan arrived at Jonas's house, he found his father kneeling on the floor surrounded by half-packed boxes, holding his mother's fragile bud vase between his old, lined hands with an expression of intense sorrow.

As Ryan looked closer, he realized that the man was actually weeping. Ryan couldn't believe what he was seeing. The emotion on his father's face was so stark, so painful, and so utterly private. Ryan instinctively backed up to the front door and knocked.

Jonas covered his expression as soon as he saw Ryan in the doorway, but Ryan knew he would never forget the sight of his father on his knees, cherishing a bud vase. The intimidating man from his youth had vanished. In his place was a lonely, frail man.

Maybe Jonas deserved to end up this way, old and alone. He had been cruel and hard most of his life. It was no wonder that the townspeople feared him more than they loved him, and that his own sons felt more wary than warm.

But as Ryan faced his father now, he knew that he no longer had the energy or the desire to carry a grudge. He felt sorry for Jonas, for all that they had had and all they had lost.

Jonas set the bud vase down in a box and cleared his throat. "I thought you had gone."

"I decided to stick around a while. See what happens with the river." *And with you.*

Jonas continued packing, ignoring Ryan, but the silence wasn't as cold as it had been before. Ryan sat down on the couch. "So how are you?"

"Fine."

"Do you need anything?"

"No." Jonas shook his head.

"Where are you putting those boxes?"

"Upstairs."

"I'll help you."

"Why?"

Ryan counted to ten. "Because I want to talk to you."

"About what?"

"About Becky Lee and Mom."

Jonas stiffened. "I don't talk about your mother."

"Fine, let's start with Becky Lee then." Ryan handed his father the masking tape as Jonas pulled the corners of the box down. "Andrew said Becky Lee had a long talk with you just before she left him. I want to know what she told you, and more importantly what you told her."

"You think I remember every conversation I've had in my life?"

Ryan smiled. "Yes, I do. Did Becky Lee tell you I was the father of her baby?"

Jonas lifted his head, and after a slight hesitation he said, "No, she didn't say that."

Ryan let out a sigh of relief. "Then Billy really is Andrew's son?"

"Yes."

"But you never assured him of that fact."

"I didn't know he had any doubts."

"Of course he had doubts. I'm sure you did, too."

Jonas shrugged. "In the beginning I thought you were letting Andrew clean up your mess, the way you always did, especially when you left town so fast. It never occurred to me that she hadn't told you she was pregnant."

"Because you liked to believe the worst about me."

"It was easier that way."

Ryan read the truth in his father's eyes. Yes, it was easier to hate than to love, and much safer. Jonas set the box down on the floor and reached for his stack of fishing magazines on the coffee table.

"There's one more thing," Ryan said.

"I told you I won't talk about her."

"Angel thinks there's a ghost at the river. She thinks this ghost is Mom. In fact . . ." Ryan dug into his pocket. "Angel found this by Tucker's Bridge." He held up the Mickey Mouse watch.

Jonas stared at the watch as if it were a snake about to strike. Finally he took it from Ryan's hand and sat down heavily on the couch. "Angel found this?"

"Yes. I threw it in the river twenty-five years ago. Suddenly it's back."

"You're not telling me you believe this crazy story?"

Ryan sat down on the other end of the couch. "Is Mom dead?"

Jonas turned white at the word. "How the hell would I know? I haven't heard from her since the day she walked out on us. Why don't you ask Kara Delaney?"

"Kara doesn't know. She didn't even know her father . . ." Ryan stopped as he saw the look of discomfort cross Jonas's face. "Her parents split up right after the flood, and although she received occasional cards from her father, she never saw him. When he finally did come back into her life years later, he was alone, and he never mentioned Mom."

"So what? Maybe Isabelle realized he was an idiot and left him, too."

Ryan pressed his fingers together. "It doesn't add up. Where is she, Dad?"

"I don't know."

Ryan gave him a hard look, trying to get past the outer shell, and for a moment he did, when their eyes connected, when he realized that his father wanted to know the answer as much as he did.

"You tried to find her," Ryan said suddenly, hitting on a truth that was completely unexpected.

"Yes." Jonas leaned his head back against the couch. "About two years after she left. I couldn't come up with anything. I kept thinking that one day she would just show up again, or I'd see her picture in a story that came across the wire, or I'd hear from some long-lost relative of hers. But I never did."

"Maybe she is dead."

"That's possible. But she's not a damn ghost. And if she were, the last place she'd haunt would be the river. She hated it almost as much as you do."

Ryan smiled to himself. "Sometimes I think I hated it because you loved it so much. I had to compete with the river for your attention, except the river always won."

"The river didn't talk back to me."

"And I did." It made sense. Jonas liked things and people he could control.

"Ryan—"

"What?"

Jonas stared up at the ceiling. "I never meant for you and Andrew to get caught in the flood. My heart just about stopped when I saw you two clinging to the roof."

"I never would have guessed. You yelled at us for not taking any drinking water up there with us."

"I didn't know how to tell you I was sorry. I knew you were scared of the water after that. But I wanted you to get over it, to see the river as I do, to feel its power, its magnificence."

"I never felt the river's power, just its anger. So much like your anger. I could never make you happy."

A second voice joined Ryan's. "Neither could I," Andrew said. He stood in the doorway, watching both of them. Ryan wondered how much he had heard. Maybe it was good that he had come now. The three of them needed to talk together.

Andrew walked forward with purposeful steps, looking more sure of himself than Ryan had ever seen. Even Jonas sat up straighter, waiting for Andrew to approach, to say what was on his mind.

"No matter what I did," Andrew said. "I either came in second to Ryan or screwed up completely." He looked from Ryan to Jonas. "And damned if I didn't try to please you. In fact, I'm still trying. But this is the end of the line, Dad. You can't run the paper anymore, so you either trust me with it or I walk away."

Ryan stared at his brother in amazement.

"You're walking out on me?" Jonas demanded.

"I don't want to, but I want control of the paper. I need to pay bills, which means I put my signature on the bank card. No one will talk to me. Everyone is waiting for you to come back and take charge. I'm tired of being treated like a child. I'm an adult, and I can run that paper as well as you can."

Jonas flushed a bright, angry red. "I ain't dead yet, Andrew. It's my paper."

Andrew's hands clenched into fists at his sides. "You will be dead if you come back to work. I spoke to your doctor this morning."

"You had no right."

"I had every right," Andrew said forcefully. "I'm your son, dammit. And I might just be the only one who cares two cents about you, so don't you think it's time you started reciprocating?"

Jonas's mouth dropped open. He was utterly speechless. Ryan felt much the same way, as if a sleepy bear had just come out of a thirty-seven-year hibernation.

"Your doctor told me," Andrew continued, "that if you don't stop working and start taking better care of your heart, you're a prime candidate for another heart attack, a big one this time. Now, I want the keys to the safe and I want your signature on these." Andrew set two bank release forms down on the coffee table.

Jonas refused to pick them up. Instead he looked at

Ryan as if he wanted his support. But Ryan would not take sides against his brother, not this time.

"He's right," Ryan said.

"What do you care? You'll be gone by morning, or as soon as you get a better offer."

"Maybe. I like the outside world, Jonas. I like meeting people who speak other languages, listening to songs where I don't understand a word. That's who I am. I have to accept the fact that you're a grumpy old man who couldn't say 'I love you' if your life depended on it. Why can't you accept me as I am?"

Jonas didn't speak for several minutes. The air was thick with tension, with words that had needed to be said for a long time. "I didn't think you cared one way or the other," he finally said.

"That's not an answer."

Jonas tried to stare him down. Ryan refused to back off.

"You're a good photographer," Jonas admitted with a trace of grudging admiration in his tone. "You don't need me to tell you that. You got the whole world. And you—" He turned to Andrew. "*The Sentinel* is the central point for news and information on the river. With the media swarming all over us, you won't be able to handle things alone."

"I can handle the writing and the other media, and—"

"And I can handle the photography and whatever else needs to be done. I did spend every summer of my childhood working on that paper," Ryan finished, not sure where those words had come from, but now that they were spoken, he was pleased. Both Jonas and Andrew looked at him in surprise. "I'd like to help," he added.

"You two ganging up on me?" Jonas asked. He looked touched, taken aback, almost overwhelmed.

Andrew glanced over at Ryan, then slowly nodded. "Yes, we are ganging up on you."

"Does that mean I can help?" Ryan asked, feeling like the little brother once again.

"I guess, but I'm the boss, got that?"

Ryan laughed. Some things never changed.

# 26

Kara waited up for Ryan that night, but she didn't hear his footsteps in the hall until midnight. Although a part of her longed to sneak into his room and crawl into bed with him, another part of her said absolutely not. So she stayed where she was—cold, shivery, and alone.

Tuesday morning brought more media and more water. Kara and her aunt spent most of the day helping elderly residents evacuate a trailer park just south of downtown. The residents were scared, some too old to walk, some terrified of losing their last few belongings to the river.

Josephine worked miracles, soothing everyone's fears with her calm, efficient manner and her no-nonsense approach. She didn't want to alarm them, but she absolutely refused to let anyone ride out the storm in the hope that the worst wouldn't happen.

Kara saw little of Ryan that day. When she wasn't setting up a shelter at the rec center and another at the high school, she was making coffee and feeding hungry sandbagging volunteers.

She tried to keep Angel busy and away from the river, but the schools had closed for a few days due to the rising water, giving Angel too much time to think about her ghost. Kara finally stopped worrying. Her daughter was smart enough to stay out of danger. Plus, Kara had about as much chance of stopping Angel as she did of stopping the river. Both were determined to go their own way.

By ten that night, Kara's worries turned to Ryan. With the thought of sleep seemingly impossible, Kara went down to her kitchen and began to bake. For two hours she mixed flour, sugar, and salt. She kneaded and rolled and cut and shaped and finally baked. The smells of vanilla, ginger, and cinnamon soothed her troubled mind. By midnight she had cakes, pies, and cookies cooling on the counter. She was just cleaning up the last bit of flour when Ryan came in.

His strong hands caught her waist and his warm mouth touched her neck. Kara silently thanked God for bringing him back for at least one more night. She turned into Ryan's arms and gave him a welcoming smile.

"Hi," she said.

"Hi, yourself. I've missed you."

His voice sounded husky. His eyes were dark with emotion. He looked at her with desire, with longing, with need. Kara knew those emotions were reflected in her own eyes, because she felt each one like a hunger pain that wouldn't go away until she fed herself, until she feasted on him. She touched his face with the back of her hand, noting the weary lines beneath his eyes.

"You look tired," she said. "Where have you been?"

"Helping Andrew get out a special flood edition of *The Sentinel*."

Her mouth fell open. "You and Andrew are working together?"

Ryan leaned over and kissed her, taking advantage of her vulnerable mouth. "Mm, you taste good. Like hot coffee and whipped cream. Can I have some?"

"I can make you a cup," Kara said, but Ryan kissed her again, making a mockery of her answer.

She pushed her hand against his chest. "Wait a second. I want to hear more about you and Andrew."

Ryan shrugged. "Andrew needs help. My father certainly can't do it."

"And you can?"

"I'm not helpless. I grew up at that paper."

"That's not what I mean. Last I heard Andrew hated your guts. And Jonas felt the same way. What did I miss?"

"I went by the house yesterday. I found Jonas packing up the downstairs. He was holding this vase of my mother's in his hand and he was crying." Ryan wearily shook his head. "When I saw him like that, I realized how pointless our feud was. When my mother left, we all lost someone we loved. Maybe it doesn't matter anymore why she left. Maybe we can't keep living our lives based on something that happened twenty-five years ago."

Kara squeezed his hands. "I'm glad you've made peace." She paused. "Ryan, when are you leaving?"

"A day or two."

"That's what you said a couple of days ago."

"Trying to get rid of me?"

"No, just trying to figure you out."

"An impossible task. I haven't figured myself out yet. You know, with all the media in town, Serenity Springs is going to get plenty of coverage. Just what you wanted."

"But this isn't what I wanted the world to know. I wanted them to see the river in its glory, not in its fury."

"You can't have one without the other. Every rose has a thorn. Every love affair has an ending."

"Is that what we had—a love affair?"

"You said no strings," Ryan reminded her.

Kara took in a deep breath. "And I meant it. I just don't know what the proper etiquette is here. I could have handled things if you had left yesterday morning, but now—now it's more difficult. I don't know how to act around you. I don't know what you want from me."

Ryan stopped the flow of words with his mouth, taking her with his tongue as surely as if he'd taken her with the rest of his body. When he lifted his head, she felt dizzy.

"God, how do you do that?" she asked. "How do you make me want you with just one kiss?"

"I want you, too, Kara. As much as you're willing to give me." Ryan flipped off the switch behind her head, plunging the kitchen into darkness. The dim light blinded Kara to the reality of her situation, to the empty future ahead. She was only aware of the storm outside, the storm within, and Ryan's outstretched hand. After a moment she took his hand, and they walked up the stairs together.

He made love to her slowly this time, gently, tenderly, tracing her body with his hands so he could remember every fine detail. He started with her face, trailing his fingers down the slender column of her neck and shoulders, her lush, full breasts, the dark nipples, the cluster of freckles that encircled her heart as if they were gatekeepers.

Ryan kissed each one of those freckles, tormenting them, wanting to erase them with his lips, wanting entrance into her heart and into her body. He moved on to her breasts, arousing her with his fingertips, then with his mouth until he heard soft cries coming from her lips. He moved his hands down her rib cage, encircling her waist, feeling the soft roundness of her abdomen, memorizing the curves of her body so he would know the way home.

He ran his fingers along the inside of her thighs, into the soft red curls that accentuated her femininity. Kara called his name. Her hands touched his shoulders hesitantly, as if she was unsure whether to push him away or hold him in place.

But there was no hesitancy in his mind. He wanted to touch her, to taste her, to take her as high as she could go. So he touched her with his fingers, then with his mouth, swirling, sucking, caressing until she cried out and her body shook. Then he slid back up her body, separating her thighs with his knees, pressing inside her hot, wet body, taking her moans inside his mouth.

And this time when she came, they came together.

Kara reluctantly left Ryan's bed just before dawn, sliding out from the warm, cozy cocoon of love into the cold, damp darkness of the morning.

She could have gone back to bed in her room, but she was no longer sleepy. Tired yes, exhausted even, but her mind was whirling, her senses tingling. She felt more alive than she had in a long time.

She let the puppies out in the light misty morning, wiping them off with a towel before she let them back in the house. By the time everyone else made their way downstairs, the heater was going and the smell of freshly ground coffee filled the house.

A half hour later, as Kara surveyed her beautiful breakfast table and the delighted smiles on the faces of her guests as they attacked stacks of pancakes, fluffy eggs, and hash brown potatoes, she knew that she had finally found something she was good at. This house was her haven, her place to shine, and damned if she wasn't proud of it.

Ryan caught her eye. He gave her a loving, intimate wink, and she blushed like a schoolgirl. Fortunately Angel interrupted.

"I heard on the radio the schools are closed again today," Angel said with delight.

Kara nodded. "I heard that, too. Don't look so happy; it's not exactly good news."

"It is for me. Now I can go down to the river and look—"

"Angel, please. I don't want to hear any more about the ghost or the necklace or anything. It's a great story, one of your best, but please find another one."

Angel appeared hurt as she sat back in her chair. "It's not a story."

Kara sighed, glancing over at Ryan. He shrugged as if to say let her be, let her have this time to live in a world of fantasy. What harm could it do? Probably nothing, Kara decided, as long as Angel stayed away from the river. She didn't want her in any kind of danger.

The doorbell rang, and Kara got up to answer it. Dirk Anders stood on the doorstep, his yellow slicker wet from the morning rain. His expression was serious, his voice gruff as he spoke.

"Is Ryan here?"

"Of course, he's just finishing breakfast. Come in."

As Kara stepped aside, Ryan came down the hall. "What's wrong?" he asked.

"The river is five steps from the lower deck at your dad's house."

Kara gasped. "It's that high?"

Dirk nodded, looking straight at Ryan. "I can't get Jonas out of the house. He has a boat, but I worry about leaving him up there, especially in his condition."

"I don't think he'll listen to me," Ryan said, frustration marking his voice. "He does what he wants. You know that."

"You have to try."

"All right."

"And Kara . . ." Dirk sighed.

"Don't say it," she said.

"You may have to evacuate, too."

"No."

"Don't make me say it twice."

"The river would have to rise at least another fifteen feet to even touch the lawn."

"Ten feet," Dirk corrected. "And she's rising fast, like an angry woman bent on taking back all of her belongings."

"The ghost lady said the river's going to flood by

tomorrow," Angel declared as she joined their conversation. "She said that Mr. Hunter, Jonas, has to leave this time."

"Well, maybe you can get that ghost friend of yours to talk to Jonas. Maybe he'll listen to her," Dirk said with a smile, tipping his head at Kara and Ryan. "I've got to move on. There's plenty of room at the high school and the rec center, Kara, for you and your guests."

"But all my things are here," she protested, echoing the same sentiment expressed by everyone who lived by the river.

"There might still be some storage lockers in the next town if you want to move valuables today. If not, some folks over in the next town are renting out their garages."

"Thanks, I'll think about it."

"Don't think too long. Time is not on your side."

"Are we going to leave, Mom?" Angel asked with her usual wide-eyed expression as Kara closed the door.

Kara knew she should say yes, but every instinct told her to say no. This was her home. This was the place where she had found love and peace and herself. How could she leave it? How could she let the river take it away from her?

"You can't stay," Ryan said. "Not if the river is rising that fast."

"Dirk is just being extra cautious." Kara reopened the door. "Look, you can see the water is still . . ." Her voice faded away as she realized the water was much closer than she had anticipated.

"My God." Ryan put his arm around Kara and Angel in a protective gesture.

Kara put her own arm around his waist. "It's okay, Ryan. It's not that bad."

"You have to get out."

Kara licked her lips. She would get everyone out, and she would box up her things and take them to higher ground, but she wasn't going to spend the night at some shelter while her house was going under. She would put out sandbags. She would move the furniture to the second floor. Her mind raced with everything that she had to do.

"Angel, start packing your things, just as a precaution," she said, trying not to alarm her daughter. Angel didn't look scared, just excited by the whole adventure.

After Angel left, Kara turned to Ryan. "I'll tell the guests that they need to move to higher ground. Where—where do you think you'll go? To the rec center or the high school or—back to Los Angeles?"

"I'm not sure."

"I know you don't like the river when it gets like this."

His jaw tightened. "No, but I can't walk away right now, not knowing what's going to happen. It would be like putting down a book right before the last chapter."

"It's easy enough to put down a book if you don't care about the people."

"Maybe I do care," he said.

"Then you should stick around to see how things turn out."

"Maybe I will."

But Ryan didn't stick around the Gatehouse. Instead he went to see his father. He had to wade through a foot of water just to get up the driveway. The river was licking the bottom steps like a hungry child with a tantalizing sucker.

Ryan felt a rush of nervous tension as he looked at the water. He hadn't been this close to it in a long while. Even during the sandbagging he had managed to keep a respectable distance. But now it was right on top of him. For a moment he wasn't sure he could take another step. The river had a way of paralyzing him. Then the front door opened. Jonas stood there, wearing knee-high boots, blue jeans, and suspenders.

He grabbed Ryan by the arm and pulled him into the house when Ryan seemed to waver, leaning, drifting, as the river hypnotized him with its movement.

"Ryan. Ryan." Jonas lightly slapped his cheek.

Ryan started at the sudden stinging pressure. "What did you do that for?"

"You almost fell in the river out there."

"No."

"I've seen it happen. You get so caught up in the movement, in the current, that you start to go with it. It's easier to go with it than to fight it."

Ryan swallowed hard. "That's the way I remember it, the way it felt when we sat on the roof and watched it coming to get us." He shook the disturbing image out of his head. Then he looked around the room. Jonas had packed up most of the things and put them upstairs. The walls were bare. Even the carpet had been rolled back and stuffed upstairs. "Are you ready to go?"

Jonas stared at him. "I'm not leaving, Ryan."

"You have to. You've been ordered to evacuate."

"I'll stay at my own risk."

"Why?" Ryan sighed. "What's the point?"

"The point is this is my home. I won't leave it to the mercy of the river."

"What are you going to do when the river comes through the walls and up the stairs?"

"She won't get that high."

"*She* is not your friend or your lover, she's an enemy. She's a body of water intent on destruction."

"You don't understand her like I do," Jonas said. "I don't expect you ever will. Go on, Ryan. Go back to your jet-setting life. I'll be fine here."

Ryan paced around the room, not knowing what to do. He felt helpless. He couldn't physically remove his father from the house, but he couldn't leave him there either.

"Why are you so stubborn?"

"Why do you care? A week ago I could have been dead for all you knew."

"A week ago I was still filled with anger. But coming back here changed all that."

"What changed?" Jonas demanded. "I'm still the same. You're still the same, and your mother is still gone. Just like when you left."

"When I left I didn't know how much I was going to miss having a family, a home. I've never hung one picture on my apartment walls and I don't own any furniture. I never wanted to be tied to a house the way you are." Ryan looked at his father long and hard, trying to see past the surface. What he saw made him realize something else. "It's not the house, is it? It's her. She's here. The little you have left of her is here."

Jonas turned away. "You're a fool."

Ryan put a hand on his father's shoulder and forced him to turn around. "Am I? You loved her, didn't you?"

"Of course I loved her," Jonas said loudly. "I worshiped her. But she left, dammit, she left."

"You sent her away. I saw the letter, remember?"

Jonas's eyes filled with sorrow. "I talked to her after I got the letter. I begged her to come back. I told her I would get you and Andrew, and we would find somewhere to stay. But she had to make her choice. And she made it. She left."

Ryan couldn't believe what he was hearing. That wasn't the way the story went. "You never told me this before."

"You weren't ready to listen then. You hated me. I couldn't have changed your mind."

Maybe not then, Ryan silently admitted. He had been too young, too full of his own ideas, too stunned by the letter to hear the other side of the story. And later . . . later he had been gone.

"None of that matters anymore," Ryan said. "Why she left, where she went, we'll probably never know.

What's important is now. Maybe we can be a family again."

Jonas's hand shook as he brushed his hair away from his eyes. "You and Andrew need to find your own families."

"That would make it easy for you," Ryan said angrily. "Then you wouldn't have to change. You wouldn't have to open your heart up again. You wouldn't have to say the words that you've never been able to say." Ryan's voice caught. "I was a stupid little kid when Mom left. I was nine years old. I missed her so much. I cried in my pillow every night for a year. Where were you, Jonas? Why the hell couldn't you be there for me? You wanted me with you. You wouldn't let her take me, so where were you when I needed you?"

"I—I didn't know how."

"They're just words, Jonas. You can't say them even now, can you?" Ryan answered his own question. "No, you can't. God, why am I beating my head against a wall?" Ryan headed to the door. "You want to stay here, fine. Do what you want."

"I'm leaving," Billy announced, stopping dead in his tracks a good twenty feet from the raging river. "We can't get any closer. It's too dangerous."

The wind blew Angel's hair across her face, blinding her view. In that moment of blindness, she heard a voice call to her, pleading with her not to leave.

She brushed the hair out of her face and stared at the river. She couldn't see the lady, but she could feel her presence, her need. "I have to get closer," Angel said.

"Don't be stupid, Angel. There's no ghost and there's no necklace. It's just a story."

"She could be your grandmother." Why didn't Billy understand how important it was to find out the truth?

"My grandmother left town years ago. My dad said

she hated this place. There's no way she would still be here."

"Maybe she got trapped. Everyone thought she had gone, so no one went to look for her."

Billy rolled his eyes. "Yeah, right."

"It could have happened like that."

"It didn't."

"You don't want to see her, do you? You're afraid."

"I am not."

"Well, I'm getting closer." She walked on ahead, ignoring his calls to come back. She felt something drawing her in, something so strong she couldn't walk away, at least not without finding out what it was.

Angel walked along the bank, calling out for the lady. She couldn't tell where Tucker's Bridge was now that the river was so high, but she could see the Hunter house just downriver and knew she couldn't be too far away.

Finally she stopped, breathless from scrambling through the bushes and a little nervous from the roar of the wind and the sound of branches snapping off the trees and crashing into the water, as noisy as a hundred kids in a swimming pool.

"Angel."

She whipped around and saw the lady floating above the water, her yellow and red scarf protecting her hair from the rain.

"I was afraid you stopped believing in me," the lady said.

"I didn't know where you were."

"Here, where I've always been. Time is running out. I must find my necklace by tomorrow. I believe it is caught in the branches of the tree that Jonas's father planted when he was born. When the water gets high enough, it will shake everything loose. You must get it for me."

"Are you—" Angel suddenly couldn't ask the question. She wasn't sure she wanted to know the answer.

"It doesn't matter who I am. What matters is that they don't end up like me. Did you warn them, Angel? Did you tell them the river will flood by tomorrow?"

"I did, but I don't think they believe me."

"And Jonas, did you tell Jonas?"

"He won't listen to me."

"You must make him listen."

"How?" Angel asked in bewilderment.

"Tell him a story," the lady urged. "A story about me. Tell him about my hair and this scarf and my ring." She held out her hand and showed Angel a brilliant blue sapphire on the third finger of her left hand. "You must convince him. I know you can do it. Because you have the words and the imagination to make him believe. Tell Jonas to leave the house before it is too late. Tell him I miss him."

As Angel blinked, the lady disappeared. But she could still see her face, her scarf, her ring.

The sound of crashing branches behind her made Angel jump. She whirled around again, this time coming face-to-face with Jonas. He was walking along the bank with his walking stick. When he saw her, he stopped abruptly.

"What the hell are you doing here?" His roaring voice was as loud as the river.

"I—I—" Angel glanced back over her shoulder, wondering why the ghost couldn't just appear now and talk to Jonas herself.

"Get on home now," Jonas commanded.

"Okay. But—" Angel licked her lips. "I'm supposed to tell you that the river is going to flood tomorrow and that you have to leave."

"Who sent you here? Your mother? One of those fool sons of mine?"

"The ghost lady."

His eyes bored a hole right through her. "I don't believe in ghosts."

"She said you would say that. She said to tell you

that she still has her ring, the blue sapphire.''

Jonas's hand shook slightly as he gripped his walking stick. "You don't know when to quit, do you, girl?"

"It's true, and she said to tell you about the scarf, the one with the yellow and red flowers." Angel tried to think of a story to go with it, but for once her mind was blank.

Jonas brushed past her, storming away so fast, Angel could do nothing more than call after him, "She said to tell you she misses you."

# 27

"Have you seen Angel?" Kara asked Josephine as she walked into the shelter that evening with two suitcases and a Hefty bag filled with Angel's stuffed animals. "I told her to stay right here until I got back."

Josephine finished wrapping a Band-Aid around the finger of a seven-year-old. "There you go, sweetie."

"I got an owie," the little girl said to Kara.

Kara looked at the Minnie Mouse Band-Aid with a somber expression. "I can see that. What happened?"

"Bobbie Webster bit me."

Kara hid a smile. "Why would he do that?"

" 'Cuz I was trying to count his teeth." The little girl scampered off to find her mother.

Kara's smile faded as she glanced around the rec center. It had been the sight of their beautiful banquet and the dazzling talent show. Now it was a shelter for the homeless. Cots had been set up barely a foot apart. Already there were children and adults huddled around radios listening for the latest updates on the weather.

"I hope that's the worst of it," Josephine said as she put away her first-aid kit.

"Why don't you go home and rest, Aunt Josephine. I'll look after things here."

"Here? And the Gatehouse? And everywhere else?

You're not a superwoman, Kara. You can't do everything."

"I'm not trying to do everything."

"Yes, you are. You have to realize that if the river floods and you lose everything, you won't be a failure."

"I know that," Kara said awkwardly, not comfortable meeting Josephine's eye.

"Do you? I don't think so. You have to be satisfied with your best, even if it's not good enough. Now, I want you and Angel to stay with me tonight, and the puppies, too. They've already made themselves at home on Ike's easy chair."

"I'll bet. Thank you, Aunt Josephine. Now I'm going back to the Gatehouse to finish packing up some things. If it gets too late, I might just stay there, so don't worry, okay?"

Josephine frowned. "Kara, it isn't safe."

"I'll be fine until tomorrow. I need more time to get things together. Even Dirk said he was just warning me to get ready, not giving an official order to evacuate."

"Kara, remember the tea leaves, the danger."

"Aunt Josephine, please. I can't argue about this. You know what that house means to me. I want to protect what I have."

"They're just things, Kara."

"Some things mean a lot."

"The Gatehouse has been flooded before, twice in my lifetime. It will happen again. Maybe not today or tomorrow, but sometime. You have to accept that."

"I don't know if I can."

"Kara, it's not the house that makes you happy. Haven't you figured that out yet?"

Kara was saved from answering as Angel and Billy walked into the shelter holding a bedraggled kitty.

"Look what we found, Mom, Loretta's cat." Angel stroked the shivering wet cat with her hand. "Do you have any towels?"

Josephine handed her a small dish towel. "Here you go."

"Thanks."

"I'm glad you rescued Loretta's cat, but I thought I told you to stay here," Kara said.

"Uh—well," Angel looked guilty. "I had to—"

Kara held up her hand wearily. "Save it for tonight, Angel, when I need a bedtime story."

Angel shrugged. "Okay."

"Have you seen my dad?" Billy asked.

"Did you try the paper?"

"Only Uncle Ryan was there," Billy said. "I couldn't believe he was working on Grandpa's newspaper."

"I find it hard to believe, too. But your grandfather certainly can't do everything himself. It's about time he realized that."

"Sounds like someone else I know," Josephine said.

Kara ignored her aunt's pointed interruption, waving to Andrew as he walked into the shelter looking tired and worried.

Billy ran into his dad's arms.

"Are you okay?" Andrew asked. "I got a call from Mrs. Murray saying she was leaving town."

"I'm fine."

"You sure?"

Billy nodded. "Yeah, I'm sure."

"Good, because I need to find Loretta."

"Is something wrong?" Kara asked.

"Loretta left the bar a couple of hours ago and hasn't come back. The roads to her house are six inches deep. I thought she might have come here." Andrew suddenly noticed the cat in Angel's arms. "Hey, that's Loretta's cat," he said with alarm. "Where did you find her?"

"Down by the river," Angel replied.

"I told you not to go near the river," Kara said.

"We couldn't just let her drown. We were careful."

"Oh, Angel, what am I going to do with you?"

"Dirk said he evacuated Loretta's street early this morning," Andrew interrupted. "I know she wouldn't have left her cat behind. Where could she be?"

"I'm sure she's around," Josephine said. "Loretta knows how to take care of herself."

"She's nine months pregnant," Andrew said. "And she's nowhere near as tough as she talks."

Kara heard the worry in his voice, the tenderness; and it suddenly became clear to her that Andrew cared about Loretta. How could she have been so blind?

"I don't know you at all, do I?" she said softly, drawing Andrew's attention back to her. Josephine discreetly led the kids away from their conversation.

"I don't know what you mean."

"You're in love with Loretta."

"Don't be ridiculous."

"I'm not." Kara's conviction grew stronger with his reaction. "I should have seen it before. She's the one who got you to admit that Ryan didn't kill Becky Lee. She's the one who got you to climb a tree and rescue her cat."

"I was just walking by. It was no big deal."

"And it was Loretta's lunch you bought at the picnic."

"I couldn't afford your lunch."

Kara pulled him over to one side, away from the front door, away from the people coming into the shelter. "Why didn't we ever make love, Andrew?"

"What?" he said with a shocked sputter.

"How could we have thought of marrying each other without being together in the most intimate way?"

"I—I don't know, Kara. I thought you wanted to wait. I thought you wanted to build a friendship first. It didn't seem right with the kids and all to do anything else."

"It didn't seem right, because neither one of us wanted it badly enough."

Andrew pulled at the collar of his shirt as if it were

suddenly too tight. "I don't want to talk about this."

"I know you don't. You never want to talk to me about anything, about your father or Ryan or Becky Lee. But you talk to Loretta, don't you?"

"She already knows everything."

"Yeah, I guess she does."

Andrew finally relented. "It's different with Loretta. I don't have to pretend. She knows all my faults. She has seen most of my embarrassing moments. I can be myself with her."

"I never asked you to be more than that."

"You never asked, but you expected it, because you have high expectations. You don't need me, Kara. You're so damn strong. The truth is you scare the hell out of me."

"I do?" Kara asked in amazement.

"Yes, you do. And so does Angel. You both need someone who isn't afraid of life, someone who wants to sit on the roof with you and count the stars, someone who wants to listen to Angel's wild stories and chase puppies around the house every night. But most of all you need someone as strong as you are. I'm not that man. We both know that."

She thought about what he had said and knew it was the truth. "I guess we do."

"I'm sorry about the things I said the other day, about your father. I know you're not him, but when—"

"When you look at me, you see him," she finished.

"Actually when I look at you I see Ryan. I see you two dancing at the banquet, laughing together, smiling at the same jokes. I see the way he looks at you and the way you look at him, and I know that you never looked at me that way. I want that look, Kara. This time around, I want that look to be only for me." Andrew paused. "I've got to go. I need to find Loretta and make sure she's okay."

Kara nodded. "Go."

Andrew called to his son. "Billy, do you want to stay here?"

"No, I want to come with you. Please, Dad. We're a team. You said so, remember?"

"Yeah, I remember."

"Besides, you might need my help."

Andrew smiled at that. "No doubt." He gave Kara one last look. "Maybe Ryan will stay."

She shook her head, fighting back a rush of emotion. "I don't think so. You know better than anyone that Ryan can't stay in this town."

"Ryan never had a reason to stay before."

"He could have stayed for Becky Lee."

"Ryan didn't love Becky Lee," Andrew said simply.

"He doesn't love me either."

"You could have fooled me."

Kara worked until late that night, packing up the downstairs of the Gatehouse. As she wrapped her belongings in tissue paper and placed each one lovingly in a box, she felt as if she were saying good-bye to her friends. Although she could take her most valuable things to Josephine's house, she couldn't take everything, not the grandfather clock in the hall or the piano or the wallpaper that she had lovingly placed on the walls.

The big house was too quiet tonight. Gone were the sounds of the guests, the laughter, the chatter, her daughter's impatient footsteps on the stairs, Aunt Josephine's raucous laugh, and Ryan's saxophone music. Tonight she was completely alone.

Angel was tucked in at Josephine's house, and the guests had found other accommodations. Even Ryan was gone; she didn't know where. Some of his things were still in his room, so she knew he hadn't left town yet, but where he had holed up for the night, she had no idea.

Finally, exhausted, she crept into bed and studied the

wallpaper pattern going around her walls as she tried to hypnotize herself into a state of unconsciousness.

Sometime in the night the wind got stronger, and the rain pounded down on the roof like a relentless drummer. Kara pulled the quilt over her head, trying to block out the storm as she had blocked out so many bad things.

A loud thunderous roar followed by the sound of shattering glass sent her upright in bed. A burst of wind and rain ruffled her hair and wet her cheeks as the sharp edges of splintered glass hit the arms she instinctively raised to cover her face. When she tried to move, she couldn't. Something pinned her down, something scratchy and dark. Horror filled her mind as she wrestled with her unknown assailant.

"Kara? Kara?" The words came from the doorway. A shaft of light entered her room, spilling in from the hall. Ryan stared at her in shock. "My God."

"Get it off me," she cried out. "Get it off of me."

Ryan ran to the bed and pulled off a heavy branch from the oak tree that had fallen through her window. When she was finally free, he drew her trembling body into his arms and held her close. "It's all right. I've got you. You're safe."

Her breath came in rapid gasps, too quick to form words. All she could do was stare over his shoulder at the broken window, at the tree that had clawed her like the bony arm of a skeleton. She shuddered again. The shadows in the room raised monsters in her mind.

Kara suddenly felt something dripping down her cheek and her arm. In a daze she looked at her white nightgown. There were splatters of red everywhere.

"Am I bleeding?" she asked bemusedly.

Ryan gave her a critical glance. "You have some cuts on your face from the glass," he said. "Let's get you out of here." He swept her up in his arms before she could think about walking and took her down the hall to his room.

He laid her on the bed with gentle hands, then got a towel out of the bathroom and tenderly wiped the blood off her face. His expression was so solemn it scared her. "Is it that bad?" she whispered.

"No, but it could have been. When I think how close you came to being wiped out by that tree . . ." His voice thickened with emotion, then turned angry. "What are you doing here anyway? I thought you went to Josephine's house."

"I had a few more things to pack."

His hand fell to his side as he stared at her. She wished she could take her words back, wipe the expression of disappointment off his face. But she didn't know what she had done wrong.

"You can't leave, can you?" Ryan asked.

"This is my home."

"It's a house, Kara. You're just like Jonas. You'll risk everything for a stupid house, including your life."

"I'm not in danger," Kara said, realizing how foolish her words sounded in light of the fact that she was dripping blood on his bed.

"You're in danger of losing yourself."

"But this house is a part of me."

"You're making it more important than it is," he argued. "My father broke up his family because of a goddamn house, and you would do the same thing, wouldn't you?"

"No," she cried out.

"Yes," he said just as loudly, just as passionately.

The air between them sizzled with anger and frustration then passion as the dark night and their heightened emotions pushed reason away. Ryan reached for her with ruthless arms, kissing her again and again and again until they couldn't breathe. Then he set her away with just as much determination.

"No, I won't come in second to a house, not again." Ryan stood up. "I won't compete with a pile of lumber and a bunch of things."

He said the word so scornfully, Kara felt as if he had cut her with a knife. "Where are you going? It's the middle of the night."

"What do you care? Do you care that your daughter cried herself to sleep tonight because she didn't know when you were coming home?"

Kara stared at him in shock. "Angel? How do you—"

"Josephine told me. She called me at the paper. She sent me over here. Your daughter needs you, but where are you? You're saving your precious house. Just like Jonas. He left me alone in the flood so he could save the house."

Kara saw the terrible memories wash over Ryan's face. She wanted to tell him that it wasn't the same thing, that Angel wasn't in danger, but she knew that Ryan couldn't hear her. He was caught up in the past. He was reliving his own terror, and there was nothing she could do to stop it.

Instead of leaving he threw his things into his suitcase. Kara sat back on the bed, watching him take his fury out on a stubborn zipper and a pile of clothes that wouldn't fit in. Finally he gave up and threw the bag across the room. Then he stormed down the stairs. She waited for the front door to slam, but nothing happened.

Five minutes later she heard the sound of a power saw. In surprise she walked down the hall to her room. Ryan had chopped off the branches of the tree and was putting plywood over the window.

She wanted to ask why, but when he looked at her with an expression so grim, so bleak, so closed off, she couldn't do anything more than say thank you. She didn't return to his room, but to Angel's room. Seeing her daughter's cozy bedroom stripped of its stuffed animals, posters, and boxes of collectibles only made her feel worse.

She curled up on her daughter's bed with an extra blanket and stared at the shadows on the ceiling. She didn't know if Ryan stayed or if he left. She just knew that she had never felt so alone in her life.

"Leave me alone, Andrew." Loretta's head tossed back and forth on the pillow of the bed as she clutched her abdomen with her hand. She started to cry as pain ripped through her.

Andrew stared at her in alarm, then looked over at Billy, who had backed up against the bedroom door, unsure whether or not he wanted to stay. It had taken them a long time to get to Loretta's house. The streets were completely flooded.

Upon arriving at her house, he and Billy had had to crawl through a downstairs window as there were already several inches of water holding the door in place. At first Andrew thought she wasn't there, then he'd heard her scream and had raced upstairs to find her clutching a pillow to her chest.

"We have to get you to the doctor," Andrew said. "Billy, go downstairs and make sure the boat is still there."

Billy ran out of the room.

"No time," Loretta gasped. "I can feel the baby coming."

"The baby can't come now," Andrew said in horror. He didn't know anything about delivering babies. He hadn't even been in the room when Becky Lee delivered Billy. She had wanted her mother with her, and he had been relieved to give up that duty. The waiting room had been close enough for him.

"It's coming, Andrew."

"What are you doing here?" he shouted in frustration.

"I came back to find my cat."

"Good God, Loretta, what were you thinking?"

"I was thinking my cat was going to drown."

"What about your baby?"

"What about it? It wasn't supposed to come for another two weeks. Ow . . ." She cried out as the pain overcame her.

"Jeez, Loretta." Andrew reached out to touch her, but he didn't know where to put his hands, what to do, or what to say. "I'll call 911."

"The phone's out," Loretta said.

Right. He had tried calling her earlier. "Let me just carry you downstairs and get you in the boat."

Loretta grabbed his arm and screamed, "Forget the fucking boat, the baby's coming now."

"It can't."

"It is."

"All right. I'll boil some water or something."

"They only do that in the movies, Andrew."

"Well, what do you want me to do?"

"Get me some towels so I don't bleed all over the bed."

Blood. There was going to be blood. Andrew took a deep breath. He wasn't good around blood or crying women.

"What are you waiting for—an invitation?"

"Okay, I'll get you the towels. Don't go anywhere."

"No, I think I'll go dancing."

Andrew raced to the door. Billy was sitting on the top stair. "Is she okay, Dad?"

"No. She's having a baby."

"Uh, what—what are we going to do?" Billy stuttered.

Andrew found strength in that halting sentence. He couldn't let Loretta down, and he couldn't let Billy down either. "We're going to help her, that's what. Why don't you go downstairs? Check the garage for a CB radio. Loretta's dad used to have one."

"Okay."

"I shouldn't have brought you with me," Andrew muttered, suddenly realizing they could be trapped in Loretta's house if the water kept rising. "What kind of father am I?"

"You're my father," Billy said proudly.

"I've got to get you out of here."

"No, I want to stay with you. I'm not afraid of the river."

Andrew hesitated, then nodded. Billy was afraid of a lot of things, and despite his words he knew his son had a healthy fear of the river, but maybe it was more important to stay together than to send him away. He would protect his son no matter what the cost.

Loretta screamed his name, reminding him there was another life at stake—make that two more lives at stake. "Don't take anything Loretta says too seriously, Billy. She's not herself."

Billy grinned as Loretta let fly a string of curses that would make him the coolest kid in school if he could remember them.

Andrew found towels in Loretta's linen closet and brought everything he could grab, including a big beach towel. He threw them all on the bed, accidentally covering Loretta's head in the process.

"Oh, jeez, I'm sorry."

She glared at him, brushing strands of sweaty hair from her forehead. "You are an idiot."

"Me? I wasn't stupid enough to go looking for a cat when I'm about to have a baby."

"Get me a knife."

"What for?"

"So I can kill you before I kill myself."

Andrew looked at her warily. "I think you should calm down."

"I think you should go to hell."

"I'm only trying to help."

Loretta's face contorted with pain, and Andrew's heart went out to her. Without thinking he put his hands on her shoulders and rubbed her arms until the pain subsided.

"I am so scared," she whispered. "What if something goes wrong? What if I hurt the baby?"

"You won't."

"I might. I always screw up. You know I do."

"Not this time."

She twisted the sleeve of his shirt between her fingers. "I can't do this alone, Andrew."

"You don't have to. I'll stay with you."

"Really? The water's coming up."

"I can swim."

"But you have Billy with you."

"He's worried about you, too."

"He's a good kid." Loretta smiled weakly. "I didn't mean it when I called you an idiot."

He stroked her forehead. "I am an idiot, stupid for not realizing how much I love you."

"You love me?" she asked in wonder.

"God, yes."

"Even now?"

"Especially now."

Her eyes filled with tears.

"Another pain?" he asked in alarm.

She shook her head. "No one ever said that to me before." She playfully slugged him on the arm. "What took you so long?"

"I had to grow up first."

"Yeah, me too."

Her eyes met his, and he knew that they had both come a long way to get to this point.

"Andrew, about the baby's father."

"It doesn't matter. I'll be the baby's father if you'll let me."

"You're a generous man. Raising Billy alone, now offering to raise my baby."

"I want a family, Loretta. The blood doesn't matter, just the love."

Loretta's face tightened as she began to pant. "It's coming again."

"Hang on. Breathe."

Loretta started to gasp deep, wrenching breaths of air that made Andrew's stomach twist into a knot. It was unbearably difficult to watch her in pain. What was he thinking? He couldn't do this. He wanted to run, to hide, to get the hell out of town. But when Loretta looked up at him with her big brown eyes, when her fingers wrapped around his, he knew he wouldn't leave her. This time he would stay. This time he would fight for the person he loved.

"You can do it, Andrew," she said softly. "I have faith in you. I always have."

He hoped her faith wasn't misplaced. He had never been anyone's hero, never really risen to any occasion, usually too afraid to try; but this time he had no choice. He would do it. He would deliver this baby. Or die trying.

His confidence soared in front of her adoring face. Then the lights went out.

# 28

"Oh, God," Andrew said as Loretta began to cry. "It's okay. I've got a flashlight." He turned it on, pointing it toward the ceiling and away from her eyes. "Billy," he yelled.

Billy came to the door with his own flashlight. "I'm okay, Dad."

"Good. We need candles. Loretta, where do you keep the candles?"

"Downstairs in the kitchen," she gasped. "Don't leave me," she begged.

He heard the fear in her voice, the sudden doubt, and knew that as much as she wanted to have faith in him, it was difficult for her to trust him. He had run from her before, every time she tried to get close. "I'm not going anywhere." And he didn't have to, because Billy was already back with the candles.

"Good job, son. I knew I could count on you."

"I found the radio and put out an SOS. I'm not sure anyone heard me. There was a lot of static."

Andrew lit the candles and set them around the room. "Billy, you might want to wait outside."

Billy nodded with relief. "Okay, I'll keep my eye out for another boat."

Loretta began to pant again, alternating between crying and screaming. She called Andrew every name in the book as he tried to talk her through the contractions. When he finally got the courage to lift her dress and spread her legs, he could see the baby's head.

There was no time for thinking after that. No time to be afraid or embarrassed or inhibited. The baby came into his arms in a mess of fluid and blood and tangled limbs. It was the most beautiful thing he had ever seen.

Andrew tenderly wiped the baby off with a towel.

"Is it okay?" Loretta asked fearfully.

"She's beautiful."

"It's a girl?"

"A beautiful little girl." Andrew felt the tears come to his eyes as the baby blinked her eyes open and a tiny scream came out of her mouth as she squirmed in his arms. "She's perfect, ten toes, ten fingers—perfect."

Andrew cut the umbilical cord and wrapped the baby in a towel, then placed her on Loretta's chest. She started to cry as she tenderly touched the baby's head. "How could anything so beautiful come from me?"

"How could it not?"

"Dad?" Billy hovered in the doorway. "Is it okay?"

"More than okay. Come on in and say hello to—I guess we can't call her Andrew," Andrew said.

Loretta smiled. "How about Andrea?"

"Perfect."

Billy joined them on the bed. Andrew put one arm around his son and the other around Loretta's head. He finally had the family he had always wanted.

When Kara woke up the next morning, the house was freezing. Wrapping the blanket around her body, she walked down the hall, stopping by Ryan's room. His things were gone. The room looked bare, as if he had never been there, as if they had never made love on the bed, never found joy in each other's arms.

But she still had the house, she reminded herself as she walked downstairs and looked out the front window. The river was almost at her doorstep. She was out of time.

Ryan was right. She couldn't stay here. She couldn't leave Angel alone, not for another second. It didn't matter that deep in her heart she knew Angel was okay, that the river would never reach Josephine's house. What mattered most was that she had left Angel alone, as her mother and father had left her alone in the shelter.

How could she have done the same thing to her daughter? How could she have made the same mistake?

Kara ran up the stairs, dressed hurriedly, and threw a few of her clothes into an overnight bag. Then she went downstairs and out the back door, up the small incline behind the house where she had parked the car, and drove into town, trying not to look back, trying not to go back, because she was terrified that the next time she came down this road, her house would be gone.

She arrived at Josephine's house just before nine, expecting to see her daughter and aunt having breakfast in the kitchen. Instead she found Ryan on the phone and her aunt pacing back and forth across the room.

"Where's Angel?" Kara asked immediately.

"She's gone." Josephine held out a note.

Kara took the piece of paper with shaky hands.

*I have to find the necklace, Mom. If I don't find it by this afternoon, it will be too late. I'll be careful.*
                                        *Love, Angel*

Ryan hung up the phone and turned to Kara with worry in his eyes. "There's no one left to look for her, Kara. The river is supposed to crest in thirty minutes. There are flash flood warnings up and down the river. Every available man is helping with the evacuation."

"I'll go on my own then."

"I'll go with you," he said, his voice carefully even, not angry as he had been the night before, but not loving either.

"I thought you had left town."

"I couldn't go, not like this."

"I'm sorry, Ryan. I was stupid. You were right. I put the house before everything and everyone. I didn't mean to. I love Angel, you know I do." Her voice broke as she thought about her daughter all alone in the storm.

Ryan pulled her into his arms and hugged her tightly. "I know you love Angel. I was wrong, too, about a lot of things."

Although she would have liked to stay in the comfort of his embrace, they were wasting time. "I have to find her."

"We will. I tried Jonas, but the phone is out."

Kara stepped out of his arms. "Jonas can't still be in his house. It's right next to the river. Heck, it's probably in the river by now."

"Oh, he's still there." Ryan's mouth drew into a taut line. "He told me he wouldn't leave, not for anything. Not even if the water rose over his head."

"He didn't mean that."

"Yes, he did. I saw it in his eyes, Kara, the same look I saw in your eyes last night. I think that's what scared me."

"Maybe he came to his senses, too."

"I hope so."

"You can take my boat," Ike said as he came into the kitchen. "It's hitched up to my truck. Drive down as close as you can, then take it in. It's a small rowboat, but you may need it."

"Not your boat," Josephine said, her eyes suddenly filled with fear. "Remember the leaves. Danger and your boat."

"But I'm not going, Josie," Ike said.

"I'm afraid. Something terrible is going to happen." She put her hand to her heart. "I can feel it."

"We're going to stop something terrible from happening," Kara said with fierce, motherly determination.

"Take care of yourself." Josephine gave Kara a quick hug. "And you," she said, turning to Ryan, "you bring our girl home."

"I will. I don't suppose your crystal ball knows where she is?" Ryan asked.

Josephine shook her head. "I think if you find Jonas, you'll find Angel."

"You have to come with me," Angel cried. "The lady says you're in danger." Angel waded through the water in Jonas's living room. She grabbed his arm and tried to move him, but he wouldn't budge.

"I told you to go away," Jonas said. "I don't believe in your ghost."

"She's not my ghost. She's your wife," Angel said hotly. "Her name is Isabelle. And she sent me to get you. Her necklace is lost in the branches of the tree your father planted. She said you could tell me which one it is. Please," Angel begged.

Jonas stared at her in shock. She couldn't be telling the truth. She was a foolish, fanciful girl with a wild imagination. She had probably heard some story about Isabelle running off with her grandfather and made the rest up. But Angel began to cry with frustration.

"Why? Why is this so important to you?" Jonas asked, holding her shoulders with his big, thick hands.

"Because she's my friend. And she's sad. She said she's sorry about everything that happened. She said she still loves you, and if I can find the necklace, you'll know what really happened. She said she wants to see you one last time."

Jonas felt his heart begin to beat at an ungodly pace. His anxiety level rose so high, he almost couldn't breathe. *What really happened?*

Isabelle had left him. She had run off with another man. That's what had happened. But what was the necklace that Angel spoke of? Could it have been Isabelle's locket? No. Now he was starting to believe the foolish story.

But this child, with her big brown eyes and her captivating voice, almost made him believe that there was some secret left to be uncovered.

"You have to come," Angel said one last time.

Jonas looked around his house. "I can't leave." And he couldn't. He had vowed to stay here till the end, to protect his home. A man had nothing without his home.

God, who was he kidding? He'd had nothing since Isabelle left, and less still when the boys had gone.

Angel slid out from under his hands and ran out of the house. He watched her struggle through the water, finally reaching the upper end of the driveway and dry ground.

He wondered if he should go after her. Or if he should stay here where he belonged.

"Isabelle." He whispered her name, remembering her bright eyes, so like Angel's, her loving nature, her ready smile, her warmth. He had wanted to control her, to keep her by his side forever. But the same passion he adored had made her want more than he could offer.

She hadn't loved him enough to stay. He hadn't loved her enough to go after her.

Now he knew they had both made a terrible mistake. But it was too late. She was gone. His sons were gone. All he had left was this house. He closed his eyes, feeling dizzy. He saw Isabelle again in his mind. He heard her voice calling to him.

This time he would go. He gave the house one last look. There was nothing here that could touch him, nothing that he could put his arms around, nothing that he could love. Why hadn't he seen that before? Why had he been such a fool?

Jonas pulled on his raincoat and ran after Angel. He knew where the tree was. He knew where she was going. He just hoped he could get there in time, because that tree was probably underwater by now.

*    *    *

Angel saw the lady again, pointing her fingers to a particular tree. Angel also saw the gold strand twisted in the branches. She could climb up there and get it. She knew she could. But the tree bent halfway over the river. By the time she reached the necklace, she would only be a few feet above the water in the middle of the river.

"Don't," the lady said suddenly. "It's too dangerous. You will fall."

"I won't fall."

"I can't let you do this."

"You're my friend."

"Jonas isn't coming, is he?"

Angel started to climb the tree.

"No, stop."

"But you said if I helped you find the locket, you would get your family back."

"That's true, but—"

"You told me to believe. You told me not to give up."

Angel didn't wait for more protests. She had to get the locket. She had to set the lady free. The tree was wet and slippery. Every inch made her body stiffen with fear, but she kept on going. She could almost see the necklace when the tree branches began to sway and crackle. The branch she was on suddenly bent in half, landing her feet in the water.

She could feel the rush, the terror, as she clung to the branch. Slowly she pulled herself out of the water, climbing onto another branch. With her hand outstretched she finally reached the locket, and with a little maneuvering, she pulled it free from the branch.

Inside the locket was a picture of two little boys and the words, *With my love, Jonas.*

The river suddenly roared, and a wave of water came at Angel so fast she froze with terror. Suddenly the tree was engulfed in water, as if a bridge had broken upstream. She looked over to where she had started her climb and the ground was no longer there. She was trapped in the tree.

Angel heard someone call her name. She saw a man in a boat. It was Jonas. He told her to hang on. Angel could do little else. She looked for the ghost, but she couldn't see the lady through the branches of the tree, nor could she hear her voice over the roar of the river.

Jonas finally got to the tree, but when he tried to grab hold of the branches, the current was so strong that the boat went out from under him and he fell halfway into the water. Angel screamed and reached out a hand to him, trying desperately to pull the big old man out of the water.

She didn't know where her strength came from, but suddenly he was next to her, clinging to the branch as she was. He gasped for breath, his eyes wide and shocked. "How did you do that, kid?"

"I don't know." She handed Jonas the locket.

His mouth dropped open. "Isabelle's locket. She swore she would never take it off, not until her dying day. But how did it get here? How?" he yelled.

The lady floated down in front of them. "I was coming back, Jonas. I knew I couldn't leave you or the boys. But the river came up too fast and the boat tipped over. I—I couldn't swim well enough. I wanted to get to you, but I got so tired. I'm sorry. So, so sorry."

Jonas stared at the image as if he were mesmerized. "My God, you're real."

"Not anymore. I haven't been real or whole since I left you. I loved you, Jonas. I was a fool to think the city or Harry could offer me more than I had with you."

"I loved you, too, Isabelle," he whispered.

The lady reached out her hand. "May I have the necklace, please?"

Jonas looked at the locket in his hand. Angel watched them both with utter fascination, hardly believing that the ghost was real, that Jonas could see her, too. But something was wrong. Jonas was wrapping his fingers around the locket and shaking his head. The lady called his name again, telling him that time was running out, that she needed her necklace.

The tree began to sway, cracking under their weight. Angel watched the branch in horror, wondering if she and Jonas were going to die here, too.

Kara grabbed Ryan's arm as she saw her daughter and Jonas clinging to a tree in the middle of the raging river. A terror so overwhelming, so debilitating, made speech impossible. She wanted to shout at Angel to hang on. She wanted to tell Jonas not to let her daughter fall. And most of all Kara wanted to tell the damn river that if *she* really were a woman, she would not swallow up a little girl and an old man.

"Kara, help me with the boat," Ryan shouted as he backed the truck up to the edge of the river and let the rowboat slide down toward the water.

Kara held on to the boat as Ryan released it, then pulled the truck away. The water was up to their knees and rising fast, a raging torrent, impossible to fight. And their boat was small. It wouldn't hold more than two people. Only one of them could go.

Kara looked at Ryan's white face as he stared at the river in fatal fascination. He was terrified. She knew that as well as she knew her own name.

"I'll go," she said.

Ryan caught her arm. "You can't. You aren't strong enough to handle the current."

He was probably right. The river was an angry monster. Ryan's monster. The stuff his nightmares were made of.

"Ryan, are you sure?"

"I'll do it," he said grimly. "I'll save Angel. I promise you that. There's no way I'm going to let this river take my family away."

Ryan got into the boat, stuck his oars in the water, and pushed off. Kara watched him go with fear pounding against her chest. She took a breath every time he took a stroke, willing him to get to the tree, not to be swept downstream. Fortunately part of the tree's branches were in the water, providing a barricade that helped Ryan stay the course.

The trip seemed to take Ryan a lifetime. With each second that passed, Kara's love for him grew beyond all bounds, beyond all of her defenses. She loved this man. More than she had ever thought possible.

He was risking his life not just for his father but also for her daughter, a little girl he had known only a week. Ryan had told her he wasn't a hero, but she knew that he was. And more than just a hero, he was the man she wanted to spend the rest of her life with.

"Please God, let him be okay," she whispered. "Let Angel be okay. And Jonas, too. Jonas and Ryan are just learning how to be father and son. Don't take them now. Please." The litany of prayers went around and around in her head.

Finally Ryan reached the tree, stopping the boat by grabbing hold of one of the branches. Kara held her breath, watching and waiting. The boat could slip at any moment. They could all be lost. She had thought losing her home would be a horror beyond words, but losing the three of them seemed unimaginable.

Ryan held on to the branch, feeling the pressure of the water thrusting the boat forward. His muscles burned with the strain, but he would not let go. He would not let the river defeat him.

"Get in," Ryan shouted.

"You did it," Jonas said with amazement and pride. "I didn't think you had it in you. I'm proud of you, son." He looked up at Angel. "Put your feet on my shoulders and climb down. Now. There's no time to lose."

"But I don't want you to fall," Angel argued.

"I won't fall," Jonas said.

Angel slowly loosened her grip on one branch so she could take hold of another. She placed her tennis shoe on Jonas's shoulder and let him take her weight.

Ryan grabbed her arm with one hand, holding the boat steady with the other as she climbed in.

"Go on now," Jonas shouted. "Get her to shore."

"Not without you," Ryan said.

"The boat won't hold all of us."

He knew his father was right. "I'll come back for you."

"Don't come back. It's too late."

"What are you talking about?" Ryan cried.

Jonas held out the necklace in his hand, rain and tears drenching his face. "She was here all the time. Isabelle. She never left."

"What?"

"Your mother never left, Ryan. She got caught in the flood on her way back to us." Tears streamed down his face. "She drowned. All this time, she was here. If I had only looked up to the sky, to the top of the tree, I would have seen her necklace. I would have known the truth, but I always looked down."

Ryan didn't know what to say. He couldn't believe what he was hearing. But the roar of the water and the wind made discussion impossible. "We'll talk about it later."

"Ryan." Jonas looked at him for a long, heartbreaking moment. "I love you. Whatever happens, I want you to know that I love you."

Finally the words came from his father's mouth. They sounded like a good-bye.

"Tell Andrew I love him, too."

"You can tell him yourself."

"There's no time." Jonas put a hand to his heart. "I can't fight anymore, Ryan. Don't be sorry. No more wasted years. No more guilt." He looked toward the sky and smiled, his eyes suddenly filled with new light.

"I'm coming," he whispered before turning to Ryan. "Go on now."

Ryan hesitated, then steadied the boat and pushed off, rowing with all the strength he could find. When he got to the shore, Kara was up to her thighs in the water. She grabbed Angel, holding her close as if she would never let her go.

Ryan turned the boat around, intent on rescuing his father, but before he could put his oar in the water, his father let go of the branch. It didn't break. It didn't snap in two. His father just let go and slipped into the water.

"No!" Ryan screamed. "No!" He moved the oars with demon speed, racing after his father's fisherman's hat, which sailed down the water like a toy boat. When he finally reached the hat, he scooped it out of the water, but there was nothing else there. His father was gone.

"Dad. Dad." His voice broke as the horror of what had happened struck home. Ryan searched the water with his eyes, desperate for some trace of his father, but he knew it was too late.

His father was gone, buried in the river that he loved. Ryan closed his eyes and stopped rowing, letting the river carry him away, letting the rain mingle with his tears.

# 29

Kara watched Ryan disappear from view with a sense of horror. "Ryan!" she yelled. Her arms tightened around Angel until her daughter whimpered in pain.

The river couldn't take Ryan. He couldn't end up in the water, in the belly of the monster. God couldn't be so cruel.

Kara ran downstream, scrambling over rocks and through bushes, but the river moved too fast, veering away from her in a path she couldn't follow. She had to get to Ryan. She had to save him as he had saved her daughter.

But she couldn't reach him. She couldn't even see him anymore. Her heart ripped in two as her imagination took her down a path she didn't want to go. What if the boat tipped over? What if the water threw him against the jagged rocks? What if he became so paralyzed with fear that he couldn't swim?

She couldn't lose him. Not now—not after realizing how much she loved him.

Finally she had to stop running. There was no more air in her chest, and no more room to run. She sank down on the ground and began to cry.

Angel's arms came around her shoulders, and Kara

buried her face in her daughter's hair as they clung together.

"I'm sorry, Mom," Angel said tearfully. "I thought
the lady would protect us, but she let Mr. Hunter
fall. . . . I shouldn't have told him about her. I shouldn't
have told anyone."

"Hush." Angel put her finger against Angel's lips.
"You're not to blame."

"I thought there was time. The water wasn't that high
when I climbed the tree. I thought I could get the locket
and get down."

"I know." Kara tucked her daughter's hair behind
one ear.

Angel took a deep breath. "I know you won't believe
me, but the ghost was Ryan's mother. She told Mr. Hunter she loved him. He said he loved her, too."

Kara stared at her daughter, trying to make sense of
her words. "Are you saying that Mr. Hunter saw the
ghost?"

Angel nodded. "Yes."

"And then he let go," Kara said, more to herself than
Angel. But there was no such thing as a ghost. She certainly hadn't seen anyone. But just before Jonas let go,
he had lifted his hand toward the sky as if to grab on
to someone.

No, that was nonsense. Or was it?

"Come on," Kara said decisively. "We have to find
Ryan. We have to catch up with him."

"Do you think he's okay? Do you think he—"

"Don't say it. Don't even think it."

Angel squeezed her hand. "I don't want Ryan to go
away. It will be my fault if he does, just like when Dad
left."

Kara immediately shook her head. "That wasn't your
fault."

"I saw him with that woman in your bedroom," Angel said. "If I hadn't gone in there, he wouldn't have
gotten mad and he wouldn't have left."

Kara stared at her daughter in shock, wondering how many more surprises were in store for her. "You saw him? Why didn't you tell me?"

"He told me not to tell you."

"Oh, Angel." Kara gathered her daughter close to her heart. No wonder Angel wanted to live in a fantasy world. But now that it was out in the open, maybe they could both heal. "We'll talk about this later, okay? A long, long talk. No more secrets between us, right?"

"All right."

"And Angel, if Ryan leaves, it won't be because of you."

"I just hope he's okay."

"So do I."

Kara and Angel headed back to the truck and drove south, trying to keep the river in view, but many of the roads were underwater and Kara found herself driving through backyards, next to abandoned houses and businesses.

They finally caught up with Ryan nearly an hour later. He had pulled the boat off to the side and was sitting on the ground, his face buried in his arms.

Kara put a hand on his neck. He jumped at her touch, his eyes wild with pain and fear. She pulled him into her arms, and he held on to her as if he could take her strength and make it his.

"He's gone," Ryan said, lifting his head so she could see his face. His eyes were red, his skin pale, and his eyes glittered with the pain of watching his father die. "I couldn't find him. I tried. I couldn't catch up. I wasn't strong enough. I wasn't fast enough."

"You did everything you could."

Ryan looked into her eyes with deep intensity. "He let go, dammit. He let go."

"Yes," she said softly. "I saw him let go."

"Why? Why?"

There were no answers to his questions, at least none

that she could supply. So Kara just held him.

"He finally said he loved me." Ryan's voice caught; his eyes filled with anguish. "But I didn't get a chance to tell him I loved him, too."

"He knew it," Kara said.

"How could he know? We fought just last night."

"He saw you coming back for him, Ryan. He saw you brave the river for him. If that isn't love, what is?"

"But I never said the words, Kara. I waited too long."

"Hush." She tightened her arms around his body, wanting to take his pain away.

"I'm sorry, Ryan." Angel's words came between them like the wind.

Ryan opened his arms and brought Angel into their warm circle. "It's not your fault."

"I didn't mean for him to fall, Ryan, honest. He said he wouldn't fall."

"I know, Angel, I heard him, too. For some reason he let go. He let the river take him," Ryan said.

"I think he wanted to be with your mom," Angel said.

Kara watched Ryan's face as he listened to Angel. He wanted to believe as much as she did that there had been some purpose to it all, but how could they believe in something they couldn't see?

Ryan turned to her. "Jonas told me my mother never left, that she drowned in the river during the last flood—on her way back to us."

"That's what the lady told him," Angel said. "He looked so happy when he saw her. I never saw him smile before, but he smiled tonight."

"Oh, God, Angel, I don't care if you're telling me another story, tell me more," Ryan said, hugging her tight.

"It's not a story. Didn't you see the locket?"

Ryan's eyes suddenly lit with excitement. "I did see the locket, Kara. It was in Jonas's hand. Maybe Angel is right. Maybe there really is a ghost."

They turned their heads toward the water in unison. There was nothing there.

"When the lady asked him for the locket, he wouldn't give it to her," Angel said quietly. "I think he took it to her."

"I think you're right," Ryan agreed.

"We'll keep looking," Kara said. "Maybe Jonas somehow got to shore."

"I already alerted Dirk and the others. But I don't hold out much hope."

"I'm sorry, Ryan."

"I think I'd like to go home now."

"Back to L.A.?" Kara asked, holding her breath. "Or back to Aunt Josephine's house?"

Ryan looked into Kara's beautiful blue eyes and suddenly understood a lot of things. Jonas had told him to find his own family. As he put one arm around Kara and the other around Angel, he had a feeling he had done just that.

Andrew arrived at Josephine's house just before five that evening. When Ryan saw him, he felt a sudden attack of nerves and another rush of guilt.

"You heard?" Ryan asked, knowing by the set of Andrew's face that he had.

"Dirk told me," Andrew said, uttering the words through tight lips. "I couldn't believe it."

"I tried to find you."

"I was at the hospital in Sonoma. Loretta had her baby last night. I just got back an hour ago." Andrew paced around Josephine's tiny living room. "Goddammit, Ryan. Why didn't you save him? You were always the fastest, the strongest, the best. You always landed on your feet. You always won. Why couldn't you win this time? Why?"

Andrew's words ripped apart Ryan's heart. He had asked himself the same questions over and over and over again. Why couldn't he have saved his father? Because his father didn't want to be saved. Deep down in his heart, Ryan found the ultimate truth.

"Jonas let go." Ryan met his brother's eyes and saw the anguish there, the disbelief, the denial.

"You're just saying that so it won't be your fault."

"He said good-bye, Andrew. He said to tell you he loved you."

Andrew's face turned white. He put his hand to his mouth and squeezed his eyes shut. When he opened them, there were tears gathering at the corners. "He never said that. Not once in all the time we were growing up."

"He said it tonight."

"God, I wish I could have heard it," Andrew said with desperate longing. "I wish I could have been there with you. I wish I could have told him how I felt."

"He knew, Andrew. You gave him your whole life. He knew that."

"But it wasn't enough. Never enough."

Ryan's heart broke at the sorrow in his brother's voice. How perfectly it matched his own pain. But then, they were brothers. Ryan took a deep breath, knowing he had to tell Andrew the rest of it, no matter how crazy it sounded. It was the only thing they had left.

"Jonas showed me Mom's locket," Ryan said. "He found it in the tree, Andrew. It was there all along."

"What are you talking about?"

"Mom never left. She died. That's why there was never any trace of her. That's why the detectives couldn't come up with anything. No bank accounts. No mail. No sign of her and Harry Cox going anywhere together." Ryan tried to speak slowly, knowing he had had hours to piece together the puzzle while Andrew had had only a few seconds. "Mom died in the river," he said again. "And once Jonas found the locket, he knew she had never left him."

Andrew sat down on the ottoman, looking suddenly weak. "She died?"

"Yes."

"But you don't know for sure?"

"I do know. Angel—"

"Not the ghost story, please." But even though Andrew said he didn't want to hear it, Ryan knew that he did.

"I don't know if it's a story or if it's the truth, but I know one thing. Mom never took off that locket. She said she would die with it on, that she would take it to heaven with her. Don't you remember?"

Andrew slowly nodded.

"Jonas looked at the sky with the locket in his hand. He told me to leave him there, Andrew. Then he let go. He didn't fight the current. He didn't swim. He just went under."

Ryan walked over to the table and picked up his father's hat. "It's all I could find. I did try. God, I tried." His voice broke with the remembered horror. He didn't think he would ever forget his father going into the water. But even as the scene played over in his mind, he saw Jonas's face again, the sudden smile, the light in his eyes, the new life in his voice as he looked toward the heavens.

"There's no hope?"

Ryan shook his head. "I called the sheriff's department. They looked for him for hours. The current was too swift, too strong. He just disappeared."

"Like Mom," Andrew said heavily.

"Yeah."

There was a long silence as Ryan thought about his parents, about the secrets, about the way he had lived his own life based on a set of beliefs that had turned out to be untrue. Andrew had done the same thing.

They had been on opposite sides of the river for so long, it had taken another flood to change things, to finally erase the boundaries between them and bring their parents back together. Maybe there was a certain symmetry to what had happened.

Andrew stood up as if to leave, then hesitated. "I don't know what to do, Ryan. I don't know where to go. The paper was Dad's paper. The house was his house. It won't be the same without him. Our family is gone."

"Not the whole family. We're still brothers." Ryan paused for a long moment. "I didn't get a chance to tell Jonas, but maybe it's time I told you. I love you, Andrew." His voice caught, and suddenly he and Andrew were hugging with the awkwardness and clumsiness of grown men overcome by emotion. It was a brief moment, but one filled with a lifetime of apologies and a future of hope.

Four days later the sun burned brightly and the river drifted downstream in a gentle fluid motion, no longer a raging monster but a loving woman, nurturing the land, feeding the wildlife, her soft currents reminding them all of the rhythm of life.

Kara took Ryan's hand as Father Miles held a memorial service on a small incline just above the river, a few yards from where Jonas's house had once stood. The house was gone, ripped from its foundation, all of its belongings swept downstream, lost forever in the river.

The Gatehouse had fared a bit better than Jonas's house. The water had come up three feet on the first floor, leaving a pile of mud, silt, and trash behind, making a mockery of the home Kara had created, the walls she had painted, the flowers she had planted. So much work gone in a moment.

Ryan let go of her hand and walked to the front of the group of mourners. Andrew, Loretta, her baby, and Billy stood off to one side, holding hands, taking comfort in one another. Dirk and his wife, Josephine and Ike, the Grubners, the Applebornes, the Woodriches, and some of the other townfolk stood toward the back, saying their good-byes to a man who had kept them together and torn them apart for half a century.

Ryan talked about his father in a simple way, about his love for the river and the fitting end to his life. He talked about families and forgiveness. At the end he took Jonas's hat and tossed it in the river, and they watched in silence as it floated downstream.

Kara glanced at Angel's face and saw wonder in her eyes as she looked toward the heavens.

"Do you see her?" Kara whispered.

Angel nodded. "They're together, Mom, for all of eternity. She won't be coming back."

"No more ghosts?"

"No."

"I'm glad."

"Me, too." Angel took her mother's hand and squeezed it tightly.

After the service Andrew and Loretta joined Kara and Ryan. Andrew handed Ryan a key.

"What's this?" Ryan asked.

"The key to the paper."

"What am I supposed to do with it?" Ryan asked.

"Whatever you want." Andrew smiled at Loretta and Billy. "We're leaving town, Ryan. We're going to San Francisco, maybe L.A., maybe New Orleans, wherever our hearts take us."

"You're leaving?" Ryan asked in astonishment. "I can't believe it."

"Believe it, little brother. I spent my whole life in this town so Dad would have someone with him and so I could prove to Mom, wherever she was, that she had made the wrong decision to leave. I told myself this was all I wanted, but you know what? I want a hell of a lot more. I want to see something of the world. I want to work on a paper that actually has news to report. And I want to live in a place where no one knows anything about me."

Ryan sent Loretta an approving smile. "I don't suppose you had anything to do with this?"

Loretta beamed with the joy of motherhood and the satisfaction of love. "I just want Andrew to be happy."

"And he will be. You're a good woman, Loretta."

"And you're a good man, Ryan."

Billy took a step forward and held out his hand. "Good-bye, Uncle Ryan."

"Good-bye, Billy." After a slight hesitation, Ryan pulled Billy into his arms and gave him a hug. "I want you to know that I would have been proud to be your father, but since I'm not, I'm glad you've got my brother, because he's the best man I know."

Andrew slapped Ryan on the back. "Thanks—for everything."

Something deep and personal passed between them, something only the two men would ever know, Kara realized as she watched them say good-bye. Maybe some secrets were meant to be kept.

Finally Ryan, Kara, and Angel were alone. They walked over to the last two cars parked on the bluff, the red Ferrari and Kara's Ford Taurus.

"I think we should take my car," Kara said. "Everything won't fit in yours."

Ryan raised an eyebrow. "What are you talking about?"

Kara walked over to the trunk and opened it. Inside there was a set of luggage. "Angel and I had a long talk, and we're going with you, Ryan. Wherever you want to go. That is, if you want us."

"If I want you?" Ryan took slow, purposeful steps toward her, stopping just inches away. He lifted her chin with his hand so she had to look into his eyes. "What about restoring the Gatehouse, rebuilding your dream, living in a small town for the rest of your life?"

"I don't want any of that without you, Ryan. You were right. The Gatehouse is just a house, and Serenity Springs is just a place. I love you, and I want to be with

you. I want us to be a family. There, I said it." She
sniffed with a tearful smile. "I promised myself once
that I would never be the one to love more, but here I
am, so completely and totally in love with you that I'll
take whatever you have to give me, however small it
may be."

"Oh, Kara, you couldn't possibly love me more than
I love you. Do I want you with me? Of course I do."
He kissed her on the mouth with tender, loving promise. Then he held out his hand to Angel. "I love you,
too, Angel-face. Promise me you'll tell me a story every
day for the rest of my life."

"If I can think of that many."

"Oh, I have no doubt that you can. You're right, Kara.
We'll take your car. I don't need a sports car anymore.
I need a family car."

With Angel in the backseat and Kara sitting next to
him, Ryan started the car. He didn't take the road toward town, but the one toward the Gatehouse.

When they arrived, Ryan turned to Kara with love in
his brilliant green eyes and said, "We're home."

"Really?" she asked in disbelief.

"Yes." He got out of the car and went around to open
Kara's door for her, pulling her into his arms as they
stood on the lawn in front of the Gatehouse, surveying
their home. The roof was damaged and the garden torn
up. There was a big hole where the living room wall
had once been, and the piano was now on the front
lawn.

Ryan started to laugh. "Looks like you'll still be able
to practice your music, Kara."

"Maybe we can make a duet. My piano, your saxophone."

"Sounds perfect. I want to live here with you and
Angel and your crazy aunt and those mongrel puppies." He laughed as the puppies came barreling across
the lawn, jumping between their legs, licking and kissing and barking with the joy that surrounded them all.

"For a man who likes to travel light, you certainly seem to have acquired a lot of baggage," Kara said. "A house, a family, a newspaper . . ."

"It's about time. I did the same thing Andrew did; I based my life on something that wasn't true."

"We all did."

"No more illusions, Kara. No more ghosts. Just kids and puppies and love—lots and lots of love."

"What about your work? I'm not sure I can see you running a small-town newspaper."

"To be honest, I can't either. Maybe it's time to have someone other than a Hunter controlling the news."

"I think so. I don't want to hold you back, Ryan. You can still travel. Just come home every now and then, okay? I'll make you apple strudel."

He grinned at her. "It's a deal. And you can run the inn."

"What about the river? Some day it will rise again."

"No doubt. I can handle the river now. My parents are a part of that river, and when I look at it, I feel their love. Now I want to feel yours." Ryan lowered his head to kiss her. "Take a deep breath, sweetheart, because I'm never letting you go."

And he didn't, not for long, loving minutes, not until Kara laughingly pulled herself out of his arms. "Let's go home." As they walked up to the house, Kara saw a scarf caught on a bush just to the side of the porch. It was a woman's silk scarf—yellow, orange, and red. "What's this?"

"My mother's scarf," Ryan said. "She took it with her when she left."

"How did it get here?"

"I don't know. Do you believe in ghosts?"

"I believe in love, and I think it lives on forever."

"Maybe that's close enough."

Angel watched Ryan bring the scarf to his lips. Then she looked up at the sky. "I don't know if you're real," she whispered. "But thank you."

## Discover Contemporary Romances
## at Their Sizzling Hot Best
## from Avon Books

### THE LOVES OF
### RUBY DEE
*by Curtiss Ann Matlock*

78106-9/$5.99 US/$7.99 Can

### JONATHAN'S WIFE
*by Dee Holmes*

78368-1/$5.99 US/$7.99 Can

### DANIEL'S GIFT
*by Barbara Freethy*

78189-1/$5.99 US/$7.99 Can

### FAIRYTALE
*by Maggie Shayne*

78300-2/$5.99 US/$7.99 Can

## Coming Soon

### WISHES COME TRUE
*by Patti Berg*

78338-X/$5.99 US/$7.99 Can

# *Avon Romantic Treasures*

*Unforgettable, enthralling love stories,
sparkling with passion and adventure
from Romance's bestselling authors*

**SUNDANCER'S WOMAN** *by Judith E. French*
77706-1/$5.99 US/$7.99 Can

**JUST ONE KISS** *by Samantha James*
77549-2/$5.99 US/$7.99 Can

**HEARTS RUN WILD** *by Shelly Thacker*
78119-0/$5.99 US/$7.99 Can

**DREAM CATCHER** *by Kathleen Harrington*
77835-1/$5.99 US/$7.99 Can

**THE MACKINNON'S BRIDE** *by Tanya Anne Crosby*
77682-0/$5.99 US/$7.99 Can

**PHANTOM IN TIME** *by Eugenia Riley*
77158-6/$5.99 US/$7.99 Can

**RUNAWAY MAGIC** *by Deborah Gordon*
78452-1/$5.99 US/$7.99 Can

**YOU AND NO OTHER** *by Cathy Maxwell*
78716-4/$5.99 US/$7.99 Can

# *Avon Romances—*
## *the best in exceptional authors and unforgettable novels!*

WICKED AT HEART
**Danelle Harmon**
78004-6/ $5.50 US/ $7.50 Can

SOMEONE LIKE YOU
**Susan Sawyer**
78478-5/ $5.50 US/ $7.50 Can

MIDNIGHT BANDIT
**Marlene Suson**
78429-7/ $5.50 US/ $7.50 Can

PROUD WOLF'S WOMAN
**Karen Kay**
77997-8/ $5.50 US/ $7.50 Can

THE HEART AND THE HOLLY
**Nancy Richards-Akers**
78002-X/ $5.50 US/ $7.50 Can

ALICE AND THE GUNFIGHTER
**Ann Carberry**
77882-3/ $5.50 US/ $7.50 Can

THE MACKENZIES: LUKE
**Ana Leigh**
78098-4/ $5.50 US/ $7.50 Can

FOREVER BELOVED
**Joan Van Nuys**
78118-2/ $5.50 US/ $7.50 Can

INSIDE PARADISE
**Elizabeth Turner**
77372-4/ $5.50 US/ $7.50 Can

CAPTIVATED
**Colleen Corbet**
78027-5/ $5.50 US/ $7.50 Can